GRACE VICE

Grudges and Revenge

To all the good girls and boys that want it all!

To all the good girls and boys that want it all!

Contents

Acknowledgments

Special thanks to the ARC readers that made this debut novel possible. You guys are the unsung heroes to new authors pursuing their dreams!

Additional thanks to my biggest fan, my crazy awesome husband. You know who you are. None of this could have happened without your undying support.

Dearest Reader,

The following story falls under the "dark romance" category. Part of what makes these kinds of books wonderful is the knowledge that they can always be put down if the story isn't for us. We read for fun, for emotional rides, for escape, and for a good time. Please take into account the following warnings, as your mental health should always come first. If it's not for you, that's okay. There is power in knowing your personal limits! I hope you enjoy this book as much as I enjoyed writing it, but as always, keep it fun.

-Grace Vice

Trigger Warning List

Abduction/Kidnapping
  Alcohol/Inebriation
  Anal
  Asphyxiation
  Blood Play
  Bondage
  Confinement/Isolation
  Consensual Non-consent
  Discipline Play
  Dominance/Submission
  Exhibitionism/Voyeurism
  Gore
  Graphic Language
  Group Sex
  Gun Violence
  Human Trafficking
  Knife Play
  Medical Procedures
  Murder
  Nightmares/Night Terrors
  Organized Crime
  Panic Attacks
  Profanity
  Prostitution
  Robbery
  Sexual Assault

Suffocation
Suicidal Ideation
Torture
Toy Use

PTSD:
Childhood Abuse
Domestic Abuse
Drug Use/Addiction
Family Abuse
Homelessness
Loss of Family Members
Sexual Abuse

1 | The Exchange

Emma was sick of Grant. A startling slam of the front door, jolted Emma up. Crashing sounds from the living room, beckoned her from the cheap foldable futon in the office. The panic of being woken so suddenly, was quickly replaced with agitation. Emma pressed a rough throw-blanket to her eyes, trying to push away the headache about to begin.

She remembered why she was sleeping in the uncomfortable space, the latest fight. Grant, her less than loving boyfriend, was probably trashing the cramped townhouse like a child throwing a tantrum. She groaned as she sat upright and pressed her feet to the floor. If she had any other options, any, she would have left a long time ago.

Emma pushed her tangled, blonde, hair away from her face, and rubbed at the leftover makeup under her forest green eyes. Her fingertips were black with yesterday's eyeliner. Great. She was about to go into round two looking like a raccoon. Her naturally dark eyebrows, against her pale skin, had a funny way of making her extra grungy when her makeup smudged too much.

She glared at the closed door with resignation. She hated pretending to care anymore, but what choice did she have? She aggressively threw off her inadequate blanket, and stomped to the door. Just as Emma's hand rotated the brushed-nickel lever, a voice could be heard from the other side. It wasn't Grant.

The strangeness wasn't lost on her. Why would he be throwing a fit in

1

front of company? Her thin, white, tank-top and black underwear wasn't exactly guest-appropriate attire. She'd have to be stealthy as she made a run for actual clothes. The door made a loud, hollow, pop noise as she pushed against it. So much for subtlety.

Two startled men, and Grant, turned to see the sliver of the woman in the office space. Her plan to discreetly catch Grant's attention to deliver clothes to her definitely failed. Her stomach dropped before she could fully digest the chaos ensuing in the cramped, open concept, living room and kitchen. Remnants of glassware littered the floor. A cheap copy of a painting that lacked any personality hung crooked against a gray wall.

All eyes shot to a well dressed stranger in a blue suit. Dark, sea-blue eyes riled at Emma's presence. His masculine jaw and intentionally groomed stubble showed off in defined angles, as he clenched his teeth together. His jet black hair had signs of usually being parted off center, but in this particular moment, was a disheveled mess. His menacing posture demanded unquestionable authority.

No one felt the weight of the man's power more, at that moment, than Grant. Grant had cinnamon-brown hair, matching eyes, and hands splayed in the air in surrender. All eyes returned to Emma, even as the dark-haired leader of the intruders steadily pointed a handgun at Grant's face.

The door handle Emma didn't realize she was squeezing, was ripped from her grip. Her heart skipped a beat. The door lurched to reveal a third man the size of a mountain.

"Great," said the large man, in a sarcastic grunt.

Long, dark-brown, hair rested in natural waves at the giant's toned shoulders. A few pronounced veins ran along the considerably large muscles that flexed beneath his rich-tawny skin. Bright amber eyes sized up the comparatively tiny woman. He looked back to the other two unwanted visitors with raised brows.

"Grab her," the leader said, with a nod.

Shock kept Emma from moving for precious seconds, before the instinct to fly or fight could be awoken. As the big man began his advance, reality finally took hold. She dashed back into the home office. She tried to slam the door shut, but it bounced off her follower as if it was made of styrofoam.

Emma looked around the room in a panic. She flung a keyboard, computer monitor, pens and paper, anything she could get her hands on. He barely bothered taking a defensive pose as he swatted away the projectiles. She seemed to be doing little more than making him irritated at the prolonged chase.

With a heave, Emma sent the entire desk toppling over. He avoided the falling furniture easier than she had hoped. Still, she had to try. If she could just get to the window, she could find help. If she was fast enough, maybe she could save Grant too.

Emma crinkled the plastic blinds out of the way. Her hands desperately fiddled with the lock on the window. She pressed her palms against the glass and pushed, only to have forgotten that a second lock prevented it from being fully opened. The frame slammed against the mechanism intended for safety purposes. A harsh tug yanked Emma away from her escape.

Even through her frantic kicking and fighting, the big man easily managed to carry the flailing woman into the living room with the rest of the party. The moment Emma's feet met solid ground, she tried to run again. She started for the front door but was cut off by the only of the trio that didn't look like he wanted to murder someone.

He stood between her and the exit. He had to have only been a few inches taller than her, and she wasn't a very vertically inclined person. Her confidence to take him on was considerably greater than her hopes to get past the other two. She tensed, readied, and before she made her move, one hand from the man stretched out in a silent plea for her to stop.

His complexion reminded Emma of a porcelain doll, and like a ceramic toy, he appeared fragile compared to his partners in crime. Ash-blond hair hung in careless, loose, curls around sharp features. His icy-blue eyes were desperate and sad. Full pink lips parted with the slightest tremble. He pushed away the hood of his heather-gray jacket, and lowered his halting hand.

"We don't want to hurt you," he said, sweetly.

Emma regarded the impish blond with uneasiness. His body language, his expression, the sound of his voice; everything about him encouraged her to trust him. Confusing emotions surged through her brain. She was terrified. She needed to run. And yet, the person before her tugged at her heartstrings. Maybe he needed help too? She turned to the large man that was just pursuing her. Maybe...

In her moment of distraction, the giant effortlessly took her hands in his. He swiftly spun her around in an almost dance-like motion. Her arm and his crossed over her head and came down around her waist. She was wrapped tight against him as he held her like a human straitjacket. She twisted her shoulders and arched her back. She tried to throw off his balance by pushing against him. His grip on her wrists tightened. She grunted and pulled to get away. Hopeless knots tied in her guts when she realized she couldn't win.

Physically defeated and breathing erratically, she yielded to the intruder. Without the fight, new room was made for more fear. A harsh gasp escaped from her lips when she realized what she felt behind her back. Her eyes widened.

She looked at the blond, who returned her stare with a lack of understanding. She looked up at her captor to confirm if she was correct, but he avoided her questioning gaze. His answer was a tighter hold that began to numb her hands. Anxiety filled her chest when she felt a hardness through his pants grow behind her. Nearly hyperventilating, she looked back to the blond with desperate, scared eyes of her own.

The blond man's attention darted multiple times from Emma to the giant. Something shifted in the smallest of the men. Like an actor switching characters in a one-man-show, he was suddenly a different person. He shook his head with the tiniest of motions of annoyance and disapproval. He knew. He understood what was concealed behind her back, and he was irritated more than concerned.

"Cut it out," the leader snapped at his men. "We don't have time for this."

Grant looked to be in another world. Emma understood that stress could do weird things to people, but he didn't even look afraid. She was certainly afraid. Grant stared at the leader in the blue suit. She could practically see wheels turning in his mind. He held the look of a person that wanted to ask a question, but didn't want to impose.

"I agree," said the blond. "We don't have time for this, so let's just go!"

Emma startled at the rough voice that rumbled from behind her.

"Toss me the gun," said the giant. "You two go, I'll take care of this."

"Or," said a self-important sounding Grant, pointer finger in the air, "Or, I could give you a head start."

The blond looked at Grant with skepticism in his eyes. The leader glanced down at the weapon, then at his large partner. The leader gave an intentional shrug, and the giant received the message. Emma's holder took her wrists in a single hand and wrapped the fingers of his other around her throat. Emma could feel her pulse pounding against his grip. She tried to swallow and panicked at the difficulty.

"Look," Grant said, as if the negotiations were going well. "I can cover for you. I can flag the cops down, tell them two, no– four men, that look nothing like you, came through here. I can tell them you went in the opposite direction."

A muscle twitched in Grant's neck when he looked at his struggling girlfriend. Emma thought of their fight last night. She wished they hadn't. She may have been in the right, but still. It would have been more comforting if she had as much confidence in Grant as he had for himself. A determined resolve made its home on his face. He straightened his shirt and addressed the leader.

"I'm not asking for much. But if you agree, I can assure you, you'll get away from… whomever you are running from. Just hear me out. I only want one thing in return."

"I have a feeling I've heard this request before," the leader said, glancing momentarily in Emma's direction. "But surprise me, what could you possibly want in return for assisting in our evasion of the cops?"

Grant postured himself a little taller, in the way men do when they've made up their mind on a moral matter.

"Kill the girl for me," Grant said, bluntly.

Confusion spread around the room like an airborne virus. The leader raised a brow and tilted his head. He was, in fact, surprised. The giant with his hand around Emma's throat, loosened his grip.

"You want to cover your tracks," Grant asked. "You want a head start? I want her gone. Kill her, fuck her, sell her, I really don't care. I just want her dead or gone, preferably both. I don't care how you do it, or what will happen in between. If you hold up your end, I can't possibly tell anyone about you, without running the risk of incriminating myself. You could kill both of us and get all the closer to being caught or, you leave her alive with me, and I'll have to kill her myself. But then I'd have to make it look like you did it, get my hands dirty… It feels like a lot of work."

The intruding men exchanged looks of alarm, disgust, and desperation. They needed to move and had already wasted too much time. Emma stood in shock with wide eyes and a slightly dropped jaw. She knew he was sick of her. She knew she wasn't anything like what he was hoping for her to be. But what he was offering was so far beyond what she could have expected.

"I'd rather simply tell the cops about the four red-headed brothers that broke in," Grant said. "They killed my girlfriend in a panic, and left me oh so sad to pick up the pieces. If you're not messy and take her with you, I can always say they took her, and said they'd kill me if I followed. So that's the deal. Leave me alive to give them time consuming, inaccurate, information. You get rid of her for me."

Rage exploded from every inch of the woman. The man restraining her was no longer holding her to keep her from running, he was saving Grant. She wanted to hit him, tackle him, scream at him for everything he put her though, and now this. She wanted to rip him apart.

"What… the… fuck!" she screamed.

Whatever strength she may have used before meant nothing. She thrashed and threw herself around. The man holding her, picked her up once more while she kicked into the air. Sure, she wanted to get out of the unknown man's grip. But more than that, she wanted to give Grant a real reason to have her killed.

"You pathetic, insecure, son of a-"

A clicking sound reminded Emma that her backstabbing boyfriend wasn't the only thing that demanded attention. She looked to her right and felt a numbness in her gut. Her face paled. The skin on her arms and neck tingled uncomfortably. Her legs buckled. She would have fallen to the ground if not for the man holding her in place to be executed.

She could barely feel him. She could barely feel anything apart from her impending death. It was possible she might have heard the blond shout protests, but she couldn't concentrate enough to be sure. An eternity of darkness could be seen at the center of the barrel. Emma looked up to see the face of its holder but couldn't fight the need to stare back into the threatening metal. Her body shook from the inside out. Angry and terrified tears unwillingly slid down her face.

"Y...you shouldn't," she said, in a shaking voice. "What if someone-" Her voice cracked through the tears.

"There is no, someone." Grant cut her off. "The neighbors are at work. She doesn't have friends, family, or anyone that will care. You gentlemen picked the perfect house, lucky for me."

Her hate for Grant was strong, but her terror was overwhelming. Emma didn't look at Grant, she couldn't. She could only stare at the weapon ready to take her life. She wanted to speak, to say something meaningful for her last words. She wished her last moments wouldn't be such a reminder of how alone she always was. But she didn't speak. As much as she wanted to, words refused to manifest.

The blond seemed to be getting louder, but Emma couldn't listen. Her holder argued about who should be the one to kill her, or something. Emma could barely make out the words of anyone over the deafening noise of her pounding heartbeat. The only sound that pierced through the panic was the sound of sirens. The room went quiet while everyone listened to the same moving sound.

"Deal," the leader said.

A sickening smile planted on Grant's face, as he pointed at the bathroom to the left of the kitchen pantry.

"There's a window that'll lead you to an alleyway. It's the only one that can see out that way. You should be in the clear if you stay off the main roads. I'll have the story ready."

"We're taking the girl," the leader directed to the giant. "Go."

The big man began to speak but was cut off.

A thunderous beat sounded at the door. From the other side, officers with kind words but harsh voices called for Grant to open up, so they could ask a few questions. Every face turned to the thumping and then back to each other. They were out of time.

"I said go! Now," the leader whispered.

Emma nearly lost her balance, as the large hands went from holding her up to pushing her forward. The giant moved her towards the bathroom, but Emma's fury knew no bounds. In one last attempt, she lunged for Grant spewing curses as she reached to ring his neck. The large man held her back by the arm. She struggled to get free, to attack the man that traded her so easily.

"If I get out of this," she seethed, "I'll fucking destroy you!"

"It's so ugly when you curse," said Grant, with a smile.

The gun found its way back to Emma's face.

"You can come with us, or you can let your dick of a boyfriend watch you die."

The leader took her hair in his hand and pulled her to him, while she was still in the grip of the giant. He moved his lips close to her ear, and whispered.

"Don't let that bastard win. Don't give him the satisfaction."

Grant sneered at Emma and chuckled to himself. The gun swung around. Grant fell back as the weapon faced him again. The leader rushed to his side. He pushed the barrel into Grant's cheek and snarled at the appalling man.

"If you cross us, remember, we know where to find you."

Grant nodded desperately and stumbled to his feet. He adjusted his shirt and cleared his throat.

"You get rid of her, and you'll have nothing to worry about from me."

The blond was the first to run into the small bathroom. He slid a metal lock attached to the side of the window to the open position. He cautiously poked his head out, and waved his hand for others to follow as he climbed out of the rectangular slot. The big man swung Emma into the room, grabbed her at the waist, and literally threw her out the open window.

The blond cursed under his breath at the unexpected person being lobbed at him. He wasn't prepared and only half caught her. He stumbled in his attempt, causing Emma to hit the concrete wall of the narrow alley. Her head bounced off the brick. Her arm grated against the rough surface, leaving a significant red scrape from elbow to shoulder. Emma's arm stung and head throbbed.

"Shit," said the blond. "Look at me."

The man held her head and tilted her chin to face him. Emma jerked herself from his grip. He reclaimed her face and gave her a stern look.

"Cooperate with me," he said, "I won't let them touch you, but you have to work with me. Now look at me!"

His glacial-blue eyes studied hers, with uncomfortable intensity. Clearly satisfied by whatever he was looking for, he turned his attention to his partner. Emma leaned against the wall and placed her hand on her forehead. She was a little wobbly. The giant shimmied one arm and most of his upper body through the opening. He was comically too large for the plan. With a little pulling on the blond's end, and a hard push from behind, he made it through quickly enough.

"Some warning would have been nice."

"What," the big man said, defensively. "You're fine, she's fine."

"You threw her at a brick wall! She could have gotten a concussion."

"I don't see why that matters."

The leader followed with a rough grunt, as he landed marginally more gracefully than Emma had.

"Elijah, cut it out!" the leader said. "I don't have the patience for your bickering right now. Matthew, he's right. You shouldn't have thrown her."

The two men looked at their leader, bewildered.

"Um, okay," said Elijah, after blowing a few blond curls away from his face. "Professionalism and secrecy be damned then?"

Elijah turned to Emma, glaring.

"Elijah," he said, bitterly. "Shitty to meet you."

The leader reached for his side and growled at his men. He must have hit the ground harder than Emma realized.

"I said, cut it out," he barked.

The sound of officers inside the building reminded the criminals that they were already cutting it too close. Matthew ducked below the view of the bathroom window. The leader made a silent command to run down the passageway, and his men obeyed.

Matthew gave Emma an encouraging push. His huge hand positioned her in the middle of the pack. With the command of the leader, they ran. The unkind and poorly maintained asphalt, darkened and tore at Emma's bare feet. Her focus was kept entirely on the ground, as she avoided broken bottles and discarded litter. Her exposed and abused body almost felt a glimpse of relief when they reached a busy street.

Parked close, was their target destination. A small, graffiti plastered, moving truck sat unaccompanied and waiting. The leader nodded for Elijah and Matthew to go ahead. They did without question. Emma took only a few quick steps before the dark-haired man shoved her against the painfully coarse wall. He let out another subdued grunt. He was out of breath, despite the short distance they had run.

"You will not scream," he scolded. "You will not intentionally draw attention to yourself. Is that understood?"

Emma nodded without making eye contact.

The man reduced the space between them. Emma tried to back up but there wasn't any room left. She felt the roughness of the gray bricks prick her skin. The man caged her between his arms. She looked up to him. He looked down at her.

"Say it. Do you understand?"

Her voice broke and cracked.

"Yes, I understand."

Dark blue eyes continued to threaten without words.

Clanking sounds came from the street. The two that ran ahead unlocked and unhinged the sliding door to the moving truck. Elijah opened it just a crack and waited. Matthew cranked the ignition and readied their getaway vehicle.

One hand of the leader moved down the wall. He slid it to Emma's damaged arm. She winced. He glanced at the scrape with a hint of concern. As if remembering his role again, his eyes darted up to hers, and then the truck. He jerked her around to face the waiting crew.

"Now!" he whispered.

Together they raced.

The baking desert sun scalded the ground between the generously shaded alley, and the truck. Her feet burned. Cars drove past. People stared at their phones. Not a soul seemed to notice anything out of the ordinary. In an area so polluted with crime, Emma was disheartened but not particularly surprised. Less than a foot before they reached the compartment, Elijah pushed the sliding door up and then brought it crashing back down in a hurry once Emma, and his leader, jumped into the back.

Emma was blind. The interior of the metal box was pitch black. Imprinted visuals of light blurred sporadically in the dark contrasting environment. The engine rumbled and the world jolted forward. Her forced companion fell back with an, "Oof!" and another painful groan.

Shuffling sounds were made while Emma tried to remain steady on her hands and knees through the unanticipated turns and stops. The skin on her hands and legs protested against the rough, splintering, wood flooring that was eventually coming into focus.

Suddenly she was blind again. A large flashlight beamed in her direction. It cut through the darkness wildly, then rested on a backpack. The leader rummaged through it and retrieved a roll of duct tape.

"Against the wall," he demanded.

Emma looked around. She was closer to the side than she realized. She sat against it. The metal wall was warm, as was the air around them. The heat basically turned the place into a large portable oven. She looked up and noticed a bar. It was fixed a little more than half way up the wall, and ran horizontally around the metal interior.

"Yup," the leader said. "Hands up."

Emma did as she was told and reached above her head. Her fingers extended to touch the hot bar. She didn't have the height to put her palms to the round rod. The man crawled on all fours to her, bracing for unpredictable driving. At the wall, he positioned her between his legs and held her wrists together above her head with one hand.

The truck shifted, slamming her hands against the wall and pushing his body into hers. Emma took in a sharp breath. The feeling of his jacket against her chest and the curves of his pants made Emma feel naked beneath him. She pulled against his hold on her wrists, but he wasn't letting go.

"Take it easy," he warned.

The man unbuckled his belt with one hand and slid it smoothly away from the loops of his pants. Emma panicked beneath him. She pulled at his grip and struggled hard. She crossed her legs and held them together as tight as she could manage.

"Wait," she started to beg.

He took a deep breath and let it slowly out. His words came out gently. Even so, she found little comfort in them.

"Shhh. We aren't all as bad as the piece of shit that gave you away."

He worked the belt around the bar and tried tying the other end around her wrists. The hard leather protested when he attempted to force it into positions it was never meant to be in. The garment was new and stiff to work with. The belt simply refused to be tied into any type of truly secure knot. The man chucked it away in irritation.

"I am sorry, truly. I was hoping to avoid using tape, but–"

The man reached behind him and grabbed the tape he found in the backpack earlier. He ripped the duct tape loudly, making Emma jump. With significantly more ease, and a frightening amount of experience it seemed, he fixed her to the rod. Cleverly, he gave her a little slack. Whether it was for her comfort or his convenience, she wasn't entirely sure. The dark man chuckled to himself in a way that chilled Emma to the bone.

"Fucking belt," he mumbled under his breath. "I apologize," he said, addressing Emma again. "I'm afraid I'm a bit distracted. I'm usually quite the professional at this art."

Another breathy laugh left the man, as he ran his fingers along the tape that bound her. His hands steadily pressed against the wall, an arm on either side of her. He held her gaze for too long. He looked down at the suggestive position he put her in, eyeing her tightly crossed legs. Slowly, he removed his arms from around her. He moved over her, then back into the shadows. Emma heard him lean against a box with another groan.

"If I let you run, right now," he asked, inquisitively, "where would you go?"

"I don't know," Emma said, and instantly regretted her answer.

She probably should have lied. Grant may have been an asshole, but there was truth in his words. She really didn't have anywhere to go, anyone she could stay with.

"Were you surprised by your boyfriend's deal?"

"I don't think anyone expects to be tied up in the back of a moving truck," she said, her aggression surprising herself.

"Just answer the question," the man said, through gritted teeth.

The tone of the man's words sent a shiver down Emma's spine despite the terrible heat. Emma didn't want to answer. She knew Grant wasn't happy with her. She knew he was getting tired of her and was growing increasingly irritated at their constant arguments. But still, who would make such an inhuman request? She didn't deserve this, no one did.

Out of sight, the man ripped more of the tape from its roll. The sound made her flinch. Whatever he was sticking it to, it required a generous amount of the material.

"No, I guess not," she finally said.

Her eyes searched the darkness, then dropped when she accepted they could never adjust enough to see him.

"Then why were you with him?"

It was a strange question from the person leading the team that was kidnapping her. Maybe he was passing the time? He couldn't possibly care about her personal life. He barely seemed to care very much for her life in general, given that he was so keen to point a gun to her face.

"He," she shook, "he was supposed to be safe. But I guess it's hard to pick safe when you've never seen what that looks like."

Emma felt uneasy about being unable to clearly see his expressions in the dark container. She shared too much. Then again, did it matter how much she said? Emma focused on the duct tape line that attached her to the truck. He had experience. How many times had he done this? Maybe he got some sort of a kick out of asking his victims personal questions? Sweat beaded and ran down her thin shirt.

"Did you cheat on him?"

"What?"

"He clearly didn't love you anymore. Why? What did you do?"

The light beamed in her direction. It wasn't fair that he could see her but she couldn't see him. She closed her eyes, tears falling as she did. Her smeared makeup started to burn, but that wasn't the reason for her wet face. She wiped her tears away with her dangling arm, sniffed, and let out a sad laugh.

"Love? Funny. Some people aren't lucky enough for love. But if I find out why, I'll let you know."

The vehicle slowed to a stop and reversed. Emma could hear her captor get to his feet. He scanned the area with the light, revealing multiple stacked boxes. The cargo was carefully tied, like Emma, to the opposite wall. He quickly found what he was looking for, a black canvas bag. He shook out its items carelessly, letting them fall to the floor. Another, smaller, sticky rip of tape sounded.

The man returned to Emma, knelt down and softly pressed the binding material over her mouth. Emma sounded a plea behind the tape. He held a finger to her lips and whispered a hush to her. He removed the silencing finger he placed over his own lips as he pulled the dark canvas bag over Emma's head.

The engine shut off. She heard the rolling of the door open and saw a faint light through the black fibers. Shoes tapped and creaked against the wood as her fellow passenger met with a new voice.

"Hey, hey, hey!" sounded a very excited new man, with a smooth Latino accent.

The slaps of masculine hugs made rounds as the men all greeted each other.

"My favorite boys! A little late, but all is good. I was almost worried. Give me a look. You always–"

The new voice trailed off for a moment. An awful silence filled the empty seconds.

"Oh, boys," he said, in a cautious tone. "I thought you knew better. We've talked about this."

"We did," said the leader, coldly. "Things didn't go as planned, so now we have this. She knows too much, and she's a fighter. Before you start, I'm not in the mood to be fucking scolded by you. I need options, El Tiburón."

Two sets of shoes stepped up to the container and walked nearer to Emma. She couldn't see them. She couldn't see anything. They weren't talking! Why weren't they talking? She regretted wanting to hear words when the new voice spoke inches from her, making her flinch.

"Someone's snappy," El Tiburón said, disapprovingly at the leader. "Still, it's interesting that you brought her here. If she made it this far, she's in too deep. I'm not in a position to hold her. You can kill her, or sell her. I know a guy. Just the once though. You know how I feel about sharing that area of business with you. I'm sure," he said with pressure, "this isn't going to be a recurring situation."

Elijah started to interject, "Absolutely not! Dame–" but was cut off.

Emma fully panicked.

She struggled to pull herself up. Her yells were muffled against the tape. She erratically pushed her sore bare feet against the rough flooring. With her last flailing attempt, an exposed nail ripped into her ankle and tore up and along her calf. Blood spilled from the wound, making the floor, her legs, and both of her feet slippery. Emma felt a chill replace the rapidly leaving warmth that was meant to stay in her body.

Curses expelled from the leader's mouth.

"She's not for sale, El Tiburón," he said, as the sound of a knife scraped from its sheath.

Emma felt the leader kneel above her. Pain and hopelessness overlapped her fear. That was it. He'd kill her. She tensed for the inevitable slice that would end her life. Would it be quick, or would it feel like an eternity? He held her hands tightly in his and cut Emma away from the metal pole. He scooped the woman up in his arms and carried her out of the truck, the black bag still on her head.

"Good talk," El Tiburón said, his voice getting further away. I'll take care of the truck, but if you start getting too messy again–"

A car door clicked open.

Emma was laid across leather seats and followed closely by another person. The car smelled new, expensive. The engine turned and it too purred like a vehicle befitting a jet setting millionaire. Elijah's gentle hands propped her legs up on his lap and tried to clean the bloody mess. The wound shot sharp pains through Emma, despite the gentle care.

"Take a deep–" he said, then frustratedly tore the dark hood from Emma and threw it on the car floor. "Take a deep bre– Dameon! Damn it!" he shot, furiously at the leader, seeing the tape over her mouth.

The dark-haired man twisted from the passenger seat to reach Emma in the back, his seat belt straining against his chest. Elijah continued to clean her feet and legs as Dameon moved his fingers against the edges of the tape that held Emma's mouth shut. She tried to look down at the damage but his hands held her face forcefully.

"No," Dameon said. "Look at me. Don't look anywhere else. Just look at me."

Slowly, carefully, with as little discomfort as he could manage, he peeled away the gray strip. A small cry forced its way out once her lips were permitted to part again. Without meaning to, Emma did look down. Her legs were drenched in blood. Elijah held a red cloth with a single clean corner that suggested its original color was actually white. She stared at the continuous leak of important liquid and felt light headed.

"No, no, no." Elijah said, in a soothing voice. "Take a breath. Just breathe, honey. It's not as bad as it looks."

Elijah was calm enough for the both of them. Emma struggled to gain a fraction of his composure.

"Damn!" said Matthew. "All that from a little nail?"

He grabbed a glance at the mess, with one hand on the sporty steering wheel. The other men in the car glared at him. A quick silence passed in the car.

"Dameon…" Matthew asked carefully. "Where are we going? If we're about to do a desert dump, we'll need gas."

The powerful engine rumbling over the highway pavement was the only sound for a while.

"We're not taking her out. We're taking her home."

More silence.

"Why? How," Matthew asked. "She looks like, well, like a lady that was just abducted, which she is."

"This is a bad idea," Elijah agreed.

Dameon reached between his legs for a backpack that had been stowed away. He pulled a piece of clothing from it and tossed the shirt back. Elijah wrapped Emma's leg with it and fastened it with more of the duct tape. It wasn't pretty, but at least she wasn't bleeding out anymore.

Dameon took an audible breath and pressed against the headrest of the seat.

"Clean her up," said Dameon. "Matthew will carry her. We'll play it off like she's passed out after a hard night of partying. We were out all morning, met her at a bar, and took the party back to our place."

Elijah scrunched his nose.

"So instead of abduction, you're going for what? Taking a, mostly naked, passed out girl to our home?"

Dameon let out an irritated sound from the back of his throat.

"Okay," he said, through gritted teeth and closed his eyes in thought.

"It does sound bad," said Matthew. "We don't want the wrong people thinking about our old habits. If they found out–"

"Shit! I know! I know, just let me think."

Dameon ran a hand through his dark hair, messing it up even more.

"Matthew will carry the girl on his back."

Dameon pulled a pair of sunglasses from the center console. He reached back to Elijah and snatched the duct tape. After ripping two pieces off, he threw the roll back to his partner. Meticulously, Dameon taped the insides of the glasses to render them useless and handed them back too.

"Put those on her. It'll keep her blind, and also help hide her identity. And give her your jacket."

Dameon picked up a water bottle, unscrewed the cap, and dumped the contents out over Emma, and Elijah by proximity. The blond jumped and swore. Dameon continued with his plan, unphased.

"She was at the pool, that'll help explain her lack of pants. She slipped and hurt her leg. Matthew will carry her on his back. We are taking her up to give her first aid. Just a bunch of good samaritans."

Swimming trunks were taken from the backpack next, and tossed back. A pair was also set near Matthew.

"What about you," Matthew asked.

"You two are enough. I met you on my way back from a separate event." Dameon said, shrugging.

Elijah placed his jacket delicately over Emma. She met his eyes and embarrassingly averted her gaze to look at the detailed stitching in the leather behind the driver's seat. She didn't realize she was watching him take his pants off until the moment of. Her cheeks would have blushed if she wasn't so pale after seeing her blood all over the place.

He was quick to change. Once seated again, Elijah pulled Emma's hips closer to him. In doing so, he gave Emma more room to get the jacket on without completely requiring her to sit up. Her fingers searched for the ends of the zipper, but Elijah already had them. A vulnerable feeling passed over her as he pulled the zipper up to her neck.

"Hood up." snapped Dameon, without looking back.

Elijah followed the orders, though the look on his face revealed his complete displeasure for the plan ahead.

2 | The Doc Is In

Darkness blanketed the car when Matthew pulled into a parking garage. Yellow lights strobed slowly through the windows. Elijah unfolded the shades and placed them in her hand as they turned into a more secluded and private section of the garage. He nodded encouragingly to her with polite instruction.

Emma placed the discrete blindfold over her eyes and took in a shaky breath. Once parked, Matthew and Dameon got out of the car and spoke in low voices. Emma clenched her jaw. She had no idea where she was, but knew it wasn't bound to be good.

She regretted ever coming to this god-forsaken desert. She even begrudgingly wondered for a moment if her father was right all those years ago, when she left home at sixteen. She certainly wouldn't be in this situation if she had only stayed a little longer. No. She shoved the thought from her mind. Even potentially facing death, she wasn't incoherent enough to give her abusive father a remotely kind thought. Her mind continued to spin with the regrets she had that led her to her current predicament.

The threat of more tears burned, despite her desire to keep them at bay. A few salty drops disobeyed her wishes. They caressed the black, plastic, rims of the glasses and rolled down to her ears where a small pool was forming. Her chest rose and fell at an increased speed with the feel of silent crying. She flinched when she felt Elijah's hand slide beneath the jacket. He moved from her hip up to the smallest part of her waist.

"Do what he says," he whispered. "And try to trust me. I have every intention of getting you out of here."

His thumb pressed lightly against her shirt and rubbed in a comforting rhythm back and forth. Emma's trembling hand slid across her middle, feeling his hand through the thin jacket fabric. Both hands jumped away when the car door clicked open. Emma couldn't risk Dameon or Matthew seeing her biggest chance to escape, and it appeared that Elijah felt the same.

An annoyed puff of air expelled loudly from Matthew. Rough hands dragged Emma from the seats, and dropped the lower half of her body to the concrete. She let out a cry that should have been small, but instead echoed in the stone building. Dameon angrily shushed in their direction. Elijah and Matthew were opposites in every sense of the word.

Matthew pulled Emma's arms and hoisted her onto his back without the slightest consideration for her pain. Her leg stung as it was used to secure her position on the man too large to wrap her legs around. He released her hands over his shoulders and wrapped her legs in his arms. She looked like a human backpack.

"It'll have to work." Dameon said.

Matthew turned and walked down a number of stairs. Every step made Emma's stomach drop. Her temporary blindness proved to be highly disorienting. They stepped into the sun. She could feel heat caress her and tempt the water Dameon dumped on her to evaporate.

An icy gust of air swirled around her. It was freezing compared to the previously scorching temperature. Emma held tighter to Matthew to steal some warmth and keep from shivering. His hands adjusted around her legs. Elijah spoke with a loudness that made Emma jump.

"There's a reason there are signs telling you not to run by the pool." he said, with a laugh.

Matthew laughed heartily in a way that vibrated through his torso. Dameon joined the inside joke, put a hand on Emma's back, and leaned close.

"Hold your hand in the air and give a thumbs up, now!" he demanded, in her ear.

Emma jolted her hand up. After a couple pats on the back he leaned in again.

"Good girl," he whispered."Put it back down,".

She did as she was instructed.

Matthew stopped. A pleasant ding echoed. He moved forward. A plastic button clicked, and a quiet thump of a door closed behind them. Emma squeezed Matthew's shirt in her fists as the floor lurched. They were moving down, or up, in an elevator. The hospitable ding returned to announce their arrival.

Dameon pulled the hood of the jacket back and removed the glasses from the bridge of her nose. They were in an entryway of some kind. They stepped out of the elevator, allowing the doors to shut behind them.

Though it wasn't a large area, it boasted an air of expensiveness with lustrous, tan, wide, tile walls. Dameon brought Emma's attention to, what she realized was, the Fort Knox of doors. Besides the elevator access, it was all that the space contained; just one gaudy, large, white door.

A keychain with a dangling gold heart jingled as it was retrieved from Dameon's pocket. A simple looking key was inserted into an average looking lock. After the first lock, he pressed a keycard to a metal plate. The card unlocked a small sliding panel on the door that revealed a sensor. Dameon held his face near to scan his right eye. Finally the door fully unlocked with a heavy metal thunk, rivaling that of a bank vault's door.

Matthew carried her through the threshold and turned to allow her to see an equally impressive amount of security on the inside as well. Dameon closed the door, locked two separate deadbolts with two separate keys, then the main lock. Another, automatically operated by a card, sounded. Then of course another retinal scanner guarded the way to shut them in.

"As you can see," Dameon continued, "There is no way in or out of this place without myself or one of my partners."

Emma looked at Elijah, who nodded his head in confirmation.

"You can scream if you want, but it won't help," Dameon said, "The entire penthouse is soundproof. You'll need one of us to get out to the terrace as well, so no disturbing the neighbors that way either. Do you understand?"

She was trapped. She was completely and truly confined in this place. Matthew straightened his spine causing Emma to slide off his back. She dropped to a cold marble floor. Elijah rushed to her side and knelt close. Sweet hands observed her impaired limb while his eyes took in her trembling body.

"If you're going to keep her here," said Elijah "you'll have to let me have her first. But I'll probably need your help to hold her down. You said it yourself, she's a fighter."

His hands gripped the jacket, pulled the zipper down, and slid it away. The cool air chilled Emma's skin. She crossed her arms to conceal the temperature's effect on her chest. The skin on Emma's arm pebbled as Elijah traced the sensitive places that bordered the large red scrape on her shoulder. She'd really have to stop letting him trick her.

"After I'm done with her we can do... whatever it is you're planning on doing with her."

A shiver shook through her body. She was cold, frightened, and without any kind of plan. Dameon gave silent permission, directing Matthew to pick her up again and follow Elijah. The loyal man scooped Emma up and carried her down a short hallway with pinkish-tan marble walls.

They stopped at an elaborate brown door. Its frame had thick, dark, carvings of crosses, snakes, and various geometric designs. Elijah twisted a brass knob to enter a starkly opposing room. Stainless steel gave the walls a sense of being uncomfortably sterile. Silver medical instruments gleamed in the windowless light. Glass jars with gauze, clear cabinets with neatly labeled pills, and a single chrome and black examination table made Emma feel as if she had just been carried into a hospital.

"On the table." Elijah instructed his accomplices, "Face down, please."

Matthew placed Emma on the faux-leather top and flipped her over with ease, pinning her arms at her sides. Emma noticed little round patterns of color in the hard fabric. The design was not something intentionally made. They were dried blood stains. Panic flooded her veins. It was useless, she knew, but she kicked and tried to wriggle out of Matthew's strong grasp.

"No!" she screeched. "Get away from me!"

"You'll be fine," Elijah said, dismissively. "Not that you'll believe me. It'll only hurt a little, and I'll be quick."

Elijah circled the table to retrieve a surgical mask from a box on the counter in front of Emma. He pinched the metal piece to form it better to his nose. A cross-armed Dameon watched him with genuine curiosity.

"Is that really necessary, the mask," he asked, with curiosity.

"At this point," Elijah shrugged, "probably not, but better safe than sorry. Besides, when have I ever passed on the chance to play dress-up?"

Dameon tilted his head with interest as Elijah took a couple of vials from the steel refrigerator with a glass door. He pulled open a drawer and took out a couple syringes. He ripped one out from its paper and plastic package, and bumped the drawer closed with his hip. He shot Matthew a wordless reminder to keep a hold on Emma. She struggled harder, sending rocking motions through the table.

"I told you we needed the table with straps," said Elijah.

"Quit playing around," Dameon said, agitated.

"El Tiburón was right," said Elijah. "You are snappy today. And I'm not playing around."

Elijah gestured towards Dameon to take over restraining Emma's arms. Dameon wasn't nearly as strong as the muscle man he commanded, but he was still much stronger than Emma. Matthew repositioned to hold her wounded leg down. Elijah pushed her healthy leg to the other edge of the table. She tried to push her legs back together until Matthew proceeded to press her knee roughly into the fabric. A stinging pain shot up her body, forcing compliance.

After the angry push, he moved to hold her foot down painfully. His other hand started at the bend of her knee then slid upwards. His thumb pressed against the skin just below her ass and stopped at her pantyline. His fingers squeezed into her inner thigh, terribly close to her crease, restricting the movement of her hips. Goosebumps surfaced over her skin again. The location of Matthew's fingers caused her pelvic muscles to instinctively contract. Matthew cleared his throat.

"What? What," asked Elijah, rapidly, in Matthew's direction.

"It's not important," he said.

Dameon's irritation spilled over and soaked his words.

"Spit it out! What?"

"She's wet," he said.

"Piss," Dameon asked.

"I really don't think so," Matthew said, simply.

Matthew's fingers tensed and pressed a measure harder against Emma. Dameon released her arms with a hard warning not to move. He rounded the table and ran a finger directly above Matthew's, just over the line of her underwear. Her skin chilled. Her heart pounded. The eyes of the men shifted from one another in a silent, private conversation. Dameon continued to circle the table until he stood in front of her.

"No," said Emma, strained. "It's... it's pee, I swear. It's not–"

Dameon seized her wrists and pulled them above Emma's head. He slammed her hands into the table, making it shake loudly. He squeezed out the slightest amount of pain around her hands. She raised her head to see dark-blue eyes level with hers. His face was only inches away and held a dangerously serious expression. Emma felt her core involuntarily tighten again. She felt a sense of betrayal in herself. She didn't mean to be wet.

"We have one rule above all others in this home," he said. His voice was gruff and low. "No lies," Dameon said.

A needle pierced Emma's ankle. It burrowed deep into her skin, her muscles. She choked on the sharp pain. She wanted to move, to run, to fight. A terrible fear increased when she realized she couldn't feel her foot move. There would be no running now. Emma tried unsuccessfully to swallow the lump in her throat as Dameon demanded her attention. His grip on her wrists tightened uncomfortably.

"You will hear only the truth in our home, and we will expect the same from you. You will follow this requirement. Do you understand?"

Emma nodded.

"Say it," Dameon snarled.

"Yes, I understand."

"No," Dameon said, coldly. "Say it. Admit what is happening between your legs."

"Dameon!" Elijah scolded.

The beginnings of Emma's, "please," was cut off by a near numbing pressure to her wrists. She tried to look back but a warning look from Dameon told her she'd regret it if she tried. She could hear the sound of scissors being snipped in the air. Emma shook as Dameon waited for her to speak.

"I don't..." she whispered, "I don't mean to be... it doesn't mean–"

A half smile graced his lips. Dameon eased up on his hold.

"I believe you," Dameon said. "Try not to beat yourself up over it, it's not your fault. It's a common enough reaction. Some bodies are quick to prepare for the worst, for what it thinks is about to happen."

He looked back at Elijah, then quickly back to Emma. Dameon's grip got tighter again. He transferred both wrists into a single hand. With his other, he placed her face in his palm and moved his lips centimeters away from hers. Emma felt something chilly spill and drip around her leg. A hot tear traveled down the side of her nose and salted her lips.

"How old are you," he asked.

"T... Twenty-five."

"Only three years younger than myself," he said. "How old does that make me?"

Emma couldn't think. It was simple, easy math. Why couldn't she think? Why was he asking her this? She felt the pressure of another needle sink into her leg. Dameon's face coaxed her to answer. She counted stupidly in her head. Six, seven, eight.

"Twenty-eight."

"Very good," he breathed. "Now, tell me your name."

"Please," she whispered.

"I said, what is your name?"

"Emma. Emma Kincaide."

More tears silently flowed. Emma closed her eyes tight and locked her teeth together. She squeezed her fists shut. She waited for more. Dameon brushed sweaty and untidy hair from her face. He cradled her cheek and wiped away the burning drops from her green eyes. She opened to see his gaze staring at her lips. He was so close. Dameon tilted his head and leaned in. She held her breath. He pulled away before making contact and bit his lip.

He was playing with her, tormenting her. Emma's breath shook out. He moved in quickly and hovered again. Dameon parted his lips and looked like he was ready to devour her. The table gave a little rock as Elijah manipulated her leg into a different position and tugged at her body. She couldn't feel what was happening. She was too numb, and she wasn't permitted to look. She begged for him to stop.

"No," Dameon said, simply. "But keep those pretty eyes on me, it'll be over soon."

More tears ran over her cheeks.

"You said you weren't as bad as Grant," she whispered.

"The honesty rule only exists inside our home. I lied," he said. "Well, mostly. There are some lines, even we don't cross."

Dameon looked back at Elijah once more. Pity and amusement dripped from his words.

"Well done, Emma Kincaide."

A startled scream left her lips when Elijah slapped the chrome table. He let out a triumphant, "Ha," and snapped something cream-colored and latex through the air that landed in a nearby trash bin. She looked at the discarded item and realized it wasn't what she initially suspected. It was a glove. It was bloody, but just a glove.

"Done," Elijah said, pridefully. "So quick, it might even be a record."

"Take a look," Dameon said, giving Emma considerably more breathing room.

Evidence that the tear in her leg had been expertly fixed, rested on a little side table. She was beautifully wrapped in clean bandages. Her sterilized leg contrasted heavily with the mess that was the rest of her body. She turned back to Dameon. She suddenly wondered if he was being malicious, or if he was trying to distract her from Elijah's work. Either way, he succeeded.

Elijah grinned.

"But really," he said. "I think stitches might be my favorite thing. There's just something satisfying about sewing it all back together."

"You're a little strange," Matthew said. "You know that, right? It's not normal to like this bloody shit."

Yeah…" said Elijah. "Because you know so much about being normal? Because anyone here knows normal?"

Dameon puffed a single laugh. He smirked at his medically inclined partner, but his eyes gave way to a look of defeat and pain as he toppled to the floor.

"Dameon!" shouted Matthew, very much distressed.

The huge man immediately abandoned his tough-guy role. He left Emma without a second thought and dropped to the ground. Matthew lifted Dameon's upper half and held his friend to his chest. His eyes were panicked and fearful. His expression was that of a lost child.

Dameon made Matthew aware that his side was the source of the problem. Matthew ripped Dameon's jacket away to reveal a bloody white shirt beneath. He tore the shirt open to find duct tape wrapped around his body in an attempt to keep the blood contained. It hadn't worked well.

"When," Elijah shakily asked.

"At the shop." Dameon groaned. "The asshole stabbed me when he realized what was up."

Elijah looked at Emma, her leg, Dameon, then Emma again. He launched out of his seat and took Emma by the arm. He practically dragged her off the table and pushed her into a nearby closet. Elijah flipped the light switch with a slap, then slammed the door behind him. Emma toppled to the floor and heard the distinct sound of being locked in.

Emma's leg was completely numb, rendering her unable to stand. At least it didn't hurt anymore. She looked around the cramped room. Shelves lined each of the walls. Boxes neatly organized in the room said things like: Steri-Strips, Trauma Dressing, and Sterile Burn Sheets. It was a mini-hospital. These people had a legitimate emergency room in their home.

Stethoscopes, even a portable AED, was in this closet alone.

Emma heard a painful shout and swearing from the other side of the door. She looked around the room for something, anything, that could improve her situation. Sterile Scalpels, IV Kits. She didn't have a plan but... she paused. Emma shot to her feet and then right back down when her leg gave out. More carefully this time, she stood on her good side and reached for the box of scalpels. She took one of the individually wrapped blades and tore open the package. It was tiny, but sharp, and it was all she had. She sat on the floor, leaned against an orange EMT kit, and waited.

Minutes passed, or maybe hours. She couldn't tell in the closed off room. The pained noises from outside subsided. She wondered if their leader had died. She wondered what they would do to her if he had. In the midst of Emma going down the rabbit hole of ways she wouldn't make it out of the closet alive, the lock clicked.

The handle twisted. Elijah and Matthew stood in the doorway. Matthew looked curiously at the tiny woman sitting on the floor and the tiny blade in her hands. She tried to keep from shaking as they looked down on her. She gripped tighter, trying to steady the scalpel. They were clearly unfazed. She noticed significant blood stains on both of them and wondered how much was hers and how much belonged to Dameon.

"You're up," Elijah directed.

Matthew nodded his head and started for Emma. She pushed herself up with the help of the shelves behind her. She swung the scalpel wildly through the air. Matthew merely leaned back a measure to dodge her attack. She lunged forward with a poorly planned step and fell, thanks to her useless leg. Emma reached out to rip at Matthew's ankles, maybe even slice a tendon.

"Hey, hey, hey." Elijah said, his voice sounding exhausted. "There's no need for that."

Matthew stomped on the tiny blade, pinning her fingers to the floor with it. Emma pulled hard at the handle of the medical tool, and cracked her knuckles whilst freeing herself. She looked helplessly around for something else. She should have made a backup plan. Emma tossed a box of gauze at the huge man, who swatted the projectile.

"If you keep throwing things at me," he threatened, "I'll start to take it personally."

Matthew's impatience grew as he waited for Emma to comply. She let a spool of surgical tape roll out of her hand, and topple to a stop at his feet. Emma trembled as he lowered to her level. He gathered her hands in one of his and lifted her to her feet.

"Don't let her walk, please," said Elijah.

Matthew respected the request and swept her legs from under her. Emma wrapped her arms around his neck in a panic. She didn't want a painful drop to the stone floor again. She felt so small next to him, so unfairly matched. Her captor didn't pause as he walked past the beautiful front door of the penthouse. She kept her eyes on the lock-covered exit until it was out of sight.

They continued down a gorgeous hallway, far from the emergency room. Matthew stopped at a simple white door with a brass handle and card reader. He awkwardly pulled out the keycard and unlocked the door, making it mechanically hum. He popped the door open with this hip, and carried Emma inside.

"This key is the only thing that can open that door," Matthew said, losing her hold and dropping her onto a bed. "Only its holder can enter or leave."

A simple room was made stunning by a wall of floor to ceiling glass. Designed like a hotel room for business trips, the decor was clean, and neutral. A wooden desk and black rolling chair nestled into a corner, with a minifridge at its side. The white walls, white sheets, and a white bedside table, made the gray throw blanket on the bed seem like an exciting color. Just beyond the bed, was a private bathroom; elegant, but equally lacking in color. Though modest in size, the view could not be beat.

Las Vegas put on a dazzling display through the enormous window. Everything could be seen; the strip, casinos, cars in the distance. They had to be at least twenty stories high. And yet, though she may have been able to see the entire city, there wasn't a person in the city that could see her. The view provided the best of everything, except for hope. There wasn't a single neighbor to see her call for help.

"It's not what I expected," she said.

Matthew raised an eyebrow. He sat next to her, and moved close. She scooted away, wanting more distance between them. Her reluctance to be next to him made him smile weakly.

"When you took me, I guess I pictured a leaky basement, maybe a dungeon or something. I didn't exactly imagine this when I was taken prisoner."

Matthew laughed.

"Prisoner huh? Sounds like someone that hasn't lived in Vegas long. Basements don't exist in Vegas, the ground is too hard. But as for a dungeon…"

He smiled in a way that made Emma concentrate on her breathing again.

"Let's just say, you don't belong in that part of the penthouse."

"Wait. You actually have a dungeon?"

Matthew's grin frightened her.

"Yes. We have our own, personal, urgent care. Is it really so hard to believe that we also have a dungeon? But like I said, you really don't deserve that kind of treatment. If you were to see the things we do, the pain Dameon loves to inflict… You think you're nervous now? You don't know us, and you definitely don't know me."

Matthew moved closer to Emma. She didn't move away this time, only cowered under his massive presence. The side of his leg touched hers. His solid arm slid behind her, as he leaned into her space. She lowered her head and tried to shrink into nothing. Emma gripped the blanket under her and tried hard to look back at Matthew. She managed a quick glance into his caramel-colored eyes but immediately looked away.

"If you think I am saying these things to make you scared, you would be right. There is no way out of this place. Start a fire? I will kill you before anyone has a chance to save you. Misbehave? You will face consequences."

Emma flinched when Matthew moved to leave her side. He stood and opened the door. He turned back to face Emma.

"It would be smart of you to be a good… little prisoner."

Emma nodded.

"Oh, and one more thing. Elijah suggested that you not get that leg wet for a few days, not that I can guarantee you'll be around that long. Feel free to shower but for your own sake, mind the leg."

He winked and closed the door behind him. Emma heard the lock automatically activate. There really was no escape.

3 | A Mind Is A Terrible Thing To Lose

Alone in the room, Emma was left with only her thoughts. It wasn't great company, considering she was completely overwhelmed, tired, afraid, and her leg was gaining an increasing amount of pain. She smelled of sweat and adrenaline, but nothing, not even a simple shower, felt comfortable. Paranoia took root as she stepped into the bright bathroom.

The thought of hidden cameras crossed her mind before undressing, and compelled her to do a quick search. She checked around the bottles of jasmine soap and opened every drawer and bathroom cabinet. She didn't find cameras, but did find extra soap, wash cloths, tampons, pads, toothbrushes and toothpaste. It was guest ready, and Emma didn't know whether to be grateful or concerned that it was so readily prepared.

Emma awkwardly wrapped her clean bandage in a clear plastic curtain, and turned the shower on. Warm water trickled filthily down the drain. The flowery perfume of soaps impregnated the steamy room as Emma tried to banish the stink of terror that lingered in her every pore. She scrubbed away the dark stains the asphalt left on her worn feet. She lightly rubbed the sore scratches on her shoulder and arm, but couldn't avoid the sting that accompanied removing the dirt.

Once somewhat satisfied and clean of the terrible day, she exited the shower and wrapped a fluffy towel around her body. Emma picked up her discarded tank top from the floor and felt the grime of it in her hands. It somehow seemed more dirty than she remembered. She hated it, but what choice did she have. She gripped her towel tighter, and returned to the room, gross clothes in hand.

On the bed were two neatly folded men's shirts and basketball shorts. A hastily written note rested on the small pile with the words, "little prisoner" on the torn piece of notebook paper. At least her captors were nice enough to provide her with clean clothes. She pulled a big, white, men's shirt over her head and swam in the fabric. It fit her more like a short dress than a shirt. The pants were so large, she decided to forego wearing them at all, at least to bed.

Emma winced as she pushed herself under the covers. The poofy comforter was more luxurious than she had ever felt. She wished she could fully enjoy the feeling, but being there against her will, and her stitches rapidly losing their numbness, made it difficult. Emma closed her eyes, and tried to force herself to sleep before her leg became too painful.

Nightmares awaited Emma. Matthew strangled her to death in the first dream. In another, Elijah thoroughly abused her before stabbing her with a scalpel. Many of her nightmares, in true dream fashion, made little sense. One involved Dameon. They were in a medieval dungeon. His eyes turned red, and magically set her on fire. She felt the burning start in her leg, then eventually consume the rest of her. Emma woke with a start, yet again and wondered if she'd ever get to stay asleep.

She panicked when she saw Elijah leaning against the desk in her room. The yellow sunrise bounced off a pair of scissors that Elijah twirled in his fingers. He snipped at the air absentmindedly, making bone chilling scraping sounds of metal against metal. Emma was getting sick of these dreams. When she moved to begin her next fight, her leg unbearably burned under the blanket, rooting her in reality. It wasn't a dream.

"Shit," she nervously whispered.

Elijah approached the bed and pulled back the covers that were hiding her naked lower half. Emma tried to throw a punch at the man. He caught her fist with devastating ease. When she went for another try, Elijah's fingers wrapped tight around her other wrist. Emma jerked and fought his hold, sounding a rageful and terrified scream.

"Shhh!" he hissed.

The white blanket bunched as he pushed her arms into the bed. The closed scissors in his right hand pressed roughly against her left arm. She kicked at her attacker, provoking Elijah to straddle her legs to keep her down.

"Stop fighting me," he said, strenuously. "You don't have to be so difficult, it's getting annoying."

Emma stopped the combatant kicks of her legs; not because she wanted to make anything easier for him, but because it hurt her to do so. Her leg throbbed and burned. Though she went into the fight with some hope, he clearly had won. Her strength was no match for his.

"Good, I hope it ruins it for you," she cried, pulling hard at his grip on her arms.

Tears ran down her face as she pressed her knees together as tightly as she possibly could. Doing so pained her leg, but she couldn't fight the instinct. Elijah tilted his head down to see Emma trying to cross her legs under him. His tone shifted and took on a greater note of irritation.

"Oh my god, girl! Stop! Use your brain. Look at me. What exactly do you think a man like me would want to do with a woman like you?"

Elijah's words hit her like a smack to the face. She stared up at him. It was only after she paused her fight, and really took in his appearance, that she noticed what she hadn't before. His shirt was flowery, feminine, pink, and quite possibly a woman's tank-top. Not only that, but his shorts were small, bright, and yellow. He raised a sassy brow and waited. He was wearing a shiny lip gloss. Did he have pink eyeshadow?

"There it is," he said. "I'm here to check up on you, not fuck you. Please, stop trying to fight, so I can stop holding you like this. There's a chance I hate it just as badly as you do."

She relaxed her muscles best she could, and Elijah responded with an eased hold in turn. Deliberately and gently, Elijah let go of Emma. He monitored her with deserving distrust.

"I'm not going to lie and say I won't hurt you. I simply can't promise that, especially if you are going to try to hit me. But you don't need to worry about me trying to–"

Elijah exhaled in exasperation.

"I just need to check my work for signs of infection."

Emma pulled the bottom of the large shirt down, trying to gain more coverage despite her realization that Elijah may not have an interest in her, let alone any woman. Elijah noticed, and a flicker of pain crossed his face. Did he feel bad for her situation, or was she merely grasping for hope?

"Please," he requested. "Roll over so I can get a good look. I don't want to unnecessarily twist your leg around and stress the stitches."

Emma did as he asked without fighting. He ran a blade of the scissors under the bandages, and undressed them with a snip. Emma flinched at the sound, then again when he ran his thumb along the side of the sensitive skin. Emma hissed in pain.

"Don't move," he said, placing the metal scissors on the bedside table with a clank. "I'll be right back."

Elijah left Emma for only a few minutes. He returned to the room nearly as quickly as he left. In his possession was a translucent bottle, cotton balls, new gauze, and tape. Elijah dispensed the items on the small table next to her and sat to the side of Emma. He soaked a cotton ball in the clear liquid, placed a gentle hand on her lower leg, and paused.

"Emma," he said, carefully. "I'd feel a lot better if you put the pointy object back on the table."

Her heart sank at being caught so instantaneously. She considered lying but knew how pointless it would be. Elijah removed his hand and glanced at the only exit.

"I'd rather not call Matthew for backup."

His tone didn't sound threatening. Rather, he sounded as if he was giving her a chance to fix her mistake. Elijah gave her a moment to reconsider her move. She didn't budge.

"Honey, I'm pretty sure he's itching for a reason to be worse than the villain you thought I was. You don't want him in here."

That sounded like a threat. She retrieved the scissors from under her pillow. The blades chattered against the wood top as she placed them, with a shaking hand, on the table.

"Thanks, because this is definitely going to make you want to stab me."

He didn't give her time to jerk away before pressing the burning cleaning agent over her wound. She squeezed her pillow and groaned loudly through gritted teeth.

"Almost done, the worst is over," he comforted.

Elijah dressed her leg in new gauze and rose from the bed.

"It's not bad, shockingly. Tetanus shouldn't be a problem after the shot I administered during the stitches, and so far there are no signs of infection. It just needs a lot of care. If you need to start antibiotics, we'll get you covered, just keep it out of water for a few more days."

Emma uncomfortably rolled over and sat up in the bed. She eyed the scissors again. It would be nice to have some sort of defense, if not against Elijah, at least against the other two.

She thought of Matthew and his erection against her before being taken. She thought of the way he mentioned her wetness on the operating table. A picture of Dameon and the memory of his forceful hands on her wrists, the sounds of duct tape being ripped from itself to bind her to the container wall of the truck. The thought of the dungeon.

"Sorry," Elijah said, picking up the sharp tool, "these are coming with me. I can't have you attacking my... associates."

Elijah trailed off for an uncomfortable moment.

"Anyway, try to relax. If things go my way, you'll be out of here soon."

The blond man was nearly out of the room when Emma found her voice.

"And if things don't go your way?"

Elijah's face resembled a marble statue, hard and unfeeling.

"Then I'm sorry, but at least you probably won't have long to worry about it."

Days had gone by. Elijah left her meals of instant oatmeal, granola bars, and the like. Every meal was some type of survival-style food left in a basket for her on the office desk. He checked her healing cuts and scrapes each day. With the passing of time, he stopped wrapping her leg. The stitches remained, but she was assured her leg was mending better than

Elijah could have hoped for.

Emma sat in the spinning office chair and counted how many full rotations she could make with a single push. She paced the room, testing the limits of the pain in her leg. She took baths and challenged herself to hold her breath under the warm water until her heart pounded in her ears, just to kill time. She stared at the texture of the white walls until she could make out shapes. She made up stories for the imaginary faces in the wall because, frankly, there was little else to do.

Emma was grateful that she wasn't being horribly harmed or killed, but the sheer nothingness was doing a number on her. In its own way, the solitude without a bit of stimulating activity was enough to count as torture. A clock didn't exist in the room. Would the ability to tell time be a blessing or curse? She had her massive window to keep track of the change from day to night, but that was all. She imagined that with a clock, she'd find herself sitting in front of it for hours at a time, counting the seconds with its ticking hands.

In her daydreams she played with thoughts revolving around what might be happening just outside her room. More often than that, she imagined scenarios leading to her escape. She made up fantasies of Elijah finding pity, and allowing her to slip out unnoticed. In her greatest moments of delusion, she dreamed of attempting to seduce Matthew or Dameon into letting her go.

She was clearly losing it. She could never trust or feel much more than fear for either of those men. Matthew was brutish and seemingly barbaric, from what she could gather. Dameon was daunting and demanded a sense of power in whatever space he was in. Not that she had seen them since the day they brought her into this prison.

Elijah was the only person she ever had contact with, if you could call coldly delivering instant meals to her contact. She wished he would at least speak to her. It always looked like he was doing the dishes or taking out the trash when tending to her. He arrived with food or medical supplies, then left with the look of having something more important to do. The interaction was so small, Emma started singing songs to herself just to keep her voice in use. If she hadn't lost her mind yet, she soon would at this rate.

Emma found herself thinking about how she got here in the first place. She thought of Grant. She remembered his charismatic smile and conversations when she met him as a waitress at a local sports bar. He was so full of optimism and promise. He became a regular, coming in nearly every day for a week, just to see her.

Grant was on an extended trip to Alabama. His goal was to expand the marketing business he was a part of. Though he returned home to Las Vegas without the business deal he was hoping for, he, instead, came back with her. Grant wanted to be Emma's knight in shining armor. She was only a paycheck away from living on the street again after a lifetime of hard luck. After running from her abusive household at the age of sixteen, Emma struggled to have the bare minimum for all of her following days. Grant wanted to take her away with him, live with him, be her savior of a boyfriend.

Emma should have known better than to get on a plane with a man she barely knew. But damn if he wasn't a smooth negotiator. It didn't help that she was desperate. The economic environment in her small town was taking a terrible turn. She was given a kind heads-up from her boss that the little bar wouldn't be able to keep her for much longer. She had nowhere to go and Grant pounced on the opportunity.

She liked him. He seemed enamored with her. Emma didn't realize until her feet hit the desert soil of the new city, that Grant was never a knight. He was a wolf on the hunt for desperation and found it in her. It only took a short time before Grant realized that he made a significant mistake. What he really wanted was someone to mold into his idea of his perfect woman. He wanted someone soft spoken, conservatively dressed, and willing to do anything he desired; after so graciously saving her from her impoverished life. Emma was nothing like what he had hoped for.

Starting their final fight, Grant was fussing over an, admittedly, flirtatious barista. The young man triggered Grant's pride, and simultaneously, his easily tapped jealousy. The working stranger assumed that of the two coffees, the fancy, sweet, cup was for Emma and the simple black pour was Grant's. It was a simple mistake. Emma didn't argue over the little mess up and wordlessly switched with Grant.

The mix-up wasn't the only mistake. Grant rotated his paper cup, revealing a phone number and cute little heart. Emma rolled her eyes. She was sick of his controlling insecurities. She didn't ask for the unsolicited number, but to him, that was an irrelevant detail. Grant criticized her saying that her eyes were too dark, her shirt too low cut. He felt that if she was more "presentable" she wouldn't get hit on.

Grant hated that she only wore the most "revealing" clothes he paid for. Emma reminded him that he wouldn't have to worry about wasting his money if he would agree to let her have a job. He was the one that got upset every time she came up with solutions.

"You're not working at that club," Grant said.

"It's a waitressing gig," she argued. "It's the only job I have qualifications for. I'm tired of you lording your financial power over me. I want the damn job."

"No! You don't know this town. You don't know the kind of dangerous people that own those places. You aren't working there. And quit cursing."

"Then what am I supposed to do?"

"We've talked about this! If you really want to work, you can work for me. I don't get why you are so opposed to staying at home, having a few kids, and letting me be the man. I wouldn't have brought you here, if I thought you'd be so ungrateful."

"Letting you be the what? Ungrateful," Emma fumed. "You're unbelievable, you know that? I can only work if it's for you. I can only make friends with the people you approve of. You want to tell me how to talk, how to dress, how to breathe! It's bullshit. I'm sick of it!"

Emma looked around the white cell of a room. It all seemed rather ironic now. She was so angry at Grant for being a controlling prick. She wanted freedom, choices, a little independence. Now she sat day after day in a colorless cage, waiting for a decision to be made as to whether she would be let go or killed.

She looked out to the cityscape and wondered if these were the terrible people Grant warned her about. They clearly had a load of money. Her mind wandered into the possibility of working at a club for Dameon. He could have been her boss. She never would have known what secrets he and his roommates hid away in their elaborate safehouse. Now, she was the secret. How many people did he interact with on a daily basis that would never suspect that he was keeping a woman locked away in their tower?

A particularly bright morning cast a shine in the room, one morning. Emma sat in the simple office chair and faced the window. Her eyes were closed, clinging to the warmth of the sun against her skin.

From behind, the lock made its little noises behind her. She hadn't seen anyone in days and was looking forward to the presence of another person, even if getting him to talk would be like pulling teeth. Still, she waited anxiously for the announcing sound of Elijah's entrance.

Emma casually swiveled the chair, with a flick of her foot, to face him with a smile. It wasn't Elijah. Matthew lingered in the doorway and surveyed the blank room. Emma's heart dropped.

"You seem disappointed."

Emma didn't answer. In her attempt to get to her feet, the chair spun out from under her. Emma fell to the floor in a thud. It sent a shock of pain up her leg. The wound seemed closed but Elijah insisted on keeping the stitches for a while longer. Even so, her healing limb was decently sensitive.

Emma stumbled back as Matthew reached into his back pocket. They had made their decision. This was it. She would die in this room. He moved closer with unforgiving eyes. Emma scrambled to her feet and backed against the window. The warmth of the glass could be felt through the fabric of the oversized shirt.

Slowly, Matthew pulled out a small, rectangular, shape. He tapped its edge against the desk twice, and left it on its surface. He grinned at Emma's darting eyes that jumped from the piece of plastic to him.

"Turns out, your stay might be staying a little longer than I would have hoped. So, I was told to bring you this."

Matthew left Emma nervously against the glass as he stepped back to reach just outside of the door. He retrieved a small microwave with a dial for a timer. A full bag of groceries hung around his wrist. Matthew dropped the appliance carelessly on the desk and plugged it in.

"These," he said, tossing the bag into the freezer portion of the minifridge, "are yours too."

Emma's heart sank at the addition to the room. She should have been relieved by the gesture. But to her, the clock-less microwave told her that she could be stuck in that room for much longer than she had hoped. Hooray for not being murdered, but this wasn't a great option either.

Matthew circled a finger around the tiny gift left on the desk as he strolled back to the door. He paused before leaving to study the woman's fearful stance and curious expression.

"Just a reminder," he said, quietly. "There is no getting out of this penthouse. You have not been given permission to leave this room. If you are caught, there will be consequences."

Emma nodded, cautiously.

A false smile found Matthew's face that terrified Emma from across the room.

"Enjoy the microwave. Don't stick a fork in it, or anything stupid."

The door automatically locked behind him as he left her alone again. Emma waited for as long as she could manage, just in case Matthew decided to make a second appearance. When he didn't, she darted to the desk. It was a keycard. She looked from the plastic, to the door, several times.

Matthew made a point to remind her that she wasn't allowed to leave. But then why would he leave a key in the room? Was it a test of some sort? He certainly didn't seem like the kind or caring type, so it was unlikely that he was taking pity on her maddening situation. Elijah made it sound like Matthew was looking for an excuse to harm her. Was this bait?

Emma glanced around at the confining boring walls. Slowly, nervously,

Emma picked up the key and let her feet lead her to the only exit. Emma used the key on the electronic lock. The mechanical parts sounded and clicked into an unlocked position. The lock stayed open for just under a minute then returned to its original locked position.

Her heart pounded. It worked. Emma put her back to the door and sunk to the floor. This was great! This was terrible! Matthew really gave her a working key to her room. It was a cruel trick. She had been stuck within these horrible walls for days and now, she was handed the chance to break the rules. She needed out, obviously, but couldn't leave. New anxieties danced in her mind at this new, exciting, and terrifying development.

Emma ran her fingers along the edges of the smooth, thin, plastic card. She jumped to her feet, leg irritatingly reminding her of its affliction. She rushed to the bed, grabbed a pillow, and shoved the key deep inside a white pillowcase.

She thought about telling Elijah the next time she saw him. But what if he didn't know? What if the key was meant to be a secret just between her and Matthew? What if by telling Elijah, she would lose the card? What if he already knew and he was waiting to see if she would turn it over?

Matthew was far from being an advocate for her safety. The man wanted her dead and didn't spare her feelings by keeping his wishes a secret. Elijah led her to believe that he didn't hold the same sentiment. He may not have been the most friendly of hosts, but he cared enough to patch her up and keep bringing her food. No, Elijah wouldn't know about this. He wanted her gone but not killed. Emma bet that Elijah didn't know about whatever Matthew's plan might be. But what exactly was Matthew's plan?

Emma sat on the bed, the chair, and the floor. She waited for the pretty blond man for a day, then two, then three. He never showed up. In fact, she hadn't seen anyone since Matthew left the card. The rations she was given were starting to dwindle. She hadn't been left alone for this many consecutive days before.

Was she expected to simply leave? What if, when she opened the door, she would discover the front door to the penthouse completely unlocked? Was she sitting in this miserable room only because she was too intimidated to

42

move, while her freedom nestled in the depths of a pillowcase? Matthew's words rang in her ears. She wasn't given permission to leave. Was that what she was waiting for, permission?

The days started to blur together the more Emma thought about how long she had been confined to the room. To the best of her knowledge, it had been over a week since her arrival. Two weeks? It was an eternity of white walls, of fear, of boredom, of instant meals, and of minimal human contact. She wished she had kept track better and understood why prisoners marked the days on the walls.

Maybe she was being dramatic. Maybe she hadn't been alone eating watery oatmeal and soggy microwaved vegetables for long. How much time did it really take for a person to lose their mind when in a situation like hers? Emma paused a quarter of the way into singing Mr. Sandman by The Chordettes when she felt a mental hand reach out to grab a fleeting piece of her sanity. She reached into the pillow just to feel the little key. It was there. It was in her hand. She couldn't sit on it forever.

Emma jolted upright when she heard the handle make the slightest movement. A hand rested on the other side. Was it Elijah? Matthew? Her mind whirled with indecisiveness. If it was Elijah, she would tell him. No, she wouldn't, she couldn't. He would be standing in front of her in less than a minute and she still hadn't decided.

Mumbling voices she couldn't quite make out sounded from the hall. Tragedy crushed Emma's heart when the handle was released. He left! He didn't even open the door. Regret nauseated Emma. She wasn't even given the opportunity to panic in person over what to tell the person on the other side. Even that would be better than her isolation.

She slid from the bed and pressed her ear to the door. Nothing. She couldn't hear anything. Emma wanted to take back her fearful thoughts. She didn't mean it. She just wanted to see someone.

"Please," she whispered to the door. "Don't go."

Forehead pressed against the door, Emma closed her eyes. She resented the pretty view of a world she wasn't allowed to touch, smell, live in. The white walls shrunk around her. The bed took up too much space. There wasn't enough floor. She was being strangled by the loathsome place.

Emma crawled to the bed. She pulled her secret-keeping pillow down to the floor with her. She traced the outline of the card through the thin fabric. Her vision blurred as she hugged the plush material and watched the unmoving door.

4 | Keys Unlock Doors

By day eight, ten, or fourteen, of Emma's stay in her personal hellhole, her hatred for her captivity overpowered her fear of the unknown. Between her erratic sleep schedule, boredom, and poor eating habits, she couldn't remember how many times the sun rose and set. She stood, arms crossed, feet from the locked door. Sorrow, self-pity, and worry were replaced with frustration and defiance.

Elijah never returned, and she had very little food left. As far as she was concerned, she didn't have a choice anymore. Test or no test, she was ready to push the limits of her nerve. If she left the room, she could die. If she stayed, she would quite possibly starve to death. Of course she was afraid, but the card she twirled around her fingers finally became too tempting to resist. Emma stared out the window, and waited until the sun had been lost behind the mountains and the city glowed again.

She pulled at the length of her massive shirt, second guessing her decision not to wear the shorts. The length would be acceptable for any short dress, but she felt insanely exposed without underwear. Emma picked up the shorts and puffed an irritated cheek of air out when looking at the waist. Even with the assistance of the drawstring, the shorts could barely stay up on her small frame.

Eventually, she decided against it, not wanting to spend every moment out of the room holding her pants up. What would it matter anyway? If anyone caught her, she doubted a loose pair of shorts would make a difference if they wanted to harm or murder her.

Emma's hand hovered over the knob. Anxiety and excitement tingled her skin. Her hands shook as she used the card to escape. The lock whirled. She pushed, and inched the door open. Nothing happened. No alarms, no one jumped out to exclaim that they had caught her. Emma moved cautiously out of the room and let the door close behind her. The lights were out but the moon bounced luminous beams off the seemingly glowing surfaces. Her barefoot steps were quiet, yet too loud for her liking. She made her way down the hall, distancing herself from the dreadful room.

Emma found herself at the center of two elaborate rounded staircases that mirrored each other. Their steps were stone, and a dark iron railing twisted with nature-centric inspiration. The circular space made up the foyer of the home, and with a simple look at the front door, she could see there was still no way out. The retinal scanner and locks made that instantly apparent.

The light of the city lit up the penthouse, courtesy of more floor-to-ceiling windows. The entire side of the multistory penthouse was made of glass, and faced the sparkling Strip. The red top of the Stratosphere pierced the sky. A white beam, shown like a beacon from the Luxor. The hotels and casinos cast a defiant glow of light pollution in the night. The view was breathtaking, as was the architecture, that she didn't have time to appreciate before.

Her heart pounded with every step she took towards the beginning of the circular stairs. She rested one hand on the cold iron. With the other, she gripped her keycard like the most valuable of lifelines. The layout of the home was open, grand, and resembled a palace in the sky.

She looked up at the open second story. The black vines of the railing wrapped around the border to the top level. A number of large, leafy, plants in massive pots decorated the second floor and could be seen from the first. A loud snap echoed through the house. Emma dropped to the ground, held her knees close to her chest, and gripped the keycard so tightly, it left little lines in her palm. She looked around, but there wasn't a person in sight. She took a quiet breath.

The noise came from upstairs. Her hand shook as she reached again for the smooth railing and took silent steps up to investigate, against her better judgment. At the last step, Emma's feet left the stone and were welcomed by an elegant carpeted floor that complemented the thorny design of the iron.

Two more quick cracking noises sounded, followed by a painful moan. This was a bad idea. It was a very bad idea. Emma considered running back to the room, but the thought of willingly going back so soon made her stomach turn. And yet, terror was still preferable over losing her mind in that place.

The second floor seemed to be made up of six or so rooms all neatly bordered by the railing. As curious as she was to look inside, she decided not to press her luck to that degree. She walked with additional care towards the other set of stairs. If she wasn't brave enough to try peeking into any of the rooms, there was little to see in this space. She had more to explore. Besides, putting some distance between her and whatever was happening to the victim on this level, was also a selling point in returning to the first floor.

The startling bang of a door being slammed open shocked Emma like a bolt of lightning. She dropped behind the cover of one of the fat plants that periodically decorated the banister. Heart beating out of her chest and fear in her throat, she tried to remain quiet. In that moment, it seemed there was little she could do to stifle her own deafeningly loud breaths of existence. An inkling of regret dripped its way into Emma's mind. What if they already knew? Emma's thoughts were quickly disrupted by the person that so violently threw the door open and strode into the hall.

"Fine, have fun. Enjoy your little game, but I'm not interested." said Elijah as he stepped close to the iron border.

He ran a hand through his thick, wavy hair. A heavy stone dropped in Emma's stomach when she saw the man. Elijah was dangerously close, unaware of her presence, and naked. Her eyes lingered for a little too long at Elijah's exposed self. He stood only a few feet away. Emma attempted to shake the momentary attraction from her brain. With as little noise as possible, she slid further into the shadows that barely provided the cover she needed to evade her kidnapper, while also providing her a view she was too intrigued to miss.

Blue hues of moonlight contoured his defined abdominal muscles. Elijah pursed his lips together and made an exaggerated, long, blink. His tight chest and arms tensed as he squeezed the railing in frustration. Emma's lower body warmed subtly at the sight despite the knowledge that he could never be attracted to her. She wondered if he had been kept from visiting her, or if it was his choice.

A white towel tightly gripped in Elijah's hand, flew through the air as he spun flamboyantly to face the dark room. His chiseled back and perfect ass made Emma feel uncomfortably turned on. A little roll of his shoulders proclaimed a sense of confidence. He was in a natural unabridged state of Elijah, and attraction aside, it was a sight to behold.

Another air-splitting snap echoed. The startling sound encouraged tattling leaves to shuffle as Emma flinched. Elijah didn't seem to notice.

"You get your stress out however you need to. I'll get mine out my way," he said.

"Go take your bubble bath, Elijah," growled Dameon, from the dark room.

"I will," said Elijah, with a snap of his fingers and a powerhouse of feminine sass. "But when I come back we're discussing the girl. I've been patient, but you're starting to piss me off. You can't ignore this mess away."

The terrifying sharp sound happened again, and was accompanied by a strained, angry, muffled moan.

"Bath. Go." warned Dameon, cooley, over the pained cries of his victim.

The thought sent an involuntary shiver through Emma, rustling the leaves once more. Despite the darkness of the hall, Emma could see an impatient eye roll radiate through Elijah's entire body. In a final act of defiance, Elijah whipped his towel in the open doorway. He immediately threw his hands in the air and backed away, giving Dameon a look of jesting regret.

"Whoa! Whoa! Woah! I'm not the one you're grumpy with, and I'm not interested in being on the receiving end of that thing. But this isn't over."

Panic raced through Emma's body as Elijah marched in the direction of her hiding spot. The man didn't notice the crouched woman. He was feet, then inches, then feet away from her.

"And maybe cool it with the ropes for a night," shouted Elijah, without turning back. "You don't always have to be so mean," he said, flinching this time at a final warning snap intended for him.

The panic was still present and strong in Emma's mind as her eyes followed Elijah. He made his way down the dark hall and into one of the rooms on the second floor. Clinging to her cover she slid to the other side of the foliage, keeping the barrier between her and her captor. Once certain Elijah was gone, she shut her eyes and let out a quiet breath of relief. With small, silent movements, Emma turned her back to her protective plant and sunk against the cold stone vase.

The door was still open. She wasn't safe yet. In her desperation not to be seen, Emma had traded hiding from Elijah for hiding from the unknown dangers of the new room. She realized that this may not have been the smartest move, but fear does not always nurture the best of decisions. She could try running back to her cage. She could pretend she never snuck out. She could return the key, proving that she could be trustworthy. And yet, curiosity bubbled inside of her like a mint dropped in soda.

Slowly, Emma followed one of the subtle thorny vines of the carpet's pattern. She allowed it to lead her eyes up to the open door. A fire's glow lightly illuminated the floor on the other side of the entryway. Up, up, she continued until she saw him, Matthew. His wrists were taped to an expensive looking, but short, oak chair that forced his long legs to bend in an exaggerated position. His mouth was sealed with the same sticky restraint.

Like Elijah, Matthew was missing his clothing. He was as Emma could have imagined. His arms, chest, abs, legs, all looked like he never missed a day at the gym in his life. If he looked big and strong before, he looked overwhelmingly indestructible now, even bound as he was. His torso proclaimed an undeniable sense of masculinity with a well groomed chest and navel. His eyes intensely fixed on a place out of her view in the room.

Mumbled words, too faint for Emma to hear, came from Dameon. She still could not see him. The unheard words were returned with a warning face from Matthew that conveyed something along the lines of, "don't you dare."

Another snap struck the air, but this time with a lightning fast visual for Emma. The end of a whip bit inches from Matthew's feet. His legs twitched hard in the chair, as did his proportionally and impressively sized dick. Elijah's average size seemed small in comparison. Then again, anyone would seem small when measured against the monstrosity that was Matthew.

It was a wonder that the giant didn't break the chair as he protested and angrily growled at his captor. In bone-chilling clarity, Emma heard a malicious chuckle coming from Dameon. Matthew continued to fruitlessly argue when out of the corner of his eye he caught her. Every cell in Emma's body turned to ice. It was over.

Matthew's eyes darted back to a still hidden Dameon, then her again. He didn't alert his captor. He didn't make any major sudden movements. Instead, Matthew raised a challenging brow and lowered his eyes slowly over Emma's body. His view was limited, between the protective shadows of the plant and her oversized shirt, but his silent intent was unmistakable. Deliberately, he closed his eyes, and opened to Dameon's direction. Anger abandoned, Matthew moaned pitiful and muffled pleas that drew Dameon into Emma's view.

Exasperation took hold as Emma wondered why the hell all three men had to be the personification of sex. Was she really so deprived of human interaction that she would want these men, or were they actually that enticing? Dameon continued the muscular trend among the three. Larger than Elijah, but not as buff as Matthew, Dameon never ceased to carry an aura of power. Now more than ever, every step nearer to Matthew was made with control and unparalleled confidence.

Slithering behind him, Dameon dragged the whip close. The weapon was long, brown, leather, and a source of some nervousness for Matthew. The huge man flinched slightly when Dameon lightly flicked it, harmlessly, between his victim's legs. Seeing the huge man flinch bred intrusive thoughts that made Emma smile. Matthew tilted his strong chin up. With a heavy breath from his chest, he wordlessly pleaded to the man that looked down on him with an icy expression.

A harsh, sticky, pop sounded when Dameon ripped the tape from Matthew's mouth. Emma clenched her jaw as she recalled the memory of Dameon taking that same material from her lips. With Emma, he had been careful and delicate. With Matthew, Dameon was searching for pain.

Emma nervously watched, sure Matthew would expose Emma's secret. She was certain Dameon wouldn't be as gentle with her if he caught her now. After all, she was warned that she would face consequences if caught. Were these the consequences? If so, what did Matthew do to deserve it? Did he know about the key?

"Rip a little harder next time," Matthew said, sarcastically through gritted teeth.

Dameon threw the whip violently across the room and bent down to Matthew's level. He held his fingers around his jaw like a vice grip.

"Am I being too gentle?"

Emma could have sworn that she saw a glimmer of nervousness behind Matthew's eyes. Warmth spread in Emma's face, and elsewhere. The fear that resided in her throat was swallowed and transformed into something resembling excitement in her stomach. A wetness began forming between her legs as a tightness grew in her core. With one hand Dameon pumped himself while the other held Matthew's long hair between his fingers.

For just a moment, Dameon closed his eyes while twisting strands of the chestnut waves. Matthew seized the moment to burn a hard gaze to Emma's eyes. He sent a quick grin to her then looked back to Dameon. Something inaudible was whispered from Matthew to Dameon, followed by an open mouth and inviting tongue.

Dameon wasted no time. He propped up his right foot and pressed it into Matthew's thigh. He tilted Matthew's head slightly and drove into his open mouth. Dameon's ass flexed as he used Matthew's throat like he owned him, drawing out strangled gagging noises.

Emma's chest rose and fell in heavy rhythm. Her legs pressed together tight. She fidgeted with the card, flipping it over and over when reality crashed into her. What was she doing? Emma shot up to her feet, a sharp pain coursing through her leg where her stitches reminded her of their existence. She sprinted through the warning pain to the stairs and quietly held the black iron railing with white knuckles. She gave herself a moment to regain some type of calm. Emma took a deep breath, then let it out. She repeated her attempt at control until her heartbeat felt manageable again.

The sound of a few deliberate coughs interrupted her attempts to gather herself. She spun and opened her eyes to see Matthew standing in front of her. His restraints were removed, along with a bit of arm hair around the wrists. Small traces of sticky residue clung to his skin. The moonlight kissed the hard lines of his body, just as it had Elijah's. The dark boxer-briefs he hastily pulled on did little to cover his hard self. Fear flooded Emma's being, and yet she still felt a warmth lingering between her legs.

Matthew closed in on her like a wolf to a doe. She moved backwards down the stairs. She took them one slow step at a time. He matched her pace until Emma's foot misstepped and slipped. Her heart leapt into her throat. She felt the fall numb her fingers and toes, and yet never tumbled down. Matthew caught Emma's wrist and held her in place, keycard shining in the moonlight.

Heat radiated from the grip which promised to bruise by morning. Would she make it to morning? The uncertain thought sent a sharp inhale to her lungs. The many warnings she was given flashed through her consciousness. He was looking for a reason to do something to her. She would face consequences if caught. That's why he left the key, he wanted an excuse to hurt her.

Matthew pulled her back up the few stairs. Once returned, he snatched the card from her hand. He smirked and tucked the card into his waistband.

"You picked an interesting night to break the rules," he said, quietly.

Emma wanted to respond but all she could muster were a few stuttering sounds. She trembled as Matthew touched her lower back beneath the oversized shirt. She made a mistake. She should have worn the shorts. His fingers followed the line of her spine to her neck. The shirt bunched below her breasts, pushing them up. Her sensitive tips increased in visibility under the clothing. Matthew jerked Emma closer into him, pulling at her waist. Instinctively, she balanced on the tips of her toes.

"Dameon doesn't like to be kept waiting," he whispered, into her ear. "He expects me to return quickly. You're welcome to have a closer look. I'm interested to see what he would do with you."

"N...no." she breathed out.

Matthew cocked his head.

"Are you sure?"

He leaned down and brushed his stubble across her cheek.

"Can you really tell me you aren't wet again?"

Emma squirmed to break free of Matthew's hold but he barely needed to exert the slightest effort to keep her in place. She was indeed wet. She was painfully aroused. Sure, Matthew was hot as hell. Sure, this was the first human touch she had felt in forever. But she didn't exactly want to have sex with the dangerous man holding her, or to be anywhere near Dameon either. She missed touch. God she missed touch! But more specifically, she missed a kind touch.

Emma looked up into Matthew's light-brown eyes and shivered. Nothing about him gave her the impression that he would be gentle. He wanted her dead and wasn't quiet about it. Even before getting her into the back of the moving truck, it was his suggestion to kill her. Certainty set in that he would hurt her in ways she could, and probably couldn't, imagine.

"Please," she struggled. "I'm not. And I'm sorry for looking... I won't do it again...I–"

In a rough pull he fixed Emma even closer. Her bare navel pressed against him, directing his hardness up and between their bodies. His massive dick strained the fabric struggling to contain him. One of Matthew's hands crawled up to Emma's hair and gave it a tug, commanding her to look up at him. His face was serious and warning.

"Lying is against the rules," he said, his tone sending a shiver through Emma. "I promise, Dameon won't be as forgiving as I am if he catches you breaking it. And don't ever apologize for the things you want."

"Is that another rule," she asked. The tightness between Emma's legs was unbearable.

"No." he said. "I just hate fake apologies."

Emma's free hand buried its fingers in Matthew's chest hair.

"I'm sorry I got caught." she whispered, testing her own audacity and his genuineness.

He responded with a raised brow but without a smile.

"That's not an apology," she said, hastily. "It's just the truth. I... I think I feel sorry for myself, that I liked what I saw, but that doesn't mean I want it."

Her eyes started to burn.

"I said I was sorry before, because I don't know what's going to happen. I don't know what you are going to do to me, and I'm tired! I'm tired of getting hurt," her voice shook. "All I want is... I just want to be held, to be told it's going to be okay."

A tear escaped alongside her embarrassment. She had cried so much in front of these men, she didn't mean to let that last bit out. She wished with every fiber of her being that she could be tough and fearless. Instead, she fell right back into being the scared little woman that got kidnapped by people that didn't want to take her in the first place, facilitated by a boyfriend that wanted her even less.

Matthew released her hair. He gently cradled the side of her face and cut off her train of thought with the warmth of his palm. His thumb lightly brushed over her lips as he softly hushed her.

"You caught me at a hell of a time," Matthew said, in a rough whisper, "and you are right to be afraid, little prisoner."

His hand behind her lowered.

"I want to hear you beg for it," he said, pulling her shirt back down, past her bare ass. "I want to hear you want me when you feel me."

Matthew loosened his hold.

"I don't know what we're gonna do with you, but I am not going to take you against your will. And if Dameon wanted to kill you, I wouldn't have caught you," he said, with a glance towards the stairs. "I would have pushed without a second thought."

Emma leaned her face into Matthew's warm hand. It was calloused and rough. She placed her hand over his and squeezed. Her tears wetted the creases between his thumb and fingers. The sobs she tried to fight off struggled in her chest.

"What are you going to do," she asked, eyes shut tight.

To Emma's surprise, Matthew wrapped his arms around her. His hand pressed her head to him as his fingers buried themselves in her hair. He pulled her so close, she could hardly breathe. His warmth surrounded her body, and his squeeze pressed her instability into something that wasn't all horror and fear.

"I'm going to take you back to your room. But, I'd highly recommend that you don't share this little moment with the others. I doubt they'd take it well."

The walk back to the room was accompanied by silence. Between the straightforward stare Matthew kept and the feeling that she shouldn't speak, Emma felt more like a prisoner than before.

An anxiety crept into her as the childish feeling like she got caught stealing cookies found its place in the air. In a rather sarcastic motion, Matthew opened the way to Emma's prison with a bow befitting a gentleman; an obnoxiously large, mostly naked, and highly attractive gentleman.

Her eyes fixed on the messy bed as she entered the room. She imagined Matthew's hands on her, and joining her in the bed. She shook the vision from her mind. Matthew wore a mischievous grin again and tapped his fingers on the brass handle of her door. Emma held her breath with reignited panic. She had so little time. Her heart broke at the loss of her key.

Before he gave Emma much time to mourn the loss, he flicked the card onto the bed.

"Do me a favor, don't get caught again. You were practically asking for Elijah to see you tonight, and I don't feel like explaining myself."

He paused, waiting for confirmation.

Emma said nothing, but nodded her head in understanding.

The door closed with a click. Emma sank into the fluffy sheets and held the key to her chest.

Her head spun with adrenaline and, frankly, an unhealthy amount of horniness. Emma gathered the card and pushed it back into its hiding place in the pillow. She plopped onto the bed, drowning in her thoughts. Dameon was a little scarier, and sexier, than she let herself imagine. Elijah seemed more irritated at her presence than he led on. Was that why he stopped delivering food? Was he angry enough at her being there to try starving her to death?

Matthew. Horrifying, intimidating, Matthew. The one she assumed to be the most brutal, was surprisingly interested in her consent. All this time, Emma thought Elijah might be her best chance of getting out of the penthouse alive. Now, she wondered if she was holding out hope for the wrong person.

Elijah kept her alive, but Matthew gave her what she wanted, something she hadn't received even long before being kidnapped. Emma pulled the covers over her shoulders and fell asleep thinking about the feeling of something so simple as a hug.

The sun beat into the room when morning came. With panic stricken movements, she checked for the key. Still there. Still hers. A rumbling stomach persuaded Emma to get out of bed and pour a bowl of instant oatmeal, again. It's funny. A girl can eat oatmeal for breakfast for weeks straight, but the second it isn't your decision to do so, it feels horribly tedious.

She slumped into the office chair, spilling a bit of the too-watery oats as she did. She was restless. She needed space, even more than she wanted it before. All she could think about was her next escape. Leaving the room might as well have been a drug, and she was already addicted to the high.

For a moment, she acknowledged the craziness of her situation. She was kidnapped, held against her will, possibly still facing death, and she was angry about being bored. It could be worse. It could be a lot worse. Yet, she couldn't scratch the itch to move. Her eyes relentlessly rested on the door, again.

"Welp," she mumbled, to no one in particular. "Guess I like to push my luck."

Emma pulled the heavy curtains closed. She snuggled back into bed and under the fluffy white blanket. She had a whole night to be awake for.

Orange, pink, and purple finally colored the sky behind great, dark mountains. Emma spun in the chair and positioned it to stare out the window. She watched the pretty sky darken. Planes scattered tiny lights over the glowing city. Gold, white, and neon polluted the darkness and signaled the beginning of Emma's evening. She stood in her dark room with the light off and made her way to the door.

She presented the key to its lock, pushed it open slowly, and took a look around. Nothing. The penthouse was silent. Emma stepped down the hall in the dark again. She touched the cold railing of the stairs. Last night's memory burned strongly in her mind. She was being reckless, but not so ridiculous to try the second floor again.

A benign glow emitted from an ever-present light under dark stained kitchen cabinets. Minding the sound of her steps, she investigated. The farthest corner room was fit for the best of chefs. Stainless steel shined from the appliances. Less walls existed than did the huge windows that showed off the city and desert. A massive dark and granite island counter boasted a tempting bowl of fresh fruit on its surface.

She took a banana, feeling a closeness to Eve or Persephone. If Elijah wasn't going to bring her food anymore, she'd have to take this time to eat something. She smiled at her audacity. It was a small gesture, but she found the tiniest satisfaction in the idea that she would steal anything from the men that stole her freedom. She looked out the great windows as she took the most delicious bite she'd eaten in weeks.

The kitchen was impressive, but she was out and about. It was time to move on. Three quarters of a banana in hand, Emma accepted that she would be back for more later tonight. She wandered back to the iron adorned staircase and passed them to a living room area. An impressive fireplace was the main attraction with deep floral carvings. Above it, was a very large television. An elegant white sofa and a green floral rug furnished the room, along with two matching green and brown chairs.

Further on, and to the right of the fireplace, a doorless room tucked itself into the darkness. Perhaps it was another living area? She entered the space but struggled to see. Emma bumped into a small table, knocking several wooden parts loose with startling loudness. Her fingers felt around to discover that it was a chess board. She shushed an inanimate bishop and replaced the fallen pieces best she could in the dark.

As her eyes began to adjust, she started to make out bookshelves and some wooden contraptions. Emma swallowed another bite of fruit. After the kinky events upstairs, she wondered if she had wandered into a room containing more elaborate props for her captors. She imagined Matthew being strapped to an X-shaped bondage structure with Dameon sadistically brandishing a whip around him.

The light of the room clicked on. Emma nearly jumped out of her skin and nearly spat out the last of her banana. She spun around and saw Matthew leaning against her only exit. She covered her mouth and managed to get the, almost expelled, fruit down her throat.

"Impressive, I would have bet against you swallowing." He smiled, looking around the room. "You didn't waste any time did you? How often did you sneak out before I caught you?"

Emma's heart raced.

"Just last night, and tonight."

Matthew's face didn't hide that he wasn't convinced. Without words he shot her a warning.

"I'm not lying." she said, a little too loudly.

Matthew humorously put a finger to his lips, reminding her to stay quiet. He laughed with low notes.

"You aren't very good at breaking rules, are you? You've been caught both times, and by me no less. Lucky you. Elijah wouldn't be happy, and Dameon, well, I'm not sure what he would do."

As Matthew took casual steps towards Emma, she mirrored him in reverse. He looked down at the board. The pieces were correctly placed, but a tad off their marked squares. Matthew let out a singular airy laugh and nudged the wooden parts to their proper centered locations.

"We've been through this dance before," he grinned.

Emma internally scolded her body for feeling warm at his words. Her panic resumed as she turned around to look at the bondage equipment. She wasn't ready to be strapped to some pain and pleasure, wooden… easels? Canvases of all sizes rested in vertical piles against bursting bookshelves. Emma tilted her head in curiosity. She placed her banana peel on a nearby desk, forgetting it instantly.

She walked curiously to the paintings and took in their different styles and subject matter. They were nice. They probably wouldn't make it into a museum, but they looked like something a well versed art student might make.

Landscapes contained empty beaches, carnivals with eccentric dancing people, palm tree lined roads, vibrant close ups of thin multi story homes squished together, and embellished churches graced the canvas'. They were delightful, exciting, and daydreamy. She reached for one of the stacks and tipped the artwork to see more. More colorful streets, more classic cars.

"Cuba?"

Matthew nodded.

"Yeah, he has a real hard on for the place. He thinks it's the ultimate end goal, or something. Not sure why. It's definitely not a friendly place for people like us, and he's about as straight as a circle. But what can you do? Can't talk him out of it, and I've tried."

Emma imagined Dameon sitting on a beach in Cuba drinking something alcoholic with a little umbrella. She flipped to another painting but was interrupted by Matthew. He rushed to the canvases and slammed them together, making her flinch.

"Um… maybe you don't need to see anymore." he said, in a way that sounded more like a request than she was prepared for.

Emma eyed the big man. It was strange seeing him look embarrassed.

Her curiosity was bubbling over.

"Please," she asked, sweetly.

Matthew rubbed his hand against the back of his neck. Whatever was on that canvas must have been something interesting to warrant his reaction. She had to know. Matthew saw the resolve in Emma and defeatedly waved a hand for her to continue. She smiled broadly and turned to the mystery painting.

She immediately found it. It was not what she was expecting. It was an amateurish portrait of the three men posing in front of the staircases in their home. Comparatively, it was not very good. Dameon's weren't exactly masterpieces, but they were objectively well done. This looked more like a child's art project compared to Dameon's paintings. Matthew pushed the paintings back against the wall, with some shyness.

"Sometimes, they talk me into painting with them. It's not my thing, but I have a hard time telling them no."

Something in Emma's chest stirred. She wanted to complement the poor drawing, or say something to make him feel better about the vulnerability he allowed her to see. She wasn't an artist by any means. She'd probably have the same reaction as Matthew if someone saw something she tried to paint. Instead she pressed on. He didn't exactly deserve her pity.

"So Elijah paints too? Which are his?"

Emma turned to the remaining unexplored side of the room. Her jaw dropped.

"So..." Matthew said, more carefully than she'd heard from him yet, "those weren't Dameon's. The Cuba and bright stuff is Elijah's. What you're looking at over there, those are Dameon's."

Paintings, charcoal, and sketches littered the walls and leaned against bookshelves on the floor. Different mediums, different techniques, but nearly half of the same subject. A girl that couldn't have been much older than a teenager was the subject of the majority of his works.

The muse appeared in some as a child, but in most she looked like a teenage girl with sad eyes. In one pastel painting, the girl had Dameon's blue eyes and dark hair. She was beautiful, freckles on her nose, long hair playing in a breeze, and wearing a whimsical blue dress.

Love emoted from every attentive detail. Emma suddenly wondered if Dameon was a father. It was a strange light to attempt to see the terrifying man in.

"Penny," Matthew said, solemnly. "His sister. Well, twin sister."

Emma felt her heart flood with pain, love, and loss. She could feel it with every brush stroke, every porous line of chalk, every harsh line of ink on the canvases.

"What happened to her?"

She turned to Matthew who echoed the heartbreak used to create the portraits. He knew her too. Or maybe he cared for her deeply simply because Dameon did.

"I don't know if it's my story to tell. She was a good person. She didn't deserve–"

Matthew made a face that revealed confliction. He was giving her information he was clearly uncomfortable letting out. His fingers brushed through his hair in one long stroke.

"I don't think I can say much more. It's strange, having you here. We never had much of an issue with our honesty rule before. If Dameon had let me kill you from the start, we never would have started keeping secrets. It's a little late for that now."

Emma attempted to subtly put a little more distance between them. It didn't sound like he wanted to harm her at the moment, but she wasn't sure. With the emotions visibly running through him, she didn't want to be too close if he were to change his mind.

"Our truth rule can be a bit much. I probably shouldn't be so relaxed about your near death experience. But it wasn't bullshit, we really do our best to follow that rule. All of it, even if it isn't what you want to hear."

Emma looked down at a dark wood floor that complemented the artsy study. It must have been killing him to keep her key a secret. The rule was important to him, yet he was breaking it every day she kept it.

"But you want me to hide the key you gave me," she asked, hesitantly.

"Yes," Matthew said. "But there's no use in asking me why. I'm still trying to figure that out."

"Can you tell me what you're thinking now?"

Matthew laughed.

"Easily. I'm thinking about Penny, and killing those responsible. I'm thinking about the banana peel I'll need to throw away to keep you from getting caught. And now, for some reason, I'm thinking about bending you over that desk and making you cum for me."

Emma's heart skipped a beat. She snapped her eyes from the floor to him.

"But," he continued, "that isn't going to happen tonight. Does that satisfy your question?"

Emma shied away from looking at Matthew again. He was right, hearing an unfiltered truth regarding the uncertainty of her lifespan wasn't easy. However, listening to Matthew's physical desires over her was terrifying, and to her discomfort, intriguing.

5 | Secrets

Elijah knocked, as he always did. Emma was sure he could hear her thump and "Ouch!" on the other side of the door. He opened the door to investigate, to see Emma pop her head up. She was on the floor behind the far side of the bed. A judgy look passed over Elijah's face.

"Still asleep? I didn't think I'd be waking you."

Emma glared for a moment, then reeled herself in. She was angry at him for abandoning her for so long, but she was still his captive. She didn't want him to be any more irritated at her than he already was. He strode in with a new bag of provisions. An oddness set in when she realized that she knew more about him than he did about her.

"Well," she said, trying to keep her tone cordial, "I don't have a clock in here. I never really know what time it is. How should I know how late it is?"

Elijah looked taken aback by the candidness of the conversation. Emma had always kept an air of timidness around him. They didn't often exchange more than a few pleasantries, maybe a smile. This time, she had more snap to her tone than usual.

"Do you need a clock," he asked, awkwardly.

"No, I don't do anything all day anyway. Why would I need to know the time?"

That one came out a little more bitter than she hoped. Elijah set her latest delivery on the little office desk. He crossed his arms and looked her up and down with a judgy gaze.

"Okay, then. Is there something you do need?"

"Underwear!" she said, firmly. "Some underwear would be greatly appreciated."

His eyes wandered everywhere except over Emma's naked body, barely covered by the comforter she wrapped around her. He picked up a neatly tied trash bag in the corner and retreated to the door. He paused before leaving.

"In my defense, I didn't think you'd be with us long enough for it to matter."

Something angry was on the tip of his tongue, but whatever it was, he held it back. Elijah left and shut the door behind him. The lock electronically sounded.

Emma continued eating terrible food in the day, and lovely fresh food in the evening. She and Matthew got into the habit of making midnight salads, an often wordless but pleasant activity.

Her adrenaline spiked the first time he handed her a knife to chop tomatoes. The kitchen light gleamed against the chrome blade. The dark handle felt sturdy in her hand. As great as it may have felt to hold, she knew she'd need a lot more than a kitchen knife to escape, so she settled for a crisp meal instead.

Her favorite part of keeping her key, unbeknownst to Matthew, was when the sun had yet to disappear over the valley. In the middle of the day, Emma started opening her door. It was just a crack. She didn't want to actually risk getting caught.

It filled her with sparks of excitement every time she did. Sometimes, she could hear the men playing video games in the living room, or watching a movie. Other times, she heard them planning out their next illegal endeavor. Listening in and learning about her captors quickly became Emma's favorite pastime.

Emma had made the entertaining discovery that they weren't simply a bunch of inexperienced kidnappers, they were, in fact, professional criminals. What Emma got caught up in, was a bad day in a string of, usually successful, robberies. She couldn't tell how long they had been engaging in the dangerous career, but it definitely sounded like they had been at it for a while. Dameon was the leader, and man with connections. Elijah was their personal medic and a miraculous grifter. Matthew was the driver and muscle.

The trio of thieves had most of their next heist planned for a jewelry shop. They decided on the getaway route, the vehicle changes needed, and the time frame in which it all needed to happen. But their plan was not without a few remaining hurdles they still needed to overcome.

Apparently, they didn't want to chance the store owner getting hurt. From what Emma could piece together, the guy seemed like a decent person, or at least someone that they deemed worth protecting. There was something about him being on the straight-and-narrow, but the details were fuzzy. Also, he had some kind of connection to El Tiburón.

Emma immediately recognized the name. El Tiburón, the man Dameon turned to for advice. The man whom they trusted enough to leave their truck-full of loot with. The man that offered to sell Emma to the highest bidder. She didn't hear them say much about him, but he definitely seemed to be a person her captors didn't want to upset. Even with her limited knowledge, Emma felt she could understand. Simply hearing his name never failed to send a shiver through her own spine.

The other dilemma the group was facing revolved around Dameon. Emma learned quickly that the three men were more than partners in crime, or casual fuck-buddies. They were wholly and entirely part of a life-long relationship. They cared for each other and supported each other in a way that was foreign to her. They irritated, pushed, played, and loved one another deeply. Seeing Dameon almost lose his life, made both of his loved ones nervous to pursue their next hit.

Emma learned a lot about the moments leading up to her abduction. She learned that their last heist involved a rather seedy pawnshop. Elijah played the role of a drug addict needing money for his next fix. Dameon took the part of a scorned, and argumentative, fiance wanting an engagement ring back that his recent ex had supposedly sold.

Elijah griped over the unfair price offered for the junk being peddled.

Dameon was loud, insufferable, and continued asking for a sentimental piece of jewelry that never existed. The chaos in the shop was going to plan. Everyone that needed to be, was perfectly distracted. All the while, Matthew loaded the back of a moving truck with a plethora of freshly stolen goods.

It was all going great, until the manager recognized Dameon. That's when the shit hit the fan. The manager shouted. Another employee brought out a wooden bat and started swinging. Elijah ducked in time, but Dameon was not so lucky. The manager shoved a hidden blade deep into Dameon's side.

They didn't have time to waste. Their easy, simple, job was blown to hell, and Dameon needed to get his partners to safety. He kicked the man hard, sending him backwards and into glass shelves. Hearing the wrong kind of commotion, Matthew stormed in, pointed a loaded gun at the manager, and fired.

While Matthew was busy committing murder, Dameon knelt below the cash register and found a bit of luck. Amongst pens, paperclips, and a heavily used notepad, was a stapler. He did what he had to do. Despite every natural urge, he stifled his agony and temporarily stapled the gaping wound closed. He didn't tell them. He didn't want them to worry. He only needed to get them home.

With Murphy's law in full effect, the thieves had to resort to the backup of backup plans. Their routes were compromised. Between the inbound police, and some kind of rivals Emma didn't catch the name of, the three were royally screwed. Dameon led the way, in a constant state of improvisation. The cops would be on them soon, and Dameon's mind was becoming increasingly unreliable due to his secret pain and blood loss.

With Dameon's orders, Matthew tossed him the gun, and burst through the flimsy door of a random townhouse. They hoped it would be empty. They hoped for one single thing to go their way. But it wouldn't. In that townhouse, they would agree to the kidnapping of a woman as payment for their escape. That same woman, unbeknownst to them, listened through the crack of her prison door, day after day, for anything she might be able to use to her advantage.

Dameon, Matthew, and Elijah didn't wholeheartedly disagree about much. The topic of Emma, however, was a significant exception. They didn't say much within earshot, but what she could hear nearly always ended in frustration, and the absence of any solution.

Elijah seemed more keen than the others to get rid of her. He wanted her gone and did not shy away from saying it to his partners. Every passing day that Emma stayed, he became more bothered by her presence. Dameon didn't say much about it. Whatever he was thinking, he never said it in earshot of Emma. Matthew was often quiet too, which led to Elijah's latest tantrum.

"What the hell happened," he shouted.

Emma pressed her ear to the crack of her door.

"When did I become the only one interested in getting her the hell out of here? You! Matthew? It was your idea to kill her, where did that energy go?"

A pause lingered.

"I'm rather curious about that too," said Dameon, sounding almost sweetly concerned. "What's up?"

More silence.

"I think she's cute," Matthew admitted, in a bashful sounding way.

Elijah let out an exaggerated groan of irritation. "Cute? So I am the only one here not thinking with his dick? And since when has that been a deciding factor? You've killed plenty of cute people! What makes her so different?"

"She's not," Matthew said. "She's no different from any other girl or guy we've hurt or killed. She's just a person, except– "

"No," Elijah interrupted. "Nope. I'm not about to listen to this. I want her out. I don't care how, but I want her gone. I'm sick of feeding and checking in on your little crush. Squash it, or her, whichever is easier."

"If you are so sick of being her caregiver," Matthew said, "I could always–"

"No." Dameon and Elijah said, in perfect unison.

"You don't even know what I was going to say," Matthew said, exasperated.

"It doesn't matter how you would have ended that sentence," said Dameon, with a stern voice. "The answer would be no. No to letting her go. You're obviously not killing her. And hell no to letting you, and your horny ass, take over for Elijah. That's just asking for trouble."

"You make me sound like a monster. Not gonna lie, it's starting to hurt."

"Hurt," Dameon asked. "Well then, how can I make it up to you?"

A few low groans were all that broke up the silence after Dameon's words. Emma rolled her eyes and quietly closed her door.

Bunnies. The three men humped like bunnies. Seriously, she could tip her hat at their stamina, but it was all the time with those three. At first, she secretly found their random sexual sessions arousing. But given her position of isolation, it was starting to get old. It felt like they were rubbing it in, and not in a good way.

Emma wished Dameon and Elijah had agreed to let Matthew take over. She started to quite possibly, even like him. Matthew had become her personal lookout. When the evening was quiet, she'd poke her head out to look for Matthew's approving or warning nod before retiring upstairs with his lovers. One evening, she couldn't hear Dameon in the living room, but Matthew made sure she saw a subtle "no-go" sign as he passed the field of vision. But her favorite nights were when he would stay.

Matthew backed away from the personal stories after their night in the library. He carried a heavy guilt over sharing too much, on top of keeping her midnight snacking a secret from the men he cared so deeply for. Emma tried not to push. She had her own secrets, after all. Part of her wanted to trust him, but she couldn't. Knowledge was power, and she was prepared to sit on what she knew until it might become useful. But in the same breath, she desperately needed to talk to someone.

One night, the secretive pair sat across from each other on one of the sofas. Matthew read a book. She tried too, but her mind wandered. She couldn't focus on the black ink that settled into the lovely smelling pages. Instead, she studied the man. He was growing out a beard. His stubble was getting fuller and more pronounced. His eyes stopped scanning the words. He knew she was watching but didn't look up from the hardcover. Emma broke the silence between them to ask what she knew would be a dangerous question.

"Why are you keeping me?"

Matthew stayed quiet for a long moment.

"You can't be trusted," he said, with a note of apology.

Anger boiled in Emma's gut.

"Why do you give a shit about trusting me," she said, with too much bitterness. "Why would you need to?"

"The cops, Emma," Matthew said, meeting her heightened emotional level. "You could tell the cops, you could tell… people, that would love to see our heads on a silver platter."

"Not if you drop me off in some other country. I know you have the ability. Look at this place! You can afford it, so why not do that?"

Flames of defiance and nervousness raced over her skin. Emma just picked a fight with the one person that gave her any real break from her isolation, and she knew it. She meant to be calm, maybe even sweet. Of course they were afraid she'd turn them in, but they clearly had the means to send her somewhere far enough to never have to worry about her.

Matthew put a strong hand on her arm and held tight.

"You," he started.

Matthew's eyes darted to his aggressive touch. His hand let go with a flinch as if he was shocked by a jolt of electricity.

He hadn't touched her since their encounter at the top of the stairs. What started with Emma being afraid, now became quite the reverse. When she got too close, he shifted back. If she reached out, he recoiled. It was maddening. She needed to feel someone's touch. Just a squeeze of her hand, one more hug, anything.

"You," he continued, in a low voice, "are more clever than you make yourself out to be. I'm not a complete idiot, Emma. I've seen it in the way you look at every lock in the house. It's in the glances you give to the knives in the kitchen. You obviously know it wouldn't work in your favor, but you never stop plotting, thinking about what it would take to get out.

69

You're keeping secrets, even now. I can feel it when I stop myself from telling you things I shouldn't, and you look at me like you already know."

Matthew pulled his hair back in a ponytail, then let it fall again after he took a breath and lowered his volume.

"You can't tell me that you wouldn't find a way to make us pay for what we've done to you." he said, with regret in his voice. "I wouldn't believe it. We could kick you out of a plane over Antarctica, and I wouldn't be surprised if you found your way back to break us. Like recognizes like, and I have a feeling you and I are more alike than you're leading on. I don't know why Dameon is so sure too, but he feels the same way. So no, we can't let you go."

Emma let his words sit against the silence of the night. He wasn't going to help her leave. She'd never get out of the penthouse. Though there was some truth to his assumption, the words still stung. He was willing to sentence her to die in that horrible white room. The hope she clung to for a chance to escape, for Matthew to maybe take some pity on her, was squashed. Having heard it spoken to her face solidified it. She was stuck.

"If you're so concerned about me doing something to you," Emma said quietly, but still keeping a pinch of anger, "why would you give me a key?"

Matthew backed away as far as he could. His heavy body pressed against the armrest of the sofa. He looked down at his hands and didn't meet her eyes when he spoke.

"When I left you the key, I wasn't in a great place. I was looking for an excuse to– I thought if you made enough of a scene, Dameon would allow me to put an easy end to our problem."

He looked back to Emma.

"I was desperate to have things back to how they were," he said, softly. "But, I don't want to hurt you anymore."

She believed him. If he wanted to harm her, he had plenty of opportunities to do it. He wasn't even comfortable touching her. He sure as hell didn't seem interested in killing her. And somehow, Emma found herself in a place where she actually didn't want to hurt him either.

"I don't understand how you can be nice to me, and still not want to help me get out."

Amber eyes searched Emma for a hint of anything disingenuous. When he realized that she meant what she said, he placed his hand over his mouth and chin. He brushed his fingers over his jawline, took a deep breath, and pressed his brows together.

"Emma, I haven't been nice," he said, quietly.

"Yes you have. I'm here aren't I? You're the only one that has cared about me. Elijah hates me. Dameon hasn't said a word to me since the day I was put here. You're all I think about! You let me out. You gave me real food. On the stairs, you could have easily killed me or–"

"That's not nice, Emma!" Matthew said, bewildered. "That's Stockholm Syndrome talk. The absence of physically hurting you, isn't nice. Meeting your basic needs for survival isn't good, it's the bare minimum. Think about any relationship you've had before being here. You can't tell me that I am the nicest person you've met."

"Yes I can!"

Matthew's stunned, pitiful, expression compelled Emma to look away. It wasn't a lie. Her past was riddled with bad luck and worse people. She understood where Matthew was coming from, but it didn't completely make him right. Okay, the Stockholm part was a little on the nose. But he was wrong about being shown anything that was much better.

Emma felt suddenly embarrassed by her words. They revealed more than she was willing to share. Matthew extended a sympathetic hand, but recoiled before any comfort could be given.

* * *

A month had passed. At least, Emma assumed it had been about a month. She never got her period, but stress, and the residual effects of her birth

71

control shot, had a pesky habit of making her skip the occasional cycle. It was probably for the best. Though she was given a plentiful supply of feminine products, it would have been miserable to go through without underwear, and Elijah never did come back with anything more than the bare-bone meals.

Emma sprawled out over the bed, letting her head hang upside down off the edge of the bed. Intrusive thoughts dreamed up a scenario in which she had somehow ended up pregnant with Grant's child. The thought was gross. Luckily, she couldn't be. It had been forever ago, and at least one period since, that they had sex at all. She wondered if Grant had already found a new poor woman to control. She hoped not, for the imaginary woman's sake.

Emma took to raiding the kitchen again, as she had almost every night. She grabbed a green apple and sat cross legged on the island's counter. Her lovely key rested at her side on the cold top. The extra large shirt had just enough coverage to keep her bare butt from touching the chilly stone. She fiddled with the remaining core and was admiring the perfect view of the city when Matthew rushed in.

"Down!" he said quietly. "Get down!"

Emma's eyes widened. In a growing panic, she started for her room but Matthew blocked her path. He swung her behind the island and pushed her head down. Emma fell to her knees, grateful for Elijah's handiwork on her leg. The stitches were gone, and the wound was almost completely healed. She was sure that the quick movements would have been much more painful if not for Elijah's useful skills, but that didn't stop her from disliking the man.

Emma hugged one of Matthew's legs. The warmth from his body distracted her terribly. Though fear pulsed through her, his nearness was intoxicating. She looked up and noticed only then that he was wearing only a pair of tight black boxer-briefs, and was hard as a rock. He looked down at her wide green eyes and allowed the fingers of his left hand to comb comfortingly through her hair.

Emma appreciated the touch so much it hurt. After all this time, he still refused. Even with an incoming threat, feeling his skin against hers provided much needed relief from the deprivation she faced while locked away. A twitch under his small amount of clothing sent flutters through her body. Matthew snapped his attention up and tensed. As he did, he pressed her closer, protectively, to his leg.

"You can't hide from me," Dameon said, slyly.

Fear surged through Emma and shot through her spine. Matthew hastily swept her forgotten keycard off the counter. As it fell, it bounced off Emma's head and made a small "tick" noise as it hit the stone floor.

"What makes you think I want to hide from you," Matthew asked, coyly.

Dameon grinned through his words.

"Come on, Matthew. You know I have special things planned for you tonight."

Matthew's grip on Emma's hair got tighter. A brief moment of silence passed.

"Don't keep me waiting," Dameon commanded.

Emma heard Dameon walk up the stairs. Matthew relaxed with the increased distance between him and Dameon. He looked down and nodded the "all clear." Emma stood to her feet and crossed her arms against her torso, already missing his hands in her hair.

"Want to watch again," Matthew asked, with a teasing smile. "Dameon rarely disappoints."

Emma looked down at her feet.

"I was only joking," he said, backtracking. "I regret saying it." Matthew put a hand on Emma's back, and said softly, "Let me take you back to your room."

He started to walk but was met with Emma's steadfast feet.

"What if I do," she asked, "want to watch?"

Matthew regarded Emma with unease.

"When Dameon is in a punishing mood, he can get a little carried away. What you saw last time was only the start. I don't– If you see what he likes, what I let him do to me, I think there's a good chance it'll make you even more afraid of him than you already are."

"Never apologize for the things you want. Isn't that what you said?"

Emma pressed on, knowing what the powerful rule would require of him.

"Do you want me to watch?"

"Yes," Matthew said, with closed eyes and looking ashamed.

"Well, me too," she said, with some defiance. "All of it this time,"

Matthew gave her a tentative look and a chance to change her mind. Emma could practically see the wheels of his mind turning as he contemplated the notion.

"Under one condition. No more of these secrets. I can't keep adding to the list of things I'm keeping from Dameon."

Matthew held out his hand to her. She took it.

Emma knew the arrangement was short sighted. Matthew would probably be more reserved than ever on their visits. He didn't want a growing list of secrets to hide from someone like Dameon, that was understandable. But Emma was done waiting for something, or nothing, to ever happen to her. Maybe it was desperation, maybe it was her sanity slipping, either way, she yearned for more than her tedious days and nights.

In all of Emma's night time adventures, she never found the courage to go to the second story again. The memory of Dameon and Matthew being up there, and the gained knowledge that the second level is where all of them slept, kept her on the main floor. As she ascended the staircase, her nerves started jumbling in her throat. She looked at her former hiding place next to the large decorative plant.

"No. Not this time."

She was confused until Matthew opened the door to the room. Her stomach dropped. He didn't wait for her to reconsider. He released her hand and led the way.

The room was beautiful. A massive fireplace lit the dark walls in a constant orange glow. Excited pops and sizzles from tree sap played at random. An ancient scent of pine burned fragrantly. A large cherry-wood bed with a dark velvety comforter accompanied carelessly tossed white, fur-like, blankets. A familiar wooden chair had a place in one corner. A large, brown, leather, chair sat off centered to the fireplace.

The space would have looked rugged, and of another time, if not for one particular wall. In an artistic display, various detailed, and oddly beautiful, paddles, floggers, whips, crops, and other sexually explicit tools proudly hung on the wall.

An amusing thought came to Emma as she took in the atmosphere. This was the room. This was the dungeon Matthew referred to on her first night in the penthouse. The thought would have made her laugh if it wasn't for the most terrifying aspect of the place standing before her.

Dameon leaned against the heavy chair, facing the fire. Dark boxer-briefs and a bare torso left nothing to the imagination. Emma tightened at the visual reminder of how attractive both of these men were. With this closer vantage point, she saw something she hadn't noticed last time. An angry, pink scar from the botched pawnshop job rested on his side.

Emma's stomach flipped more than a gold medal gymnast. This was not what she thought Matthew meant by "no more secrets." She thought he meant that he didn't want any future secrets. She wasn't prepared to face Dameon, and the thought sent waves of fear through her entire being. Emma wanted to blame Matthew for being unclear, but if she was being honest with herself, maybe she only heard what she wanted to hear.

Dameon turned to Matthew, initially smiling until he saw Emma by his side. His glare was hotter than the burning flames next to him.

"What the fuck are you doing," he scathed.

Dameon rushed to Emma's side and created distance between her and Matthew. The absence of the man that, over time, came to feel like her protector made Emma feel incredibly vulnerable. Dameon closed in on her and held her upper arm.

"Listen to me. You are under no obligation to be in this room." Dameon's tone was harsh, despite the care in his chosen words. "I will not tolerate you being threatened to come up here, and you have my word that no one will hurt you for returning to your room."

He looked at Matthew and pointed a loaded finger in his direction.

"We are talking about this when I get back."

Dameon proceeded to drag Emma out of the room.

"Wait," she begged, suddenly worried for Matthew.

Dameon froze.

"He didn't force me to be here, I asked."

Blue eyes looked hard into Emma's. It was as if he could smell any potential lie, but there were none to be found. Emma did ask, maybe not for this exactly, but she was more than vocal about her desire to break up the monotony.

"And how would you know about any of this, if he hadn't told you about it first? I doubt you got up this morning and decided you wanted a painful threesome with two of the three men holding you captive."

"Wait, I... I don't–"

Emma's confidence wavered and her body nervously trembled. She turned to Matthew. She wondered if the end of their hiding was the only miscommunication between them. Had he planned for more than she expected? Did he want her to jump in bed with him and Dameon after being so carefully avoided?

Emma squeaked slightly when she spoke.

"I just wanted– I don't want you and him to–"

Matthew tried to go to Emma, to reach out, to explain. Dameon pressed a stone hand against his chest, stopping Matthew in his tracks. He made himself a hard barrier between him and the woman. Matthew didn't make an effort to get past. Though he had considerable height and bulk on Dameon, the dominating man still seemed to tower over the giant.

Matthew attempted to keep a strong and unintimidated composure. To a degree, he did. But there was still that gleam of concern behind his brown eyes.

"Matthew," Dameon said, livid. "What the fuck!"

"She never said she wanted us to have sex with her," Matthew responded, calmly. "And she knows... because this isn't her first time out of that room. She's been sneaking out for a while. On her first night out, she saw you in the middle of punishing me, the night with the tape."

Emma felt a sense of betrayal at Matthew's honesty. Her little bit of freedom was on the line, and he was carelessly throwing it around. Emma was worried about what Dameon might do with the information, what he might do to her, to him. Something clicked in Dameon's mind. He looked back and forth between the two. His glare fixed on Matthew.

"And how could she have done that?"

"I gave her a key." Matthew admitted.

"Ahh," Dameon said, as he released the nervous woman's arm. "I suppose that would explain your poor sleep habits lately. And how often have you been fucking her?"

Both Matthew and Emma overlapped with verbal denials. Dameon let the two squirm with their words, while he took in the guilty parties. His silence beckoned them to continue. Slowly, the disappointed furrow in his brow subtly shifted to acute interest. Dameon took a step towards the small woman. Matthew held his breath.

"I only wanted to watch." Emma said, feeling nervous and awkward. "But if it would make you uncomfortable, I can leave."

Dameon's blue eyes were on fire. "If it would make me uncomfortable? You are worried about me, your captor, the man keeping you locked away in a tiny room, uncomfortable?"

Emma nodded.

Dameon laughed in a way that chilled her bones.

"Fine," he challenged. "You two want to play games? Alright, let's play."

Emma's stomach dropped when she saw Matthew's face switch from guilt to concern. His eyes widened with Dameon's words.

"It's not a game," Matthew said. "It doesn't have to be a game. That's not–"

Dameon raised a finger in Matthew's direction. It silenced him immediately. Dameon took a very deep breath and offered a wicked half smile to Emma. He pointed to the large leather chair and spoke sternly.

"Sit."

Emma moved cautiously past him and Matthew. She sunk into large furniture that was more comfortable than it looked. Her toes only brushed the floor, so she pulled her knees up and tucked her feet into the side of the cushions. Dameon rotated the chair to face the bed, turning its back to the fire.

Both of his hands gripped the soft armrests as Dameon knelt before Emma. He forced an intimidating, and challenging, amount of eye contact.

"Rules," he said, with the demeanor of a negotiating king. "Matthew and I have an understanding, I can demand what I want and he will obey. Your consent means something to me, so answer carefully. Can I demand things of you?"

"No," she said, her voice cracking.

"Can I touch you?"

"No," Emma answered, quickly.

Dameon grinned.

"Can your friend, Matthew, touch you?"

Emma looked in Matthew's direction. He didn't hold her gaze for long. His hands seemed to be clenched. Emma wondered if he was regretting his decision to bring her here. Her heart was pounding. Dameon scared the hell out of her, but she was in need of more than just edible food. She wanted to be touched. She wanted Matthew's skin against hers. She took a moment to answer,

"No."

Matthew let out a breath of relief. Dameon clearly heard Matthew from behind. His attention shifted away for just a moment, before his blue eyes snapped back to Emma. He smiled with his teeth in a way that evoked incredibly anxious feelings in Emma's chest.

"That was a smart choice," Dameon said. "I would have made you regret it."

Emma squeezed her knees together.

"Do we have permission to look at you, acknowledge you?"

Emma thought this was an odd rule to establish, then again she was never a participant to watching two people have sex before. Maybe this was a standard boundary to set. Maybe some people wanted the active members to pretend the watcher wasn't there at all. She really was out of her depth with this.

"I don't see why not."

Dameon's face looked wicked. Matthew closed his eyes. She chose incorrectly. Matthew opened his eyes and stared at the ceiling. Second thoughts entered Emma's mind. Before she found the courage to share her uncertainty, Dameon spoke Matthew's name to regain the nervous man's attention. He motioned for him to shut the door to the room. Matthew did as he was instructed without question.

"The safewords are yellow then red. Not everyone conducts their activities like we do, but in our little group, it works. We have found that two words have been better than one. Yellow is for a warning; when you're thinking about throwing in the towel. Red is for the full stop. Say them, please."

"But why would I need safewords if I'm not going to be touched," Emma asked, nervously.

Dameon leaned in closer.

"Trust me, there's always a chance you'll need them with me. So, the safewords, please."

"Yellow and red." she timidly repeated.

The enclosed space flooded with anticipation, anxiety, power, and submission. Dameon straightened and stood before her. The light of the fire licked at the curves of his body. He gestured a deliberate pointer finger, instructing Matthew to come to him. Dameon followed the demand with a snap and pointed to his boxer-briefs. Matthew obeyed. He stood behind Dameon, inserted his thumbs into the band of his underwear, and pushed them to the floor.

Dameon's ready-self was level with Emma's face. She sank slightly lower into her seat. Matthew remained on his knees once the clothing rested on the floor. Dameon stepped out of the cloth and let a hand run its fingers through Matthew's long waves as Dameon positioned himself lazily on the edge of the bed. He was behind Matthew, whose eyes were firmly planted on the floor.

"Look at her," Dameon said, sternly.

Matthew stayed on his knees and looked up at Emma with his sweet light-coffee eyes. Dameon's gaze studied Emma's reactions.

"State why you deserve to be punished tonight."

Matthew looked as if he was punched in the gut. He opened his mouth a few times to speak but nothing produced.

"You brought her here, and you didn't think I'd let her know why you will be getting this treatment? Matthew, my love, don't make me ask twice."

Matthew's face flashed an air of defiance.

"I was caught jerking off, and you got jealous."

Dameon lunged at Matthew. He wrapped a strong hand around his neck and began to squeeze. Emma pressed her back firmly into the leather. Matthew didn't struggle.

"You're skipping the good part," Dameon threatened, "What were you thinking about when I caught you?"

Matthew's voice came out strained under Dameon's tightening grip. "Her."

Dameon released Matthew, who choked on the new air. He chuckled at the sounds of Matthew's struggles. He rounded the large man and made his way back to the impressive bed. Dameon returned to his previous position.

"Face me," the scary man demanded.

Matthew did.

"Open up."

Matthew did.

"Good boy. Now, show her how you like me to take you."

Emma's insides buzzed. Matthew placed his hands on either side of Dameon and licked from base to tip. He took Dameon with his mouth. His large hands pushed into the bed. He moved up and down the long shaft. Matthew's breathing quickened. He let little wanting moans send subtle vibrations up to Dameon who also let a groan of satisfaction slip out.

Emma felt her own tongue secretly move against the roof of her mouth. She imagined the feeling, the taste. The hard tips of her breasts grew visible through her shirt, and she was thoroughly aware of her lack of underwear. Dameon looked down to Matthew and played with his hair again. Matthew groaned in appreciation.

"Good boy." Dameon whispered. "But my love," Dameon said, as he steadily pumped himself in Matthew's mouth. "she can't give you this, can she?"

Dameon proceeded to slowly push deep into his throat. Matthew's back muscles contracted and flexed. He gripped the comforter with so much force, little ripping sounds came from the stitching. He quietly gagged on Dameon's intrusion. Just when Emma's intrigue started to slip into fear, Dameon released him in perfect timing, masterfully balancing the line between worry and want. Matthew fell slightly in his recovery.

"You're little friend can't give you that, can she," Dameon taunted, cruelly, tilting Matthew's chin up to look at him.

"No."

"No," Dameon confirmed. "Get on the bed. You're going to show her what else she can't give you."

Matthew continued to do as he was told. Dameon moved back, ensuring Matthew remained between him and Emma. On his hands and knees, Matthew faced the woman in the chair. Dameon readied himself. He let a methodical hand move half way up Matthew's spine and back down. Matthew shivered. Dark-blue eyes stared down Emma, whose chest was rising and falling with an increased pace.

"What was it you whispered when you spilled your cum all over the shower?"

Matthew swallowed hard, as Dameon's fingers yanked at the waistband of Matthew's underwear. He pulled until the band stretched around his knees. Matthew stared down at the smooth bedding.

"Look at her! What did you say? What did you call your innocent friend, when you thought no one was listening?"

Matthew shot apologetic eyes up at Emma.

"My little prisoner," he said, hoarsely.

"Yes," Dameon said. "Your little prisoner. What do you think, little prisoner? What does it do to you, seeing your kidnapper like this? Do you like seeing your secret friend as vulnerable to me, as you are to him?"

Emma struggled to speak as Dameon retrieved a bottle of lube on a near end table. He generously dispensed the liquid and stroked his impressive dick in his hand.

"You don't have to answer!" Matthew burst out. "You established rules. He can't make you say–"

A painful, guttural sound, came loudly from Matthew, that ended in a desperate and pleasurable groan. Dameon's chin tilted up as he took in his ecstasy. He pushed deeply and mercilessly into Matthew's ass.

Emma wanted to comfort him. She wanted him to take it. She wanted to feel his free, hanging cock fill her lustful need. She wanted to kiss his pain away. She wanted to hear him gasp deliciously for Dameon. She wanted.

Her legs dropped, her knees stayed pressed together while the bends of her feet locked. Matthew grunted and gritted his teeth at the pleasure that rode through him. Dameon slowed. He pulled out, still very hard.

"You want her," Dameon asked.

He moved from the bed to behind Emma's chair. She looked up. His blue eyes were fixed on Matthew who laid, catching his breath, on the bed from Dameon's exit. He was so close to her. Emma thought back to the way Dameon teased her on the operating table with the empty promise of a kiss. He leaned against the back of the chair and gripped the leather.

"Come over here. You're going to give her a taste."

Matthew's head popped up. He looked terrified.

Emma shared his anxiety. She suddenly wondered if he would ever refuse Dameon. Would he touch her if Dameon told him to? Would he take her? She wondered if Matthew feared the same questions.

"Dameon, you wouldn't."

"Only figuratively, my love. No touching. Boundaries were made. But I told you to come here. She wants you. She's soaking the fucking chair for you. Crawl to her."

Emma dug her nails into the leather arms of the chair. Matthew crawled out and away from his underwear. He closed in, one hand in front of the other. He paused at the foot of the brown furniture.

"Up, Matthew," Dameon said, coolly.

He did as he was told. Matthew crawled onto the large chair, caging her with his body. Each of his legs rested on either side of hers with less than an inch of clearance. His hands pressed harshly into the leather near her face. His dick was hard and hung just above her navel. Emma tried not to stare, but she couldn't stop her eyes from bouncing from his eyes to his lower half.

"Good boy, Isn't he," Dameon whispered in Emma's ear.

She involuntarily let out a small whine without ever opening her mouth.

"Look at how badly he wants you."

Dameon slid a hand down the chair. He moved past Matthew's hands, down to the armrests. He popped up once to avoid contact with Emma's, then found Matthew's knee. He traced a line up his muscular thigh and took a handful of his impressive cock.

Matthew let out a begging moan with a quiet curse. Emma inhaled audibly and sharply. Dameon pumped Matthew with slow tight movements. His grip made the inner workings of the chair creek under duress. Emma's need was becoming unbearable. She wanted it, wanted him.

"Yellow!" Matthew said, through gritted teeth.

Dameon instantly released him, and chuckled.

Matthew's caramel eyes revealed a starvation for her. She was so close, yet untouchable. He anguished in the control he was trying to maintain. He breathed roughly through his mouth and squeezed his eyes closed in concentration. When he opened them again he looked hungrily at Emma. He looked up to Dameon, who moved behind the chair again. Panic paled Matthew's face. He looked down to Emma, then back up.

"Wait!" he said, quickly. "Wait, Dameon!"

The plea was disregarded as Dameon rushed behind Matthew. He fell to the ground gripping Dameon's arm with one hand and tried to remove a rope around his neck with the other. Emma brought her knees to her chest. With impressive speed and strength, Dameon elaborately bound Matthew around the neck, down his arms pressed together behind him, and around his ankles in a rough brown rope. He was forced into a sitting position with his legs folded beneath him.

Fear tore through Emma as she watched the nervous man before her. The more Matthew struggled, the tighter the rope squeezed around his neck. His chest rose and fell rapidly. When he tried to speak, his voice was raspy and broken. At first, nothing comprehensible came out, but Matthew managed to growl out enough.

"R...rules! She– Don't!"

Dameon turned away from his partner on the floor. Remaining in his hand was a thinner, sleek, black, rope. He wound and unwound it around playfully in his hands, and grinned at Emma. He took a step towards Emma, then another.

"Can you guess what this one is for, little prisoner," Dameon asked, with a hint of insanity behind his words.

Matthew struggled and Emma realized he was having trouble speaking loud enough to be heard.

"Yellow!" she said, in a near screech.

Dameon laughed.

Emma's heart was beating out of her chest. Matthew couldn't have been enjoying that. Were the rules even real? Matthew couldn't say the safewords if he wanted to. Would Dameon touch her? Would he take her with the same roughness he displayed when taking Matthew? She wasn't ready for that. She was too afraid of him.

Dameon took another step towards her, still delicately toying with the dark rope. Emma balled up tighter. Terror filled her. It was for her. She knew it. Matthew was hurting.

"Red!" she screamed. "Red! Stop! Please! Red!

Dameon let the smaller rope drop to the floor. He held his hands up, surrendering as if she were a cop telling him to freeze. He smiled smugly. A visible shiver ran through Emma's body. Dameon looked terribly pleased with himself.

The door to the room opened with a violent force. Elijah stood in the doorway with soaked hair, a hastily wrapped towel around his waist, and puddles of water pooling around his feet. He took in the embarrassing scene in the light of the hallway; Dameon with his hands up, Matthew

bound in the harsh rope, Emma looking traumatized. He slammed the light to the room in the on position.

"No!" Elijah scolded.

Elijah snatched a sharp knife from a nearby shelf. He frantically sawed at the thick rope that bound Matthew in place. Elijah carried a measure of concern, but overwhelming his feelings of worry, was pure outrage.

"Oh come on," Dameon complained. "I'm not going to have any good ropes left if you keep ruining them."

Elijah pointed the knife at Dameon in an angry, but mostly empty, threat. "You know how you get with ropes. You always get carried away!"

Dameon interrupted the beginnings of Elijah's rant with a nonchalant attitude.

"I didn't do anything he didn't enjoy," Dameon said, nonchalantly.

The harsh line fell limp, allowing Matthew the ability to cough and massage his neck.

"But her!" Elijah continued at a shriek, pointing the knife at Emma. "What the fuck! Why is she here? Maybe I'm wrong, just maybe, but I didn't think you two were the rapey type. What the ever-loving shit? And even if it's not, we talked about this, Dameon. Matthew? Dameon!" Elijah was practically bursting with rage.

"She asked for it." Matthew strained.

"What the shit did you just say," Elijah screamed.

"I did," said Emma, taking Elijah's full attention.

Elijah looked dumbfounded and did a double take as if he had forgotten that she could speak at all.

"I wanted it, liked it… most of it. It just got a little–"

Dameon didn't say anything but studied Elijah. Shaking hands physically tried pushing a growing headache away. The wet blond man was nearly hyperventilating, and beyond pissed.

"Come on. I'm taking you back to the room." Elijah said.

Emma shot a worried look at Matthew. She pressed further into the chair as Elijah made several swift steps to take her away. Her hands hadn't stopped shaking, and neither had his. Elijah stopped just short of yanking her off of the chair and out of the room, when he paused to assess Emma's behavior. Emma looked at Elijah, then Matthew again with more unspoken pleas.

"He won't hurt you." Elijah said with annoyance, misreading her concerned face.

Emma shook her head.

"I'm not afraid of Matthew. I'm... I'm scared of you. You're pissed, and I have a feeling that you're more pissed at me than you are at them. Can Matthew take me back, please?"

Elijah clapped his hands together and looked at the ceiling in mock prayer and said sarcastically, "Give me strength!" He looked at Matthew and bobbled his head to look back at Emma.

"You know what, I don't know if I really care right now. Fine. Pick the guy here that spent days pouting, because he wasn't allowed to splatter your brains on the walls. I have no idea what's happening! Dameon, you are about to tell me what the hell is going on around here, okay? What is going on? What is happening right now? Dameon! Fucking help me!"

Dameon's demeanor melted from a dominating force of intimidation to that of a compassionate, loving partner. Something shifted in him, as he watched Elijah shrink from anger to overwhelmed and vulnerable. Dameon's satisfied, and falsely indifferent, attitude dropped with his shoulders. It evaporated with the smallest, sad, sigh. He dragged one of the furry white blankets off the bed and wrapped it around Elijah's wet body.

Elijah fought against the warm restraint. Dameon squeezed his arms tighter around Elijah's smaller frame, and overpowered the wiggling blond.

"Shush," he whispered. "I'm sorry, Angel."

Dameon kissed his wet forehead tenderly.

"I shouldn't have let it get this far. I should have spoken with you first."

Dameon combed Elijah's hair back with his fingers. Slowly, Elijah relaxed under Dameon's pressure and buried his face in Dameon's neck.

"Shhh." Dameon whispered. "Let me get you to bed. Let me hold you."

To Emma's relief, Matthew gestured for her to meet him at the door.

Emma unfolded her legs and moved for the exit. She stepped with as little detection as possible, tip-toeing around the abandoned ropes on the floor. Her gut twisted. She felt like she was intruding on an incredibly personal moment; something private, even sweet, and not meant for her.

Matthew shut the door behind them. He was still naked, but not as hard as before. A guilty knot tied itself in Emma's chest. The walk was uncomfortably familiar. Matthew accompanied Emma down the left set of stairs. They stopped by the kitchen, picked up the fallen key, and continued down the hallway. Matthew opened the prison door for her, and followed her inside.

She didn't turn the light on. The glow from the city lit up the room plenty. Emma stood near the glass, looking out at the green, purple, and other colorful metallic buildings. She felt Matthew's presence looming behind her.

"Did we– Did I hurt you?"

Emma spun around.

"No!"

"The way you called red, Elijah said it looked like rape. I didn't mean for it to be that way, but maybe it was. I'm not a good person, but I swear, I didn't want to hurt you. I'm sorry. I shouldn't have let any of this happen."

Emma's heart melted. She took a step closer to him. He was hard again. He reduced the space. Her eyes moved down his body, then up again. The intense want Dameon conducted inside of her returned. She wanted to comfort him. She wanted Matthew to comfort her, to hold her, to fill her.

"I was scared for you," she said. "It looked like he was hurting you."

Matthew pulled Emma to him, pressing his whole self against her. He held her in a deep embrace and teased the air between their lips with his. His kiss was a fraction of an atom's distance away. She could feel his breath against her lower lip.

"Rope burns heal. Seeing you so afraid, Emma, knowing I put you there, that's what really hurt."

Emma bathed in the warmth of his body through the fabric of the t-shirt. She couldn't resist. She moved up to his waiting lips. She burned under the pressure. Matthew took her hair in his hand and explored her mouth with his tongue. She returned his exploration with her own, familiarizing herself with his taste. He pressed hard against her. With caressing hands, he lowered her down to the soft bed.

He touched his lips to her jaw, to her neck, to her collar bone. He lifted her leg and held tight. Her shirt bunched up to reveal her bare lower half. Matthew looked down and bit his lip. Dameon was right, she was so very wet. Her sex ached for him. A longing sigh broke her heart and begged for more. She spread her legs further, offering the entrance they both wanted. Over the shirt, Matthew cupped a handful of one of her breasts and teased her hard nipple beneath his thumb.

"Do you trust me," he asked.

Reality crashed back into existence. He was being serious, not alluring, not sexy, just genuinely asking. She didn't know how to answer.

"Please, don't lie to me. Do you trust me not to hurt you?"

Emma tried to think. It was a difficult task when all of her brain cells seemed more concerned with Matthew's, no longer moving, hands. He was so close to giving her what she wanted.

"No." she finally admitted. "But I don't care."

Matthew leaned in and kissed her hard, passionately. He released her breast and leg. One hand cradled the back of her neck and lifted her into a seated position. He stood, hunched over and hovering just out of reach. Then slowly, terribly, he let her go.

"I want you, Emma. But Dameon was right, you can't give me what I need right now."

Emma's body inaudibly screamed in frustration.

"Wait, because I don't have a dick," she asked, a little spitefully.

Matthew let out a half-laugh and shook his head. He returned to her mouth and kissed her harder than before. His tongue made promises the rest of him wasn't willing to act on. She really did want him. He seemed to want her. Dameon could see it, but then again, he was also the one to point out the many things she could never give him.

Maybe she misunderstood Matthew from the beginning? Maybe she was projecting her own fantasies onto him? Emma thought about all the times he avoided her touch. She initially thought it was out of guilt, but perhaps it was simply because he knew he didn't really want to be with her.

"It has nothing to do with what your body can or cannot give. I need to know I have your trust. If you can't give me that, I can't do it."

Frustration exploded inside of Emma. She didn't misunderstand anything! It wasn't a lack of desire, or penis, that made her inadequate. He was upset because he needed her fucking trust! So he was fine with sex even though he didn't trust her, but not the other way around?

Matthew showed himself to the door and smiled sweetly. She wanted to smack the smile off his face. He was being immensely unfair, surely he knew it. He left Emma in the glow of the city night painfully unsatisfied and frustrated at his poorly placed concern. Emma looked around the empty room and realized, to her horror, that he had taken her key with him.

6 | The Light Of Day

A tragic attitude made its home in Emma's bed. The sun had been up for a while already, but she didn't feel like getting up. Being rejected by Matthew and losing her freedom again was the worst hangover she ever experienced. Matthew wanted something she was unable to give anyone, and she was being punished for that.

Eventually, Emma slipped on a black shirt that was too big, as always, and tore apart her room. She hunted for her card, telling herself that she might have imagined that part of the night. She looked under the bed, in the sheets, the pillowcases, on the stupid little office table with shitty oatmeal. It really was gone. She wondered how long she would be trapped this time in the shrinking room. Would Elijah be angry enough to finally stop bringing her food completely?

Emma sat in the black office chair and spun a few times. She rested her face against the cold desk and opened a package of dry food. She tore the top from the tiny container, and let its contents spill messily onto the table. Emma held the empty package lazily between her and the sun, mindlessly staring at the illuminated brown paper and black ink of backwards and forwards instructions. From her angle, the directions were about as clear as the state of her current situation.

Two knocks rapped at the door. She recognized the distinct sound, and knew it was Elijah before he entered the room. Suddenly embarrassed by her tantrum, she ran her hands through her hair in a hurry and swept the powdery food mess into a less conspicuous corner of the desk. When

Emma saw Elijah's face her temper returned. She was annoyed with herself that she would want to make anything presentable.

She didn't ask to be in that horrid white room. She was, as Matthew reminded her, their prisoner. The words of both Matthew and Dameon, teased and kissed at her thoughts. Their little prisoner. She stuffed the thoughts away in a box and kicked them angrily into a corner of her mind. Elijah looked around the room surveying the damage. It was actually quite a bit worse than Emma had wanted to admit.

"Busy?"

Emma scowled at his insensitive joking tone.

"Aw, poor little harlot." he said, with moody eyes and a pout. "With your key gone, you must feel so understimulated, now that you can't fool around with my lovers. It must be unbearably frustrating."

Retaliating words of irritation, and hurtful intent, twisted in her brain. Instead of letting out her distaste, she crossed her arms, sat in the chair, and let her forehead rest on the desk with a thunk. Elijah stepped closer. Emma jolted up, wondering how much fight she had in her to take on a potentially murderous Elijah. With a sassy air-blown kiss, he swung a bright, striped, canvas bag. It landed on a relatively clear place in the disheveled bed.

Emma looked curiously at it.

"I'll be in the hall. Knock when you are ready."

Elijah left, the hints of a secret at the corner of his mouth.

With the door shut and locked again, Emma approached the bag cautiously. She couldn't fathom what Elijah might have left, but she wouldn't put it past him to drop off something malicious. Emma pulled at a strap with a single finger and peaked into the bag. Spandex-looking fabric filled the sack to its fullest extent. Swimsuits, it was loaded with swimsuits.

Emma tapped lightly against the door. Activated electronic noises sounded and unlocked before she finished knocking. Elijah looked Emma up and down, and laughed.

"Now you're shy," he teased.

Emma clamped a wrapped towel firmly to her body. The pieces he picked out were skimpier than any lingerie she had ever owned. For a second, she grappled with the thought of returning back to the room. Why would he want to dress her in so little? Her first guess was that he wanted to humiliate her, make her as close to naked as possible to prove some kind of point.

"They're all a little, small."

Elijah looked genuinely taken aback. He looked almost dumbstruck that his offerings could be insulted in any way, or that his guess at her size might be incorrect. To be fair, all of the suits were highly adjustable. She couldn't blame him for not believing her.

"It fits," she clarified. "But they're lacking in... surface area. Besides, you're wearing a towel. Why can't I?"

With a wave of his hand, and a dismissive laugh, Elijah encouraged her to follow him down the bright hall.

Once past the staircases, she looked to her right towards the kitchen and to her left to the living areas. There wasn't any sign of Matthew or Dameon anywhere. She wished she knew where they were. She may have been irritated at Matthew, but she still felt he might try to protect her if need be. Elijah on the other hand, felt like walking side by side with a venomous reptile; ready to strike just for the fun of it.

The penthouse was a different place in the daylight. Sunlight bounced off the marble flooring. The tame pink and tan colors on the walls glittered with little embedded specs in the tile. The black iron of the stairs contrasted hard and beautifully against the brightness of its surroundings. Emma never considered the desert to be necessarily beautiful, but she could see the inspiration it provided all over the elegant space.

Elijah and Emma walked past the inviting kitchen and living room. Then, to her surprise, he opened a massive glass door that led out onto the balcony. The tiniest breeze brushed through Emma's light hair. She breathed in deeply, filling her lungs with a burst of fresh air. The sun warmed her shoulders, face, and soul. In the comfort of the heat, Emma let a piece of her frustration and fear fall away with her towel.

Her swimsuit was indeed small. The black bottoms were strappy and cheeky. The matching top held up two black triangles with thin strings. Despite the bag full of wearable options, her pick was actually the more conservative of the bunch. In this moment, however, she could give a pass to Elijah's inappropriate choices. The summer caressed her legs, stomach, and chest in a cozy embrace. It felt so good to have the sun directly kiss as much of her skin as possible.

Emma was brought back to reality and flinched when Elijah spoke.

"Sunscreen," he said, bluntly.

A bottle of SPF 30 flew through the air. Emma juggled it from one hand to the other in a clumsy catch. It seemed like a strange precaution for someone he didn't care for. After the secret, escalating, desires Elijah held over wanting to get rid of her, sunscreen was not something she thought he'd be concerned about. Maybe it was more of his inner medic talking.

"Don't look at me like that," he said, with a roll of his eyes. "Sunburns are a bitch, and cancer aside, it'll keep that blinding complexion of yours safe. Tanning is overrated. Health is hot."

Emma did as she was instructed, rubbing the white lotion on her arms and over her face. The tropical, yet slightly chemical, smell soaked into her skin and filled her nose.

"Put extra over your scar," he added, looking down at his work. "It may look like it's done healing, but it's not. That skin is new, and will need more protection."

Emma turned her leg so that she could look at her formed scar. It was pink and angry looking. It was only at the most random moments that a reminding sting would shock her into remembering it was there. Once Dr. Elijah was sure that she wasn't at risk of developing an infection, he seemed to have checked-out even more than before, if that was even possible. Still, she did as requested, and added another layer of sunscreen to the nasty reminder of that day. Once Elijah seemed satisfied, Emma was given a moment to appreciate her warm surroundings.

Even the outdoor area of their home in the sky was extravagant. A fully stocked and shaded bar, sink, and grill stood to the right. To the far left of the enormous balcony, sat a raised fire pit with rounded benches.

The crown jewel, however, was a magnificent rooftop pool. Expensive lounge chairs with colorful pillows bordered the extravagant feature, with permanently placed umbrellas behind, and slightly off center, to each seat. Mini tables stood next to each chair graciously waiting to hold a drink or two.

Elijah smoothly slid a wall of seamlessly concealed windows to the side, creating little distinction between the inside and out. Emma gawked at the terrace contained within the clear bordering railing, with intricate white balustrades, and dark wood trim. It shocked Emma, how much she never noticed in her sneaky evenings.

If she wasn't the victim of being held in this place against her will, it would most certainly be the vacation of Emma's dreams, but that she could never afford. It was in every sense of the word, luxurious. She wondered how long she had been staring at her impressive surroundings, when Elijah whistled for her to join him on a neighboring chair.

Emma sat hesitantly back on nearly horizontal pillows. From a cooler at his side, Elijah pulled out a square container. Inside were grapes, sliced apples, crackers, and various types of cheese. He opened the lid and set it on a table between them. Emma eyed the food then looked back at Elijah with a little uncertainty.

He laid back casually with his arms up, and rested his head against his palms. She almost forgot how fit he was. He may not have had the bulk of Dameon or Matthew, but he was lean and still very muscular. Short avocado-green shorts with white trim clung to him. They left less to the imagination than a pair of boxers. Suddenly, Emma didn't feel particularly out of place with her own lack of clothing.

"Don't hold your breath, honey. I have significantly less bisexual tendencies than my partners."

"Less? I thought you said you were gay?"

Elijah smiled mischievously.

"I never said I was. You heard what you wanted to hear, well in that case, needed to hear. You were panicking, and I nudged you in the general direction towards the truth. What better way to calm a woman's fear of being violated, than to let her think that you have no interest in women to begin with?"

Emma's eyebrows pressed close.

"I thought you couldn't lie?"

Elijah rolled his head to look in her direction.

"I never lied. I was vague, and you assumed."

Emma thought about pressing further but decided against it. Elijah pointed at the enticing food and instructed her to eat. Emma took a few of the purple grapes, and popped them into her mouth. They were delicious, sweet, and perfect.

"You've lost weight since being here. Not that I blame you. I'll admit, I've been feeding you like an unloved pet."

A small, bitter, laugh escaped through Emma's nose.

Elijah lowered his sunglasses to the tip of his nose to ask what she thought was funny. Emma ignored the glance. She closed her eyes and soaked in the beating rays. A subtle lightshow of colors danced around her shut eyelids.

"Are you suggesting that I could be a loved pet," she asked, cheekily.

Elijah made small rustling noises, signaling his return to a relaxed state.

"Perhaps. Are you house trained?"

Emma played along with an unintentional smile.

"Reasonably."

"Do you bite?"

"Only when provoked."

They both laughed softly.

"Fair enough," he said. "But can you sit, stay, and come when told?"

Emma became quiet. She thought about all of her sneaking around. She thought about Matthew's seemingly complete submission to Dameon. She thought about the provocation of Elijah's ambiguous use of come, or perhaps cum. Emma wasn't sure if she wanted to answer. The question felt like bait for a set trap.

Elijah let the silence linger while Emma's mind wandered. Eventually, she asked what she thought was a relatively simple question.

"How did you come to meet Dameon and Matthew?"

Emma could feel Elijah's eyes on her. She didn't return his gaze, only waited in growing anticipation.

"That seems like something you could have already asked Matthew."

"No," Emma said. "Matthew never wanted to talk about anything personal, so I didn't push. I didn't want to risk burning the only bridge out of that room."

Elijah was quiet. Emma wasn't sure what was going on through his mind, but he wasn't taking the question lightly. She wondered if he too would avoid any insightful information about him and his partners. The longer the silence, the greater her anxiety grew, that he might throw her back into her prison.

An exhale left Elijah's chest, as he surrendered his account of a night, seven years ago.

Green lasers sliced through a foggy atmosphere, while strobing lights pulsed silhouettes to life on the dancefloor. Music blasted through speakers and thumped through a young Elijah's cardiovascular system. Paid women and men danced in cages for crinkled bills. Tourists and locals, celebrating the death of their bachelor days and/or birthdays, packed themselves inside the cramped club. Each one, blissfully unaware of the sticky-fingered thief in their midst.

Elijah, wrapped his arms around the closest body. A playful pull danced the person by the belt loops to his groin. The man, or maybe woman, grinded back to the beat of the electric music. Light hands snuck into back pockets and grabbed a willing ass, never realizing that as Elijah's hands slid back up, so came their cash and cards.

Sleepy, high, eyes looked onward to the next victim. The blond with barely enough years to call himself a man, stumbled around the crowded room. He looked like any other poor soul in the place. Elijah swayed, appearing thoroughly inebriated from alcohol and drugs, but in truth, he was far from it. His mind was sharp, and he was hunting.

A bump into the person on the left, another twenty bucks gained. A kiss to a sloshed bride-to-be, and quick dip into her clutch, offered a bigger win. Sixty dollars in cash, whatever. But a bag of weed? Yummy. The smart thing to do, would be to sell it. The party princess seemed like the type to get her hands on some maliciously laced stuff without realizing it. Obviously smoking it would be a bad idea… but did he really mind?

Any other night, he may have enjoyed muffling his pathetic life in stimulants and depressants, but he was running low on cash again. They say beggars can't be choosers, but he wasn't exactly begging. Elijah was an accomplished taker with a taste for the finer things. It's what he was born for, what he had always been used for. He had been well trained, as leeches producing more leeches often are. So he did what he did best, what he was groomed to do since he could remember.

Expensive shoes and a well tailored suit sat casually at the noisy bar. The young, twenty-something aged man was money, and cute money at that. Elijah spied from the other side of the room. The rich boy was spoken for. A bodyguard of a bear touched the smallest of his fingers to the side of the prince's hand. The bear was nervous, newly out of the closet, if at all. The prince didn't look like he knew what the word, "nervous" meant. Perfect.

A snatched flute of champagne balanced precariously in Elijah's fingers. One intentional trip over his own feet later, and the stolen drink emptied over the target's pants. Elijah's pained and embarrassed face looked up at the man that looked like a dark, scruffy, Fabio with caramel eyes. Scrambling hands grabbed a wad of napkins to correct the mess. The clumsy twink apologized profusely while his cleaning hands brushed against an outline of the victim's dick.

"I'm sorry! I'm sorry! I'm sorry!"

A wandering hand quickly slid a number of cards from the bear's pocket. Just as Elijah shoved the latest loot into his own pants, a harsh hand gripped his wrist. The blond snapped sober eyes up to the bear and prince.

"Pay up, Matthew," Dameon said, with a grin. "I told you, the little shit would be ambitious."

"He's the one with my money," Matthew chuckled, holding Elijah tight.

"Why don't you ask him for it?"

Elijah's knees buckled. His eyes widened and pleaded. A free hand slid up the leg of the expensive fabric of Dameon's pants. Phase two was in progress.

It was the same old play he set up ten times over. He wanted the targets to feel that they had the upper hand. They caught the thief. Jetsetting, trust fund, babies loved to flaunt their power, and Elijah was sure this one wouldn't be an exception. The prince would threaten to get the police involved. Elijah would offer himself for the night, and the rich boys could never resist indulging in the idea of being owed a good time.

Like clockwork, Elijah's mark would take him to their motel. It might be a little rough, a little weird, but he could take it. Everyone sleeps eventually, and when they did, Elijah would snag everything of value before the sun rose the following morning. The scam was almost always a big payday. Still, this one was already starting out a little different. Big targets didn't usually notice his unlawful activities until they were personally affected. Regardless, the con would work, he was sure of it.

"Don't get me kicked out, please," Elijah pleaded, taking his first prod at a possible kink to exploit. "I'm underage, and they'll ban me for life!"

Dameon's eyes narrowed.

"Don't pull that bullshit, it's gross."

"No way you're a minor," Matthew said, full of intimidation. "The truth, now."

Ouch. Rude. Elijah was sure he didn't look older than he was. Well, maybe just a little. His lifestyle may have added a year or two to his face. But not that much! Technically he was underage. He wasn't exactly a minor anymore, but he couldn't order a drink without one of his fake IDs either.

"Does it matter," Elijah asked, with a bite of his lip. "If you don't rat me out, I'll be whatever you want me to be. I can be your virgin, or a whore. I can be a devil, or an angel. I can be anything you say, just... please?"

Matthew adjusted his grip on Elijah, and tightened.

"Your age," Dameon demanded.

"Sixteen," Elijah said, with icy-blue, doe, eyes and a questioning inflection to his words.

Further pressure was applied to his wrist.

"Ah! Fu... Nineteen! I'm nineteen, I swear."

"Who owns you," Dameon asked, disgust coating his words.

Uh oh. Elijah went chasing a squirrel, and found himself barking up the very wrong tree. He didn't target a pretty boy. He targeted a man with connections. "Are you a prostitute," was a question he heard often enough. "Who, specifically, is your pimp," was another question, entirely.

"No one owns me," Elijah said, breaking his composure for a moment. "But that doesn't mean I don't know a few tricks of the trade."

"You know a lot more than a few tricks," Dameon said. "Watching you dance around the room, shifting to create an individually curated grift for each person, robbing nearly half the room in just a couple of hours; you aren't new to this. So, I'll ask one more time. Who do you–"

"Me," Elijah said, angrily. "I only work for me. I've been down that road, being told when and who to fuck, it wasn't for me, thanks. But when you're good at something, you don't do it for free. Not all of us have had the privilege of sucking on a silver spoon."

Another quick look was shared between Matthew and Dameon.

"Would you like to," Dameon said, in a hushed voice.

"Wha... what," Elijah asked, nerves in his throat.

"Suck on a silver spoon," Dameon repeated. "The saying goes 'to be born with a silver spoon in one's mouth, but I think I like yours more. You're pretty, you're talented, and we've been watching you. We aren't in need of a virgin or whore specifically, and we certainly have the devil part covered for ourselves. But an angel? I can't say I've ever had the pleasure. So, what do you say? If you want to see how a silver spoon can really taste, I've got plenty."

"That's a lot of spoon talk," Elijah said, carefully. "I don't mess with– If you want to party, that's fine. I'll play however you want, roofie my drink for all I care, but I won't touch heroin, or fentanyl. I... I–.

Dameon raised an interrogating brow. He took Elijah's chin, with his less aggressive hand, and tilted to see the black of his eyes.

"How long," Dameon asked.

"What?"

"Sobriety," Matthew chimed in. "How long have you been clean?"

"Fifty-three days," Elijah said, with a swallow of anxiety.

"Twelve step," Matthew asked.

"No," Elijah admitted. "I watched my mo– my old manager, go down that path. I won't end up like her. I can't."

Dameon's thumb stroked the edge of Elijah's jaw. His knees felt weak. The pressure of his grinding teeth loosened. Regret soured his stomach. Not only did his con fail miserably, but he shared way too much. He wanted to melt into their laps, to be real and vulnerable for a single second in his life. Who the hell were these men?

"Even thieves need a night off every once in a while," coaxed Matthew, loosening his grip. "Come back to our place."

"No drugs." Dameon said. "Only the high of sleeping somewhere safe. We won't even touch you if you say the word, just let us spoil you for the evening. Forget this shitty world for the night. I have a feeling, we have much more in common than you may realize."

Elijah yanked his face and hand free. They were good, and he was in danger. Elijah knew better than to trust sweet promises. The greater the kindness, the higher the cost. Lies were a given, but these were too much. The cost would surely be his life. If he let them take him to the second location, he was sure he would meet the violent end he had always expected for himself.

White sneakers gripped the sticky floor, as he lunged for the exit. The thin blond pushed and shoved his way, frantically, through the crowd. A final, unnatural, twist to free himself from the dancefloor emptied the fullest of his pockets. His earnings of the evening littered the floor with plastic and valuable paper. When he looked back, the men weren't at their seats. He lost them. He didn't have time.

A heavy, metal, door slammed behind him. Dim lights illuminated a sketchy alley, where warm air facilitated a putrid smell of garbage and ammonia. Elijah tried to catch his breath, but the stench assaulted his nostrils and mouth. Tears welled up in his eyes. His money was gone, he probably just caught the attention of a couple of serial killers, and the stink of the alley was definitely seeping into his clothes.

"Elijaahh," sang a particularly unfriendly dealer, with cigarette breath. "Did ya think that just because you quit on me, ya wouldn't have to pay your tab?"

Elijah was barely given time to wipe his eyes before being shoved against a stucco wall. It really wasn't his night.

"Fuuuck me," Elijah half cried.

"I've seen where your ass has been. I'd rather have cash. But something tells me, ya don't have my money, again."

The disgruntled supplier pulled a knife from his waistband. The tip hovered, ready to pierce Elijah's empty stomach.

"I warned ya. Can't let people think I'm the type to get walked over. Nothin' personal."

A strong hand pulled the dealer's brown coat back with an immense amount of force.

A grunt emitted from Matthew, as he swung the would-be murderer around like a rag doll. The flung body came to a sudden stop, as his head smashed into the wall. Pieces of stucco cracked and revealed a white color beneath its khaki paint.

The arms of the dealer shook, as he attempted to pick himself up from a particularly filthy gutter. The bottom of Dameon's shoe found the center of the man's back and pressed. The struggling arms collapsed under Dameon's pressure, falling pathetically, eyes rolling to the back of his head.

Dameon knelt low. His aggressive foot dug deeper and deeper. A pained sound gurgled out of the broken individual.

"Mine," Dameon growled.

Dameon stood, straightened his jacket, and casually brushed away a stray piece of stucco that found the cuff of his wrist. When the dealer attempted to speak, a shriek replaced his words as Matthew slammed the heel of his boot into the man's ankle. A crunch and snap pierced the air when the dealer's foot bent in an unnatural direction.

Dameon zeroed in on the trembling blond. Elijah pressed into the prickly, rough, wall. He cowered under the approaching man, shoulders up, head dropped, chest heaving. A slip of a whimper sounded in Elijah's throat when his chin was lifted with Dameon's curled finger.

Confident curiosity burned in Dameon's eyes. His thumb traced the edge of Elijah's jaw as he examined him like a rancher might his next bovine purchase.

"How much," Dameon asked, never looking at the damaged man on the ground.

"I'm not his pimp," the dazed man on the ground. "You'll have to ask his mommy for that."

"Not that. What's his tab? How much does he owe," said Dameon. "Don't make me ask again."

"Asshole owes me three-hundred," the dealer said, with a cough.

Dameon pulled a wallet from his jacket pocket, and produced well over five-hundred dollars in fresh bills. He waded the money into a ball, and tossed the payment to the pavement. The dealer snatched up the money much like a mouse to scraps.

"N... no refunds," he studdered. "When ya realize you wasted your money, no refunds. Don't know what lies he sold you, but Elijah will burn you the second he gets the chance. He always does. Not even his mother could make a reliable whore out of him, and she was a cold bitch, so good luck to ya."

"Elijah," Dameon repeated, drawing out his name as if he was tasting every letter on his tongue.

Finally addressing the broken man on the ground, Dameon knelt to his level again.

"I have a job for you," he said, coldly. "Tell whoever is unlucky enough to associate with you, that Elijah is untouchable. He officially belongs to Dameon Lazarus. Do you understand?"

"Laz... Lazarus?"

Any color in the dealer's face that remained was drained with the mention of Dameon's name.

"You mean like–" he said, "Lazarus? But I thought–"

Matthew's foot swung hard, and audibly cracked a number of ribs. The broken man gasped for air, holding his side in agony.

"I said," Dameon repeated, "do you understand?"

"Yes," the pained man wheezed.

Elijah's spine tingled as Matthew's eyes locked onto his. Litter crunched under the giant's shoes, as he took Dameon's place in front of Elijah. Terror shook his knees. The closer the massive man got, the lower Elijah sunk down the wall.

"No, no, no, no, no," Elijah pleaded, with shaky breaths.

When Matthew's hand lifted, Elijah felt a flinch so hard, it jolted his entire body. Past the crook of his arm that rose to protect his face, Elijah peaked at the source of his fear. A large hand extended, offering assistance to the scared young man. He pulled Elijah upright, and placed a guiding hand over his shoulder.

"Time to go, Angel," Dameon said, with a grin. "You're coming with us."

Emma's arms crossed over her torso.

Elijah was an indifferent asshole to her for weeks. He advocated for her death when he didn't think she could hear. She didn't like him, and yet, the second-hand trauma she felt for him broke her heart. She didn't have the best childhood either, but his? Part of her wanted to give him a hug, until she remembered just how much he hated her, and that it would probably be unwelcome anyway.

"When they brought you back here," Emma asked, "did they mean what they said? They obviously love you now, but then? You were afraid they would hurt you, but they didn't, did they?"

Elijah chuckled to himself.

"Oh sweetie, they did much worse than that. They tortured me in ways even I didn't know existed. They broke me down and put me back together, in more ways than one."

Emma held her own body tighter. Elijah arched his back and rolled his shoulders, looking for a relieving pop that eluded his stretch. Emma snuck a quick glance at the blond next to her. He looked pensive as he stared off into the clear sky through his dark glasses.

"They made me feel, for the first time in my life, like I could actually be loved. Even after I tried taking Dameon's wallet the next morning, he showed me mercy I had never known before. He rolled over and caught me in the act. I was ready for him to take back every kindness, every sweet word, he said. I waited for him to command Matthew to beat the life out of me. But he wasn't mad, neither were. Dameon's only request was that I stay... So I did."

Elijah rolled over to face Emma. She mirrored his movements to face him. He removed his shades and took in the sight of her; warm, being cared for, looking more like a human rather than some caged bird.

"I didn't want to keep you," he said, simply. "I wanted to drop you off in Mexico, and wish you the best of luck. Matthew wanted to put a bullet in your head for a while."

Emma moved uncomfortably in her seat.

"Dameon," he continued, "he wanted to keep you locked up for who knows how long. I don't actually think he has a real plan this time."

Emma's eyes dropped to the cushions beneath her. She studied the stitches and woven fibers of the bright cloth.

"But," he said, "now that I think about it, it makes a lot of sense. He has always had a thing for taking in strays."

A question came to Emma's lips, and she asked with curiosity more than defensiveness.

"What makes you think that I am a stray?"

Elijah smiled, with a pucker to his lips.

"Honey, I know a fellow stray when I see one. Can you tell me that you have a family out there looking for you right now? Your pathetic boyfriend isn't looking. Do you have friends in this city, anyone?"

Emma's answer revealed itself in the form of a subdued frown, that twitched in the corner of her mouth. She tried to hide it, but knew instantly that she didn't succeed.

"There wasn't a single picture of you in that place you called a home. If

I didn't know better, I would have guessed that you never lived there at all. You woke up in an office instead of a bedroom. You stayed in a home that wasn't yours, with a man that asked us to do unspeakable things to you. The asshole wasn't the least bit concerned that anyone would miss you. No one is looking for you. Honey, sweetheart, you are a stray."

Emma's eyesight blurred, as she pursed her lips to keep them from quivering.

Elijah stood up, pushed the little table away, and pulled his chair to hers. He sat back down and wrapped an arm around her. He pulled her body close to his. A quick hand positioned one of her legs to wrap around him, and squeezed tight over her thigh. So much skin touched skin. She might have felt uncomfortable, if she hadn't been too busy feeling heartbroken.

"I'm sorry, honey. I can get a little mean sometimes."

Emma concentrated on keeping her breathing from becoming too shaky. She didn't want to cry, but she was failing despite her best efforts. A sweet, apologetic, hand from Elijah moved up her leg. Emma's emotions caught in her throat. Distrusting, worrying, eyes watched his creeping fingers. She followed them as they went further up, over her arm, then lost sight as he pressed gently between her shoulder blades.

"Oh sweetie," he said, with a soft kiss to the top of her head. "You've been through too much to also put up with me. I'm sick of seeing you cry. I'd much rather see if you can swim."

Before Emma had a chance to be confused by the rapid change of subject, Elijah picked Emma up and threw her into the pool.

The cold water shocked her system. For a moment, she was completely disoriented. Whooshing sounds under the water indicated that Elijah had jumped in after her. Emma swam to the surface and loudly gasped at the air. She quickly made her way to the edge of the pool and looked over her shoulder to find Elijah. She flinched at his nearness to her, mere inches away. He placed his hands over hers and pushed her front against the smooth tiled wall.

"I'm sorry." he apologized, as he kissed her wet cheek. "I'm afraid this pet does bite sometimes. Us strays can have trouble adapting to domestication, can't we? I'm sure you've noticed. It's hard to admit what we were before them. It's hard to stay in one place. It's hard not to bite when nervous. That said, we had a long talk last night. We agreed that Matthew had the right idea about you."

Elijah gracefully turned her body to face him, pinning her hands again to the edge.

"Not to kill you obviously, but to let you out of your cage. That's why we are here. You need some air. You need space to stretch and breathe. I know. But honey," Elijah said, venomously, "if you do bite, I promise to bite back much harder."

Elijah kissed her cheek again. His full lips lingered a little longer than the previous time. Emma's heart fluttered next to her persistent fear.

"No one here wants to break you, any more than we already have. But apparently, we can't let you go either. I love these men with every cell in my body, and I will do anything to protect and keep them."

Emma tried to turn away, but Elijah's eyes caught hers and guided her attention back to him.

"I understand," she said, softly. "And I don't blame you."

Elijah heard the unspoken words in her understanding. Of course she didn't blame him. She would do the same if she had someone that made her feel loved and secure. Instead, she had them.

Dameon and Matthew joined the outdoor party. Both wore tropical, long, swim trunks that hit their knees. Dameon made his way to the bar as if nothing unusual or different was occurring in their home. Matthew split off from Dameon's side, and lazily slid into a chair. A tilted umbrella shaded his naturally tanned body.

"Summer Collins, who else needs one?"

The two other men raised a finger to the air. Dameon nodded in acknowledgment and mixed a concoction of gin and lemonade. He poured the cocktail over four glasses with ice without asking Emma if she also wanted to drink. Balancing two glasses per hand, he offered one to Matthew, who accepted the drink with a, "Thank you my good man," and a tip of an imaginary hat. Dameon placed two more on Elijah and

Emma's table and found a seat for himself in the sun.

"What, we aren't good enough for poolside service?"

Dameon kicked a splash at Elijah.

"If you have the energy to pick on our guest, you have the energy to get your own drink."

Elijah rolled his eyes.

"Uh huh. Yeah, I'm the one guilty of playing around."

"But you are the only one guilty of intentionally trying to starve her," Matthew teased.

"Starve is a little harsh," Elijah said, casually. "Pardon me for not wanting to share my culinary gifts with her right away."

Matthew rolled his eyes as he sipped a long drink from his glass. Elijah released Emma's hands, and pushed himself up and out of the pool. He turned back to Emma and reached out with a kind smile to help her up. She took his open hand, held tight, and pulled with all of her might, sending Elijah crashing into the water. She rushed out of the pool before he could surface, unsure of his reaction. Matthew and Dameon laughed. Elijah shook the water from his hair and grinned broadly.

"Does this mean you forgive me," Elijah asked Emma.

"Forgive," Matthew asked, concern in his voice.

His body became rigid, as stress replaced his previously relaxed state. For valuing trust so much, the three men seemed to have a lack of it when it came to her. Emma almost felt guilty for causing such an upheaval in the men's relationship. They clearly weren't used to keeping anything from each other, however, if they wanted a solution to their troubles, they could always let her go.

Matthew's nervousness over Elijah's words didn't leave his face. He clearly didn't like the idea that Elijah may have done something, potentially, unforgivable.

"What did he do, Emma?"

Elijah scoffed, and proceeded to float on his back.

"Calm down big boy, I didn't do much. I just let my inner bitch get the better of me. I also may have thrown her into the pool without knowing if she could swim. Fun fact, she can!"

Dameon laughed. The sound startled Emma, not because it scared her this time, but because it was strange to hear. He sounded content, almost happy. Emma took a gulp of the sugary, alcoholic drink. Though tasty, she shivered at its strength. Elijah snapped his fingers at her and pointed to the food on the small table.

"Food! Eat!"

He was right, but that didn't keep her from rolling her eyes. Emma took a few bites of cheese, crackers, and glorious crisp slices of apple. Some petty part of her didn't want Elijah to be satisfied with himself for feeding her real food. Secretly, she savored every bite of the beautiful combinations. Though, out of the corner of her eye, she saw him flash a grin at the enjoyment he knew he had given her.

Emma wandered to the edge of the terrace with her new allowance of freedom, and leaned against the clear railing. In the wonderful light of day, the penthouse gleamed with life and promise. The view of the city, however, did not share the same appreciation for the revealing sun. The Vegas Strip was made for the night. The glowing neon and flashing lights lost their luster in the large valley. Little orange and brown roofs surrounded a crowded mess of tall buildings. The mountains were breathtaking with their gray, blue, and speckled surfaces, but the city paled in the day.

Steps grew closer, behind Emma. Matthew took her hands in his, and slid them along the top of the smooth barrier. Her arms stretched out until fully extended, and Matthew wove his fingers with hers. He guided her into a position of sensuality, and lowered himself to be cheek to cheek with her. Emma could feel the eyes of the other men on her. The ability to fall off the roof suddenly felt like a potential threat.

Emma opened her mouth to protest such an open display of, whatever it was Matthew was doing. Being affectionate?

"Elijah is a feral king of emotional manipulation," he whispered.

Emma shivered at the feel of Matthew's words in her ear, despite the warm atmosphere.

"He's never been good at dishing out physical pain, but emotional? He will keep digging until he hits a reaction that satisfies him. Sometimes he doesn't even realize he's doing it. Other times, it's a game to him. Just like he's playing games with me, by putting you in that suit."

Emma wanted to hold on to the rail as if her life depended on it. Maybe it did. But she was in a rebellious mood, and didn't appreciate being toyed with, at the moment. Elijah may enjoy his mind games, but Matthew wasn't being much better at the moment. He knew she wanted him, and that he would tell her no, despite wanting her too. Well, if he wasn't going to play fair, she didn't want to either.

Emma pulled her hands away from his. She turned around, back to the short wall, chest to Matthew's toned torso. She ran her fingers through his chest hair, and looked up at him with her big green eyes. Matthew inhaled a breath of control.

"And is this your game," she asked, softly. "Would you say I'm closer to losing, or winning, on a scale of falling off a roof, to being set free?"

Matthew ran his hold up her arms and then down the sides of her until he found her waist. His hold compressed her like a corset.

"You may want to reconsider your words," he said. "Games usually mean something a little harsh in this home. But if you really want to play–"

Emma's feet went numb as her toes left the concrete. Matthew lifted her only a few inches off the ground, before Emma gasped and threw her arms around him. Her stomach tingled. Her panic fully took over as she closed her eyes and grabbed a fistful of Matthew's hair.

Matthew laughed through her strangling hold. He didn't let her linger long and quickly returned her feet to the stable terrace floor. When the initial shock of thinking she was about to be thrown off a building subsided, Emma caught a number of breaths.

"Matthew!" Dameon scolded.

Matthew threw his hands in the air, similar to the way Dameon had last night. He turned to his accuser and defended himself poorly, claiming it was a joke. Elijah added his own outrage to the conversation. While Elijah and Matthew started bickering, Emma let herself slide down the clear barrier, giggling in light hysterics. Dameon's piercing eyes stared at her, demanding answers to questions he had yet to voice.

"Elijah," she finally said. "It's fine. If he wanted to push me to my death, he would have done it the first time he caught me sneaking around. Isn't that right?"

She looked up at Matthew with a devious smile. She let out another breathy half-laugh.

"But for someone that is so concerned with trust, you sure like to play with mine."

Dameon leaned back in his chair, and sipped his drink.

"How often did you say you two were having your friendly get-togethers?"

"Fairly often," Matthew admitted, with a frown.

Dameon eyed the woman, still trying to regulate her heartbeat.

"You've never lied to me before, Matthew," he said, never taking his hard blue eyes off Emma, "but, it's a little hard to believe that you spent all of that time together, and you didn't fool around."

Emma felt a strange sense of validation. She looked at Matthew who looked down at his feet. If this was all a game, she won this round, sort of. Matthew looked unsure and regretful. He trapped himself with his ridiculous excuse when she was ready, consenting, and literally begging for him. Emma could see him questioning last night. She enjoyed it.

The rest of the day outside was spent eating, drinking, and mostly lounging in and out of the pool. Emma caught herself for a few seconds at a time, forgetting her position in the penthouse. These were her kidnappers. She couldn't truly believe that they wouldn't do her harm if they wished, or if they felt too inconvenienced by her presence.

At the end of the day she would be returned to her room and locked away until they felt like letting her out. If they decided not to give her food or were too busy, she wouldn't eat. If she were to get sick, she would have to rely on them to manage her care. Maybe they would, maybe they wouldn't.

Elijah had been right, so had Grant. She didn't have any friends or loved ones. It was pathetic that this was the closest she had come to enjoying herself in a long time, yet here she was. She swallowed a little more of the numbing substance than she probably should have, and Dameon was quick to refill her glass.

That night, Emma, Dameon, and Matthew sat around the firepit. Matthew slumped into the back of the bench with his feet resting at the fire's edge. His arms crossed over his body and he looked to be half asleep. Emma's wet hair dripped chilly pool water down her back, making her shiver and her chest harden abundantly clear under the bikini top. A teasing gentle breeze that moved through the terrace did not help either.

Emma felt Dameon's eyes through the orange glow as he noticed Emma's discomfort from across the pit. The way the fire and shadows played with his body made her think of last night's events. He was incredibly sexy, intimidating, and in a recent discovery, loving when he wanted to be. He might not be loving to her, but he carried an abundance for his men.

Dameon stood and unwrapped his towel from his waist. He moved in, and sat very close to her. Emma found herself trying not to show how anxious he made her. Dameon placed the dry towel around Emma's shoulders. She accepted the kindness, but tensed when he rubbed her arms to get some additional warmth into her. The desert nights got so much colder than she would have expected, but that wasn't the reason for her unintentional shiver.

Elijah rejoined the group with expertly balanced plates of food. Matthew awoke with a jolt as the aroma hit his nose. Savory herbs and buttery smells made Emma's heart ache with joy. Elijah looked pridefully at his creations, and distributed the plates.

When Emma took a bite of the garlic-buttery pork bites, they melted in her mouth. A side of asparagus was cooked to absolute perfection, not too crunchy, but not completely soft either. Medic, grifter, and phenomenal cook; was there anything Elijah couldn't do? Matthew made noises of satisfaction that put a smile on Elijah's face.

"Damn," Matthew said. "Who would have known that arsenic could taste so good?"

Dameon chuckled and reached for his lemony drink. Elijah looked annoyed.

"Don't worry, Emma," Elijah said. "I take too much pride in my cooking for that."

"Oh that wasn't my concern," she said, sweetly, as she examined a piece of pork on the tip of her fork. "I was more conflicted over how good your last abductee tastes. You must have taken better care of her, than you have been of me."

Dameon choked on his drink and coughed out a strained laugh. Matthew's eyes were wide at her unexpected joke. Elijah shared Matthew's surprise. The alcohol's magic encouraged her to disregard what remained of any held back words. It also began to make her lips and cheeks tingle and heat.

"Do you think I'll end up tasting this good, when you're sick of keeping me," she asked, as she popped the bite of meat into her mouth.

"I'm sure you'll be delicious," Elijah said, eyes narrowed as he stared at Emma challengingly.

After the cannibalistic joking subsided, Emma's mind lingered on yet another question. Dameon clearly valued honesty above just about anything else. It wasn't just some intimidation technique of his. He really did want the truth to be told at all times under his reign.

"So, jokes don't count against your honesty rule?"

Her genuine tone gave Dameon pause. He thought on her curiosity for a moment, taking the question seriously. He placed an empty fork onto his plate with a small clinking sound.

"No, they don't count. The use of sarcasm and joking around is a pretty significant part of our relationship. But, while jokes may remain an exception, the honesty rule can extend to things unsaid as well."

Matthew and Elijah picked up on something Emma didn't. They passed an anxious glance to each other, but Dameon ignored their sideline looks.

"Of course, we can choose to make it known if we would rather not talk about a subject. But intentional, secretive, omission of the truth? That breaks the rule. Elijah still struggles with that one sometimes, but old habits die hard. And apparently with your arrival, Matthew had a moment of weakness as well."

Emma absorbed that last detail, and felt a twinge of guilt.

"You, however, seem to have taken decently to our rule. Would you like to share your opinion on it?"

Emma took a minute to think about it. She wanted to give an answer as authentic as his own. It seemed only fair.

"I think it is refreshing, but also difficult. There is a hell of a vulnerability to it."

Dameon nodded his head in agreement.

"Yes, it can be hard at first. And as we have seen with the nightly visits between you and Matthew, even the most seasoned of us can slip."

Matthew's guilt burdened his features. He caught Dameon's eye, who didn't exactly offer a forgiving look. Matthew looked back down to his own plate. She could see why he was so eager to get their secret meetings out in the open. To hide anything from Dameon was a dangerous and personal affront to the man.

"Over time, it gets easier," Dameon said. "It can even become close to feeling second nature."

"Do you think I will have the time for it to feel that way? For it to be second nature?"

She asked her last question with a bluntness that even took her by surprise. Matthew and Elijah both eyed Dameon. They seemed to want to know what he would answer as badly as Emma did.

Dameon nodded his head, not concerning himself to look up from his nearly empty plate.

"Yes, I do."

The last bite of asparagus was bitter sweet. She had her first freshly cooked meal in a while and it was wonderfully satisfying. But with that last bite, she knew what was coming next. The sun had set, reviving the lively cityscape in all its glory once again. Dameon took Emma's empty plate and handed it politely to Elijah. Matthew and Elijah gathered the empty glasses, utensils, and plates and shuffled off to the kitchen to clean up. Dameon stood with Emma to escort her back to her room.

She took a few steps and noticed that she had become slightly dizzy. Maybe she had more to drink that she realized. Dameon held her arm with a steady grip. Emma closed her eyes to reduce the world's rocking. Even then, when he had given her reasons to believe she might be safe, Dameon made her skin buzz with nervousness. He led her patiently through the glass doors, past the stairs, down the hall, and to the room.

Dameon allowed the heavy door to close behind him. With the introduced privacy, he closed the space between him and Emma. Emma's fuzzy mind wondered why he was hanging around. He had been so distant with her before. The only exception being, when Matthew practically ambushed him into being in the same room with her. He didn't seem too happy with him for it. Dameon slid the towel that was around Emma's shoulders, to the floor.

A fast hand slid up the line of her back and found the knotted black string. He pulled the stretchy line, and continued to the top knot at her neck with even more speed. She gasped as he pressed her barely clothed chest against his, not allowing the free top to fall. His fingers trailed down her ribs, her waist, her hips, and pulled at more strings. The still very wet swimsuit made a splat as it hit the floor.

Dameon pushed her onto the bed with him, never giving enough space for her top to fall until she was secure against the mattress. Her breath quickened, the room spun. She knew she wanted to relieve her frustrations, but she was having trouble concentrating. Dameon grabbed the center of her top and ripped it away, throwing it to join the bottoms and towel.

He never broke eye contact with Emma. New air chilled the places the removed damp suit previously covered. Her breasts, her core, her everything felt so needy– and unstable. She could practically feel his lips against hers. Did she? Was she kissing him, or was she imagining it? Her knees started to gain distance. Her legs relaxed with an unnatural numbness. Her knees parted. Were the movements Dameon's doing, or hers? The fuzzy world felt too confusing.

Emma's stomach still managed a backflip when Dameon pulled a soft blanket over her naked body and wrapped it in a way that restricted her arm movement. Even without the ropes he used on Matthew, he managed to make her feel very much bound. She wondered how restricted Matthew felt. The world began rocking again. Hands that didn't belong to her, rolled Emma onto her side. What was he doing? Did she care? She was so tired.

Dameon rose, with a pillow in one hand. She wondered why he wanted her pillow. Didn't he have pillows? She didn't need it. Maybe he'd try to smother her to death? She somehow managed not to care as the acid in her stomach expressed discontent. Emma's rambling thoughts started to make less and less sense to her. Why was she thinking about pillows? She followed the cruel man with her eyes and watched as he opened the door.

"Sweet dreams, little prisoner," he said, coldly.

Dameon let the pillow fall. He left. Emma clearly heard his bare feet step away and up the stairs. She thought about that for a moment. She clearly heard. The pillow prevented the door from shutting. No barrier existed to muffle the sounds of his feet. The lightest glow from the deserted hallway lit a sharp line where the door did not meet the wall. A single tear ran freely from Emma at the sight of reassurance that she wasn't trapped. Nearly instantly, she fell asleep.

7 | A Deal With Death

Sunlight woke Emma once again, but this time with new promise. A subtle throb annoyingly made itself present in her brain in protest over the night's alcohol consumption. The headache, however, didn't stifle her excitement when her eyes darted to the door. She didn't dream it, her door was open.

Emma leapt out of bed and into the shower. She scrubbed the pool chemicals from her hair and body with floral soaps and optimistic speed. She wrapped a towel tightly around her wet hair and brushed her teeth quickly. She rushed to her allotted clothes when she noticed another large canvas bag placed barely inside her room. A note, in pretty cursive, was pinned to the bag saying, "Sorry it took so long."

Emma looked inside to find brand new women's clothes. Camisole tank tops in white, gray, and black were folded neatly over a few new pairs of underwear and leggings. Emma had never been so happy to hold a pair of panties and leggings.

Emma caught a glimpse of herself in the mirror and smiled at her very human appearance. Her hand hovered above the cracked door's handle, afraid that once she held it, she might wake up and be locked in the small space, wearing an oversized t-shirt, staring at another bowl of instant oatmeal. She touched the cool metal and walked through the doorway.

The little freedom was so sweet. She felt like she was doing something wrong or breaking some rule by stepping out into the day without surveillance, but she was too excited to let it hold her back. She had spent so much time changing her sleeping patterns to be awake in the night, she felt a grogginess from moving about in the morning, or maybe that was the hangover?

The smell of roasted beans saturated the air. Emma inhaled deeply, taking in the warm, bitter smell. She wondered what, exactly, she was allowed to do now. Could she grab a cup at her leisure, make eggs and toast? The last time she had a cup of coffee, she got into a life-changing fight with Grant. She missed it terribly. The coffee, obviously, not Grant.

Elijah apparently felt the craving just as much as she did. He poured himself a mug when he spotted her, and gave an odd smile.

"Coffee?"

"Yes, please!" she practically moaned.

Elijah tilted his head teasingly as he poured her a cup.

"With this can of worms, officially open," he said, not so casually, "I wonder how long it will take for the fish to really bite. Dameon clearly wants a taste, but my money is on Matthew breaking first."

Emma pretended to ignore him. It's not like she didn't try with Matthew. She pretty much threw herself at him, but he refused. Dameon on the other hand– She paused at the thought. Something like an elusive dream lingered in Emma's mind, something about last night. They kissed? It was fuzzy.

"Now that you're out and about in the day, it will only be a matter of time, I'm sure. Matthew told me the way you were all over him the other night. Poor guy. He was so pent up after rejecting you."

Emma felt a twinge of annoyance at Elijah's game. He waved his hand for her to follow him out of the kitchen. He spoke as he passed her, leading the way.

"Consider it a compliment, honey. The only reason those two haven't given you "the D" yet, is because they actually care. When we do end up sharing you, it'll be because those two will have finally accepted that you really are, just as thirsty for them as they are for you. But don't worry, they'll let themselves admit it eventually. If I can, they can, and they will."

Emma stopped and stared at Elijah. After enough unaccompanied steps, he turned to look back. His eyes searched to see whether or not he won the latest round.

"When we share you? If you can, they can? What is that supposed to mean?"

Elijah rolled his eyes. He returned to the kitchen with slow and deliberate steps, and closed the distance between him and Emma.

"Would it have made you feel better," he prodded, "knowing that each of the three men that trapped you here, were horny as hell for you?"

Elijah paused for Emma to think about the question. Her eyes moved as if reading the words coming from his mouth. She watched for some sign that he was kidding, but was only given a wicked smile.

"You were already scared enough, I wanted you to take comfort in the thought that at least one guy in this place wasn't thinking about getting in your pants."

Emma stood in slight shock.

"But you said–" she started.

Elijah moved in closer. Emma stood her ground. Elijah raised a brow and continued to tease. Matthew had warned her. He told her yesterday that Elijah was very good about getting into people's heads. Is that what he was doing? Trying to mess with her? Scare her?

"You're going to have to start listening a little more carefully, honey. Have I ever said that I was not attracted to you, or did I allude to ideas that brought you to that conclusion."

Elijah moved his eyes over Emma, making her insides squirm.

"I do have less bisexual tendencies than my partners, it's true. They find a great number of women more attractive than I do. But just because I am more picky doesn't mean I have zero attraction to women. And yes, I wish you weren't here, but that doesn't mean I never thought about the body drowning beneath Matthew's ginormous shirts. And don't think I didn't notice every time you used them as short dresses."

She didn't think about it before, but the idea that Elijah wasn't interested, did in fact, provide a sense of safety. The new information changed her view of him in an instant, like he knew it would. He was right. It was overwhelming.

"By the way, this," he said, gesturing at her outfit, "is sooooo much better. It's nice to see you in something more... flattering."

Elijah led Emma back to a space she hadn't spent much time in during her nightly explorations. Two white, semi circle, sofas lined curved windows of a sitting area. It was just beyond the main living room and flaunted a unique 240 degree view of the city and desert. At the center of the space, a circular, dark, coffee table completed the round theme of the small room. It reminded Emma of a weirdly modern adaptation of King Arthur's table.

Elijah cleared his throat, with the intent to silence the conversation being had between Dameon and Matthew. The two were chatting in hushed, yet enthusiastic, voices about something. Both immediately cut off their discussion with Emma's added presence. Matthew welcomed her with a warm smile and slid over to make room. Dameon looked out the window, deep in thought.

Emma stared at the pondering man and tried to remember bits of the night before. If her memory was a puzzle, it would be safe to say that her inebriation definitely caused some of the pieces to be misplaced. She remembered her door being open. She remembered Dameon leading the way to her room. But something muddled in between her moments of recollection. She remembered him leaving. Elijah mentioned that Dameon wanted her, but he also seemed confident that his partners had no intention of violating her. But she woke up naked, and definitely didn't remember getting undressed.

"Dameon," she asked, nervously.

Dameon made a passive sound to indicate he was listening, but continued to stare out the window.

"Did we– I can't remember last night."

A devious smile spread across his lips. A stone dropped in her stomach. Dameon surveyed the uncertain woman before him. Elijah found a place next to Dameon, wiggled in close, and proceeded to observe his own colorful nails. He was obviously listening to the conversation, but pretended not to care. Dameon looked amused by the discomfort that enthralled Emma.

"See," he said, with a tone of arrogance. "This is why the honesty rule matters. When the reliability of another person's word is all you have, the ability to believe them becomes pretty important doesn't it?"

Emma and Matthew met each other's eyes. She looked back at Dameon.

"When you and my love Matthew here, decided to omit the truth from me, you gave yourself reasons to believe that I might do the same to you. So even if I told you I didn't fuck you, tell me, would you believe me?"

He leaned over the table and demanded the attention of both.

"Matthew already knows this, but you, Emma. Don't ever lie to me again. I will always find out, and I have a vicious habit of holding grudges."

Elijah couldn't disassociate from the conversation any longer, his face a mix of concern and seriousness. He didn't like what Dameon was saying. If Elijah wasn't simply playing with her again, he truly didn't believe that his partner would do anything like what he was being suggested.

"But to answer your question," Dameon said, "no. What makes you think I took advantage of you?"

Shame from her lies, and anger at the feeling of violation, mixed poorly with her coffee.

"I didn't wake up with clothes on," she said.

Dameon didn't respond, only smiled as he relaxed further onto his side of the sofa. Matthew stared hard at Dameon. Something bordering a line between anger and disbelieving denial waged a war in his eyes. The uncomfortable silence that formed was broken by Elijah.

"Dameon," he nudged. "You wouldn't do something like that."

Despite the absence of questioning inflection in the words, Elijah's statement was definitely asking for reassurance. He needed to hear an explanation that would make up for the terrible behavior, and he wasn't the only one. Dameon took Elijah's hand and gave it a squeeze.

"No, Angel." he said, with all the comfort he could muster.

He wrapped an arm around Elijah's chest and pulled him back to lay against him. He positioned Elijah between his legs and cuddled him gently.

"Not exactly. I took her to her room. I undressed her, with some flourish, admittedly. Then I put her to bed. Untaken, no stolen kisses, no intrusive tongue, and no penetration to be found. Only the removal of her wet suit, leading to the covering of an inebriated girl. I didn't even take a peek at the naked body I helped undress."

Elijah nestled in closer.

"Still. You shouldn't have undressed her when you knew she wouldn't remember, just to prove a point. That's really messed up, even for you." Elijah said.

"You're probably right," said Dameon. "I let my feelings over her secret keeping get the better of me. But I can't say I'm sorry. I'm not. I wanted to scare her. I wanted to remind her that keeping secrets in this house is dangerous. If she's going to have free reign here, she needs to know that. But you're right, Angel. It was a very cruel move to make."

Emma believed his story, but she still felt taken advantage of. Maybe not as much physically, but his emotional abuse was unacceptable. Her anger and hurt boiled over, heating her cheeks. Fine. She would give him what he wanted. No more dishonesty. Self-preservation be damned.

"If you don't want any more secrets," she said, forcefully, "why don't you keep talking? About your plans to rob, what was it, a jewelry shop? Or am I the only one that isn't allowed to keep secrets?"

A silence chilled the room by multiple degrees. Matthew's face turned hard and unreadable. Elijah's anxiety was back in full swing. Dameon held a gaze of calculation. Whether or not he was thinking about throwing her back in her cell, or planning to murder her, he looked on edge.

Emma pushed down her fears and regrets over speaking up. One voice in her head told her to quit talking and start running, but another screamed, "fuck it," and let the anger out. Where would she run to anyway? There was nowhere to go. She lit the stick of dynamite, and there was no stopping the explosion to come.

"I've been listening to you, when possible, with the door cracked. I know you are thieves. I know that Matthew murdered a pawnshop guy during your last heist. I know that Elijah, eventually, wanted me to die next. I know that you, Mr. Honesty, still haven't told your partners why you are keeping me here!"

Emma's heart pounded in her chest and in her ears. Her well fitting cami, that accentuated her feminine body, suddenly made her feel naked and vulnerable. Adrenaline lifted Emma to her feet. She stood with balled fists at her side, looking like she was ready for a fight.

"You talk about secrets and telling the truth, but what about you? I can't have a few secrets to keep my sanity, but you can hide what you please from me, from your lovers?"

Matthew's hand twitched and Emma flinched dramatically at the small movement. He touched her arm lightly with the tips of his fingers. Her muscles tensed. She was on a roll and wasn't about to stop now. Even if she wanted to, her outrage had taken over any rational thought process.

"You want honesty? Well, I'm honestly sick of waiting around for nothing. I'm sick of playing spy. What are your plans with the heists? Why are you stealing things, when you already have so much stuff? When the hell are you going to let me go, or finally decide to kill me? But you won't give me any answers, will you? Because your rule doesn't actually apply to you, does it!"

Emma closed her eyes tight, and shamelessly let tears of frustration fall. She didn't regret her decision to speak up. It was an incredibly idiotic move that probably signed her death certificate, but if Dameon could lose his temper, why not her? What more did she have to lose?

Dameon swiftly retreated from the room, leaving Matthew and Elijah without direction. Matthew moved to be near Elijah. He pulled his long hair through his fingers. When Dameon returned, he closed in on Emma with speedy purpose.

"No!" Elijah screamed.

White knuckles wrapped around a large kitchen knife. Dameon went for Emma. Matthew held Elijah back, as Dameon grabbed a fistful of Emma's hair. He yanked her head back, slamming her over the back of the couch. Warning glares were shot in Matthew and Elijah's direction, instructing them to keep their distance. Matthew ensured that they both would obey.

Dameon pressed the blade to Emma's throat. She felt the cold metal steal her temperature as it touched her skin. He held her brutally, her head pulled back, her neck over the sofa, exposing her throat to the most vulnerable angle. Her spine arched. Her legs were uselessly angled, rendering her helpless. Her hands were free to hold Dameon's arms, but his rage only added to his overpowering strength.

"Spying," he seethed at her. "Interesting choice of words. Tell me then, spy, how long have you been on Tony's payroll?"

Emma cried freely under the blade. The knife pressed further, the pressure at the cusp of breaking her skin. Dameon pulled her hair with greater violence in response to her lack of answers. Pain at her scalp encouraged the production of more tears.

"How the fuck do you know Tony!" he screamed.

"I don't!" Emma screeched back. "I don't know who that is! Please! Please! I don't know!"

Matthew placed a careful hand on Dameon's shoulder. He moved slowly as if approaching an unstable and wild animal. Matthew spoke in a calm and, attempted, soothing voice.

"I don't think she belongs to him."

Dameon jerked his head around to look at Matthew. The angry stare startled Matthew enough to remove his hand from Dameon.

"We picked her place at random. How could he plan for that? What are the odds that he would have someone ready in the random house we just so happened to bust through?"

Dameon removed the knife from her neck and threw her violently on the marble floor. Emma balled herself up into the fetal position when she saw that Dameon wasn't done. He knelt to her side and pressed the flat of the blade against her cheek, pointing to the corner of her mouth.

"If you aren't telling the truth," he said, shaking in fury, "I will cut your tongue out and shove it down your throat, so that you can choke to death on your fucking lies."

Dameon backed away. Matthew received the enraged man. He held him in a crushing hug and kissed his temple. Emma watched him whisper into Dameon's ear. For Emma, Matthew's actions felt like the most devastating of betrayals. Matthew, the closest thing she had to a friend, treated her attacker as if he were the victim.

Elijah knelt beside her. Emma hid her face and balled up even tighter. If Matthew hadn't taken her side, Elijah definitely wouldn't. She braced for the unknown.

Elijah leaned over the tightly curled woman and put a hand gently over her tender head. His fingers carefully brushed along the hair Dameon used against her.

"Is that who hurt your sister," Emma asked, without looking at Dameon. Elijah's fingers froze.

She braved a peak and wished she hadn't. Elijah paled. She really was trying to get herself killed. Dameon's dark eyes burned and threatened her existence.

"And how would you know about her," he asked, "but not about Tony?"

"Me," Matthew said, quickly. "She asked who was in your artwork. I told her Penny's name, but not much else. Only that she was gone. That was me."

It took Emma a few tries before her nerves allowed her to speak.

"Is that why you got mad when you thought Matthew threatened me into coming upstairs? Is that why, until last night, you avoided me and were so concerned with consent, why your partners were so sure you'd never do something like that? Is that what Tony did to her?"

Dameon inhaled deeply and breathed out a curse. He gathered himself for what felt like a long while. Eventually he managed to speak.

"I'm sorry."

The knife fell to the floor with a clank that made the room flinch. Dameon sank into the sofa and held his head in his hands.

Elijah pulled Emma onto his lap. He held her, with his arms criss-crossed over her chest. Comforting, stroking, movements were made against her shoulders by Elijah's thumbs. Emma reached for an arm, and held him with a desperate need for security. He understood her wordless request, and held her tighter.

"Tony never, directly, laid a hand on Penny," Dameon said, without looking at her. "But he did kill her."

Dameon looked at his victim with oceans of regret. Elijah slowly guided Emma to her feet. He transferred her from the floor, back to the couch with him. Matthew sat close to Dameon on the opposing sofa. Elijah never stopped holding Emma and massaging her scalp. The movements against her head stung, but the care overpowered the minor discomfort.

"How did–" she started, but was cut off by a warning shake of Matthew's head.

Dameon took his partner's hand and squeezed.

"Emma," Dameon said, with sincerity, "I'm sorry. I overreacted. Tony's psychopathic nature knows no limits, so it wouldn't surprise me to learn that he planted the perfect person in the right place to get to me. But you asking if sex was a factor between him and my sister–" he exhaled a false attempted laugh. "No. You clearly haven't met the man. Sex has never been his driving force. The man is obsessed with power but not that kind."

Emma prepared herself to ask another question but was cut off again.

"I don't want to say more," Dameon sighed. "I'll give you everything you want to know, just not right now, please. Can you accept that?"

Emma nodded.

"I shouldn't have attacked you. It was a poor way to repay you for the honesty I demanded."

Emma nodded again in acceptance of Dameon's apology, but he was clearly unsatisfied. Elijah asked tenderly if Emma would feel safer in her room. Emma's anxiety spiked when she thought of being locked away again. She still didn't have the key. She needed Elijah. She needed to be held. Being imprisoned in that awful room, alone, would be unbearable after being attacked, after just getting the freedom to come and go as she desired during the day. It was too much.

"No!" she said, quickly. "No, please, or thank you. I... I just got out!"

Dameon stood to his feet, making Elijah and Emma jump. He angrily marched behind a well stocked bar to the left of the fireplace. He spun the top of a whiskey bottle and let the lid fall, and roll around on the floor. He grabbed a glass, dug ice out of a small freezer below the counter, and poured.

Matthew sat on a brown and brass barstool, but Dameon didn't look up from his glass.

"Don't," Dameon warned. "I don't want to hear it."

Matthew calmly tried taking the drink from his hand.

"If you know what I'm going to say," Matthew pushed, "then you know what to do. Put it down."

Dameon slammed the glass on the bar, splashing liquor as he did.

"Fuck off" Dameon shouted. "A single drink to take the edge off isn't going to hurt anyone."

His voice was different. His untouchable presence wavered. Dameon's glassy eyes fastened to the liquor hugging square ice.

"Sober me already has that covered," said Dameon, under his breath.

Matthew reached over the bar. Dameon's shirt twisted just below the neck, in Matthew's fists. His speed was quick, his grip unbreakable. He pulled Dameon over the top, knocking glasses against glass, and sending full bottles to the floor. Before Dameon could get his bearings, Matthew slammed his partner, his indomitable leader, into the wall.

Dameon's fingers pried at Matthew's. He threw a shoulder forward, but Matthew pounded Dameon's attempt back into the wall. Matthew wasn't backing down, and it was clear how physically unmatched they were. The disobedience enraged Dameon, and the knowledge that he could do nothing to gain an upper hand only added fuel to his fire.

Elijah held Emma tighter. She wasn't sure if he was trying to give comfort anymore, or looking for it.

"Look at me," Matthew demanded.

Dameon's eyes glared off to the side.

"Look at me!" Matthew's booming voice rattled the remaining, intact, glass at the bar.

Dameon complied.

"You made me promise!" Matthew shouted. "Your bullshit is out of control, and you're spiraling. You took an innocent woman from her home, imprisoned her, manipulated and abused her. And now you just want to drink your mistakes away? Who do you sound like right now?"

Dameon bared his teeth at Matthew.

"Your father would be proud," Matthew said.

"Take that shit back," Dameon growled.

"I can't do that. It would be a lie."

"That's fucking low," Dameon said, without releasing his clenched jaw. "I'm not–"

"Then prove it. Fix it!" Matthew barked. "Be vicious, be good, just don't be him."

Matthew relaxed his grip without fully letting go. Dameon threw himself into Matthew in a desperate hold. Matthew squeezed the man. He whispered something in Dameon's ear, only for him. Whatever it was, it made Dameon painfully smile. He held the big man tighter. Dameon said something private in return. Matthew almost looked like he was shaking. Whatever the man said, it made Matthew look sick.

"My love," Dameon said, with a kiss to Matthew's cheek. "This is me, fixing things my way."

Matthew nodded his head in understanding.

Dameon brushed his hair back with his fingers. He straightened up, and exhaled the temporary vulnerability. He closed his eyes and regained the rest of the composure he had lost. He turned to Emma, his gaze back to being sure and sharp.

"Take Elijah to the kitchen, Matthew. I don't want an audience."

Elijah held Emma closer. Dameon walked over to the abandoned kitchen knife on the floor. He picked it up and turned to Emma.

"I changed my mind!" Elijah protested. "I know I said some things before, but I was just frustrated. I want to keep her, Dameon! Dameon?"

The leader of the two men sat on the edge of the coffee table, and looked past Emma to Elijah.

"Let her go," he demanded.

Elijah shook his head.

"Angel, go with Matthew. I need you to trust me."

Elijah's hands trembled. Slowly, and with visible regret, he abandoned

Emma and listened to his partner. He removed her from his hold, and stood to uncomfortably join Matthew. Dameon grabbed Elijah's hand on his way, and kissed it, stopping him briefly to tell Elijah he loved him.

Then they were alone. Only Emma and Dameon remained in the room, and they stared at each other hard. Emma felt much like she did when they first met; angry, scared, and defeated.

"I can't let you go," he said, with finality.

Angry tears rolled down Emma's face.

"It's not right," he said, bringing the knife closer to her, "and it's not fair."

Emma gripped the cushions of the couch, with wide eyes. Dameon reached out with his empty hand and took hers. He placed the knife gently in her possession.

"I took you from your home, because I panicked. I brought you to mine, because I wanted you, in the simplest of ways. Something triggered in me when your boyfriend made his request. You, Matthew, and Elijah have so many similarities. I was bleeding out, and somewhat delusional. I wanted to save you, but also keep my loved ones safe. I didn't know how to do that at the time. I still don't. I'm in over my head because I stupidly thought it was the right move."

Dameon wrapped her trembling fingers around the knife.

"If you never want me to touch you," he said, "speak to you, look at you, then it will be so. Give me your demands, or take from me what you feel you are owed."

Dameon slid his hands away and sat across from Emma. He looked at the knife. He looked at her.

"Do what you need to do. I've already taken so much from you. Matthew and Elijah will not retaliate, and I won't fight back. I can't un-kidnap you, or take back the many ways in which I have hurt you. I can't exactly offer an eye for an eye, but I can offer you a little revenge. If I was in your place, I would want to kill the bastard responsible. So feel free to inflict the pain you feel you are owed from me, or tell me how I can fix my mistakes."

Dameon sat up straight. He gripped the side of the coffee table, and tilted his chin slightly up.

"I won't stop you. Whether you decide to damage only what Elijah can fix, or to take everything, I'm not going to stop you. The power is yours."

Dameon's face was full of resolve. His knuckles were white as he prepared himself. She swallowed hard. Emma moved the shaking knife up to Dameon's throat. It barely touched his skin. She got to her feet, and stood over him.

He clenched his jaw and breathed in slowly. Emma closed her eyes and took a moment to enjoy the power Dameon relinquished unto her. She believed the man. He wouldn't fight her, or at least to the best of his ability. When she opened them again, she caught a glimpse of fear behind the unmoving resolve in his eyes.

The knife became steady in her hand. She watched his reaction as she slid the metal lightly under Dameon's chin where his well manicured stubble met his neck. He inhaled sharply when a small amount of red graced the steel blade. He didn't move away as she tested his commitment. His only objection came naturally, in a small hiss of pain. Emma placed one foot on the table, leaned close and gripped the knife with increased aggression.

She slid the blade down to his chest without making a cut. She moved lower until it rested above his groin. Emma pointed the tip downward. Dameon swallowed hard. He swore repeatedly under his breath but didn't try to run. He didn't grab. He didn't try to stop her, just as he promised. Instead, he moved his knees farther apart to give her better access.

His breathing turned rapid and audible. The table creaked in protest to the pressure it received from Dameon's grip. Emma tilted her head. Fearful anticipation gleamed in his eyes. She looked down and ran the blade back up. She repositioned it, ready to plunge straight into his stomach. She wondered if Elijah could fix a wound like the one she threatened to make.

"Promise," she said, with all the strength she could find. "Promise me that you'll never attack me like that again."

Dameon's eyes started to water but didn't give way to tears.

"I promise."

"Promise me you'll never lock me in that room again."

"I promise."

Emma pressed a measure closer, creating a tiny hole in his shirt as she twisted the knife.

"And promise me that I will walk out that front door. Promise me that I won't spend every second of the rest of my life here. I'll go to the store, or a park, or anywhere that isn't here."

Dameon shut his eyes. He wasn't quick to answer. When he did, he opened his eyes to stare into hers.

"I swear to you, I will find a way."

Emma dropped the knife in Dameon's lap. As she did, he took in a sharp breath of relief. Emma fell to the couch. Her arms and legs trembled from the adrenaline. Dameon stared at the woman for a while, waiting for her to reconsider. He expected more. More bloodshed, more pain. A part of Emma wished she had the will to give him what he thought he deserved. A part of her knew that she didn't want to. He rose slowly and towered over her.

"Can you promise me something as well?"

Emma waited.

"If I do anything to hurt you like that ever again, you will not show me this mercy twice?"

"I promise."

"It's a deal then," Dameon said, with a smile

Dameon ran his hand along his shallow cut, and toyed with the blood between his fingers and thumb. He looked back to her.

"You're a better person than I am. It's much less than I would have taken."

Dameon picked up the knife and slid the droplets up and down its sharp end. He quietly laughed to himself in amusement.

"And for what it's worth, I'm grateful. Matthew and Elijah would have put together a whole damn funeral to mourn the loss of my cock."

He looked at her once more, smiled wryly, and left for the kitchen.

Emma didn't move. In her mind, she watched, and rewatched, the events that had just transpired. What the hell just happened? It wasn't long before Elijah practically fell over himself whilst rushing into the room. His eyes were slightly puffy from crying, and the blue of them shone shockingly bright through the tears. He approached Emma with caution in his steps.

"He said to trust him." Elijah said, guilt coating his words. "I had to."

Elijah sniffed, on the verge of tears yet again.

"But I tried to come back, for you, and for him. Then Matthew told me what Dameon was doing and I–"

Emma noticed the faintest pink outline of a hand around his mouth. Another printed itself on his arm. Behind the scenes, Matthew had restrained him. He held Elijah back while Dameon, in his psychotic way, attempted to right his wrongs.

The white cushion next to Emma depressed as Elijah sat. His eyes fixed on the floor, and arms wrapped around himself. Elijah spoke in a low mumble.

"Can I... would it be okay if I hugged you?"

Emma answered with an embrace that pressed a devastated gasp from Elijah. In return, he practically smothered her; pushing his face into her hair, arms surrounding her, and hands gripping and afraid to let go. She needed his touch. She needed someone to hold her, to care, to pretend to love her. As she felt the intensity of his pull, she knew he needed something too.

"Thank you, Emma," he whispered. "You could have killed him. He would have let you. I don't know what I would do without him. We... I really don't deserve it, but thank you."

Elijah leaned back and wiped the tears from his cheeks.

"Dameon is a stupid asshole for making me cry like this," he said, with an attempted laugh. "He's lucky I skipped the eyeliner this morning. I would have been a much bigger threat to him than you, if he had ruined it. "

He looked back at Emma after a couple of heavy blinks.

"I'm sorry, Emma. Dameon has always had a rough side, but that? None of this was supposed to happen, none of it."

Emma tried to give a comforting smile.

"I know," she said, quietly.

Elijah's breathing picked up speed. Panic bubbled under his surface. Out of the corner of his eye, he had only just noticed a smear of blood on the couch. Wide eyes expressed a combination of accusation and worry. He fumbled to his feet, ready to provide the aid Dameon might need.

Emma reached out, and took his hand. Conflict weighed down his shoulders. His gaze bounced from her to the kitchen.

"It was just a scratch. He's okay, really."

Elijah's knees started to buckle. Emma guided him back to the sofa, rolled him onto his side, and pulled him to her. Emma scooched close, making herself the best big-spoon she could manage. She pressed her cheek to his shoulder and breathed in deep and deliberate breaths. Her hand pressed against his chest, feeling the hard thumping of his anxiety.

"I hate this," Elijah said, softly. "I should be the one coddling you right now. He's always been in control. He's never hurt us, not really. This? And you could have– I don't–"

Elijah trailed off. A deep breath in and out released Elijah's nerves. Emma could feel the tension leave his body, but it was replaced by something else; something wild and defiant.

Elijah spun around. Two startled gasps inhaled past Emma's teeth. He wrapped his leg over her lower half, and squeezed her like she was his personal body pillow. His lips touched her neck, where Dameon had held the knife. Delicately moving fingers, touched her jawline and cheek. Another hand pressed against the small of her back.

Sparks ignited. His lips were smooth as rose petals. His hold pushed comfort into her bones. Quick distrust dripped into her mind, despite the serotonin being released with his touch. His lips parted, letting his breath send a shiver through her body.

"I'm sorry, honey. Being sad and scared is overrated. I think I want something sweet instead. How about you?"

Emma could barely keep up. Less than a second ago, Elijah was terrified and hurt. Now, he exuded energy and impulsivity.

"Elijah," Emma squeaked. "I'm not sure–"

"Shush, shush, shush," he said. "Cookies. I want to make cookies. Sweets make everything better."

Emma wriggled a hand between her and him, ready to push Elijah off the couch if she needed to. His change in tone was jarring, and she needed a moment to process the sudden change.

"Please," he begged. "I can't take much more of this uncertain mess. I don't like it. Am I being gaslight-ish, or lovebomb-y, or something worthy of relationship counseling? Probably, but I literally don't know what else to do. We're in the middle of a shit sandwich, and that kind of meal doesn't exactly satisfy a sweet tooth. Forgive me. Don't hate me. Please? Cookies?"

Emma smiled.

"That sounds nice," she said.

Elijah popped up from the sofa, extending a hand to Emma. When she took it, Elijah pulled her to her feet and wrapped his arms around her again. He squeezed her, and tried for a few more calming breaths. A touch of his emotional overcorrection toned down before he led Emma by the hand to the kitchen.

When they rounded the corner, the two heard a thump. Elijah and Emma exchanged nervous glances. The kitchen looked bare, but Elijah was clearly expecting Matthew and Dameon to be there. Emma and Elijah speedily searched the kitchen space until they found the missing men.

Behind the island, Matthew and Dameon were found on the ground. Matthew sat against the lower cabinets, while Dameon straddled the giant. Both had clothes on, but for how long, it was hard to tell. The pair kissed each other hard, while Dameon grinded and breathy sounds came form Matthew.

An intense grip was kept on the back of Dameon's shirt by Matthew. Out of the corner of his vision, Matthew finally took notice of Emma and Elijah. With a look of startled bashfulness, Matthew pulled a previously concealed hand from Dameon's pants.

Dameon looked up, catching his breath, and taking in the two onlookers. He adjusted his pants and grinned upward at them.

"Don't look at me like that," he said to Elijah, his natural demanding and confident voice back. "I looked into the face of death, and she gave me a second chance. It's Christmas fucking morning, Scrooge. You can't tell me that near death experiences don't make you horny as hell."

"Did you just refer to me as death?"

Emma meant for it to sound like a joke, but a crack in her voice made it come out wrong. Dameon smiled at her and chuckled.

"Yes," he said, matter-of-factly. "I have given you an open invitation to kill me. Any time, for as long as I keep you imprisoned, you have the power to make the call. No second chances. Promises were made. So I figure, it's just a matter of time before you decide that you've had enough of my bullshit, and take my life. Or, perhaps you'll decide to go through with your original plan to separate my dick from the rest of me to Matthew's dismay. Either way, I'm at your mercy."

Elijah squeezed Emma's hand. She squeezed his back.

8 | Best Laid Plans

A carton of eggs slid precariously over the island countertop. Sticks of butter slapped the granite. Flour and sugar clinked in aesthetically pleasing glass jars. Spices and treats littered the workspace as Elijah chaotically tossed kitchen items through the air.

Dameon and Matthew took places atop leather-cushioned barstools to watch the baking show that was about to commence. Elbows leaned on the stone counter, and arms crossed as they watched the man on a mission get into his groove. Elijah tossed a metal bowl in Matthew's direction, who caught it with an echoing "ding."

"If you're going to sit here," Elijah said, "You're going to bake. We're not doing all the work, for the boys to reap all the rewards."

The two men smiled and agreed to Elijah's terms and conditions. Emma was shuffled to a place at Elijah's side, and handed a measuring cup.

The plan was set. Each would make their own cookie dough, following a simple base recipe, and customize their creations with their own flavors and extras. The task seemed straightforward enough, though Emma quickly found herself understanding the saying, "too many cooks in the kitchen."

Right off the bat, Matthew and Elijah had begun arguing over the proper amount of flour needed for cookies.

"I'm telling you, that's too much," Elijah stated, in annoyance.

Matthew was clearly and intentionally pushing his buttons. His posture and tone resembled that of a kid taunting with the classic, I'm-not-

135

touching-you, game. His nose scrunched and his smile looked to be barely holding back a giggle.

"Maybe you don't have enough," Matthew teased.

Elijah reached into a glass container with his bare hand, and grabbed a small, unmeasured, amount of the powdery ingredient.

"Is this enough," Elijah asked, with a snarky pout.

Before he was given a chance to answer, Elijah blew a puffy cloud of flour in Matthew's direction.

"You ass!" Matthew laughed, shaking his shirt clean.

Elijah stirred his mixture with false innocence and a goofy whistle. When he turned to grab vanilla from the counter-space behind him, his return was met with an explosion of white powder that had been catapulted through the air. The creases at his eyes left little clean lines in the coat of flour on his face, while he blinked in disbelief and Matthew's audacity.

Elijah lunged for the jar of flour. The two frenzied, snatching handfuls, grappling over the container, and throwing powder carelessly over the counter. Dameon and Emma ducked for cover, but it didn't matter. Flour coated nearly every inch of the island and the surrounding floor.

Dameon's head slowly rose from behind his side of the island. He didn't survive the warzone unscathed. Flour dusted his dark hair and his shoulders. Elijah didn't have a clean spot on him, and neither did Matthew. The white of the ingredient stuck to Matthew's eyebrows and beard, and sent Emma into a side-splitting laugh.

In spite of the shenanigans, four batches of cookie dough somehow made their way to baking sheets. Dameon and Emma's sheets weren't terribly remarkable. Elijah's, however, had perfectly neat and uniformly spaced balls of dough. Matthew's were a hodgepodge of large, small, and generally irregular-shaped, rolled dough.

While Elijah nit-picked Matthew's work, Dameon walked two tiptoeing fingers over the counter towards Elijah's pan. Noticing Emma's watchful gaze, he sent a quick wink her way and continued on with an added pep in his fingertip's steps. Elijah's hand shot out to smack away the intruder, but not in time.

Dameon still managed to pluck one of the perfect balls of dough from the pan. A smug smile played on his face before he stuck out his tongue, a bit farther than was necessary, and placed the sweet, unbaked, good in his mouth. Elijah glared at the man's taunt.

"So, not only are you a thief out there, but you're a thief here too," Emma asked, with some instigation.

Dameon wanted to answer, but literally bit off more than he could chew. Nothing about his situation was particularly attractive, and Emma couldn't help but laugh at his struggle. She waited patiently until the man eventually got the last of the loot down his throat and grinned at her.

"Absolutely," he finally said. "What's not to love about stealing kisses, the breath of a loved one, and the occasional unbaked cookie? I won't apologize for that."

She wasn't sure what she wanted to accomplish, by bringing up the men's illegal activities so soon. Maybe she wanted to test him, to see if he would fly off the handle again. But his relaxed answer, and seeming acceptance in regards to her awareness of their unsavory profession, settled some piece of her lingering anxiety.

Still, an awkward discomfort hung between the four. Elijah's baking idea may have been temporarily distracting, but it wasn't enough. Emma could see the traces of guilt that hid behind Dameon's attempts to be casual. She caught Matthew's worrisome glances from the corner of her vision. And Elijah, she wasn't sure what to make of his devotion to avoidance of the situation. He almost felt like a different person compared to the man that came to her aid with sorrowful experience behind his eyes, and who trembled in her arms only moments ago.

When an elongated and high-pitched beep alerted the kitchen dwellers that the proper temperature had been reached, Elijah transferred the pans into the double ovens stacked into the wall. He set a timer with rapid clicks, and surveyed the disaster they made.

"Every time," he said, smiling with irritated jest.

After attempting to become somewhat flour-free, Dameon, Matthew, Elijah, and Emma sat around a dark wood, rectangular, table. A single dividing wall separated the formal dining room from the kitchen. A marble statue of an unknown man stood in the corner, and warm-colored paintings of nature left the room feeling more business-like than cozy.

Emma fidgeted in the silence. She had questions. She was never good at keeping her thoughts to herself, and the unbearable thickness in the air begged for words to be spoken. Dameon promised to never harm her. They had rules about honesty. Dameon promised.

"I want to talk about the next heist," she said, with the same tone one might use to suggest a new television show to watch.

Matthew and Elijah noticeably tensed, and waited for Dameon's reaction to the blunt demand. Dameon leaned back in a matching wooden chair and crossed his arms. His head tilted to the side and slightly up, his face hard to read. His papercut of a wound had closed quickly, but a bright pink line was very much visible.

"What do you want to know," he asked, calmly.

"Your jewelry store owner," Emma said, "he's a good person with a family, and that's why you don't want to hurt him?"

An antagonistic smile crept across Dameon's face. Emma couldn't quite tell if he was unhappy with her depth of knowledge, when it came to their plans, or if her question excited him. Emma pressed on.

"I haven't met many "good" people," Dameon said. "I don't know if I would consider Riel to be one of them, but he has been out of the game for a while now."

"Woah," Emma said. "You mean to tell me you are on a first name basis with the guy you're trying to rob? I don't get it."

"We know enough about him through a mutual friend. He, however, knows almost nothing about us. He's made a quiet, boring, disconnected life for himself and his family. We all would like to help keep it that way."

"But then why—"

"Because it's not about him," Dameon said, quickly. "It's about sending a message to someone else with a vested interest in his business."

"Tony," Emma asked, cautiously.

If Elijah and Matthew weren't concerned before, they certainly were now. Both looked to each other, then to Dameon. They were antsy, chairs inching back, fingers arching, feet ready to pounce if control was lost for a second time that day.

Dameon only stared, face intentionally blank. Emma understood what his lack of expression likely meant. He wasn't disinterested, rather, he was maintaining a forced and calm composure. He took a breath, did not speak, and nodded his head in confirmation.

Emma's nerves were on fire, but so was her desire to be heard. She spent so much time in her prison thinking about this. She wasn't going to stop over a little old thing like Dameon snapping again.

"I only caught bits and pieces from the room and from what you've told me. It sounds like this man is trying to live the American dream. He owns his own business. He is living on the straight and narrow. I'm guessing he probably has 2.5 kids, a wife with her own career, a white picket fence, and I'd be willing to bet that he even has a dog to complete the picture. Am I right?"

"Yes," Elijah said, with an interested inflection. "He does. The wife's a nurse. He has four kids and, you nailed it, a golden retriever too."

"Perfect! Then, if it's not even about the guy, and you don't want him to get hurt, I have an idea."

Sparks of curiosity prickled around each of the men, attentively waiting to hear Emma's next words.

"You can always hit the shop when he isn't there," she said, happily. "Unless you need him to be present for some reason."

Dameon nodded patiently.

"Ah," he said, with a gentle tone and underwhelmed smile. "That's a... good idea. No, he doesn't have to be there, so we think that would be the best course of action as well. However, it all has to go down during business hours. We're looking for attention, not stealth."

Emma raised her brows in exasperation and the irritation at Dameon's condensation. Hoping he'd redeem himself, she stayed quiet to hear the turn around.

"Our issue is," he continued, "how can we make that happen? When we make a plan, we need to include a few more details. How do we get him out? Sick kid, car trouble? There are a lot of options, with moving variables for each. It's not a bad start, though."

Emma crossed her arms. Nope, it didn't get better. What in the mansplaination was that? Matthew and Dameon, both, seemed to be over cautious about underestimating her. She'd already be free if they weren't so worried about her retaliation. Dameon assumed, "make sure he's not in the shop," was it? Did he really expect so little? Was that all it took to spook him? Is that what was keeping her locked inside their penthouse?

"Yes," she said, not hiding her irritation. "Obviously. That's why– you know what? No! Hold on. Did you really think that was it? You thought that was all I had to offer?"

Dameon managed to look offended at having offended Emma. Defensive and apologetic expressions fought for space as potential responses stumbled over themselves. Elijah smirked at his flustered partner.

Matthew stayed rigid. He locked eyes with Emma. He knew she had more, and she knew what revealing her plan might cost her. It wasn't an elaborate concept, but it was enough. Saying it out loud could solidify his suspicions. She just might be the threat he believed her to be. His stare was warning, yet not deterring. He wanted to hear it, regardless of the expense.

When Dameon looked as if he had finally found the right words to say, Emma cut him off. With an aggressive snap of her wrist, she pointed an authoritative finger in the air, commanding his silence. Her mouth opened to give him an earful. Words didn't manifest before she sucked in her cheeks and pursed her lips.

Dameon rested an elbow on the table and weaved his fingers together. An incredulous smirk and arched brow put a pause on Emma's resolve to tell him off. His pupils dilated. His jaw tightened. A muscle in his neck twitched. Emma's mouth suddenly felt dry.

"Sorry," she said. "That was a little rude."

"Liar," he lured. "You're definitely not sorry."

Behind his words, Emma could feel the unspoken ending. Yet. She was not sorry, yet. Dameon's tone was playing in the realm of minor chords, but Emma wasn't persuaded to dance along.

"Guess you're right," she said, holding on to her streak of boldness. "I'm really not. Still, it was rude."

"I don't blame you for being snappy," he said. "I insulted you. I was disappointed with your underwhelming solution, and jumped to the conclusion that I may have over estimated you. The apology is mine to give."

"You're not going to actually say sorry, are you," Emma prodded.

One of Dameon's fingernails clicked against the wood surface.

"No, I won't. But I do want you to correct me, Emma. The floor is yours. Show me what you have to offer. What suggestions do you have that might provide a solution to our predicament?"

Emma locked her hands together, bit against the nail of her thumb, and shimmied her shoulders. An excited smile crept onto her face.

"I'm glad you asked."

The Plan

Riel loves his dog. Even if that's not completely true, his family does. For him, that means a walk every morning before work. He doesn't mind too much, but he is also a busy man. He works long hours, but that doesn't mean he isn't present for his family. Walking the dog is one less thing for his wife to worry about, so that's what he does.

On his typical route, he finds himself walking the same path as a new stranger. The unfamiliar man has three dogs of his own; leashed, happy as can be, and tails wagging. The professional-looking person is dressed in khaki pants and a blue polo shirt. He has a friendly smile on display, and is wearing a nametag with a cute little pawprint next to his name. The dogwalker's face belongs to Elijah, but the name on the little silver magnet says Chris.

Chris reaches out for a handshake. He compliments Riel on being such a great owner, expresses his admiration for his healthy routine, says whatever is needed in order to make Riel feel comfortable. Over the course of a few weeks, Chris engages in enough small talk to map out Riel's typical daily schedules, as well as that of his family.

"What do you say," Chris smiles. "I have an open spot later in the morning. And because I already love your fluff bucket, I'll give you the first week free. You deserve the break. Take the hour to have breakfast with the wife. Or get a coffee by yourself, and let the Mrs. think you're still walking the dog. I get it," he says with a wink.

On game day, Riel wakes up with the feeling that something is off. It's not completely uncalled for. Most people feel a little strange when their routine has been switched up. The odd itch that he has forgotten something scratches at his brain when he turns his pet over to the man.

He's not one to trust people so easily, but Chris doesn't come off at a threat. Riel couldn't help but see him as a bit of a sissy boy with some of that peppy, entrepreneurial energy. He even had a fancy-looking website with schedules and exciting popups about charity donations to local shelters. So, Riel shakes the feeling away and heads off to work.

At the shop, everything is just as he left it; jewelry in glass cabinets, cash register ready to go, security cameras perfectly functional. The minimum wage employee wanders in unenthusiastically, but never a minute late. A glowing neon sign repeatedly displays the letters: O-P-E-N, flashing in the window.

Just as a spray of cleaner hits one of the glass cabinets, Riel's phone rings. He tosses a damp microfiber rag to the side, and looks at the phone. It's Chris. Riel second guesses his decision before answering the call. He can't afford to babysit the guy. The whole point was to give himself some free time. Sure he didn't utilize that time today, but maybe tomorrow he would.

"I'm sorry!" Chris sobs. "I'm so sorry. He wriggled out of his collar. The truck didn't stop in time. The driver just kept going! I'm so sorry!"

"What? Are you saying you killed my dog?"

"I'm sorry! It wasn't my fault. The driver wasn't paying attention. His collar was too loose."

"What am I supposed to do? My wife is at work, I'm at work. She is a nurse, she can't just leave!"

"Please come get him," Chris cries. "I don't know what to do. This has never happened before. Do I call the police?"

"No," Riel shouts.

An old, familiar, panic hits his stomach. If that kid calls the police, Riel will have much bigger problems to worry about. He made a home for himself, for his woman, for his kids. He could lose all of that if Chris invited police to poke their noses in his life.

"I'm on my way. Don't call the cops. They'll just be pissed at you for wasting their time."

"Okay. Okay. Just hurry, please. I don't know what to do."

Furious, and a little more heartbroken than he'd like to admit, Riel grabs his keys and rushes to the exit.

Before leaving, he reminds his employee that she is temporarily in charge of the shop. The young woman shrugs and takes command with a dispassionate nod. She isn't paid well enough to care. Riel knows this, but he doesn't have the time to start a lecture about her generation's lazy work ethic.

The store is left in silence.

Rarely do people stop by the shop in the morning hours. If her boss was present, she'd subject herself to busy work. But now, her boss is nowhere to be seen. She uses the uneventful time to pull out her phone and look at a list of job openings. Watching her thumb scroll over a rectangular screen, she catches a glimpse of customers walking her way.

Unfortunately for her, they aren't customers at all. Two men with black masks over their eyes and white and black striped shirts burst through the entrance. Empty sacks with green dollar signs printed on fabric accompany both of the armed robbers.

"Put the phone down," says Dameon. "and push it off the counter."

The woman does as she is told.

"Now, hands in the air," Matthew says, pointing his firearm in her direction.

Dameon gets straight to work, grabbing everything that isn't nailed down. He shoves every bit of merchandise he can into the expanding moneybags.

Matthew keeps his gun on the woman, reminding her not to be brave. The poor girl, who everyone should definitely feel sorry for, because being in that position is scary as hell, and she didn't ask to be kidna– robbed at gunpoint. Anyway, she keeps her hands in the air. She isn't about to put up a fight for a store she has no investment in, and certainly isn't willing to die for.

When the faceless bad guys can't possibly take anymore loot, the evil robbers wave to the security cameras and skip, arm-in-arm, away from the scene of the crime. The woman is quick to dial 911, but because the immediate danger is gone, she is told it may take a moment for them to respond.

Next, she makes the call to Riel. He never answers. It isn't until he walks in with his dog, tongue lazily out and healthy as can be, that he discovers what happened during his absence.

"What the hell?"

"Two cartoon characters with guns robbed the store," she says, with a baffled expression and almost monotone voice of disbelief. "What happened to you? The dog seems fine."

"No, yeah. He's fine. The dumb dogwalker mistook mine for another one."

Riel matches his employee's dumbfounded energy, still confused about the ordeal. He puts a hand to the back of his neck while surveying the empty store.

"Actually, I'm not sure another dog got hurt at all. I think... I think it was just a smashed package of ground beef on the road. There wasn't even an empty leash. I think the guy might have had a mental breakdown or something."

"Hum. That sucks. I had a gun in my face. So, I guess we both had a bad day."

"Yeah," Riel says, in the middle of his ransacked shop. "A bad day."

Emma grinned ear to ear. Her fingers wiggled with finale jazz hands posed around her face. Matthew and Elijah sat with their mouths slightly open.

144

"Well," Emma asked. "What do you think?"

"You just came up with all of that," asked Matthew.

"Not just," Emma shrugged. "I had a lot of time to think about it. Your dilemma was my main source of entertainment."

"My favorite part was Dameon and Matthew's dastardly attire," Elijah said, with a snort-giggle. "If we don't incorporate that, at the very least, I'll be heartbroken."

"Not happening," said Matthew. "Get out the ice cream, and queue the emo music, because I'm not wearing it. It's hard enough for me to blend in."

While Matthew and Elijah bickered over Emma's use of comic relief in her otherwise serious plan, Dameon's eyes burned into the smooth table. He fixated on a spot of flour, with the aimless motion of a single finger.

The timer buzzed. The cookies were done. Nobody moved. Dameon's silence put the room on edge yet again. He appeared to be deep in thought while the people around him waited in anticipation for his response.

"Elijah, the cookies are going to burn." He said bluntly. "Matthew, he'll probably need help."

Matthew stood first and put a calm hand on Elijah.

Elijah rolled his shoulder from Matthew's lazy hold, and didn't budge from his seat. His hands gripped the sides of his chair, and eyes avoided contact with Dameon.

"No."

"Angel," Dameon said, sweetly. "I just want a private moment. No secrets, no anger. But I would like to speak with Emma without seeing your antsy asses worry while we have, what could be, an uncomfortable talk."

Emma placed her hand on top of Elijah's. His knuckles were hard under her palm. Her fingers nuzzled their way into his grip, and coaxed him to relax. When Elijah looked up at her faint smile, he returned a grim one of his own. Behind those sweet soft-blue eyes, was a fear infused boldness, that knew action was the only way to apologize for his abandonment of her earlier.

"It's okay," Emma said, softly.

Elijah tightened his grip.

"You can go. He'll be safe with me," she said, with a wink.

Her false confidence couldn't be more transparent, but it was the permission he needed. Elijah looked to Dameon. He gave a nod to his angel, a signal displaying his sympathy for Elijah's actions and reluctance to follow orders. Elijah stood to join Matthew's side, and left Dameon and Emma to their conversation.

"Did I meet expectations," Emma asked, willfully.

Emma startled at the sound of Dameon's chair screeching closer to hers. With another frictional noise, he rotated hers to face him, sending a vibration from its legs to her back against the chair.

"I'm trying to trust you, Emma," he said, sternly. "I hope you can appreciate how hard that is for me in this situation. I want to. But knowing you've been secretly listening to our conversations, then hearing you give us, what sounds like, a decent plan all based on a guess that he even had a dog to begin with? It sounds a little coincidental. It sounds like deception."

Emma felt an involuntary shiver run down her spine.

"You said you wanted to hear it! Now you're mad because it sounds too thought out? That's... that's not fair."

"I'm not trying to be threatening. I'm giving you my point of view. If I was Tony, I would instruct my plant to do exactly what you have done. Gather information, cause friction, insert yourself into our schemes, and lead us right into his hands."

"I was bored," said Emma, with a little too much desperation. "You might not want to hear it, but I was going crazy in there. Elijah didn't speak to me. Matthew felt so damn guilty about keeping secrets from you, he tried avoiding any real conversations. And yet, if he hadn't let me out at night... I ate, I slept, and I listened. That's all I had every day in that stupid room."

Emma tried to calm herself, but adrenaline infected her body as she preached her defense.

"You think the dog scenario was the only one I came up with? I had dozens ready to go. I didn't know if, when– From sunrise to sunset, every single day, I wondered if you would kill me, if Matthew would take my key, if Elijah would stop bringing me food. I needed to think about anything else. If I hadn't, I would have lost my mind!"

Realizing it too late, Emma noticed that she was absentmindedly rubbing the place where the knife met her neck. A bruise was beginning to form, marking the place where Dameon lost his temper the last time she voiced her displeasure.

"Part of me wonders if I already did, a little."

The amusement on Dameon's face faded. Emma's nerves disturbed the acid in her stomach. He reached for her hand that was preoccupied with his evidence of lost control. Emma fought the urge to pull away as he gripped her fingers tight, and stroked his thumb over the top of her hand. His stare was piercing and stringent.

"I need to hear you say, you wouldn't knowingly put Matthew and Elijah in harm's way."

"Of course not," Emma said, as confidently as she could. "If you think my idea is too risky, toss it out. It's not like I expected you to praise me and throw all of your eggs into my jankity basket of an idea. If you think it would be too dangerous for them, don't do it."

Another of Dameon's hands folded over hers and warmed her skin. Emma's heart jumped into her throat when he applied a pressure that overlapped her constrained fingers.

"Convince me. Killing me is one thing, but those two getting hurt? Tell me why I can trust you. You may not have taken me up on the offer this morning, but I'm not naive enough to confuse that with forgiveness. Say something to make me believe that you won't make them suffer, for what I have done to you?"

"I can't. What could I say? You won't believe me, not really. If you do intend to keep me around forever, I guess you'll just have to see for yourself. You don't have to be afraid of me. And for the record, I don't hate them."

"Another lie."

"Damn it, Dameon! Where," Emma asked, exasperated. "Where is the lie this time? I don't hate them. I'm not entirely sure how I feel about them, but hate isn't it."

A crooked smile inched up to the left side of Dameon's cheek.

"Sweet, but not what I was referring to."

Confusion brought Emma's brows together.

"You're being dishonest, Emma. I don't have to be afraid of you? Little prisoner, I should always be afraid of you."

Dameon pushed his chair back with another loud screech against the floor. Emma jumped, and cradled the hand Dameon had been holding. It wasn't that he hurt her. It was more of an instinctual move, like what one might do when a large dog barks from the other side of a flimsy fence.

Dameon lifted his chin, and shouted to the kitchen.

"Are they burnt?"

Elijah yelled back, "No, but Matthew's suck!"

Matthew peaked around the corner with an ear to ear smile.

"They actually do," he whispered. "But we've got to pause the rule, just for today, and only in the spirit of pranks. Pleeeeease go with me on this?"

Dameon gave Matthew an approving nod.

"My cookies are shit," Matthew said, excitedly. "But eat them. Tell him mine are better than his. He'll shit a brick."

"You have my undying support," Dameon said, playfully.

Elijah's cookies were a bite of pure heaven. Little violet specks peaked through the bright cookies with masterful balancing of lavender and lemon flavors. Dameon made an attempt at a snickerdoodle-type of cookie, but his proportions were a tad off. Still, the taste was pleasant. Emma went for a mix of colorful chocolate candies. Her creation wasn't fancy and the flavor was simple. But they were pretty, fun, and still a delightful treat that Elijah was quick to complement.

Exaggerations were not made on behalf of Matthew's abomination. Matthew created the most bland, flour-tasting, repulsive cookies Emma ever had the misfortune of eating. If displeasure was a spice, his cookies must have been made with cup-fulls of it. But, with the straightest faces they could manage, Emma and Dameon played along.

"When did you learn to bake," asked Dameon, with a smile. "Damn Elijah, Matthew might actually give you some real competition."

"Oh, wow," said Emma, struggling with the imposter of a cookie. "It's really something. It might be one of the best cookies I've ever tasted."

Elijah did indeed, "shit a brick." He ranted and raved, throwing his hands up in massive protest. The flustered man went on talking about "poor taste" and how they were, "a terrible excuse for anything edible!" He kept on until Emma couldn't keep her laughter, or the cookie, in her mouth any longer. Matthew and Dameon broke instantly after.

Elijah stared down Emma, challenge in his eyes.

"Oh? You're ready to play," he coerced. "Okay. Well game on, honey. We have a whole day ahead of us."

Matthew's cookies quickly made their home in the garbage bin, to no one's objection. After a final sweep of the kitchen, Dameon suggested some time in the pool to get away from the ovens that heated the space a number of degrees on the hot summer day. The group agreed whole heartedly, and Elijah and Matthew disbanded to change into their swimming attire.

Once up the stairs, Dameon stopped Emma with a gentle clutch of her hand. Emma jumped slightly at his unexpected touch. From the pocket of his jeans, he retrieved her key and placed it in her hand.

"I promised," he said, seriously. "It'll never be taken from you again."

Emma felt the thin edges against her fingers. That little piece of plastic felt more valuable than if it had been made of gold.

"Thank you," she said, softly.

"Don't thank me for correcting a mistake that should never have been made," he said, and with the smallest squeeze of her hand over the card, he too retreated up the stairs.

Under the burning sun, Dameon floated on a blow-up purple raft. Elijah sat on an underwater bench, wrapped under Matthew's arm. The two were having a conversation, when Emma returned to them after changing into a new swimsuit.

"Elijah," Dameon said. "Was that really the best we could do? Don't get me wrong, she looks great, but did we really not have any swimsuits that were less… revealing?"

Emma looked down at the white suit. Her ass was very much on display, as the bottom half was basically a thong. The top was similar to the black one she wore last night, with the exception of the decorative straps that bordered the small triangles and further accentuated her breasts.

She certainly would have preferred to wear something that covered a little more, but after the events of last night, she felt uneasy wearing the same black suit that still laid on the floor of the room.

"I can put on a t-shirt if you're uncomfortable," Emma said, earnestly.

All three men replied in quick unison.

"No."

Emma's insides squirmed, suddenly considering getting a shirt for her own comfort. Elijah wasn't wrong. Knowing that all three felt a considerable amount of desire for her, was a lot to handle. The three shared subtle looks of embarrassment and disappointment in each other.

"Well done men," Dameon said, sarcastically. "We don't sound at all like a bunch of horny frat boys."

Emma smiled and forced a half laugh as she entered the water. Matthew squinted at Emma's top, which looked an awful lot like he was ogling her chest. His stare was so hard, she also looked down, just to be sure she hadn't popped out of the suit. Nope, still covered.

"Why is that swimsuit so familiar?"

Elijah didn't need time to think about Matthew's question. His answer was immediate and casual.

"The swimsuit model. It was hers. They all belonged to her."

Matthew snapped and pointed his finger at Elijah. "Yes! That's it." Matthew's face dropped. He scrunched his mouth and looked disheartened at the memory of the suit's previous owner. "Oh yeah..." Matthew said, grimly.

"The swimsuits belonged to someone else?"

"Yep," Elijah said. "Luckily, they're made to fit a variety of sizes. So it worked out."

"Why did you keep them," Dameon asked, curiously.

Another simple, and shameless, answer came from Elijah.

"I wanted to wear them. Some of the tops were fun, but none of the bottoms even remotely worked. They're really nice though. I didn't have the heart to toss them. Never know when they might come in handy, and look, they did!"

"Ah," said Dameon, satisfied with his answer.

Emma felt odd in this other woman's clothes. She wanted to learn more, even though she knew she might not like what she heard. Was she a girlfriend? Why did Matthew look so unhappy when thinking about her? Was he attached to the woman? Emma mentally shrugged at the idea of disliking the answer, and asked away.

"So this woman, she stayed here?"

Elijah and Dameon smiled, Matthew did not.

"No, not here," Dameon said. "We met up in different casinos and hotels all over town."

"And you guys used to–" Emma asked, awkwardly.

Dameon laughed a little too hard.

"Emma, are you about to ask about our sexual histories? I'm not sure this is a road you're going to enjoy going down, but if you want to hear it, we'll tell it. No more secrets."

"Yes," she said, with some defiance. "If I'm going to be here forever, I might as well know everything."

Dameon took a moment and passed the story telling to Elijah.

Elijah explained, with no remorse or shame to be found, that each of the men had a pretty high body count. Matthew with the least, and Elijah with the most by far. Thanks to protection and a few miracles, they all remarkably remained STD, and child, free.

Only twice, did the men come across a woman that they all found attractive. With ground rules laid, and clear boundaries set, two one-night-stands occurred in the penthouse. Though Elijah claimed it was fun, they each learned quickly that they weren't comfortable making such a thing a recurring pastime. They enjoyed being loyal to each other, and knew that such activities would eventually lead to hard feelings. So they agreed early on never to casually sleep with other people again, as a group or individually.

The newly acquired information played in her ears on repeat. It was no wonder Elijah took her intrusion the other night so personally. They vowed to be true to each other, and the idea of Matthew and Dameon being with Emma probably felt like a huge betrayal. Emma couldn't help but feel bad for suggesting her desire to watch. If she hadn't, Matthew wouldn't have brought her to the room.

Grumpiness overpowered her guilt when she grappled with the absurdity of her emotions. If she hadn't, she'd still be in her room, limited to temporary freedom after dark.

"Was the model one of the two?"

Dameon's face turned grim. Elijah passed a questioning brow to Dameon, waiting for permission to continue. He was met with the return of an accepting shrug and the nonverbal confirmation for Elijah to continue with their story.

The answer given was a simple and matter-of-fact, no. Unfortunately, the majority of their sexual encounters were of a very different nature. Poor intentions accompanied the majority of their endeavors, and were entirely malicious. The swimsuit model fell under that category.

The model knew people of interest, people under Tony's umbrella. Without her figuring out what they were up to, they manipulated her into revealing a plethora of useful information. They used men and women, like her, to gain intel on Tony, until their use ran out. When that happened, the people too close to Tony, or people that were apparently worse villains than themselves, would be killed by Matthew.

"So," Emma asked, uneasily, "I'm wearing the swimsuit of a murder victim?"

Elijah shook his head, with a chill smile.

"Nope. She was just a hell of a busy-body. She knew all the gossip around Tony, and his men, but she wasn't close enough for us to need to eliminate her. She, and others like her, got off the hook. When we were able, we'd scare them enough to not be a problem."

Emma had to ask, she always had to ask.

"Then what sent her running?"

Matthew spoke before Elijah could answer.

"Me," he said, solemnly. "We used to take turns being the bad guy. I played the part of the jealous lover. I acted like I hated that she slept with other people. Dameon took her to bed a few times, Elijah too. We all pretended not to know each other. I "caught" her with Dameon."

Matthew's eye drifted to the shimmering water.

"After I "scared him off," I yelled, trashed things, and made a whole scene. When a guy that looks like me acts out of control, possessive, and angry, it's often enough to make people head for the hills. She was no exception."

Dameon lightly splashed his way.

"Sorry lover. It was your turn. She was fun though."

Each of the men in the pool agreed, and all three stared off into dreamland.

Emma's jealousy started to rise. She pushed it down, knowing she got what she asked for.

"But you let her go," she said. "Even though she could rat you out, turn you in, tell Tony?"

The pool went silent.

"I see where you're going with this, Emma," Dameon said. "But she was different. She was planned. She never saw our home, knew who we were, and was weak. To her, we were random fucks, that she didn't even expect to be criminals. She didn't have the knowledge, or rage, that you do."

"You're so damn sure that I would turn you in." she said, with irritation. "Why didn't you try scaring me away like you did her?"

Dameon let a long silence linger. Emma watched him brush his fingers along the cut on his neck. He didn't look at her as he did. It seemed more of an absent minded movement while he searched for his next words.

"I saw it, Emma," he said. "I saw it when your ex asked us to get rid of you. By the time my mind was right, it was too late. I was clearly right, when I saw it in your eyes today. You may have spared me for now, but I felt the rage you have. Even when scared, you're not weak. You didn't kill me, but you wanted to, probably still want to."

Water swooshed and flowed with momentum around Emma's moving

153

legs. She sat on her lonely underwater seat and watched, as bright little waves circled around her gnarly scar. His words angered her, but she knew her temper would only confirm what Dameon was saying. She tried to keep her face straight as a board, so as not to prove him right.

"There are fighters and runners. Matthew and Elijah told me about your resourcefulness, after they locked you in the med closet. The way you tried using a scalpel to attack him? Runners don't do that. Runners also don't go for their betrayers throat, despite having a gun in their face. Can you look me in the eye, and tell me you wouldn't hunt down your ex for what he did to you? That you would just let him live his life, thinking he won?"

Emma knew her answer but didn't say it out loud. After finding her footing again, making Grant pay for putting her through all of this would be at the top of her list of things to do. He wasn't totally right though. Emma was a runner, at least in the past. Sure, she was just as vengeful as he thought, but she was most definitely a runner too.

"That's what I thought," he said. "Now tell me with honesty, that you would let us go after killing your stupid ex."

Emma didn't answer again. Wrong again. She could never be a killer, but everything Dameon said resonated with her. She did want Grant to pay, and when she was done, maybe with some distance and her Stockholm feelings behind her, she'd want them to pay too.

"So you sleep with people to get information," she asked, instead.

Dameon chuckled at her lack of information returned, and grinned.

"I thought we established that withholding the truth was very similar to lying. You seem pretty interested in asking questions without answering mine."

"There's a chance," Emma said, "That I've been a little revenge-happy in the past. Congrats, you got me. But I'd rather not dig up my own trauma right now, if that's acceptable to you."

A sad smile crossed Dameon's face as he nodded.

"Yes, of course. You've been through too much today as it is. I won't push any further, for now. But full story? We don't sleep around anymore. We put an end to that years ago. We learned fast that there are better, less risky, less complicated ways to get what we needed. So if you're feeling jealous, you can rest easy knowing we aren't the sluts we used to be."

Elijah lifted himself out of the pool with a huff.

"Alright, that's enough of that." he said, and went behind the outdoor bar to grab drinks.

"Elijah," Dameon called out. "Make mine a virgin?"

Matthew glanced, lovingly, in Dameon's direction. Dameon saw, and returned a sweet smile. Elijah came back with purple drinks. Dameon's was given with a quick kiss, and reassurance that alcohol was not included.

Emma took a large blind sip. As she did, the smell smacked her in the face, her tongue revolted, and she immediately spit it back out. The discarded drink polluted the pool water. Dameon laughed himself off his raft, spilling his drink as he fell. Matthew took a cautionary smell, winced, and placed his cup to the side. Elijah sat smugly on the edge with his legs crossed.

"What's the matter, honey? Don't like it?"

Emma looked at the glass in disgust.

"What the hell is in it?"

Elijah hopped in, and swam close to her.

"The letter of the day is G, for grape and garlic! With your taste in cuisine, I assumed you'd love it."

Emma glared back at Elijah's satisfied face, and chugged the remaining contents of the horrific concoction. Her stomach heavily disagreed with her choices.

"Loved it," she challenged, slamming the bottom of the glass onto the concrete.

Elijah closed the distance between them. A hand found her waist and pulled her into him. His lips were inches from hers.

"Your breath is vile," he teased.

"Good," she breathed back, with a little extra air to her response.

"Elijah," Dameon warned.

Caught off guard, Elijah backed away without fully letting Emma go. He shot Dameon a disorientated expression.

"Maybe not today," Dameon suggested. "It's been an eventful one."

Emma tossed a glare in Dameon's direction. She was pissed at the self righteous interference.

"Trying to kill me and protect me, all in the same day," she asked, with bite. "How noble."

Emma grabbed the sides of Elijah's face and kissed him hard. She placed herself around his waist, and with a few grinding motions of her hips against him, felt him harden beneath her. He pulled Emma closer and kissed her back with increased enthusiasm. She pulled away harshly, and stared down Dameon.

"You should have been protecting him," she said. "My breath really is awful."

Emma removed herself from Elijah's grasp and lifted herself out of the pool. Defiance in every step, and without turning to see their reactions. She felt their eyes on her near bare ass as she walked to the doors of the penthouse, and did her best to let them watch the show.

"Where are you going," Elijah called after her.

"To brush my teeth!"

9 | Slumber Party

Out of the wet suit, showered, and newly dressed in black leggings and a white cami, Emma sat on the edge of the bed to gather her thoughts. Dameon was right. It had been a very long day. She took a deep heath and tried to process the chain of events that led to this point.

Emma looked around the room and spun the key between her fingers. God, she hated that suffocating, blank room. They couldn't possibly keep this up forever. She imagined looking into the bathroom mirror to see wrinkles on her face and grayed hair. She couldn't be hidden away until she was an old lady, a captor for the rest of her life. She would have to leave someday, even from a logistical point of view, it wasn't feasible.

Yet, Dameon's words rattled in her head. She hated to admit it, but they knew the truth, and so did she. She was dangerous to them, as much as they could be to her. If they killed her, their lives would be simpler. But then, given everything that happened that day, she was gaining a genuine belief that none of them actually wanted to do it.

Each of them seemed to be growing sentimental towards her, at an alarming speed. A twinge of self-pity pinched her emotions when she realized she cared too. If she didn't, she would have killed Dameon when she had the chance, but she didn't. Her heart ached for Elijah whenever he started to look overwhelmed. Matthew... Matthew was complicated.

The idea that Dameon, Matthew, and Elijah might be the most sincere people she'd been around for any significant length of time, was depressing. They weren't without a laundry list of red flags. They were murderers, thieves, and conmen, but here they were honest. For better or worse, they could be trusted to tell her the truth, and that was a unique security she couldn't remember ever feeling before.

After showers and a quick change, the residents of the penthouse regrouped in the living room. Elijah offered to make a late lunch, or early dinner, reminding Emma that the only thing that she had in her stomach was coffee, cookies, and the worst mixed drink of her life. Elijah's pitch to make food was met with distrust on Dameon's end. He didn't want to fall victim to another of his pallet-punishing pranks. Emma and Matthew agreed wholeheartedly.

Elijah toyed with a smile on his own face that gave validity to their fears of being fed something truly awful. Dameon followed the mischievous blond to the kitchen, and out of sight. Matthew and Emma trusted Dameon's watchful eye, and held back alone.

Matthew gestured to the living room sofa and invited Emma to sit next to him. She felt a jumbled mess of emotions fighting for dominance. Seeing Matthew handle Dameon so lovingly after hurting her soured her image of him as her protector. But then again, he did shock the hell out of her when he aggressively called Dameon out on his violent behavior. In the end, she didn't know what to feel for the person she'd spent the most time with during her incarceration.

Though she felt his weight in the cushion next to her, a hint of loneliness and uncertainty invaded her chest. It didn't elude her, that he never quite let go of the weight he still carried from the conversation about the model. A shadow of guilt clung to him in a way she didn't expect from the main murderer of the group. She didn't like the wall being built, and her need to understand him better demanded the wall to be chipped at.

"Matthew, did you really think I would kill Dameon?"

He looked down at his hands, a wash of shame overcoming his expression.

"I hoped not. I hoped that you would just fuck him up a little, but at least give us something Elijah could still put back together."

"And you would have let me?"

Matthew nodded and looked at Emma.

"Yes," he said. "When Dameon makes up his mind, nothing can stop him. If I hadn't let him repent in the way he wanted, he'd have found another way, a worse way, to get his point across."

Emma's eyes drifted to the place where Dameon threatened her, where he offered to sacrifice himself to even up the score. It felt strange, tainted. Her eyes turned from the round sofas where she was sure she'd die, the place on the floor where Dameon threw her, at the coffee table where she let him off the hook.

"He went as far as he could to distance himself from his father. That man wouldn't have lifted a finger to save someone that didn't have something to give him in return. His father was manipulative, a drunk, and extremely violent. Dameon always had his ways to cope with the parts of himself he inherited from his sperm donor, but he crossed a serious line this morning."

"You hurt me today," Emma said, confidently as she could.

Matthew looked her up and down, panic in his eyes.

"When you hugged him, after what he did to me– I had a dumb idea in my head, that you might keep me safe. I get why you chose him, but the truth is, it hurt."

A sad smile upturned on his face.

"You're adapting fast to our rule."

Emma shrugged, waiting.

"I'm sure I did. I wanted him to come back to us, the real Dameon, the one that's better than his blood. It might be hard to believe, but he's always been the best of us. He's certainly a lot better than me."

"Matthew," she readied, again.

He looked uneasily at her. He braced for the onslaught of questions that were bound to be tough to answer. Matthew wasn't allowed to keep the distance he previously maintained against personal conversations. Emma guessed, judging by the look on his face, that he already had an idea as to what she was about to ask.

"How many people have you killed?"

"My body count for the people I've slept with, is much smaller than the other body count I've racked up. But even if I wanted to, I couldn't give you an accurate answer. It's not that I don't remember them, but there have been a few… situations, when I'm not sure how many I actually killed at once." he said, hesitantly. "Does that scare you?"

Emma didn't answer.

"I've noticed that you're the only one directly called out when they talk about murdering people. Why?"

"Because I'm the only one that can do it," Matthew frowned. "Dameon wants revenge for Penny, so do I. I grew up with the girl. Though she had every reason not to be, she always managed to stay kind. It's a rare trait for people that grew up like us. But Dameon, despite his demons, has never been able to pull the trigger. I could. Elijah can't. But I can. They can act like me when they need to, but deep down, they aren't me."

Matthew ran his hands through his long, dark, hair. Emma noticed he did that a lot when he was upset.

"I know what that makes me. I'm… I'm not a good person. I'm a monster. But I hope you can believe me when I say, I really don't want to hurt you. At least, more than I already have."

Emma scooted closer and placed Matthew's arm around her. She took his hand and examined it, palm up. He nearly filled the space of both of her hands while she followed his lines with her thumbs.

"You shot them all," she asked, softly.

Matthew closed his hand around hers.

"It's what I prefer, it's quicker. But no, not all of them, some were stabbed. One, I killed with a bat."

A smile flickered briefly at his memory of the murder victim whose life ended with the swings of the baseball equipment. A serious frown regained its place.

"A few of them, I… It takes longer than you might think to strangle another human being. But I've done that a handful of times too."

Emma gently placed herself in his lap, her eyes never leaving the large hand that ended multiple lives. She guided it up and opened his hand to press his palm against the flat of her chest. Her heart beat hard against him.

She slid him up, to rest the center of his hand over the side of her neck.

Once loosely wrapped, his fingers caressed below her hairline, his thumb hovered in a place to feel her pulse. His was faster, she could feel it.

"Wh…what are you doing," Matthew shook out.

He kept his touch as light as humanly possible. He trembled under her direction. She didn't. She felt herself swallow against the weapon that choked the life out of others. Matthew asked her again what she was doing, in a voice that sounded almost afraid. Emma leaned back and rested against him, keeping his hand in place.

"Trusting you," she said.

Emma clearly noticed a hardening under Matthew's sweatpants.

"Are you scared," she whispered, with a slight laugh, "or turned on?"

He became fully erect. His thumb pressed further to feel her rapid beat.

Matthew moved quickly. Emma gasped. He shoved her down to the sofa. He pressed her back flat, and pinned her. He was over her, hard between her legs. His hand remained around her throat but he didn't give himself permission to tighten his grip.

Emma's heart raced. Matthew's demeanor was much like the one he had on the first night she caught him and Dameon together. It was the same look he had when he pulled her from the stairs, caught up in his cravings and want for her.

"Yes," he breathed. "To both."

Apparently, Dameon's trust issues over Elijah's cooking meant that no progress would be made in the kitchen. Even with insistent hovering over him, the man still managed to tease enough to make Dameon want to abandon the endeavor all together. Elijah really did seem to enjoy his mental games, and pranks were apparently his time to shine.

When they entered the living room, Elijah was happily poking fun at influence over Dameon. Matthew's position over Emma was caught by Dameon, who cleared his throat loudly in warning before Elijah was close enough to see. Matthew's face shot up to his partner. He released Emma from his grasp and backed away speedily.

With his retreat, Matthew unintentionally applied extra pressure to her neck as he pushed away. Emma let out the small, high-pitched, grunt her windpipe was naturally inclined to make. Matthew's face twisted with concern at the sound. As she tried to regain control over her energized breathing, Dameon rounded the couch and gave Emma a raised brow.

"Is it your mission to play with fire today," Dameon asked.

Elijah looked at the still worried man, and Emma, with a returned nervousness. Emma let out an exaggerated breath. She smiled sweetly at Elijah, calming him a bit. She looked back up to Dameon from the sofa and felt her defiance return.

"Well," she said, with a mean smile, "is it your mission to cockblock me at every turn?"

Dameon chuckled in a way that made her spine tingle. Elijah didn't like any of it. Was it concern he was feeling, or jealousy? She wasn't entirely sure.

Dameon made the announcement that, to prevent Elijah from any kitchen-related shenanigans, he ordered pizza for dinner. Elijah perked up at the admission of defeat, and did a little shimmy as he planted himself in one of the green chairs. Dameon took the other seat across from the sofa.

She didn't mean to, but her eyes kept drifting back to the hallway that contained the white room. A startled flinch shot through her body when she realized Dameon was watching her mental reluctance to return to the room.

"You don't have to sleep there," he said, with some remorse in his voice. "I could make up a bed for you elsewhere, until we can figure out a better solution."

Elijah tilted his head and puckered his lips to the side. His eyes lingered on Dameon, ready to object to the idea.

"Not to sound too inhospitable, but where exactly did you have in mind," Elijah asked.

"Don't be so selfish, we clearly have plenty of space," Dameon said. "But, I was thinking of having her sleep in my bed."

Emma's eyes widened, along with the other two men. They threatened to murder each other earlier that day. It would be madness for them to share a bed after that. Was this his challenging way of getting back at her for her "cockblock" comment?

Matthew and Elijah exchanged looks of disapproval.

"I don't know," Matthew said. "Don't you think that could be a little much?"

"Umm," Emma said, cutting into the conversation, "I'd like to believe that the decision would be up to me. I'm fine sleeping out here on a couch."

Dameon looked at Emma as if she declared the grass to be purple.

"That's ridiculous," he said. "You can't sleep on a sofa for the rest of your life."

"Not forever," she argued back. "Just for now."

"Yeah, no," said Elijah, also making the solution sound completely absurd. "You're not sleeping on the couch, but you're right. It would be weird to have you sleeping with," Elijah said, waving a hand around Dameon's vicinity, "all that."

Emma didn't mind the dismissal on her behalf this time. It may have been a double standard of sorts, but she didn't fully like the idea of sleeping next to Dameon. Elijah or Matthew, maybe? Yes? No. Maybe? But Dameon? She most definitely wasn't ready for that. They may have had a deal, but she needed more time before she could trust him that much.

"It's really fine. I'd rather just watch a movie and fall asleep here. It's been a while since–"

Elijah made a dramatic show of falling out of his chair and pushing Matthew to the side. He wiggled his way between the two of them and put a hand over her mouth. His sky-blue eyes were bright, and were accompanied by a hopeful smile. Excitement electrified his expression.

"Hear me out…" he said, nearly bursting. "Slumber party!"

He removed his hand and pouted, in an exaggerated face full of the word please. Emma looked at the other two. Dameon smiled broadly, and attempted to hold back a loving burst of laughter. Matthew regarded Elijah with a sweet kind of pity.

"Please," he begged Emma. "It'll be fun! We could paint nails, watch a lame scary movie, play games? Pizza is already on the way! It would be more than acceptable to sleep on the sofa if it were in the name of a sleep-over. Matthew and Dameon never do that kind of stuff with me. But you! It's been forever since I've had someone to do fun girlfriend stuff with. Pleeease? I promise, no more pranks for the rest of the night if you say yes."

Emma couldn't suppress a giggle at the pleading man. Elijah bit his lower lip. He slipped strategically off the couch and placed himself on his knees and between her legs.

Without breaking eye contact for a single moment, he ran his hands up the sides of her legs and pressed against the sides of her waist. He pulled her forward, closer to the edge of the sofa. Her heart skipped a beat. Emma looked at Dameon, expecting to hear his command for Elijah to stop, but all he did was watch with amused interest.

Elijah waited for her attention to return to him. When it did, he begged with the largest puppy-dog eyes. She warmed at the sight and feel of him moving lower. Elijah pressed his lips into her inner thigh. The fleeting thought that she wished she wasn't wearing leggings, crossed her mind as he inched a bit closer, switching to give attention to her other thigh.

Elijah pushed her knees together, interlaced his fingers over her, and rested his chin on his hands. He made a pleading promise that he'd be good if she would only say yes.

"Sure," she said, shakily with a laugh. "If you want to that badly, I guess it would be fine to…"

Elijah released her, and raised his triumphant arms in the air with a huge grin. A drawn out, "yesss," brought smiles to Dameon and Matthew. Emma wondered how often Elijah's sensual begging worked on them too. Probably every time. Dameon's eyes followed his smallest partner, with complete adoration and affection. He clapped his hands together and got up with a stretch.

"Well, if you want to do this," Dameon said, "let's do it right."

Dameon gestured for Matthew's assistance, and began moving the chairs from the center of the room. Matthew stood and pushed the sofa backwards with Emma still on it. Elijah put his hands over his heart.

"You too," he asked, looking genuinely moved.

"I'm not about to miss this," Dameon said. "But I'll skip the nails, thank you."

"Same for me, please. No nails, but a scary movie sounds fun."

Emma couldn't help but feel a hint of joy when she took in Elijah's excitement. He jumped to his feet and practically squealed. His happy spark was contagious.

Dameon unlocked the many security features of the front door, and headed out to meet the pizza boy in the lobby. Elijah ran up the stairs to "get his things," while Emma was assigned popcorn duty. The microwave beeped, hummed, and rotated an expanding bag while she waited patiently for the popping to begin.

"It means a lot to him," Matthew said, causing Emma to jump.

She thought he was still in the living room, preparing the space for Elijah's ideal slumber party ambiance. Matthew took a step back, his caramel eyes looking for any traces of crossed lines.

"Sorry," he said. "And, sorry for earlier too. I already regret it. I shouldn't have held you like that, especially after everything."

"It's fine," said Emma. "You just surprised me is all. And don't regret it, I don't."

Emma ignored the popping and subsequent beeping sound of the finished popcorn. She reached for Matthew's hand, and he held tight at her touch. She wrapped an arm around his torso and pulled him into a caring hug. Up, onto the tips of her toes, she stood. Briefly on the cheek, she kissed him.

"Sometimes," she whispered, "I wish I was more afraid of you. Instead, I think I might just be crazy."

A hard pull lifted Emma closer, bringing her up to Matthew's waiting lips. He surrounded her in an all encompassing hold that warmed her body and tightened her core. He kissed her hard, with an open mouthed kiss. Her rising leg jerked upwards as Matthew's hand wrapped beneath the bend of her knee. She could feel his hardening dick under his denim pants.

Both nearly jumped out of their skin when they heard the sound of the front door opening. Emma's heart pounded in her ears, and she was sure Matthew's was doing the same. Without words, Matthew guided her leg back down and created a distance between them.

She wanted him. He wanted her. So why weren't they doing it? She knew why. Dameon. He didn't even need to be in the same room, for both of them to know that he wouldn't approve of any hanky-panky tonight. Emma blew out a breath of acceptance and smiled. Matthew left Emma to continue her popcorn-centric mission and left the kitchen, adjusting his pants as he did.

When Emma returned to the living room with multiple bowls of popcorn in her arms, Matthew and Dameon were on the second floor. The two grunted, lifting the massive dungeon mattress over the iron railing. With a final push, the heavy thing slapped the ground in a loud crash. They really were going all out.

Elijah waited giddily at the bottom of the stairs. A silky, light-blue, dress stopped just above his knees. Matching silk-lined heels with fuzzy accents, added at least six inches to his height. Emma smiled at the man who she thought looked down-right adorable.

Under his arm, was a clear container of brightly colored nail polish and manicure-essential items. When she got closer, he threw a blush-pink nightdress her way. The knee-length, thin, t-shirt material was soft, and had a wide neck meant to expose one shoulder.

"Don't worry," he said, with a smile. "That one didn't belong to any dead people, or otherwise. It's mine."

Emma smiled appreciatively, and went to the room to change. When she returned, Dameon and Matthew stared strangely at her. The outfit wasn't particularly revealing in any way. The comfortable fabric hung rather loosely on her small frame, though it did look very cute. She tugged at the end of the shirt-like dress for more length, when met with the eyes in the room.

"What," she asked, somewhat defensively.

"You look..." Matthew couldn't find the word.

"Authentic," Dameon said. "Natural."

"It's the color. We haven't seen you in anything other than black and white. The pink is fabulous."

Emma smiled at the complements. There was a sweet nature to their words, more than there was any kind of lusty suggestion. They just seemed happy to see her in something that made her look a little more like a guest, rather than the prisoner she was. Emma had to admit, she liked it too.

"Thanks. And Elijah, you look–"

"Gorgeous? Hot? Like a "my wealthy husband died under mysterious circumstances," lovely, lady?"

"Oh yes, absolutely. But I was also going to say, impressive. I don't think I could walk three feet in shoes like those."

Elijah looked down at his heels, then popped his head back up to stare down Emma.

"You're telling me, you don't know how to walk in heels?"

"I never said that! I can, somewhat, hold my own, in a less sky-high version. But I don't think I've even tried to attempt anything as tall as those."

Elijah's eyes twinkled, and his hands clapped together excitedly.

"Oh my God, I'll be right back."

He flew up the stairs and ran, yes, flawlessly ran around the second floor.

"Size?" he shouted down. "Shoe size, what are you? Please say seven!"

"Right on the money," Emma yelled back.

An ecstatic, "yes" sang through the penthouse. Elijah hurried back with a pair of shoes that made Emma's jaw drop. They were too pretty to actually wear, and looked more like they belonged in a display case, than with any outfit. The thin sole and straps had a silver shine, and the bottom half looked as if it was made of perfectly clear crystal.

Elijah extended the shoes to Emma, but retracted them back in a hug.

"Obviously, they don't fit me. But these are my Cinderella shoes. I love them more than Dameon and Matthew combined," he said, with a wink to his partners. "These heels are made from genuine diamonds. They are my favorite things ever, but this seems like a worthy cause."

Emma was nearly speechless.

"I can't possibly wear those!"

"You can, and you will. I'll be damned if I let you live here, knowing you can't walk properly in heels."

"Pretty sure," Dameon teased, "you're already pretty damned."

Elijah stuck his tongue out at Dameon. He offered his prized possessions to Emma and grinned ear to ear.

Emma, carefully, strapped the shoes to her feet. When she stood, the floor might as well have been turned into a trampoline. Her ankles threatened to roll, but Matthew and Elijah rushed to her sides to offer support. Once some balance was achieved, Elijah flipped his hair and puckered his lips.

"Like this, baby."

Elijah strode with the grace and experience of a runway model. Emma attempted to follow in his footsteps, Matthew holding her arm along the way.

"No, no," Matthew said, and put his hands on her lower waist. "You have to roll your hips as you go. If you simply walk straight, you'll be fighting the whole way. You need a little more of this."

Matthew guided her hips around, as Emma tried again. It was better, she was better, but she still stumbled. She giggled at her incompetence, as did the other men.

"You know what," Elijah said. "I think you need a more elaborate example. Matthew, help me out."

"No."

"Yes! I won't stop asking, until you do. Please? Please? Please? Please? Plea-"

"Fine! I'll do it. But only because I know you'll never shut up if I don't."

Matthew marched upstairs like a grumpy child, and came back down with an enormous pair of shoes as tall as Elijah's. Emma's jaw dropped yet again. She couldn't believe her eyes. As the masculine, muscly man, slipped on the heels and towered over everyone. He was already huge, but the added height made him inhumanly tall.

"This is how you do it," Matthew grinned.

Absolute shock filled a dumbfounded Emma. Matthew, freaking Matthew, stepped, one foot in front of the other, rolling his hips and stomping over the stone floor.

"Come on lover," Elijah coaxed. "Gimme more!"

Shock nearly sent Emma into cardiac arrest, as loud music blasted from the living room speakers. Elijah was quick to steady her, as Emma's legs wobbled like a baby deer. Rainbow lights beamed in place of the previously normally lit room. Emma looked at Dameon, who lounged back into a chair to watch the show.

Matthew flipped his long hair around, and shimmied his shoulders. A hard bass beat pounded, as he strode with a sass that was on par with Elijah's. Dameon whistled, as Elijah led Emma to the make believe runway. She followed the advice and loosened her stride, moving with the unnatural curves of her feet.

She did it! She made it! An audience of three, clapped and cheered over her success. Emma bowed in an exaggerated curtsy, almost losing her footing again, and laughing at the clumsy mistake.

The music bumped, the lights gently strobed in alternating colors, and the three people in heels strutted their stuff like they were being paid to do it. Elijah spun at the end of the pretend line, and held out his hands triumphantly, before returning. Emma miraculously got the hang of it, and ended her pose with a confident tap of the diamond against the marble floor. When Matthew reached the end, he put a hand on his hip, bent at a surprisingly flexible angle, and snapped back into a towering standing position.

Their sides stung with the pain of laughing. It was too much. Never in Emma's wildest dreams, could she have imagined Matthew in such a position. Even better, he was loving it. Elijah squealed more than once with absolute joy.

Just as Emma's feet began to ache, Dameon turned the music down, and transitioned back to their formal setting. Matthew kicked the giant heels off, and melted into Dameon's neighboring chair. Emma removed her own, with more tenderness than that she might have given to the cutest puppy. Elijah took them, kissed the insanely ornate footwear, and quickly returned them upstairs.

Mountains of colorful blankets and pillows piled atop the large mattress. The rearranged furniture framed the impulsive sleeping arrangement, allowing Dameon and Matthew to prop their feet up from the comfort of their green chairs.

With minimal push back, the two bent to the will of Elijah yet again, and changed into matching fuzzy robes and slippers. Elijah laid out a towel to protect the blankets from any stray polish. Matthew passed around pizza, and Dameon picked out a movie.

The chosen cinema for the evening was the 1982, gem of a cheesy scary movie, Creepshow. It wasn't actually scary or realistically gory in any way. Matthew protested, wanting a modern slasher, but Dameon quickly put his foot down on the idea.

"The answer is no."

"But why? I did the walk! I think I'm owed this."

"I said, no."

"It drives me crazy! Bodies don't decompose that fast in the water, and what's with the grass alien thing? What even is that? At least pick something with a realistic color for the blood."

"That's the point. After this morning, we're watching campy and corny, not traumatizing and triggering. We'll have plenty of time for that in the future."

"Gee, thanks," Emma said, jokingly.

Past the sarcastic tone, Dameon sent a quick wink at Emma's, genuinely appreciative, crooked smile.

"Fine," Matthew said, with an inauthentic grumble.

Elijah patted the towel, inviting her over to his work station.

He got straight to work with a smile that pulled at Emma's heart strings. He went for the whole manicure experience. Elijah's nails looked far better kept from the start than her own did. Neither mentioned it, knowing that much of the reason was due to her captivity. Emma picked a sparkly purple color that looked blue at different angles. Elijah picked a metallic, bright blue to go with his dress.

Elijah filed her nails, fixed her cuticles, and painted with expert precision. When the movie was about to reveal one of its creepy conclusions, at the end of the first of its short stories, he even massaged her hands. When it was his turn to be pampered, Emma gave his hands the same attention and care he imparted on her. Though perfectly innocent, Emma felt a closeness and comfort in making him look so happy.

After Elijah's turn was finished, he convinced Matthew to let him and Emma paint his nails too. They went for a black nail polish at Matthew's request, but Elijah couldn't resist throwing in a bright pink nail while the large man wasn't paying attention. The two painted like giddy teenagers while Matthew watched the movie.

Poor Matthew was internally dying, and rolled his eyes at the film's cheesy effects. Occasionally he'd throw an exasperated hand in the air, much to Elijah's dismay, who would snatch his canvas' fingers back to complete his work of art.

Dameon, however, was far less invested in the movie. He smiled fondly, as he watched Elijah and Emma playfully torturing Matthew with their activity. They were having fun, Emma was unexpectedly relaxed, and Dameon was drinking in the moment of tranquility in his home.

"Truth or dare," Elijah said, blowing against Matthew's wet nails.

"No," Dameon said, quickly.

"What? Why not," Elijah pouted.

"Play nice, Angel. If you want to ask a question, feel free. But we aren't doing dares of any sort tonight."

Emma passed another grateful look to Dameon. Elijah rolled his eyes.

"Party pooper," he said, reluctantly. "But you're putting this on."

Elijah tossed cucumber facemasks to Dameon and Matthew. Both made faces of objection, but decided to play along anyway. Neither wanted to rain on Elijah's parade, or disappoint Emma's budding excitement.

On the count of three, each of the four slapped gooey masks onto their faces and revealed the fruits of their participation. Laughter exploded in the room until their sides hurt. The beauty product was highly unflattering as the sticky sheets plastered their skin.

Matthew grabbed Elijah by the arm, and yanked him into his lap. The brute teased relentlessly, asking for a kiss through the sticky mask. Elijah playfully fought back, but eventually gave in to the demands and kissed through the slits of the paper.

The credits rolled, the popcorn bowls were emptied, and three pizzas had been thoroughly devoured. Elijah and Emma moved the paint and self-care items off the bed and propped up pillows to take in the view of the city, through the wall of windows. It really was beautiful. Emma and Elijah stared out at the lights and took turns asking questions back and forth. She leaned her head against Elijah's shoulder while he traced the edges of her fingers with his own.

"Favorite date you've been on," Emma asked.

"Easy! Dameon and Matthew took me to see an adult-rated circus show. They spoiled me rotten all day with shopping, fine dining, and surprised me with great seats. It was super early into our relationship, and I couldn't believe it."

Dameon laughed.

"My wallet didn't see you coming," he said. "I'd never met someone as enthusiastic as you, over designer fashion. I don't regret a thing, but I definitely learned a lot about you that day."

Elijah blew a kiss in his direction.

"Okay, my turn. Have you always lived here? If not, why come to Vegas?"

"Nope, Alabama. I grew up there. I spent most of my life in a small town, a really small town. It… wasn't a great time. I left home a little young, and kind of made my own way. I came here because, well, because of Grant. He offered me a place when I was down on my luck, again. He made big promises and looked like a way out. I believed him, so now I'm here with you."

"Sorry," Elijah said. "I probably shouldn't have asked that one."

Emma shrugged.

"Do you own a lot of feminine clothes," Emma asked.

"Yes," he answered, with a bit of guilt. "I should probably apologize for that too. You didn't have to wear Matthew's stuff, but I was grumpy. I was mad at Dameon for keeping you, and didn't want to share any more of what was mine. I didn't want you here, let alone in my clothes or enjoying my culinary masterpieces. It was petty of me to make you feel like such a prisoner, but I didn't want to think of you as anything more."

"And now?"

"I think I'm getting pretty attached to you, honey," he said, moving closer. "I can't pretend you're a temporary thing anymore, and I don't hate it. Don't get me wrong, I wish you had more of a choice to be here, but I like you. I think you might be fun to keep. So, no more crap food or prison clothes, scouts honor. Unless you piss me off of course."

Emma looked up at Elijah. Apprehension turning her stomach with the threat over her volatile predicament. If she didn't keep any of the men happy, she really was liable to go back to staring at walls with oatmeal for breakfast, lunch, and dinner again. Dameon cleared his throat, warning eyes fixed on Elijah.

"Only kidding," Elijah said, hugging her and grinning at Dameon. "We're not putting you in that position ever again," he said, turning to Emma. "It's not gonna happen."

But it could. Even if Elijah was serious in his assurance, that he was joking. Emma would always be at the mercy of them for as long as they kept her. If she made them angry enough, they could make the rest of her life hell.

Even with the deal she made with Dameon, she was sure they could find a loophole to make her miserable. She probably should have made better demands when given the chance. Not attacking her, not confining her to that room, and getting the chance to leave the penthouse at some point, were the all she could think of in the spur of the moment. Hindsight is twenty-twenty.

"Thanks," she said, eventually. "For this, I mean. It's nice feeling like a person."

"No, thank you. It's been a long time since I've been able to have this kind of fun. So, sports?"

"No, not really," she answered, sleepily. "Just chess for me. My parents didn't approve of a girl in sports."

Elijah and Matthew eyed Dameon. The dark-haired man grinned at the new insight to Emma. Though judgmental and slightly apprehensive glances passed back and forth between the men, Emma ignored their wordless conversation. She didn't have the energy to dig into whatever they were thinking about.

"I have a question," Emma said, with genuine curiosity. "The room I was put in. You said you haven't brought anyone back to this place in a long time. Why have it so prepared if you weren't expecting guests? I mean, all the soaps, even feminine products. Why keep it so stocked when you didn't think it would be used?"

Dameon's mouth twitched in a way that suggested he was still very upset about forcing her to stay in that room for so long. It bothered him, and Emma couldn't help but rather like that it did. Hopefully, she was safer from being locked away than she was giving them credit for.

"For emergencies," Dameon said. "In our line of work, you never know when a close friend might need a place to lay low. One can never be too prepared."

A little "huh" of acceptance at the answer, along with a shrug, was all Emma gave. She supposed it made sense. She began wondering just how many "friends" they had for the men to keep a room for such an occasion.

Elijah pushed the potential for a heavy topic away, and continued to take turns asking more casual questions. Elijah's favorite dessert was opera cake, both to make and to eat. Emma liked strawberry ice cream. If Elijah could pick a super power, it would be the ability to walk through walls, or super speed. When asked why, he simply stated that they sounded fun and imagined the ease it could create for robbing a bank, or setting up further pranks for his partners.

"What about you," Elijah asked, turning to Matthew. "What would you pick?"

"Invisibility," he said, with a thoughtful expression. "It'd be nice to not have eyes on me all the time. People always seem to keep an eye on the big guy. I think it'd be nice to slip under the radar sometimes." How about you," he asked Dameon.

"I don't need super powers," he said, with a cocky bob of his head.

The entire room groaned.

"You have to pick something," Elijah coaxed. "Come on."

"Fine. Mind reading. Practical, and could be fantastic when applied in the bedroom."

"Lame," Matthew groaned.

"It's not lame," Dameon said, defensively. "Imagine knowing every little thing going through your partner's head when having sex, knowing exactly what and how they want it. Imagine knowing the perfect limits of your partners. I'd be the god of sex!"

"Sounds like an awful power. I don't think I want to know what goes on in your brain when having sex," Elijah laughed. "And you're already a sex god, but I think you just wanted to hear us say it. So yeah, Matthew is right, lame. Next!"

All eyes rested on Emma.

"I don't suppose teleportation would be a valid answer," she questioned.

"Only if you also use it to create some epic fight scene before making your escape," Elijah said. "Swoosh! Ninja chop to the face! Swoosh! Proceeds to kick Matthew's invisible ass!"

Emma laughed at Elijah's karate-impersonating hands in the air.

"Done," she said. "Epic fight scene, no problem. But first, I'd have to pop over to Grant. It'd be nice to zap him over an active volcano. I do have priorities, you know. And what's a proper vigilante story without a list of people that wronged you?"

"It's almost relieving to hear you admit your desire to watch us burn," Dameon said, with a sly smile. "I was beginning to wonder if I'd ever hear it."

"Only Grant gets the volcano," Emma corrected. "Super-me might spare you though," she said to Elijah, "as a thank you for the perfect nails."

"Aw," Elijah squeaked. "They are cute, aren't they?"

"They are," Emma said, dramatically admiring her hands. "Definitely worthy enough to keep you from being dropped into shark infested waters."

Elijah put his hands over his heart.

"I think that's the nicest thing you've said to me."

With a few taps against the screen of a tablet controlled by Dameon, he dimmed the lights and selected a playlist of relaxing lo-fi music.

Emma's attention buzzed with the change of the atmosphere. She looked at the tablet, then Dameon. The instrumental music was far from threatening, or sexy, but the lighting deposited feelings of nervousness. Familiar emotions stirred in Emma's chest.

It felt like so long ago, that she watched Dameon retreat to the shadows in the back of the truck, as she sat duct taped and scared. Overlapping the memory was an urgency that compelled her eyes to the tablet. If it had a connection to the internet, maybe she could use it to her advantage.

Picking up on her plan in an instant, Dameon gave an apologetic frown.

"Sorry, Emma," he said. "It's just for the house. It doesn't have web browsing, no messaging or email. It's just an oversized remote."

Emma's heart sunk, but not greatly. She should have expected as much, and allowed him to see a disappointed scrunch of her face.

"A girl can dream," she said, tolerantly.

She looked over to Elijah, and only just realized that he and Matthew could barely keep their eyes open. The long day had taken its toll on all of them. Dameon turned the music and lights a few taps lower. In the kitchen and down a hall, he left a soft glow. Matthew slid lazily down to the mattress, and moved in to cuddle up next to Elijah.

"Careful," Elijah said, with closed eyes. "First to fall asleep gets a dick drawn on his face."

Matthew chuckled and pulled Elijah in tighter.

"I dare you not to fall asleep in my arms," Matthew said. "You know you can't resist."

The city and moon shone bright into the room through the wall of glass. It looked a little strange to Emma. They were so relaxed, caring, and flagrantly affectionate. Her big bad captors looked so non-threatening, and remarkably human, in their sleepy state. She couldn't help but smile at their sweetness as they almost instantly drifted off.

There wasn't enough space on Matthew and Elijah's side for Dameon, so he grabbed one of the many blankets from the bed, and laid on the sofa his legs were too long for. His feet propped up on the armrest, and hung in the air. Emma watched the man closely.

He really was content to sleep in a position that promised significant neck and back pain the following morning. Despite having plenty of room next to Emma, he willingly chose to give her space. He closed his dark eyes and attempted to get comfortable, unsuccessfully.

"Dameon," Emma whispered, so as not to wake the sleeping men near her.

He didn't look at her, and responded with a "hum?"

Emma hesitated.

"Would you rather sleep here?"

"Of course I would like to, but no, I'd rather be here. You really don't deserve any more intrusion on my part. I'm perfectly fine where I am."

Dameon turned his head to watch Emma, curiously. She pulled her own blanket close, wrapped it around her, and placed a separate blanket over an empty space on the mattress.

"Please," she asked.

Dameon moved slowly to the more spacious sleeping area. He was careful to keep as much distance as possible between them.

The man kept his attention on Emma while covering himself with her offering. She shifted towards him, and closed the space he was trying to keep. He backed further into the side of the sofa. She moved closer still. He tried to keep his distance but there wasn't an inch more to give, unless he were to retreat to the undersized couch again.

"Emma," he said, sounding concerned. "What are you trying to do?"

Emma reached out and touched his neck. She ran her thumb over the thin, pink, line that healed like the papercut-wound it was. Her touch was lighter than a feather, but Dameon took in a sharp breath. He didn't try to stop her, but reached back to grip the sofa cushion. Her touch couldn't possibly be painful, so she could only assume that she was making him nervous. Yet in his apprehension, he raised his chin to give better access to her handy work.

"All of you were so sure I would do more," she said.

"I deserved more. I'm still surprised that you didn't. However, if you regret going easy on me–"

"No," she said. "I don't. You may not think I was violent enough, but I've never hurt anyone before. At least, not up close and personal like that. I'm sor–"

"Don't," Dameon said, grabbing her wrist. "Don't say it. You don't want to hurt me? It sickens me, what I've done to you. It wasn't my intention when I took you, and it isn't my intention now. I lost sight of that, and I will not listen to you tell me that you are sorry. I will, however, listen to that past you are hiding from me. Few people have the spark I saw in your eyes. Such a thing doesn't exist without a past, and your curiosity seems to be rubbing off on me."

Emma's heart raced. She looked from him, to her wrist. Her fingers closed to a fist in his grip. Dameon let her go. Emma moved closer. She let the front of her body lean against his and pressed an ear to his chest. She listened.

His heart pounded. Dameon rested his hand on her head and buried his fingers in her hair. Her scalp was still sensitive, and his touch made her tense. He lightly rubbed the spot and kissed the top of her head. She looked up at him.

"I don't like admitting it," she said. "but you were right, what you said in the pool. I have made someone pay for hurting me in the past. I don't really want to talk about all of it yet, but my father–"

Dameon put a thumb to Emma's lips, preventing her from saying more. He looked from her eyes, to her mouth, then back again.

"If you aren't ready, then don't. Also, I realized that maybe I'm not ready to hear it. You don't need to see me get angry twice. I can tell by the beginning of your story that your father is about to make me feel particularly murderous."

Emma swallowed her words.

"We'll have plenty of time for story swapping. But know, there's not a person here that walked away unharmed by their bio-families. Matthew, with his physically abusive father. Me, with mine. And Elijah... the deepest levels of hell are too good for what his did to him as a child. We may have some trust issues for you, but not one of us can blame you for whatever it is you did to the people that deserved it. Those that inflict abuse can't be shocked when they finally have to face the consequences of their actions."

Dameon followed a strand of Emma's blond hair from its root to the end. He moved the back of a gentle hand across her cheek, down her neck, and just past her collarbone. Emma shivered at the light touch. She hoped her slight movements went unnoticed. It was clear they hadn't, in the way Dameon subtly clenched his jaw. Lines of remorse formed before speaking in a soft voice.

"I wonder if our abusers ever felt a sliver of the remorse that I feel from hurting you. I am the last person that deserves to touch you," he said. "I deserved so much more than a little scratch."

"I don't understand you, Dameon," Emma said, in a whisper. "If you're so worried about being near me, why would you offer to have me sleep with you, in your bed, earlier?"

Dameon chuckled quietly.

"Oh little prisoner. You're cute. You think I meant for you to sleep with me? After, as you put it, I cockblocked you all day? No. I meant that you could sleep in my bed, alone, safe."

"Are you saying I'm still not safe with you then?"

Dameon's teeth could be seen brightly in the gentle glow of the night.

Gently, he lifted Emma and pushed her a more appropriate distance away. He rolled onto his back, shut his eyes, and pretended to be asleep until his act became reality. Emma tugged at her blanket until it covered her shoulders, and found her own way to a dreamless sleep.

The sun warmed the side of Emma's face on the living room floor when morning arrived. She looked to her left and right to see Matthew and Elijah still asleep, but not Dameon. He rounded the corner from the kitchen, with two cups of coffee. Dameon winked and motioned for her to join him in the study.

Stealthy as she could manage, Emma rolled away from the two men at her side. She silently stretched, and followed Dameon into the room of books and art supplies.

Her interest peaked when Emma realized Dameon's intentions. He took a seat facing the chessboard that Emma bumped into nearly a month ago. Of course he played chess. So that is what his partners were telepathically talking about last night. He gestured for Emma to join him.

"Lady's first," he said.

After a morning yawn and a sip of coffee, Emma moved her first smooth, white, pawn.

"My father was a piece of work," Dameon said. "He hated my defiance, but loved my usefulness as a prop for his image. A son to pass his empire along to, not that he did. Very early on, he realized I wasn't as eager to please him as my twin. He knew he could manipulate Penny into doing anything to make him proud."

Pawn met pawn, knights entered the arena. White's pawn took a knight. Black's rook took white's bishop. Emma listened to Dameon's story as the game took shape.

"This building is only mine, because it was demanded by my cancer-ridden mother. She didn't like me any more than my father, but at least liked having a daughter to dress up and show off. Apparently, a soon and expectant death softened her towards me in the end."

Black's pawn took a pawn. White's king moved. Black's pawn continued his raid and took another piece.

"My father disowned me, and used this tower as a birthday parting gift the day we turned eighteen. Penny's birthday present was being told that she would, without argument, marry some kid the same age as us, Greg."

White took black's bishop, black's remaining bishop took hers.

"The forced fiance, was the son of a rival business owner and fellow amateur mobster, Tony. He and my father may have hated each other, but they couldn't deny that their partnership could make them both the ultimate force in this town. Penny only met Greg a few times, real rich kid vibes. I only met him once, looked a little similar to your ex. I mean, if Greg was older, way more fit, and well... not dead. Poor kid was unfortunately just as accommodating to his father as Penny was to ours."

White's queen came to play. Black's rook defensively moved to protect the king.

"Well, the not so happy day came. Our father didn't show, which was not out of character for him."

Emma looked up from the squared and satisfying clicking pieces. Dameon appeared momentarily lost in his thoughts. Emma slid her hand from her side of the board to his, lightly touching his fingertips. He met her in the middle and held her gently. Her heart skipped a beat at the vulnerability.

"I walked Penny down the aisle," he said. "She was beautiful. The dress was the only thing I think she picked for herself out of the whole damn ceremony. She looked like one of the little woodland elves from the stories I would read to her, when daddy-dearest would hit the bottle too hard. She was too young to be married, she deserved so much more than to be used as a cold business transaction."

Dameon squeezed Emma's hand subconsciously. Emma allowed it.

"They said their vows, had an awkward reception, and got into a limo to fly off for an undoubtedly awful honeymoon. But–"

The pieces stopped moving. Dameon cleared his throat.

"Tony's men plowed through them on the way to the airport. The limo was totaled. He killed Penny, and his own son. In a stroke of fucking coincidence, my father caught a stray bullet to the head earlier that morning. He died before the wedding. I didn't hear about it until after Penny–"

A familiar look of murder and vengeance stroked a fire behind Dameon's deep blue eyes. He ran a hand through his dark hair.

"With my father dead, everything he owned would go to Penny. With Penny gone, all assets would be transferred to her husband. With Greg dead, you can guess who got the whole thing. Tony gained millions in a single day."

Emma wanted to hold him, comfort him. But Dameon kept a measure of rage that silently warned her to tread lightly.

"I didn't even get a body to bury or say goodbye to, there was nothing left. Tony orchestrated every detail down to the minute. His only mistake was being stupid enough to try to scare me, by admitting his part in everything at her funeral."

Tremors of hate and bloodlust shook from Dameon to Emma's hand. They scared her, but she didn't try to pull away.

"Matthew and I tracked down every one of Tony's men that had a hand in murdering Penny," he said. "We killed them all, and many of those in our way. It took years to get up the gall to do it. Then about four years ago, we started stealing from Tony's businesses, low level things."

"The pawn shop and jewelry store," Emma asked.

Dameon nodded.

"Those are a few, yes. He "protects" them. Every month, he gets a cut of their profits in exchange for his services. Tony loves money above all else, so naturally, that's what we target. Over time, word will get out that he's not the gangster he used to be; that he can't keep his own businesses safe. And only after he loses his credibility, respect, and everything he loves, will I personally take his life. Not Matthew, me."

Matthew sleepily made his way to the study. He rubbed the sleep from his eyes and stretched his arms above his head when he noticed the game. His eyes bounced back and forth frantically between the two and the board. His jaw dropped and his stare turned into a hard glare.

"What the– Dameon!"

Emma looked around, confused over the upset tone in Matthew's voice.

"You can't be serious," he said, in an awestruck tone. "After everything that went down yesterday? You thought this would be a good idea?"

Emma wondered why Matthew would object so heavily to Dameon finally telling her the details that surrounded Penny. She felt Dameon had been pretty clear that he wasn't going to continue to keep secrets from her. It shouldn't have been that big of a surprise. She looked cautiously at her opponent who only offered a cocky half smile.

"Don't worry, Emma. He's overreacting."

Matthew looked flustered.

"Um, no. I'm really not."

Dameon looked Matthew up and down. Dameon's dominance was definitely back in full swing.

"I'm afraid," Dameon said, returning to the game, "that Matthew believes I am an incredibly sour loser. Not that he has anything to worry about, I've already won."

White's queen took black's pawn. Black's bishop took white's queen. White panicked. Black took another pawn. White's king moved frantically as black chased like a cat cornering a mouse. Checkmate.

Dameon startled Emma when he quickly stood from his chair. She reflexively withdrew her hand from the table. He offered an open palm for her to shake. Despite the abrupt end to the game, she took his hand.

"Good game," he said. "You seem almost as good as I am, and I am very, very good at these games."

The praise brought a smile to Emma. Between him and Elijah, she wondered when games weren't being played, be it traditionally or mentally. With the addition of Matthew's commentary, she wondered if this game might have been both.

10 | Initiation

The days passed with ever increasing comfort. Emma could come and go from the white room as she pleased. She decided, on her own accord, to sleep in her former cell after the living room slumber party. With the power she held, as a personal owner of a key to the space, she gained a sense of security in knowing she always had a way out. Even so, she continued to avoid spending any more time in the room than necessary.

Elijah showered Emma in clothes that were too big, but also made her feel sweetly cared for. All the same, she favored the built-in bra shirts and leggings. It felt nice having something to wear that was only ever hers. She ate when and whatever she desired, with the exception of dinner. Every evening, Dameon, Matthew, and Elijah made a point of eating together as a family. She couldn't exactly say that she felt like family, not that she knew what that might actually feel like. But dinner became her favorite part of the day, regardless. The event was always filled with warmth, jesting conversations, and Elijah's impeccable cooking.

On a much awaited morning in the home, and after weeks of preparation, the air was thick and tense. Metal spoons tapped against glass bowls of cereal. Muffled crunching on granola pieces provided the only conversation during the otherwise silent breakfast.

Matthew examined a handgun, looking for any imperfections or causes for concern. Minuscule sounds clicked around the weapon. Satisfied, he tucked the gun into a low profile holster, hiding beneath his dark jacket.

Dameon also wore a, discretely designed, kevlar jacket and jeans, matching Matthew. Elijah sat next to Emma. The con man was deeply concentrating on the role he was about to play, wearing the light-blue polo and khaki pants of Emma's design.

Emma eyed the gun peaking out from under Matthew's jacket. She remembered the feeling of staring into it, the fear that Dameon was about to take her life. That same weapon had already murdered a pawnshop owner, and who knows how many others.

Emma was nearly its latest victim. Grant looked into that very same barrel. The knowledge gave the gun a contaminated, dirty, feeling. It was almost as if she risked being infected by its deadly repercussions if she looked at it for too long. It invisibly connected her to a line of, who knows how many, people that met their end staring into that same piece of metal.

Dameon cut off her train of thought when he excused himself from the quiet company of Elijah and Emma. He rose to rinse and put his bowl into the dishwasher. Dameon scrunched the arm of his jacket and shirt to check his watch.

"It's showtime," he said, in grim seriousness.

Matthew and Elijah straightened their spines. Emma followed suit, though she didn't exactly have a reason to do so. She wasn't the one about to rob a jewelry store. She would be waiting around in the penthouse, while they launched the finale of her design. Something about it felt a little unfair, though she wasn't particularly keen on the idea of robbing anything herself. Even if she had a choice, would she really do something like that?

Dameon unlocked the front door and held it open with his foot for Matthew and Elijah. The two silently exited their home. Matthew called the elevator and stood in its open doorway. His strong hand prevented the moving parts from retreating back to the main floor, giving Dameon time for a few parting words. Elijah ducked under his arm, and into the impatient elevator. They both looked back to Emma with hopeful smiles.

"Don't answer for anyone that isn't us, regardless of the story they give you." Dameon said, seriousness coating his words.

"Don't worry, daddy. I won't open for strangers," Emma said, trying to lighten the mood.

"Ew," Dameon laughed. "Don't call me that."

His face reclaimed its somber attitude.

"But seriously, our enemies won't think twice about harming you. To review, we will never order a pizza to be delivered to the door. No packages will need signing. We are the only people with access to this floor. If any one knocks–"

"I'll be okay," Emma said, smoothly. "And if the cops show up, I'll give them every detail, and thank them for their profound bravery for the rescue."

Dameon shot Emma a look that stated he wasn't in the mood for her sarcastic remarks.

"As hilarious as you are, don't forget that Tony owns plenty of cops. I'm not saying it for our sakes. You can't trust anyone, even a cop. But if they do show up–"

"Dameon," Emma interrupted. "I'll be fine. You don't have to worry about me. I'm in the most heavily secured safehouse to probably ever exist. Just worry about the job. And… be careful. I'd really hate for you to get stabbed again."

Mathew airily laughed at her concern. Elijah reinstated a face of focus. Dameon smiled sweetly at her.

"We will see you before dark," he said.

"I'll be waiting."

Dameon waved a good-bye salute to Emma, then locked her in the penthouse before joining his men for the way down.

The tablet rested on the kitchen counter. Emma picked it up and played music through the speakers, in every room of the home. The modern playlist provided a much better alternative to the terrible silence of the morning. Pop and hip-hop beats loosened the stress that was building in the center of her shoulder blades. She looked around the empty home and wiggled her shoulders, rolled her head side to side, and got ready to do whatever she wanted without the pressure of watchful eyes.

Emma found herself in the library to try her hand at painting. She found a blank canvas, a few messy used bottles, and picked a brush that seemed suitable enough. Some brushes were pinpoint small, some were sponge-like, others like fans. She wished she watched more Bob Ross growing up, not knowing how to properly use any of the tools that didn't look like an elementary school kit.

In her mind's eye, she envisioned a realistic painting of the Vegas skyline. It was exciting and beautiful with vibrant colors against a dark night sky. What she got were lopsided rectangles, a wonky pyramid, and a dangerously oval ferris wheel. As it would happen, she and Matthew apparently had a similar aptitude for painting.

Accepting her defeat, she took a tube of Dark-Dameon-blue, Light-Elijah-blue, and Matthew-amber, acrylic paint. Emma chuckled at her unofficial name for the colors. She squeezed each tube along the top of the canvas, and let the gravity pull the colors at its will. Next, she generously dipped her brush in a number of neon colors and flicked them onto the masterpiece. It was messy and yet, somehow better than she expected after the rocky start. Emma categorized the style as amateur abstract, and left the canvas to dry.

Music rumbled in the empty home, as Emma moved her party for one upstairs. Even with her newfound freedoms, uncertainty still gnawed at her brain when it came to that part of the penthouse. She tried the handles to multiple rooms with no luck. A few had retinal scanners like the one on the front door. She wondered if those rooms were only able to be unlocked by Dameon, or if the other two had access as well. Only a few doors lacked locks, and opened hospitably.

A room opened with mirrors lining two of the four walls and held two treadmills. A few stationary bikes, a bench press, yoga mats, large balls, and a set of weights, hid behind the unlocked door. Two mounted television sets opposed the side of the room with the largest of the equipment. A tv remote was left in the cup holder of one of the treadmills. Emma pressed its power button.

Wide-eyed, giggling, and with haste, she turned it back off when a pornographic scene between two men lit up the left screen. Interesting choice of inspiration. She returned the remote and tried her hand at lifting a few of the smaller weights. Quickly bored, and slightly humiliated by her lack of strength, she moved on.

Emma's attention was pulled to another room with its door barely ajar. One of the fancy scanners accompanied its lock. The lack of security looked accidental. It was most certainly never intended for her nosiness. Naturally, she pushed open the heavy door.

It was a bedroom. The simple space was not incredibly unlike Emma's. It too had a wall of glass, though this one looked out to a desert landscape and blue mountains. She initially felt like they were holding out on her by keeping this spare room a secret until she realized that this place was clearly occupied by another person already.

Nostalgia littered the room. Neatly folded blankets, movie tickets, random knick-knacks from casinos, and pictures of Matthew, Dameon, and Elijah held places atop white levitating shelves. On a bedside table, a large lamp replicating a detailed moon sat next to two framed pictures. One photo was of Mathew and Dameon as teenagers. The other was of Matthew and Elijah, shots in their hands at a blue-lit club.

Emma looked around with a trace of awe. This was Matthew's room. Since the discovery that the three were in a relationship, she assumed they all shared a single place to sleep. The trio ended nearly every night, retreating to the dungeon. Why would Matthew have a separate bedroom? Did they each have a private room? That would make Dameon's offering of "his bed" have a totally different kind of connotation. Everything about the offer suddenly made a lot more sense.

She looked around the room with a new perspective. The closer she observed the carefully kept clutter, the more she realized he didn't seem to throw away any items with a shred of sentimental value. Her curiosity heightened when she noticed the spines of over a dozen beautifully bound journals. Emma picked the oldest of the diaries and opened the leatherbound item to discover poor handwriting and dates scribbled in the corner of each page.

Emma flipped to the first page.

"Dameon thinks writing in a journal could be good for me. He gave me this one. I like it. I hope I don't lose it or let it get stolen. I don't know what to write, so I guess I'll just go for it. Tonight I've made camp in the tunnels again. I don't like it here. It's so dark and I can always hear footsteps, or people having sex, or shooting up. I can't even see my hands when I turn off my flashlight. At least it's better than anywhere downtown.

I miss Dameon. Once a week isn't enough. It's probably shitty of me, but I almost wish his dad made him work at the shelter more. At least then I could see Dameon without his dad getting pissed. I wonder if he's okay. It sounds like his dad is almost as bad as mine was. I know he hates the way the guy uses him. "Hey, look at my son feeding the poor. Look at what a good father I am. No, I don't beat my kids." I wonder if Dameon thinks about doing what I had to do? Probably not. He's a good person. A good person doesn't kill their dad.

I probably shouldn't write about dad. Evidence or something. Oh well. Don't care. Asshole deserved it. If he didn't want a bat to the brain, he shouldn't have hit so damn hard. I can still feel the crack of his skull. I'm thinking of telling Dameon. I don't regret it, but I'm afraid it'll scare him. I don't know how writing this is supposed to help.

I hate the dark. I'm so tired. I'm afraid to sleep. ~~I wish I was home.~~ I wish I had a home."

Emma looked at the corner of the page. The entry was made 13 years ago. Emma would have been about twelve years old when Matthew had written that. He and Dameon looked close in age. She imagined a fourteen, or sixteen, year old Matthew, scared, alone, living on the street. He was a child, and the murderer of his own flash and blood.

Her fingers trembled as she stroked the page of the journal. Intrusively, she could hear the sound of her own father's voice.

"Disgraceful, pathetic excuse for a daughter."

Emma fiddled with the purity ring strangling her finger. The simple piece of jewelry felt tighter than her confining dress, buttoned all the way up to her neck. She knew he'd be upset. When wasn't he? Her mother meticulously washed dishes in the tiny kitchen, pretending not to hear the booming voice that filled the house.

"It was just a kiss," a young Emma said, quietly. "It's not like I–"

"Kissing leads to mistakes like you," shouted the man of the house. "It leads to unholy, ungrateful, girls. Last I checked, I wasn't raisin' a whore!"

Her mother glanced up from the sink to cast disapproving eyes in her only child's direction. Those eyes weren't the only ones casting judgment. Pictures of religious figures, and decorative pieces, littered the walls in every direction. It was as if the inanimate objects knew all about the sins she'd been hiding.

It was far from the first time she kissed a boy. In the backwoods of Alabama, when the summer nights were humid and hot, Emma would run. She would open the only window in her room, sneak away in the light of the moon and stars, and chase her freedom. She ran until she felt the relief of the cool river near her family's double-wide. She ran until she found it in soft clover patches in the night. And sometimes, like that night, she ran into the arms of the boy down the road.

Zachariah was a scruffy boy, with dusty hair and light eyes. She didn't love him by any means, and she was sure he felt the same way. But they were two rebellious teens, desperate for the thrill of some autonomy in their overbearing community. For them, that was enough.

When Emma's father caught his sixteen year-old in the act of a hot and heavy kiss, she knew what would follow. The yelling, the threats, the further limitations on her already sheltered life, it was inevitable. She'd never see the closest thing she had to a friend again. She'd never get a break from the soul crushing control her father demanded.

Two more years. She'd only have to endure the bastard's rule for two more years. If she could stick it out, she'd be off to college. She'd be away from the mother that enabled her cruel husband, regardless of how often his hand found the side of her mother's cheek. Emma could be away from the people that wanted perfection out of a child that didn't have perfection to give.

She'd be rid of the sorry excuse for parents that took offense to her constant questions about their faith, and to her growing habit of smiling in the face of abuse. With her rising hopes of the future, Emma felt her expression turn. The ghost of a smile provided an inner comfort that could barely be seen in the corners of her mouth. It was enough.

Emma's thoughts were interrupted by a sudden, stinging, slap to the face. Her mind blurred in total shock. Her father had hit her mother before like that, but never her. Her mother's eyes widened. The woman remained silent, but seemed just as surprised as Emma. Through unstable vision, she watched the woman that birthed her, the human being biologically obligated to protect her, return to her chores.

Something broke in Emma. Two years was too long. Her stare burned into her father's green eyes, a mirror image of her own. Heat surged through her chest, her palms pained with the feeling of her nails digging in as she made a fist. With every ounce of strength she possessed, she swung at the unsuspecting man.

Before he could recover from his own shock, Emma launched in the direction of her room and pulled down her secondhand dresser, blocking its weak opening. The hinges bulged and snapped, as her father pounded on the other side, shouting murderous threats through the cracking wood.

Emma didn't dawdle. She unzipped her high school backpack, littered the floor with loose papers and books, and shoved all the practical clothes she could fit into the bag. She grabbed her life-savings she had hidden away beneath her mattress, nearly two hundred dollars, and crinkled it into the front pocket. Emma opened the window and she ran. Faster than her bare feet had ever flown before, she raced for the safety of the thick woods beyond the river, and away from her hell.

For the one-year anniversary of her flight, Emma returned to the place she swore never to see again. She wasn't crawling back for help, because she missed or regretted leaving her parents, or to gloat about her better life without them. To say she struggled as a homeless teen, without a community, without family, without support, would be an understatement.

She slept in homeless shelters much of that year. She worked odd jobs, saving enough for her first rented room in a major city, far from the scope of her old, tight-knit town. Her latest job at a mom-and-pop restaurant promised reliable income, and they never pried when it came to her personal life, or age. Emma was proud of how far she had come, though the road was definitely a tough one.

No, she didn't go back to brag, or ask for help. She came back for curiosity's sake. What had come of them since her escape? Did they have another child? Maybe they replaced her with a dog they could better train. Not knowing was the thief of so many night's sleep. Her unanswered questions kept her from a desperately desired, romanticized, idea of closure. So when the stars and moon were all that lit her forest sanctuary, she sought out the answers that could only be found at the place it all began.

Emma approached her childhood home with the light feet of a walking wolf. When a light suddenly illuminated her parents' bedroom, she instinctively crouched into the nearby bushes. Mentally, she noted that she would have to check herself for ticks later. At least that was one thing she didn't have to worry about anymore in the city.

The shades were open. Emma silently snuck close, and peaked into the room. Her father sat on the edge of the bed, a bottle in his hand. He looked awful, unkept, and as though he aged far more than simply a year. The sight gave her a sense of satisfaction, though she acknowledged that she had also aged quite a bit in the short time.

"I'm sorry," the drunk said, loud enough for the rest of the house to hear. "I shouldn't have. It's my fault."

A sickly amount of gratification coursed through Emma's veins. Good. He felt regret. It would have been better if he had figured it out sooner, but it still felt good to hear.

Her mother was, no doubt, about to come in and comfort him. She would pat his back and tell him that it was Emma's fault for being a bad child. Yet, as Emma watched, she never came. It was only after minutes ticked by, that she noticed a new frame in the room.

On the bedside table, next to an ordained bordered, pristine, picture of her mother on their wedding day, was an urn. Her father patted the container of ashes affectionately before taking another swig of alcohol.

"If you just did as you were told," he sniffed. "I wouldn't've had to correct you if you had just listened better. I wouldn't have– If you just remembered–" Her father straightened up and pounded a fist to his chest. "If you could have remembered, that I am the man! I wouldn't've had to– You'd still be here."

Emma's father sloppily knocked the urn into his lap, lid fully secure. He rocked back and forth, holding the container as if she could feel the embrace through her burnt remains.

Emma's heart pounded in her ears. Her blood boiled, and teeth ground together. When did it happen? What if he killed her for finally standing up for herself? What if it was because she actually defended her daughter, after Emma ran? Why wasn't he in prison? Did the town help cover it up? Did his cop friends help? The town had a habit of covering for their own, but she didn't think they would turn a blind eye to killing her mother.

Emma watched the rotten man toss the urn back to the table. It swayed with the clumsy move, and rested next to the ring of dust from the place it last sat. He glugged at the nearly empty bottle of alcohol, and lit a cigarette from his pocket. He inhaled a deep breath of smoke, causing the end to glow in red and orange. He exhaled a great puff before setting the little white stick on an ash tray, and walked away.

The purest form of loathing flooded every inch of Emma's being. A flame she hadn't felt since her father's hand made contact with her face, returned with dangerous rage. Her palms pressed against the window and pushed it open.

Emma crawled through the window pane. In the near bathroom, she could hear the shower sputter to a start. He closed the door. Vapored evidence of the hot water crept between the gap of the floor and the door. Her nose wrinkled in disgust as she made a wish for him to slip and break his hip in the process.

The unfinished tobacco smoldered in the porcelain gift she made in her elementary days. Emma picked it up, and rolled it between her thumb and pointer finger. She sat in the dent of the mattress that her father made, and looked around the depressing room. It smelled uncomfortably like him, alcohol, smoke, and home.

Emma touched the lit end of the cigarette to the worn bedsheets. The fabric began to darken and smoke. She pressed it further until a small flame took form. She watched it with repulsion and anger. The spark of heat grew, with exponential hunger for the rest of the bed.

A little blinking light caught Emma's attention. She rose incautiously, and removed the batteries from a smoke alarm before it could begin to wail. She lifted the upper-right corner of her father's mattress, and found what she was looking for. Rubber bands squeezed rolls of money, thousands at least. It was his entire life savings, thanks to his distrust of banks. She slid the rolls into her pockets, bra, socks, and waistband.

The entire bed was soon engulfed in flames. Smoke billowed in the small room, as the greedy fire took the curtains next. Paisley wallpaper bubbled, melted, and welcomed the invasive destruction. Emma should have coughed, shielded her eyes, anything. Instead, she stood in the center of the damned room, letting the heat warm her skin. She hoped he fell. She wished he would burn.

Emma left from the window in which she came. She watched, between the trunks of the thick trees, as the building of terrible memories lit up the neighboring dry brush. Emma's eyes glowed with the reflection of the cracking roof, as it folded in. An ounce of remorse couldn't be found in the girl.

She watched until the distant sounds of the fire department could be heard. As she fled, unseen and unnoticed, she saw the silhouette of her father escape. Emma couldn't help but feel a little disappointed. The man bawled and screamed at his loss. Everything he owned, all he cared about, burned before him. Emma smiled at the sounds of the popping fire and the cries that filled the air.

Emma's gaze wandered around the room, packed with Matthew's memories. She looked down at the journal, closed it, and returned it to the shelf.

Matthew killed his father. It could have frightened her. Instead, she understood. If anything, part of her was almost jealous that he got to finish the job. Hers got away.

Emma understood why he never threw anything away. It's hard to trash anything of the slightest importance after being homeless. It all feels like treasure. Of course he was unquestionably loyal to Dameon. He was Matthew's lifeline in a sea of shit. The closest thing she had to anything like that, was Zachariah, then later Grant. Matthew had Dameon, someone that loved him in return, someone that cared.

Elijah's poolside chat rang in Emma's mind. Matthew was homeless and running from a past that anyone else would find reprehensible. Elijah was a desperate thief, trading his body and soul in the hope to survive another day. Emma was an unwanted woman, thrown at Dameon's feet to be killed, or sold into slavery. Elijah said he had a thing for collecting strays. She heard him. She thought she understood. It wasn't until then, that she truly felt the gravity of his words. She was like them, and Dameon knew it the moment he made the delirious decision to take her.

Emma retreated from the room, desperate to shake the emotions of her trip down memory lane. She made her way back downstairs and turned on the local news, hoping to catch wind of any progress the men might have made. Nothing but politics, and worries about the ever imploding economy, could be found. Emma blasted the music over the speakers, trying to drown out the emotions creeping up on her.

Emma made herself a late lunch of pasta with basil, mushrooms, and cheese. She rolled her hips in the empty space to the beats of a pounding bass lines. She took a bite, rocked her shoulders, poured herself a coke, and attempted to dissociate from the world.

She fumbled, and nearly dropped her cold soda to the floor, when a report of a robbery at a little jewelry store flickered on the television. She ran to the living room. She muted the music and cranked the channel's volume up, until the hosts were shouting around the penthouse.

According to the reporter, two gunmen burst into the store. The armed thieves scared the employee half to death.

"When they pulled the gun on me, I saw my life flash before my eyes," she said.

Emma took a drink of her bubbly cola.

"Tell me about it," she said, to the trembling girl on screen.

The reporter stated that no one was hurt, and that the store owner was desperate for anyone to come forward with any information.

The camera panned out, showing Riel, and a happy golden dog. The reasonably distraught man sat on a chipped yellow curb, just outside the store. One hand pressed against his head, the other scratched at the gleeful pet's ear, wagging his tail without a care in the world. Unbeknownst to Riel, an anonymous donation would be waiting at his home address in an unmarked envelope to set him up for years to come. That part was Dameon's idea.

Emma cheered at the top of her lungs, and threw her arms in the air. They did it! She did it! Her plan worked! Emma felt a pride in her chest, as if she just watched her favorite team win the Super Bowl. She turned off the television, jumped on top of the round coffee table, blasted the music, and celebrated her victory.

When orange and pink hues glowed through the windows, Emma watched with heavy anticipation. Slowly the city woke up with the darkening sky. When a mechanical sound clicked through the penthouse, Emma nearly jumped out of her skin. She hurried across the hard floor to meet a smiling Dameon, Matthew, and Elijah.

A suffocatingly strong and energetic hold smothered Emma, as Matthew and Elijah they squeezed her. Both tossed dark bags carelessly to the floor. She could barely breathe in their embrace, but she didn't mind.

"I watched the news," she said, when finally permitted air. "It worked?"

Dameon grinned broadly, his eyes wild. He took Emma from his partners and held her face in his hands. Before she could comprehend what he was doing, he pressed his lips, hard, onto hers.

Shock kept her eyes from initially closing. She hadn't expected that kind of reception. He kissed her! Emma wrapped her arms around Dameon, and kissed him back with the same ferocity. Adrenaline pumped through her veins. When Dameon pulled back, he took her hand and spun her around. He pressed her back against his chest, locking her close to him.

Emma watched the other two. Their faces were just as electric. They bounced, shouted, and ran around the penthouse, the excitement from the event, still drugging them into a state of exhilaration. Dameon bent down and reached for a bag. He held it in front of Emma and asked her to hold it. From behind her, Dameon kissed her neck and reached in with both hands, to reveal fistfuls of precious metals.

"Look at what you've done, Emma."

He let the expensive items fall where they pleased, as Dameon searched for something specific. He found it. A gaudy, silver, and sapphire necklace hooked onto one of his fingers. Other pieces of jewelry clung to it. Dameon gave it a shake, letting gold, silver, diamonds, and gemstones fly recklessly.

He unclasped the necklace and wrapped it around Emma's neck. He fastened the silver, and admired his work. The elaborate piece covered the blue and green bruise on her neck. It extended down past her collarbone, in an expensive mess of diamonds, silver, and blue.

Matthew addressed Emma with awe and a serious sweetness.

"You look like a princess."

"Wait, wait, wait," said Elijah.

He practically shoved Matthew aside, and dove his hands into the bag. Elijah retrieved a silver tiara and placed it on her head. She felt ridiculous until she saw the very real gleam in Elijah's eyes when he smiled.

"I don't know if I can really be a princess, if I'm also your prisoner," Emma said, in a teasing, challenging voice.

Dameon squeezed her middle, making her gasp, and more than her waist tighten.

"On the contrary, little prisoner, we intend to worship you like the royalty you are."

Elijah ran off to the bar and returned with champagne. He shook the green bottle, and popped it messily. Before the bubbles completely subsided, he moved intimately close. Elijah took her chin in his hand, and tilted the carbonated alcohol close to her lips, letting it spill over her clothes.

"Have a taste," he said.

A heat grew between Emma's legs at his words. She stuck out her tongue as Elijah dragged the neck of the bottle along her accepted invitation, tasting the sweet flavors. He tipped it carefully to spill the drink into her mouth.

Elijah's sky-blue eyes gazed hungrily at her wet lips. He bit his lip, placed a hand just behind her neck, and sampled the champagne throughout Emma's mouth. His tongue played with hers, taking her breath away when he set her free.

"We've never been more nervous on a job," Matthew said. "We couldn't help but wonder if we were about to walk into a trap."

Emma's chest rose and fell rapidly, as Dameon's thumb found the waistband of her dark leggings. He moved along its line.

Elijah barely gave enough room for Matthew to plant his own passionate kiss on her lips. When Matthew released her, Elijah took her mouth with his again. Dameon's hold got tighter. Matthew lowered himself, his knees on the marble. He looked up at Emma's tortured, wanting face.

"You gave us more than jewelry," Matthew said. "We want to give you something in return. If you want us," he said, playing with the openings of her pockets. "Just say the word, because we are done waiting."

Matthew gave a warning tug, pulling her pants ever so slightly down. The smallest muffled cry of approval sounded. Elijah ceased his consuming kiss to hear her answer.

"But only if you really want it," Elijah teased.

Her sex buzzed and craved what they offered. She could feel Dameon's hold, as he inched lower. Matthew kissed her inner thigh through her thin pants. Elijah's lips hovered just out of reach, looking drunk off her presence. She nodded her head, but Dameon took her chin. He tilted her head to look at him.

"You have to say it, Emma," he said, sweeter than he had ever spoken to her before. "We won't take you unless you say it."

"Yes! I want you. Please..."

Dameon pushed down the band of her leggings. Matthew pulled at the pockets to rip the pants the rest of the way down. Elijah took a swig of champagne, then chucked and shattered the bottle, leaving a sweet smell in the air.

Matthew guided her feet, and tossed the leggings to the side. Elijah and Dameon pulled her shirt over her head. The tiara fell to the floor, but the necklace stayed in place. It was the only thing left on her body, apart from them.

The three had her undressed in seconds. Just as quick, they frenzied over her body. Dameon's tongue explored her mouth. He twisted her for access, arching her back. Elijah took a handful of her exposed breast with one hand and rounded the tip of the other with his tongue. Matthew swung her left leg over his shoulder and kissed, licked, sucked, and teased her clit. Emma moaned in Dameon's mouth from the overwhelming attention consuming every part of her.

In one, nearly synchronous motion, the trio released her. She would have fallen if not for Dameon's supporting hold. She had no warning. Her body was wordlessly screaming at the sudden loneliness.

"Are you sure you're ready for this, Emma," Dameon asked. "Are you sure you want us?"

"Yes," she nodded, breathlessly.

Dameon loosened and released his hold on Emma. Matthew took her hand in his, and led her to the center of the living room.

Dameon took her face in his hands and kissed her forehead. Elijah's arms wrapped around Emma's body, his hands playing with her exposure. Dameon's hands moved over Matthew, and pulled the shirt from his large body. He knelt before the giant and continued to undress the man's lower half.

"Tell us what isn't allowed, princess," Dameon said. "What boundaries do you have for us? What do you need to feel safe?"

Emma reached to touch Matthew, but he backed away, teasing her desire.

"Nothing," she said.

Elijah laughed, dangerously.

"Everyone has something, honey," Elijah said, tossing his blue polo away.

"Nothing! Please. There's nothing I don't want from you."

Elijah kissed her neck, as he kicked his khaki costume out of the way. His lips brushed the back of her neck as his fingers journeyed from her back, to her ass, to a previously untouched intimate place.

"Are you saying that I can have this," he asked, teasing its entrance. "Do you have a lot of experience in letting someone fuck your ass?"

Her arm shot up to grab a hold of Elijah's blond hair.

"No," she said, shakily. "I mean, yes. But no, I've never let anyone– But I want you to. I want everything."

Elijah laughed softly in her ear.

"So needy."

"Yes," Emma breathed.

Dameon chuckled.

"Okay little prisoner. What about two in your cunt, or two in your ass? Do you want that?"

A glimmer of fear appeared next to the hunger in her eyes.

"Yes," Emma said. "If you think it's possible. I want what you think I can take."

An invasion of light pain, and new pleasure, slid up Emma courtesy of Elijah's fingers. Emma let out a small sound of shock and initial discomfort.

Dameon laughed darkly.

"Shhh, little prisoner," Dameon said, kissing between her shaky breaths.

Elijah's fingers moved in the previously unexplored place.

"Don't worry," Dameon said, "you can trust us to take care of you."

He moved his own hand to her wet crease, and slid a finger inside. She gasped as he slid another of his fingers into her. Dameon kissed her ear.

"Emma," he whispered, "little prisoner, my princess. Please forgive us, but we plan to love you."

Matthew rested back in a green chair and watched his partners taking Emma's ass and pussy with their hands. At Dameon's command, Matthew was instructed to stroke himself. Emma clenched as she saw the pleasure Matthew gained in hers, and made Dameon swear as she did.

"Don't worry, honey. I'll be back," Elijah whispered.

Slowly, Elijah released her, extracting a high moan from Emma at the motion. Before she could wonder where Elijah went, Dameon introduced an additional finger. Emma dug her nails into Dameon's shoulder as her body accepted the preparation for what was to come.

Elijah returned to the room, and motioned for her to move nearer to Matthew. Dameon switched positions, and stood behind her. He fondled her breasts in front of Matthew. She leaned back into him, as his fingers tightened around her nipples, forcing her to softly whine.

She looked down at Matthew, readying himself for her. He really was a large man. Emma began to second guess her overconfidence. She'd never been with more than one person before, and wasn't sure what to expect. Elijah knelt next to Matthew's side and gave Emma a wink, as his slick hand took over Matthew's movement. Matthew groaned with Elijah's perfect strokes.

"Trust me, sweetie," he said, adding a few more drops of lube to his hand and placing the bottle to the side. "You'll enjoy yourself a lot more with this."

Dameon guided Emma onto the chair and placed her just above Matthew. Emma gripped the armrests, butterflies swarming in her stomach.

Dameon forced her to look his way and roughly kissed the breath out of her. A hand of his, slid hand down her navel to her wet slit. His fingers spread her for Matthew.

"Tell me you want him," he growled.

Emma's heart raced.

"I want him, please."

Dameon placed his other hand on her hip and pressed, moving her down slowly onto Matthew's waiting cock. A strained moan escaped from deep within Emma's chest. Dameon hesitated.

"More," she begged. "Please!"

Dameon squeezed Emma's side, giving her what she asked for. She sounded a strangled hum as Matthew filled her. He had so much to give, and she wanted every bit.

Emma began to ride him, finding his pleasure and taking hers. He felt so fucking good. She didn't realize her eyes were closed until Elijah caused them to shoot open. She hadn't realized that he had taken Dameon's place behind her. His teeth bit at her neck. His lips pressed over the tenderness he created on skin, in dishonest apology.

Elijah's hand glided against her back with a pressure enough to make her lean forward, until she rested on Matthew's chest. She could hear his heart pounding. Matthew swept stray hair from her face and, letting go of every bit of restraint he once maintained, ravaged her mouth.

He moved his hands down her body, as he pumped his hardness as deep as her body could allow. Elijah's thumb circled and pressed into the place on her body that only he had ever entered. He pulled away his thumb to graciously ready her with his fingers. She tightened around Matthew's dick, making him groan beneath her. Elijah released her only to press his own lubed up dick to the entrance of her ass.

Emma nervously squeezed Matthew's biceps in anticipation for Elijah. Matthew wrapped her in a tight, reassuring, embrace, and kissed her cheek.

"Are you ready," Matthew whispered.

Emma nodded.

"Do it, Angel," Dameon said. "Show our princess how talented you can be."

Slowly, sweetly, inch by inch, Elijah filled her. Emma shouted out in equal measures, pain and pleasure.

She held Matthew for comfort, and he gave it. Elijah gripped her waist and thrusted into her smoothly. Lustful moans left Elijah's lips as he took her from behind. Matthew resumed his own penetrating movements, making the stolen necklace around Emma dance and shimmer. Emma felt the unbearable inner friction from the two overwhelm the lower half of her body. She loved it, and loved the sounds of them loving her in return.

Dameon stepped around Matthew's chair, and ran his fingers through the long, dark, waves. Matthew rubbed his head into his palm and kissed his hand as Dameon passed Emma to show Elijah some love. He pressed a thumb around Elijah's neck and kissed his angel.

"Mmm," Dameon hummed. "That's my good boys."

Elijah whimpered at the praise, and increased his speed in Emma. Emma moaned, holding even harder to Matthew.

Dameon's hand lifted Emma's chin next, and demanded a piece of her attention for himself. She panted under the movements and looked up at him drunkenly desperate. Without a second thought, she took over the work his own hand had started. Dameon groaned and gently ran his fingers through her hair. She pulled him close and hungrily took his cock with her wanting mouth.

He shut his eyes and dug his fingers viciously into the chair's cushions. His hand in her hair trembled with restraint, as he maintained the most gentle of holds on her. Her core tightened. She held a power over Dameon, even in this position of submission, and that control was driving her mad with ecstasy.

They felt so freaking good. She wanted more, more! Matthew and Elijah thrusted in every way she needed. Dameon teased her gag reflex, as she sucked him greedily at her will. As her orgasm neared, she took control of each of the men. She seized command of the pace against Elijah and Matthew, grinding and filling herself with them at her will.

"Fuck!" Elijah cried, "I don't think I can–"

Matthew moaned through gritted teeth.

"I know. Fuck! I know!"

Hearing their closeness only served to fuel Emma. She rode them harder, faster, deeper. She moaned around Dameon's dick, causing him to hold her tighter and thrust himself into her, losing his careful control.

"Fuck!" Elijah practically screamed.

He pulled out. Warm cum ran down her back and ass, dripping down to Matthew's balls.

"Emma," Matthew begged, "Dameon! I'm–"

"Not yet my love," Dameon groaned.

Dameon pushed himself deeper, forcing a tear to run down her cheek reflexively. He swore and pulled himself from her mouth. He messily finished on Emma's shoulder, the chair, and a bit of Matthew in the process.

Emma chased the climax of her orgasm. She rode Matthew, panting and whimpering at the waves that threatened to crash around her. Matthew tightened his jaw and strained to keep from finishing inside her. She didn't offer him mercy. She pushed him, drawing out his desperate, pleasure-filled begging.

"Fuck!" he said loudly, "Dameon, please! I can't hold on much longer."

"Not until our princess gets what she needs, my love."

Matthew gripped the chair, that creaked under the pressure.

"Emma," Matthew groaned. "Emma!"

That was it. She felt the rush of pure ecstasy. Her pussy pulsed, her legs pressed hard around him. Her heart pounded in her chest. She was cumming so hard on Matthew, she could barely catch her breath between the overwhelming crashing waves.

As Matthew attempted to pull out, she grabbed his body, and shoved him deeper still. She felt his cum fill her cunt, and it sent her over the edge to pure bliss.

The sounds of spent breathing of the four people filled the room. Only after her pulsing subsided, and the peak of her climax had passed, did Emma allow Matthew to retreat. He pulled her close to his chest, rendering her immovable.

"Good boy," Dameon said, as Matthew collapsed into the chair.

Once his breath was caught, Matthew slowly adjusted Emma in his arms. With one fluid motion, he lifted her to carry her up the stairs. She didn't pay much attention to where they were going, until she realized they had entered the dungeon. A hint of worry found her face. Elijah bent from her side to kiss Emma's head, having seen her anxious expression.

"Don't worry, honey," he said, with a touch of femininity. "We aren't planning on a round two. There's always tomorrow to play, and the next day, and the next."

Emma smiled.

Through the dungeon, they entered a bathroom. It was just as impressive as everything else in the home. A massive shower with three showerheads, and a large bench, closed itself off with a glass wall and door. Two sinks and five cabinets lined the other wall. Framed mirrors were fixed above the sinks, conveniently facing the shower for an entertaining view. White tiled flooring and walls were accented by beautiful black fixtures and lights.

Matthew deposited Emma carefully onto the stone shower bench. Elijah removed the shimmering necklace, promising as he did, that she could have it back later. Dameon detached a showerhead from the wall and bathed Emma in warm water. Matthew and Dameon bubbled up sudsy loofahs, and gently cleaned every crevice of her body. Elijah took to washing her hair with the massaging technique of a professional hair stylist. Each took turns rinsing the soap from their areas of concentration.

Sweetly, cruelly, Dameon whispered in her ear.

"You are our princess. You deserve every drop of love we can give and more. You are fucking adored. And, Emma, my darling, you are very much wanted."

Emotion swelled in Emma's chest.

Elijah instantly recognized her inner conflict. He joined her on the bench and cradled her wet, naked body. She wrapped her arms around him, and buried her face in his neck.

"I know," he said. "Trust me, honey. I know."

Emma couldn't hold on tight enough. She was exhausted from fucking and being fucked, from cumming, and from the feeling of having so much emotion pulled from her soul.

The men dried her with soft, fluffy, towels. Matthew resumed carrying Emma, and placed her into the bed. He joined her to the right, Elijah to her left, and Dameon on the other side of Elijah. Dameon played absentmindedly with Elijah's wavy hair. Matthew wrapped an arm around Emma's waist, pulling her close. Elijah took her hand, pressed his lips to her fingers, and didn't release her until they both were asleep.

11 | Steak, Eggs, and Windows

The dungeon was a windowless room. The sun never rose, making time uncomfortably irrelevant again. The three men slept soundly when Emma woke. She shimmied out from between Elijah and Matthew, leaving the large bed.

She quietly made her way to the bathroom and splashed cold water on her face. Hanging near the sinks were multiple silk robes. Emma wrapped a luxurious tie around her waist to fasten the robe that draped a little too long over her body. In hushed movements she popped open the bedroom door and closed it with a tiny click behind her. The midmorning brightness of the world granted her eyes only the ability to squint from the edge of the railing.

The stark contrast between the dungeon and the rest of the penthouse required a moment of adjustment for her body and mind. Once focus could again be obtained, Emma's attention swept over the lower floor. The place was a mess. Shards of broken glass from the champagne bottle littered the floor, and the thoroughly abused chair had seen better days. Bare feet made terrible sounds as partially dried, sugary, alcohol velcroed to her skin. Her hands quickly found a broom in the kitchen pantry and swept the glass in a neat pile.

Emma didn't wake up because she wanted to clean. She was awoken by the need for food, and was reminded of this fact by angry growls that sounded from the depths of her empty stomach. The evidence of the night before would have to wait. The handle of the broom was placed against a wall as it was decided that breakfast would need to take priority.

Emma opened the fridge, took out a carton of eggs, and grabbed a small pan from one of the lower cabinets. Her skeleton nearly jumped out of her skin at Elijah's unexpected presence against the opposite side of the island counter. She apparently wasn't the only one good at sneaking around the penthouse.

A full white shell fell from her hand and cracked against the stone floor. Viscous yellow mixed with the clear of the uncooked egg, while Emma's distracted and delayed thoughts slowed her speed of reaction. Elijah put a hand to the back of his neck and rubbed as he looked from the woman to the newest addition to the mess downstairs. The blond man was wearing a pair of red briefs that didn't leave anything to the imagination. Emma wondered, when she glanced at the attire, if wearing so little would become a standard around the house now that she'd seen every inch of each of the men anyway.

"Were you cleaning," Elijah asked, in his accusatory, sassy, tone.

Emma shrugged, ripping a paper towel from its roll to clean her butterfinger mistake. Elijah snatched the sheet from Emma's hand with a kiss to her cheek, and picked up the result of his unannounced entrance.

"So," he said, wiping the yolk up from the floor, "you wake up after an orgasmic night, you sneak out of bed without saying a word, then come down to clean? I've seen how you've kept your room, honey. You aren't a neat person. So tell me, what's on your mind? Afraid of a little morning sex, trying to erase a mistake, play housewife? What's up?"

The remaining undamaged ingredients found their way to the stove as Elijah insisted on cleaning the mess on the floor. Fluffy yellow food formed in the hot pan as she scraped the spatula around without looking up or saying a word. Elijah, switched off the heat to her rapidly burning eggs. Emma placed the utensil on the counter but her attention remained downward, avoiding Elijah's questions.

"Emma," he said, softly, as he placed a hand near hers without touching. "Are you okay?"

A small, "no" moved her head from side to side without speaking. Elijah's hand distanced with some concern, but was stopped by Emma's. She interrupted his retreat and squeezed her fingers around his. She tried to swallow the lump in her throat, but she wasn't winning.

"If you're playing me," she said, quietly. "if you're using me, or if this is just another game for you—"

Elijah, delicately put pressure on her shoulder. He turned her to face him and wiped a wet tear from her face with the back of his fingers. He pulled Emma into a strong embrace and petted her unbrushed hair.

"No one here is pretending anything, sweetheart," he said, gently.

Elijah led her carefully past the missed glass on the ground, and onto the white loveseat. He poised her to lie lengthwise on the cushions and hovered over her. He wrapped an arm under her waist and cradled her neck and head sweetly with his other hand. Slowly, he lifted her nearer to his lips and held her gaze for a long moment. He turned her face so he could kiss up her jawline to where he whispered, close enough for her to feel his mouth against her ear.

"I told you, didn't I? Being loved, it's harder to accept, for people like us. It's easier to believe we're just being used."

A scary warmth from deep within Emma's chest stirred at hearing Elijah's words. It was a reaction she wasn't sure she wanted to feel at the moment, but that didn't make it any less real.

"I don't know what to do with this feeling," she said. "It's so hard to believe, it almost hurts."

Elijah halted her ability to speak with a quick, sweet, kiss to her lips. He trailed his mouth down to her neck, to her collarbone, to her sternum, back up to her neck, and then to her ear again.

"They didn't deserve you. Not your shitty family, not a single co-worker, and definitely not the fuckwad that asked us to take you. But just because they couldn't see your value, doesn't mean you have none. We don't deserve you either. But as you know, we aren't allowed to lie. So, sweetheart, you can bet that when we say we care for you, we mean it."

Elijah took a deep breath. Emma closed her eyes and followed his lead.

"I'm afraid of ending up like the other people you've slept with. I'm afraid that this is just another game, and I'm losing," she said, weakly.

Elijah kissed her, with a soft chuckle in his throat.

"If this was a game," Elijah said, "we've all lost. This wasn't the plan, but Emma," Elijah smiled and held her face in his hand, "I don't mind losing this one."

Emma wrapped her arms around the blond, and clung to him. He kissed her hair and held the small of her back.

Dameon put a hand on the back of the loveseat. He grinned down at his two strays and ran a finger along Elijah's spine.

Elijah popped his head up. He hadn't heard his partner come downstairs either. Emma felt embarrassed by her red eyes and blotchy cheeks. Dameon either didn't notice, or intentionally didn't address the emotional state she was in. He slid a finger under the waistband of Elijah's underwear and gave it a playful snap. Elijah laughed through gritted teeth and a hard flinch.

"And here I was thinking that you'd still be tapped out after last night. Already asking Elijah for more?"

Elijah wiggled next to Emma on the small sofa, then positioned her, chest to chest, over him. Her naked lower half straddled Elijah, nearly rendering her covering a useless gesture. Without actually exposing her, he lifted the edge of the silk robe higher, teasing Dameon with the idea of her bare ass. Emma silently pleaded her objection with her gaze.

"Don't worry honey," Elijah said, only for her to hear. "I'm just giving him a little tease. He knows he has to be good. He knows you need a break."

Dameon fell right into Elijah's trap. Emma could feel his eyes on her, burning away the thin fabric. Her spine tingled. From below Elijah's body, and out of Dameon's sight, she held tight.

"He'll be good," Elijah breathed. "He really does want more than your body, honey. Watch."

Dameon ran his fingers down the length of Emma's back and stopped at her waist. He gripped a good chunk of the robe in his hand. The cinched fabric revealing the slightest bit of additional skin. No more than a centimeter more, and she would be exposed. Dameon groaned, wordlessly threatening to rip it away. Emma tensed. Dameon let go and smoothed the robe back down.

Elijah smiled with a wordless, "I told you so."

"We need food," Dameon said, eyeing the burnt eggs on the abandoned stove. "Get her done up; hair, make up, the works. We're going to Huevos."

Elijah practically pushed Emma off of him, his butt meeting the floor in the process. Emma almost went down with him, as he hit the stone and quickly recovered to his feet.

"Wait, what," he said, excitedly.

Dameon retrieved a mop and bucket from a closet, and continued nonchalantly.

"You, me, Matthew, and Emma are going to Huevos for breakfast. Unless you'd rather stay home."

Emma's eyes widened and heart raced. She was going outside? She looked frantically between the two men. Elijah's fingers tapped against his thumbs, numbering off the steps to an imaginary list in his mind. He looked her up and down several times before speaking.

"Grab..." said Elijah thoughtfully, "A black cami and black leggings, but don't put on the shirt just yet. Meet me upstairs. We've got work to do."

Emma, too full of excitement to ask questions, ran off to the room to snatch the requested pieces of clothing. Once there, she propped the door barely open with a previously worn bundled up shirt. She really wasn't the most tidy of people. Still, she couldn't shake the uncomfortable feelings that accompanied that door being closed. She slid into the stretchy leggings at the speed of light, grabbed a top, and rewrapped the robe around her chest for a little modesty.

A new door was open upstairs. Elijah waited inside.

A single accent wall was wallpapered in a pink, white, and black botanical print. A black leather bed with white sheets was pushed against the pretty wall. Blush-pink pillows of various shapes and sizes lined the headboard. Colorful, somewhat abstract, paintings of Dameon and Matthew in the nude had a home on the other, less colorful, wall.

The new room, also, had floor to ceiling windows and were lined with numerous hanging plants. Green foliage, open racks of clothing, and brightly colored decorations were everywhere. The Barbie-pink vanity would have looked strange in another room, yet here looked perfectly natural. Elijah met Emma at the entrance and directed her to a matching stool in front of the round, pink, mirror. He clapped his hands together and tapped the tips of his fingers rapidly.

"Alright honey, I'm gonna have to get a lot of skin, so no shirt for this first part, okay?"

Emma nodded and removed the robe, leaving her chest bare. Elijah cleverly put Emma's hair up and under a wig cap. He checked for any stray, stubborn, blonde hairs and tucked them neatly away. He then put a glove on one hand and retrieved a canister that he shook vigorously.

"Close your eyes and don't breathe in three, two, one."

Elijah thoroughly sprayed the mist all over Emma's hands, arms, chest, neck, face, and ears. When she was told she could open her eyes, she nearly screamed in laughter. She was amazingly, horribly, fakely tanned.

"Don't worry," he said, laughing with her. "This stuff is pretty easy to wash off, but it's great for an on-the-fly change."

Elijah placed a medium-long wig, with black hair, over her cap.

"This," he said, pulling out a number of colorful pencils, "is going to make you totally unrecognizable."

Emma held very still while Elijah worked his magic. By the time he was done with the lipstick, liners, the eyeshadows, pencils, fake eyelashes, and an unbelievable amount of contouring, Emma really was unrecognizable. Her lips were too full to be hers, cheeks too round. Her jaw was redrawn and her eyes were too big. The only things that held true to her natural identity were a pair of green eyes. Elijah had a plan for those too.

He opened two circular containers to reveal brown colored contacts. It took a few tries, and the reapplying of some makeup, but eventually, Emma got it. If she had been unaware that a mirror was right in front of her, she wouldn't believe that the woman she locked eyes with, was indeed her. Elijah looked like he might explode with pride.

"I am," he said confidently, "the baddest bitch at this shit, I swear."

Carefully her black shirt was pulled over the new Emma. Elijah stretched the neckline low, and slid his hands down her shirt, sticking two heavily enhancing silicone bra halves onto her chest. He clasped the bra together with a click of a plastic mechanism, having successfully added at least three cup sizes to her breasts. The ajar door swung open as Matthew barged into the room.

"We're really going to Huevos? All of–" he started, but trailed off at the sight of Emma.

He looked in shock at the exaggerated woman in the chair. Elijah placed a conquering foot on the table of the vanity, and posed triumphantly.

"Tell me you would recognize her," he challenged.

Matthew pursed his lips and shook his head.

"Didn't think so!" Elijah gloated.

Matthew bowed out and retreated to let Elijah finish his work. Emma looked amused and a little uncomfortable at her reflection.

"You're good," she said. "But is all of this really necessary? I mean, you said it yourself, no one is looking for me."

Elijah passed a chunky, blue, crop top to Emma. She pulled it over her cami with one shoulder exposed. It reminded her of the oversized night shirt she wore for their slumber party. Elijah began meticulously putting his tools away, while he spoke to the borderline-orange woman.

"Imagine running into your ex," he said, "the man that expects you to be dead or at least in the hands of some human trafficker by now. Would be a little awkward, don't you think? If anyone recognized you, we could be in for a serious mess."

Emma rose from the seat and took in the aesthetic of her new body. Elijah moved close and pulled her waist to his. It wasn't exactly assertive, but rather with a hint of sweet desperation.

"Rules are rules," he said. " So, I think I need to speak up about something. Emma, I'm nervous. Taking you out in public is a big risk for us. You'll have the power to screw us over. If you decide to run off, call for help, or–"

Emma braced for the expected threat. She thought of all of the things they might do if they did catch her, if she tried to escape and failed. Elijah leaned down to be all the more close to her. He spoke, barely over a whisper. Though he was playing according to house rules with his honesty, what he had to say, he clearly wanted to be just for her ears.

"I wouldn't blame you," he said. "We've put you through something most only have nightmares about; kidnapping, death threats, forced isolation. I don't have a right to ask, but Emma, please? Please, don't hurt us out there."

Emma stretched up and balanced on her toes for a kiss. Elijah quickly backed away, not allowing their lips to meet.

"Makeup, sweetheart. I'm pretty desperate, but did you really think I'd let you ruin my masterpiece," he said, with a pouted lip.

Emma and Elijah descended the staircase hand in hand. The place smelled of cleaning supplies, courtesy of Matthew and Dameon. When they reached the floor, Matthew closed his eyes and sucked in his lips, trying not to let out a laugh at Emma's new look. Dameon on the other hand remained perfectly serious. He circled Emma like a lion on a zebra, and ended his inspection with crossed arms before her.

"Open up," he said.

Emma's skin tingled.

"Your mouth princess, open."

She looked around the room for a better understanding, but was only met with calm, encouraging, faces. Emma parted her lips and waited. Dameon pulled out a stick of gum and placed it on her tongue.

"Good girl. When we are out, chew obnoxiously. You'll get attention for it, but it'll be for the wrong reasons. It will be an additional distraction when hiding your identity, Amy."

Emma gave Dameon an unconvinced look.

"Amy?"

Matthew laughed and shrugged. "Yeah, it's kind of like Emma, but backwards. I thought it was fun. Anyway, put these on."

Matthew handed Emma, or Amy, a pair of black flip-flops. The fit was fine, but the simple shoes were definitely lacking in quality. The cheap plastic cautioned against long-term wear as they rubbed between her toes, threatening potential blisters. Perhaps she was over-thinking it, but the shoes felt appropriate for the flight risk she was.

The air around the four was prickly with nerves when Dameon retrieved his golden keychain with the little dangling heart. He unlocked each of the steadfast barriers and led the little prisoner out the front door.

A peculiar thought crossed Emma's mind as she stepped with her guards to the elevator. Her feet had never touched that floor before. The last time she was in that space, Matthew was carrying her and wishing for her death. A pleasant DING sounded as the sliding doors opened.

Mirrors covered the majority of the elevator's interior. It was larger than she expected. She wondered if that's how they managed to get bigger pieces of loot up to the penthouse. Matthew pressed the button for the ground floor and released a deep breath.

"Our rule does not exist out here," Dameon said, grimly.

Emma looked up at him from behind her black hair and brown eyes. He looked tense. Clearly, Elijah wasn't the only one that was unsure of the plan to let her out into the world. Matthew, though tense as the rest, looked as if his excitement might have outweighed his nervousness at the moment.

"Take our words with a grain of salt," Dameon said. "If we hurt you, it is to keep you safe. If we make promises, they could be hollow and only to sell a grift. We may have a truthful conversation in one moment, and feed you lies in the next."

Emma nodded.

"The place we are going to is relatively safe. Well, safe for us. But there will always be risk. To most out here, Matthew, Elijah, and myself are simply friends, spoiled roommates. Sometimes we don't know each other at all. Other times, we might appear to be enemies. We live in lies outside, and I would greatly appreciate it if you would do the same."

Emma nodded again.

"But," Matthew said, with an edge of chaotic playfulness, "have fun."

"And find Amy," Elijah said. "I made her face, but you are the only one that can truly be her."

Amy looked back at Emma in the elevator mirrors. She looked timid, despite her excitement to be out in the world. She stared hard at her brown eyes, her large chest, and her unapologetic outfit.

Expensive shades on top of Dameon's head caught her eye. Amy reached up, snatched the sunglasses, and took them for her own. She smacked her gum loudly.

"Mine," she said, with attitude.

The ring of the elevator's end, sounded. Amy placed the shades over her shirt and tucked the folded plastic between her cleavage. She flipped her hair as the door opened, and practically pushed Dameon to the side to lead the way. A smile reached every man in the elevator.

The lobby was enormous. Amy looked around the elaborate, rich, atmosphere with an unimpressed face. Massive stone statues proudly stood, bordering the entries and exits. Sitting areas were graciously offered for waiting people, that appeared to have been purchased for looks more than comfort. Amy found a revolving door and walked to it with confidence. Emma may have wanted to gawk at the ground floor of her prison, but Amy couldn't be bothered to care. The harshly-tanned woman looked back at the men, a little dumbstruck by her chameleon approach.

"Um, coming," she asked, impatiently.

Matthew looked excitedly at his partners, and was the first to rejoin their new companion. Dameon gave a subtle nod to the doorman, and watched the woman with a studious scan. Elijah caught the corner of Amy's eye and mouthed the smallest, "Thank you," as they exited the building.

The desert air warmed Emma's skin. She was out! Tears were ready to flow but were not permitted release. Amy wouldn't be emotional over something so simple as walking out outside. Plus, Elijah would be furious if she ruined his makeup in so little time. Emma did her best to hide the feelings that overwhelmed every inch of her being. Not long ago, she wondered if she would ever live to experience something so simple, so freeing, ever again.

"A block down to the right," Matthew said, casually.

Matthew stuck to her side like glue. Elijah and Dameon were right on their heels, perhaps to hide her, or maybe in preparation for an escape.

An out-of-place building with the name, "Huevos" written over the door, butted up to the wide sidewalk. A line half a block long formed at its simple entrance. Amy huffed in impatience. Emma didn't mind waiting. The longer the wait, the more time she had out of the Penthouse.

Dameon took the lead, nodding for Amy to follow. She did as instructed, as the men bypassed the many waiting people. A bell rang and announced the presence of the group. Emma wondered who they were to the people of this restaurant to warrant the special treatment. A familiar voice called from the crowded establishment.

"My favorite boys!"

Emma's blood chilled.

"And a girl," the voice inquired.

A tall Latino man with dark-olive skin pulled Matthew from Emma's side and greeted him with open arms. The two patted each other's backs in a masculine hug.

The last time Emma heard that voice, she was taped to a moving van with a bag over her head. This very man offered to take her off their hands to be sold into the human trafficking world. He was older, probably old enough to be their father. His hair was silver with bits of pepper. If she wasn't so afraid of the man, she'd admit that he was shockingly dashing, even sexy if she was honest. Dameon smiled broadly and shook his hand.

"How's it going El Tiburón," Dameon said, in a low voice.

"Good, good. But I could ask you the same." the man said, staring uncomfortably hard at Amy.

"Yeah, it isn't bad!" Matthew said, casually, "This is my girlfriend, Amy. Cutie, isn't she?"

El Tiburón's eyes trickled down the length of the woman's body. His knowing stare intentionally revealed his ability to see right through her disguise. He knew exactly who she was. He remembered her. He cast an appraising look over Emma, wordlessly examining her aesthetic, weighing her worth.

They wouldn't give her to him now, would they? Emma thought again of the men's past conquests, the ones that learned too much about their secret lives, the ones that lost their value after giving them what they wanted, the people they couldn't set free.

"Yeah," El Tiburón said, "not a bad catch."

Amy smacked her gum, diverting his analyzing eyes to Amy's face.

Dameon cast an approving smile in her direction. El Tiburón smiled as well, but Emma noticed a brief piercing glare of interrogation pointed at Dameon. With a welcoming arm extended to the restaurant, Dameon ignored the look and led the other three to a secluded booth at the far end of the establishment.

El Tiburón offered a menu to Amy, but not the others.

"Stiff coffee for the nerves," he asked the table. "Might help. It's a big morning, kids. Maybe a little extra something for the girl? Looks like she might be the type to need a little, calming inspiration."

Dameon nodded and slid into the space next to Elijah. Matthew took the outermost seat of the booth, blocking Emma in. Before her fingers could touch the laminated list of options, Dameon smirked and denied the gesture.

"That's really not necessary," Dameon said, cordially.

"Didn't think so," El Tiburón grinned. "You brought her to me. I trust you wouldn't have, if she wasn't a good addition to our little family."

The daunting man left after another brief evaluation of the woman. Emma scrounged for a bit of courage and composure, but her tears were becoming difficult to hold back.

"El Tiburón," she asked.

The three exchanged serious expressions. Dameon was the first to respond.

"Sebastian Fonsesca," he said. "You may only use that name in private conversations. Anywhere else, you'll address him as El Tiburón. He's not known for his mercy, and is "The Shark" for a reason. He's well connected, respected and feared. We value his advice, and he has helped us fix mistakes more than once. But you'll have plenty of time to get to know him. Now, Amy, you'll need a little more than a name. Where are you from? What's your story to sell?"

Emma couldn't answer. Her throat was too busy dealing with the acid in her stomach. Her eyes darted around the room, having lost track of the silver man. She swallowed hard. A shake, that could be mistaken for being a little cold, trembled through her fingertips.

They lied. They all did. They used her plan for the heist. They confirmed she wasn't a spy. They had their fun, and now they were done. They used what she had to offer, gave her a fake name, a fake face, and were getting rid of her like they did the women and men before her.

Matthew's wandering gaze fell on Emma's hand. He caught the subtle flinch when their eyes met. His expression turned. She was so scared, she could barely see straight. He shot a look at Dameon and Elijah. Dameon's own interest and raised brow nearly mirrored Matthew's.

Only Elijah showed something that could be interpreted as empathy. His eyes anguished when they met hers. Maybe he'd call it off? He shook his head, leaned over the table, and attempted to reach for her hand. Emma recoiled before he could touch her.

"Shush, shush. Don't panic. Don't run."

"You…" Emma stammered, "You said–"

"It's not what you think," he said, in a hushed voice. "Just stay calm. You're not going anywhere."

Dameon's temper flared, but it wasn't directed at Emma. Elijah was in his sights, and he was not happy. He demanded an explanation in hushed words, so as not to draw too much attention to themselves. Elijah narrowed his eyes at the accusation, that it was his fault Emma was about to melt down in public.

"I swear," Elijah whispered. "Sometimes, you two can be the most oblivious men on the planet. It's not just me, it's us. She thinks we are here to sell her!"

"Huh," Matthew asked, clearly missing something. "Why?" He looked back to Emma, repeating his question to be directed at her. "Why?"

"Because she thinks we're done with her," Dameon said. A following curse left his lips. "She thinks we've taken her to El Tiburón's doorstep to get rid of her. Think about the only interaction she's had with him."

"Yeah, and you can't blame her. Telling her what to call him in private, El Tiburón calling her an addition, offering something "calming" to put in her drink? This absolutely looks like the set up for a trade, trust me, I remember that shit. I still get nightmares from..." Elijah's quiet voice cracked. "Emma, this isn't that. He's just a friend. This is just breakfast. The man was just offering an extra shot. We'd never! You're safe, I fucking swear. No one— You're safe, Emma."

A frown replaced Matthew's lost look. He really was shocked that she would think such a thing, but what did he expect? Embarrassment nestled in Emma's gut. She was so sure she was unloveable. It was easier to believe that they were using her. She was so quick to assume the worst.

Before Emma could react, Matthew grabbed and bound her in a bear-hug that forced the air from her lungs. Elijah's protective words berated Matthew for the intense hold, telling him to let her go, that she needed only careful touches at the moment. He tried to explain, on her behalf, that she needed time to take things slow, a moment to remember that she's safe with them.

Emma shook her head when Matthew started to back away.

"No," she whispered. "Don't let go."

It turned out, Elijah wasn't right about everything. What she needed most was this, Matthew's tight embrace. She needed the warmth of his chest that could be felt through his shirt. She needed the sound of his heart in her ear. More than anything in the world, she needed that reassurance, that smothering care, telling her she was wrong.

Slowly, Matthew released Emma. Her chin rose to look up at the large man. It pained him to know how fragile her faith in them still was. Emma wanted to say that she was sorry for overreacting, but was she? She may have been wrong about them getting rid of her, but they really were moving fast. Was it such a jump to believe that it all might not be real?

Dameon's rage simmered down, but the smallest flame remained. She was beginning to recognize that look. He wasn't mad at her. He was angry with himself. He was pissed that her reaction was completely valid, and a result of his own doing. Emma waited for him to speak, but when he did, it wasn't what she expected to hear.

"Where are you from, Amy?"

Amy. She was Amy, not Emma. Amy wouldn't be doing any of this. Her eyes scanned the room, but no wandering eyes seemed to lend a curious glance in their direction. Amy cleared her voice, and tried on her best accent.

"Jersey," she said, adding a slur of vowels to the city's name.

Dameon nodded to Elijah to take lead on the lesson, while he regained his composure. The blond took a deep breath and shook his head.

"Accents are a bitch. Are you sure?"

He wasn't asking, he was instructing.

"Cali," Amy corrected, with questioning inflection.

"Where from in California," asked Dameon, politely.

Amy was from San Diego, California. Her parents still lived there. She finished high school and wanted to go to college to be an artist. She dropped out when she figured that college didn't teach her anything useful. She was going to make it big as a popstar with the help of autotune or land a gig on a reality show, whichever came first.

She was popular in school and met Matthew in a bar with Dameon. Amy was thrilled to have found Matthew while she waited for her career to take off. She always knew she'd find a good man to take care of and support her. Elijah smiled at her progression.

Sebastian, with the assistance of a waitress, broke up the chatter with their presence. Four massive plates of steak and eggs were dispersed to each of the men. Sebastian's bright eyes focused on Amy, as he personally placed her plate on the table before her.

"You need sauce for that cutie," he asked, smoothly.

Emma's discomfort resurfaced with Sebastian's attention. In a burst of determination, she shoved Emma to the side, along with her fears and insecurities. Amy looked down at the meat then back up to El Tiburón. She pulled the shades from between her oversized breasts, and played with the frame between her teeth.

"Is the steak good," she asked.

El Tiburón cast an icy stare at Amy. Emma tried to suppress a shiver but failed. Her blood chilled, as she realized how very aware he was of just how nervous he made her.

"It's perfect. You have my guarantee."

Determined to redeem herself, she made the quick decision to lay it on thick. Amy puckered and spoke sweeter than sugar.

"Then, like, why would it need sauce? If it's perfect?"

"It's a pleasure to see that you have good taste," Sebastian purred.

His smile wasn't that of a friendly host. It belonged to a man that knew far more than he led on. He was a man of secrets, of power, and she wasn't fooling him. He knew exactly who she was. Her delivery could use some work, but El Tiburón seemed to find considerable enjoyment in listening to her try to cover up her true identity.

Sebastian slapped Matthew's shoulder and laughed loudly.

"Well done, boy. You'll have your hands full with this one, I'm sure of it." he said, and left the group to their meals.

Dameon seemed surprisingly, and visibly pleased with Emma's attempt to keep Amy going. Without more than the passing of a minute, he and the others turned their attentions to the incredible breakfast plates that graced the table.

Each of the patrons dug into, what may have been, the best steak and eggs Emma ever had in her life. The slab of meat was huge and accompanied both, scrambled and over easy, eggs. The steak was cooked to absolute perfection with just the right amount of pink in the middle.

Dameon secretly offered his Irish coffee to Matthew, who quickly chugged the contents before Sebastian could return. Emma wondered if Dameon didn't refuse the drink out of some unspoken sign of respect. Maybe El Tiburón wasn't the type to take kindly to the denial of a free drink? Maybe Dameon simply didn't want the outside world to know about his personal decision to quit drinking? Whatever the reason, Matthew took a hard breath after downing the heavy handed drink and continued with his own.

Emma eyed the drink in front of her. She wanted to believe them. She wanted to trust them. She took a sip, her eyes squinted, her nose wrinkled. The warm drink was more whiskey than coffee. The alcohol tingled her tongue and throat. She covered her mouth and tried to suppress a giggle at the ridiculous morning cocktail. Matthew laughed, and switched his and her drinks sympathetically.

Conversations turned light and relaxed as everyone stuffed their faces with the delicious food and powerful coffee. Good-hearted jokes were thrown around over the terrible Jersey accent. The four mimicking the botched attempt with increasing humor. Matthew was definitely the winner, with words so exaggerated, they barely sounded like English.

When the laughter died down and each began to slouch in their seats, Emma contemplated her next move. She didn't know what kind of response she would get, but after the meals were finished, she knew she might never get another chance.

"Can you move, baby," Amy asked. "I need to use the lady's room."

The three men stiffened. She was playing a risky game. Emma wasn't asking to use the restroom. They knew that. She was testing the waters, seeing how much they would trust her out in the world and on her own. By this time, she actually did have to go, but she wanted to see if they'd trust her enough to let her out of their sight.

The ever faithful Matthew waited for Dameon's permission and stayed in his seat until he received a nod. Slowly, he let her out of the booth. They all watched as she strode away from the group.

"Hey," Matthew called after her.

Amy turned back to look back at the table. They really were trying their best to stay casual.

"You better not think of running out on me," he said, playfully.

Emma could hear the inner plea behind his words.

"Baby, you know you can't tell me what to do," Amy said with a mean grin.

She turned away, with enough sass to rival Elijah, and walked through the bathroom door. The single-person bathroom had a beautiful, welcoming, tempting, square, window.

Emma locked the door behind her. She used the toilet and washed her hands. As she dried them, she stared at the frosted glass. Her fingers brushed against the latch, and the exit popped open eagerly. Fresh air filled the room.

She could fit. She could crawl out the window and run. It wouldn't be the first time she escaped from a bad situation with this method. Emma perched herself up in its frame, half of her body in the free world. She could leave and never look back. Who would ever willingly choose imprisonment? She needed to run. The sidewalk was right there. She was good at running, always had been.

Emma closed her eyes. Her hands shook as she gripped the window frame. Seconds felt like minutes, knowing Dameon, Matthew, and Elijah were waiting on pins and needles for her return. Emma swung her legs and landed on the ground. Her feet hit the awful bathroom tile. She fixed Amy's shirt, smiled a fake, wide, smile and unlocked the knob with a click.

Dameon was in mid stride, on his way to check in on her, when she opened the door. Elijah and Matthew were clearly worried. Both let out a breath of relief when they could see their princess returning. Dameon's face revealed a different story.

He started off with a face of stone, ready to hunt her down. Even if his feelings were real, he couldn't just let her go. When he saw Amy, he flashed a smile that quickly dissolved into seriousness again. He looked at her, and silently instructed with his eyes to look behind her. She did. She had left the window open.

Emma's thoughts lingered on Dameon's temper and his determination to keep her from leaving. What would he do if he knew how close she had come to running away? Amy confidently walked up to Dameon. She reached into his pocket and retrieved a new piece of gum. She popped it in her mouth and smacked it as loud as she could. She rose to the tips of her toes to whisper into Dameon's ear, with Amy's valley girl voice.

"Don't tell the others, 'kay," she requested, trying to cover her tracks. It's totally embarrassing. I'd avoid going in there if I were you."

Two crisp hundred dollar bills were left on the table. As the four got up to leave, Sebastian and Dameon bickered over the hefty tip. Sebastian won the battle of generosity and gave a friendly smile to his boys.

"I'll hear from you real soon, yeah?"

Dameon gave a mock salute to the man with a nod. Sebastian glared when he discovered that Dameon had sneakily placed the money into the pocket of his friend's denim pants. With a huff and roll of his eyes, the older man smiled and returned to his busy restaurant.

The street was packed, bumper to bumper. The sidewalk was bustling. No one paid attention to anything besides their own conversations or their phones. Emma wondered just how many pretend people with fake lives could be walking around the city like her. How many secrets were these people carrying? How many could be thieves, murderers, victims. She had always been decently aware of her surroundings before, but something shifted in her world view with this new life.

She came to the revolving door and entered as if she owned the place as much as Dameon actually did. The doorman, with a bored expression, bowed slightly at their arrival. All three men ignored the employee. Amy waved her fingers while smacking her gum.

Matthew, Elijah, Emma, and even Dameon all seemed to release a breath, after the bulky elevator door shut behind them. Still, no one spoke until Dameon unlocked the vault of a door with the gold keychain. The mood lifted when they all were safe inside. Elijah grabbed her face and kissed her hard, stamping some of her lipstick on his own mouth.

"I'm so sorry," he said, pulling her into a hug. "Fuck, I'm so sorry we made you think we'd just sell you off like that."

Emma held Elijah back, gripping his shirt in her fists. Elijah leaned back to better see her face.

"But honey, the way you snapped back into Amy? That was incredible! You're a natural."

"Guys," Matthew smiled, with a yawn, "Emma, you're seriously awesome. You're a natural. But guys, Sebastian didn't make a light drink. I think I'm at least six, or seven, shots deep. I'm full, I'm a little... a little sway-ie, and

I'm ready for a post-Huevos nap. So–"

Matthew's feet trailed up the stairs backwards, nearly tripping along the way. Elijah rushed up and hung onto his arm. He reached up on the tips of his toes, and gave the big man a kiss. Emma smiled at their affection.

"Yeah, nap," Dameon teased.

"What," said Matthew, defensively. "I'm gonna… we're gonna take a nap. Maybe we'll have a little fun first, but we definitely are going to take a nap too. You're always welcome to join if you're jealous. Emma, you too? We can make it a party."

Sex on such a full stomach wasn't as appealing to Emma as seemed to be to Matthew and Elijah. Just as she began to wave her hand to decline the offer, Dameon grabbed Emma's waist and pulled her into him.

He reached into her shirt, slowly ripped the accentuating bra from her chest, and tossed it on the sofa. Despite the intrusion, he was careful not to leave her exposed. She may have been shocked by his audacity, but her bare, natural, chest against the softness of the tank-top was immensely more comfortable.

"Maybe I don't want to share," he said, darkly.

Elijah turned to Matthew with an inauthentic pout, and sounded a playfully pathetic voice.

"It hasn't even been twenty four hours and he's already being selfish. Why do we put up with him?"

Elijah unbuttoned his partner's pants and pushed his hands into the back of his partner's jeans. The outline of his greedy finders could be seen gripping Matthew's ass beneath the denim.

"Sometimes, I don't know," Matthew teased. "He really can be so mean,"

Dameon bit at the air in their direction, making a single click with his teeth. Emma felt a twinge of anxiety at the sound.

"Aw," said Elijah, noticing her face. "Sorry honey, unless you want to come with us, you're gonna have to fight him off on your own this time," he said, sending a wink in her direction.

Elijah pantsed Matthew and got a head start up the stairs. Matthew quickly grabbed at the waist of his pants and ran competitively after him,

225

his butt very much on display. Emma smiled and giggled at the juvenile game, watching until they disappeared into their shared room.

Dameon carefully removed the black wig and cap from Emma, then tussled her blonde hair. He took her hand and started walking. Emma's stomach turned upside down when she realized where they were going. He was leading her to that room.

He promised. He promised he wouldn't lock her in there anymore. Sure, she thought about running, but she didn't! Dameon paused at the closed door and gestured to its new lock.

"We installed this while Elijah was getting you dressed up," he said, tapping against the change to her bedroom handle.

The key was replaced by a retinal scanner like the one at the front door. He motioned for her to use it. After it processed the new information, the door unlocked. Dameon explained that she was officially the only one with access to this room.

Emma hesitated as she stepped into the space. The four walls felt confining and cold. He remained in the doorway. Even with the kind gesture of increased privacy for her, she couldn't hold back her expression of distaste for the room. Dameon held a smile that managed to resemble more of a frown.

"We all have a room here that is our own private space. As much as we love each other, everyone is entitled to a little time for themselves. I know you've had enough alone time here, and that you justifiably hate it, but I would like to make it yours. We can paint, decorate, refurnish it, however you want. I'd like to try to change this room from a prison into more of a sanctuary."

Emma looked around at the blank walls and overly neutral palate. It was hard to imagine making the room into a place she willingly would want to stay in. Dameon cleared his throat, looked down at his feet, then up at Emma.

Dameon looked like he was waiting on her for something, but she didn't know what exactly he wanted from her. Was he hoping for a thank you, for officially relabeling her prison cell? Maybe he was waiting for her to verbally confirm what she nearly did at the restaurant.

"It's your room, Emma," he said, coyly, "It's not mine to enter without your permission. So what do you say? Do you permit me?"

Emma couldn't help but smile at his vampiric behavior. The vulnerability of being potentially rejected, added a tension to Dameon's casual facade. The authority over the space gave her a precious piece of autonomy. Though she wasn't happy in the room, it suddenly felt a lot closer to becoming the place of security Dameon hoped it could be.

He leaned against the doorframe with crossed arms and a hopeful smile. Emma mirrored his failed attempt at a nonchalant attitude, with crossed arms of her own. When his gaze sharpened, her teasing stalled and fuzzy nerves came back.

"If I said, no? What would you do?"

An annoying amount of confidence returned to Dameon. She didn't even give him a sure answer yet, and he was suddenly sure that she'd willingly invite him into her space. His devilish smile chilled Emma's skin.

"Then I will walk away."

Emma eyed the man, patient and plotting.

"I'm not in the mood for sex," she said, quite simply.

"Is that still all you think I want from you? Or, are you suggesting that's all you want from me?"

Emma's heart skipped a beat. She walked right into another game, she could feel it. Emma eyed the man with uncertainty. If he was serious, she could exercise her newly gained power. She could tell him, absolutely not. Maybe she wanted a nap too? Maybe she wasn't interested in playing games? She could tell him to leave.

"You can come in."

His pace was a strange combination of leisurely and focused. His eyes were fixed. Emma's heart started to race again. She recognized that walk. She saw it first hand, when Dameon was toying with Matthew in the dungeon.

"Get undressed," he demanded.

Emma stood her ground.

"I said I didn't want to—"

"I know what you said," he interrupted. "I said, get undressed. Unless you would like me to leave? The choice is yours."

A shiver ran through her spine. Was this what Matthew and Elijah felt every time Dameon asked anything of them? Did he think that just because she agreed to have sex once, that he would be entitled to her forever? He may have said that she had a choice in the matter, but then why did she feel like it wasn't really up for discussion?

Emma pulled the layered shirts over her head, revealing her heavily contrasting fake and natural skin tones. She stripped her leggings and underwear down to the floor, and kicked them off to the side.

"The eyes too. Get rid of them. I want to see yours."

She wasn't used to wearing contacts, and needed the assistance of a mirror. So, she turned her naked back to Dameon and went to the bathroom for a better chance at getting the foreign objects out of her eyes. It took a few tries to grab the tricky circles, and it made her eyes water terribly. The tears smudged the caked on makeup, disrupting the illusion with pale streaks.

Dameon's hands pressed against the top of the counter, trapping her from behind. She gasped and winced at his unannounced presence. His fingers slid from the stone to her fingertips. His palms continued to trail up her arms to her shoulders, where he carefully squeezed and pressed his thumbs to the back of her neck. Emma's eyes closed with his massaging pressure.

When she opened her eyes again, Emma was met with a bizarre reflection of Amy melting away. Behind her, Dameon pressed his hands around her stressed shoulder blades. Her eyes widened. He had taken his clothes off while she struggled with the contacts. She hadn't noticed in her preoccupied state.

"Bold," Emma said. "Do... do you think it's a wise decision, after I said no? We made a deal. You said If I—"

Dameon spun Emma around. He was so close. His gaze didn't give special attention to her naked state, only her green eyes.

"Do you want me to leave?"

"I'm not sure I believe you would, if I said yes."

"I am a naturally dominant person, Emma. Our deal isn't going to change that. But don't you ever think for a single second that you don't get a say. Your consent is valued and important. Never forget that."

Dameon's touch lifted. His hands slowly dropped to his sides, as he straightened his posture. Serious resolve blanketed his face and body.

"I'll go," he asked, more than stated.

"I don't want to be alone," Emma said, softly.

Dameon's mouth twitched briefly down. His hand traced the drawn lines of Elijah's remaining work. He grimaced at the tan that transferred onto his skin. With a reach back, he closed the shower curtain and turned on the water.

"Then get in the shower, little prisoner. I intend to show you what it means to be mine."

Emma felt Dameon's eyes on her as she stepped into the tub.

After Dameon's hand tested the water multiple times to ensure it was set to a comfortably warm temperature, he followed her in. He put his hands on her shoulders and guided her into the steady stream. The warmth trickled against her back as she faced the intense man before her.

"Close your eyes," he said.

She did, but not without some apprehension.

For too long, nothing happened. The tension between her legs, and in her chest, grew with every passing second. Emma flinched as she felt a sudsy cloth touch her stomach. It passed her chest, caressed her neck, and gently scrubbed the caked makeup. He moved in caring circles around her eyes, her cheeks, her mouth. The scent of jasmine filled her nose. The warm cloth rubbed the back of her neck and went back to massaging her muscles into a relaxed state.

"Deep breaths princess."

He guided her into a sweet standing meditation.

More soap married the cloth. Dameon pressed the fibers against her shoulder blades, down her spine, up again to her neck. She inhaled the floral steam as her head rested back. Her breathing quickened as he moved to her chest.

Conflicting feelings complicated her relaxation, as sensual energy was fed to her body. Emma's resolve not to have sex after her substantial meal was beginning to wash away with Amy's makeup.

The cloth stopped. The raining shower cleared the slippery bubbles from her face and torso. Emma opened her eyes, and found Dameon in front of her, staring down at her neck. He brushed his thumb along the healed, no longer existent, line he had given her.

"My temper can get the better of me," he said, in a way that sounded more like a statement than an apology.

"I've noticed," she said, feeling her words touch the tip of his thumb.

"And I have a habit of getting carried away, of taking things too far," he said, before pressing his lips to the bruise.

"I know." she said

"I made you think that I'd give you to Sebastian. Even now, you still believe I'm prepared to take what I want, regardless of your feelings. You don't trust me, fear the control I demand and anger I can be quick to succumb to, and for good reason."

She could feel the pressure of his mouth against her voice. A small moan was let out with Emma's exhale. Dameon made a groan of his own, sending little vibrations through her skin.

"But I need you to tell me the truth, Emma," he whispered, kissing her shoulder. "Did you try to run today?"

Emma's heart raced.

"Yes. I did."

Dameon turned her around, allowing a distance between his chest and hers. He gently ran his hand up, and into her hair. He massaged the place he hurt the last time he suspected her betrayal.

"What stopped you?"

Emma touched Dameon's hand against her hair. He let her lead his hand down to the shoulder he was previously giving attention to.

"I don't know," she said. "It's not some lazy answer, or untruthful. I'm actually not sure why I couldn't leave. Maybe fear, but I don't think that's it. I think some part of me didn't want to go. I could have. You would have chased me, but I might have gotten away. But, for a moment, I didn't want to."

Dameon's expression crossed between pity and overwhelming desire. He moved to her lips and brushed against them with his. She found herself following him. The fear trickled down the drain with the clean water.

"If I asked to have you right now, what would you say," he asked.

Emma started to speak but was cut off again. Dameon pressed Emma against the shockingly cold shower wall. The sudden shift in temperature pebbled her skin.

"Just me. No Matthew or Elijah to hold me back. Would you want me to take you, after everything I've done? Despite all the terrible things you think I'm capable of doing to you?"

Emma was cold, hot, and wet for reasons unrelated to the drops from the showerhead.

"Yes, I would say yes," she breathed.

She reached for his kiss, but Dameon moved just out of reach. He lowered himself to kiss her neck instead.

"But..." he said, letting Emma feel his teeth against her, as he smiled, "you said you weren't in the mood."

Emma reflexively swore under her breath. Dameon stepped away from the shower and grabbed a towel for himself.

"You performed well this morning," he said, to the tortured woman in the water. "With a little training, you might even give Elijah a run for his money. They weren't blowing smoke, you do seem to have a natural talent for playing in the con game, even after the trauma of believing that I would discard you so easily. I clearly, and understandably, have a lot of trust to earn."

Emma glared in devastating frustration.

"So," he said with a grin, "am I safe for another day, or have you decided that I deserve the fullest extent of your wrath, princess?"

Emma crossed her arms angrily.

"Both," she seethed. "You're safe, but that doesn't mean you don't deserve a little wrath."

"Well," he said, cheerfully. "You know where to find me. And for what it's worth, I'm grateful you didn't choose the window. It's nice to hear that, at least a piece of you, chose us."

12 | Partner Up

Emma efficiently, albeit less satisfyingly, finished up where Dameon left off. The man was a total and complete ass. And yet, he kept surprising her. Maybe he wasn't as merciless as she thought? Intrusive, arrogant, unnerving? Absolutely. But under the surface, there was more to him than she expected.

He caught her. He knew she thought about escaping. Her fear of him being sent into a blind rage didn't come to fruition. She was so afraid of what he would do to her when she confirmed his suspicions. Instead, he seemed almost grateful.

His irritating early departure was an attempt to prove his caring regard for her, and her honesty gained a fragment of his trust. It felt good, reassuring. She wanted to believe that he actually cared about her, and wanted that hard-earned piece of him. Between her successful plan, and her decision to stay, she imagined it might actually be achievable.

After a double check to ensure all of the fake tan and makeup was gone, Emma agreed with Matthew's plan to take a short nap. The quick orgasm, and huge steak and eggs breakfast, threatened to send her into a coma. The house was quiet, the pillows were soft, and sleep came quickly. She awoke in a haze a few hours later. Her dream of a spicier version of her last moments with Dameon, evaporated faster than the steam of the shower.

When Emma opened the door to her room, the sounds of yelling and spirited shouting filled the hall. It sounded like fighting. Her heart sank. Would there ever be a calm moment? What could possibly be the newest trouble now? Nervously, she peaked around the corner.

Matthew and Elijah were on the edge of the sofa's seat in the living room. Dameon slouched in the freshly cleaned green chair. Each of the men were in their underwear, confirming Emma's hunch that a more relaxed dress code would be the norm in the home. She couldn't help but feel that it was rather sweet that they felt so comfortable now, and that they were so adamant about dressing appropriately before.

They greeted her absentmindedly when she entered the room, their attention entirely on television. A car racing video game of some type was displayed, the audio roaring as a new round began. Elijah was in the lead, Matthew was close behind. Relief calmed Emma's concern, grateful that the shouting was competitive rather than combative.

As the race progressed, Elijah quickly glanced at Matthew and shot him a look that combined panic and frustration. Significantly far from the pack, Dameon swerved his car on a gravel track, just trying to stay on the road.

"No! No! Damn it!" Dameon yelled, at the large screen.

Matthew jumped from the sofa and made a thrusting motion with his hips. He gloated triumphantly over his win with the most unsportsman-like behavior possible. Elijah grabbed him by the band of his boxer-briefs and aggressively pulled the winner back to the couch.

"Again!" Elijah demanded, already setting up another round.

Dameon deflated into the back of his seat. He held the remote out to Emma, extending an aggravated invitation.

"Just get another controller, don't be a bitch just because you lost," said Elijah, his eyes remaining on the screen.

Dameon rushed Elijah. He straddled the blond and pinned his body against the back of the cushions, knocking the controller from his hands.

Elijah gave Dameon the attention he demanded, but with a type of defiance Emma had yet to witness. Elijah didn't hold the slightest trace of anxiety in his face. He only looked annoyed at Dameon's interruption.

"First off," Dameon said, "I hate this stupid game. Second, are you challenging me," he asked, hotly.

Elijah raised his chin defiantly. Matthew watched with activated attraction. He slid away from the couch and placed Emma between himself and the two gladiators. Emma nearly laughed in disbelief as he comically used Emma as his personal human shield. Matthew wrapped his arms over her shoulders, flashed a playful smile, and went back to watching his two lovers.

"Maybe I am," Elijah taunted.

Dameon glared down at his prey. He was feeding off Elijah's defiance, amplifying his dominating presence. But Elijah didn't waver.

"You just hate that this is the one thing you suck at," said Elijah, with bite in his words.

Dameon's devilish, half crazy grin returned. Elijah raised his chin higher, not backing down. Dameon dragged his tongue along Elijah's defiant jawline.

"I think you know this stupid game isn't the only thing on which I can suck."

Dameon pecked Elijah's lips with a short, mean, kiss. Matthew bent down and whispered in Emma's ear.

"It's fun when it's not you they're playing with, isn't it," he said.

Emma didn't admit it out loud, but yes, she was very much enjoying the show. Seeing Elijah hold his ground against Dameon was exciting. Watching Dameon's sexually explosive behavior turned her on, though she wasn't exactly proud of that fact. Elijah glowered at Dameon.

"I'll take your punishments," he said, fire behind his eyes. "It'll be worth it to see you lose to me again, and again, and again, bitch."

Dameon released Elijah and retrieved a fourth controller from atop the mantle. Dameon plopped it into Emma's hand, clearly insisting her participation. She took the controller, while admitting in advance that video games weren't her strongest suit. Dameon ignored her disclaimer and instructed Elijah to continue setting up the race.

Emma played her best. She struggled initially to gain her bearings, but caught on quickly to the logistics. While in theory, it was simple enough, Matthew and Elijah were clearly the better players. Even through her struggle, Emma surprised herself by placing better than Dameon time after time.

Dameon placed better than her only a few times, but after placing in dead last in the latest round, Emma felt like a break was due. She dropped out of the game and strolled off to the kitchen. She popped open the stainless steel refrigerator door, looking for something to drink.

Emma's skin sparked when Dameon, surprisingly, kissed the back of her neck.

"I couldn't help but notice that you ended on a loss. Either you're a sore loser like me, or you are nervous about potentially joining Elijah tonight."

Emma shimmied away, with an air of confidence.

"Neither," she said. "Maybe, just maybe, I didn't want to feel bad about beating you again. You're kind of awful. It's almost sad."

Dameon pulled Emma out of the fridge, slammed the door closed, and pressed against her. Her exposed skin chilled against the steel. His groin met hers in a single push. Elijah hopped onto the counter and crossed his legs. All he needed was popcorn to complete his look of enjoying his own personal show.

Dameon wrapped his hands around her wrists, and pressed her palms over his bare chest as he teased.

"Since you seem to enjoy that stupid game as much as I do," he growled, "is there anything else you'd rather do?"

Emma thought seriously about the question. She wasn't massively fond of the video game, and she was horny as hell, but there was a comfort in participating in an activity that didn't directly involve sex. She wanted more of that, something fun, something... Dameon noticed the lightbulb that flashed figuratively above her head.

He raised an inquisitive brow, and released her. Emma hurried off to retrieve the penthouse tablet. She pulled up the endless choices of music, and handed the device eagerly to Dameon. Matthew peaked over Dameon's shoulder to see what Emma had in mind.

"I would rather dance," she said.

Emma felt a little self conscious. She couldn't place why, but her request suddenly felt like a childish alternative in comparison to what Dameon was clearly suggesting. Matthew leaned over the counter, crossed his arms, and stretched his back.

"What kind of dancing did you have in mind," the large man asked, intrigued.

"Anything really. I mean, I don't know how to ballroom dance, or anything like that. If you're going to ask, dancing sounds... nice. But now that I say it out loud, it sounds a little silly."

Dameon, Matthew, and Elijah exchanged excited smiles. Emma pessimistically wondered if, whatever they had in mind, was about to dash her hopes of the different kind of intimacy she was looking for.

Dameon's finger scrolled quickly, and found its target. The sounds of piano keys, brass, woodwinds, strings, and percussion instruments bounced off the walls. The classical style was not what she was expecting. As she listened more closely, she realized that the song was a clever, wordless, cover of a modern pop hit.

Her heart filled with excitement as she watched Dameon give an exaggerated bow to Matthew. His partner returned the gesture, and the pair linked up to dance. They looked like absolute professionals, smooth, graceful, and shockingly knowledgeable. Elijah bounced off and away from the counter. He picked Emma up, dangled her feet, and spun her around. She leaned against Elijah as her feet found the floor again.

"Follow me," he instructed.

The palm of Elijah's hand pressed gently against hers. With an instructive push backwards, her right foot mirrored his left, to step behind her. A pull to the side swept Emma to the left. Then with a little pull, he guided her forward. Emma's happiness forced a giggle, as Elijah counted steadily to three. They repeated the pattern to the right and back, to the left and forward, over and over. Their feet, mimicking the shape of a box.

Elijah approvingly smiled at her natural inclination.

"This is a waltz. They are some of the simplest steps. A good con man always has the basics in his back pocket."

They followed the sweet sounds, gracefully, with minimal error. Elijah directed her from the kitchen, to the dining room. They ended up in the circular space between the grand staircases. Her expectations were blown out of the water. She loved this.

The music shifted. As it did, Dameon flawlessly cut in and took the lead of Emma. She needed a few moments to readjust to the new, quicker, feel of the Cha Cha. Dameon patiently and playfully corrected her feet, until she found the natural rhythm of the dance. Matthew and Elijah spun more elaborately and showed off with glee. Emma smiled freely and genuinely, with the burst of serotonin the quick spins provided.

Dameon laughed sweetly at the sight of Emma enjoying herself so fully, and spun her over and over until she lost her balance. She tripped over his feet, falling into him, as he held her and waited for her world to stop swaying. Emma's dizziness invited a hard laugh of her own. Dameon pressed his hand to hers and continued their playful routine.

When the music switched again, Matthew took his turn. His cocky expression sent flutters to her stomach. He pulled Emma closer than the rest. His hand pressed against her upper back. One leg invaded the space between hers.

"And this is how we Tango. It's my personal favorite."

He never let more than a few inches separate their moving bodies. Her right foot stepped back, then left, right, left, to the side. The slow, slow, quick, quick, slow, rhythms created a sensual nature greater than the previous dances. Emma wasn't sure if her quickening heart rate was due to the dancing itself, or the feeling of Matthew being so incredibly close. When she looked into his golden eyes, Emma could swear she saw a glimmer of the same feelings just behind his gaze.

Sultry sounds went on and on, and led the participants in a glorious trance, encouraging them to dance for the remainder of their lives. Nevertheless, Dameon led with a promenade, and elegant turn, back to the tablet. Each step hit in time without a pause to his own perfect execution with Elijah. Matthew and Emma followed their lead, Emma pursing her lips together in an attempt to hold back another joyful laugh. The playlist slowed to a close.

Before Dameon picked a new set of songs, he lifted Elijah and sat him atop the large island counter. He jumped, and lifted himself up, to sit next to his partner. Matthew lifted Emma at the waist and added her to the collection, then joined them to complete the set. Dameon's next pick was an explosive change of pace. Electric guitars blasted through the penthouse speakers.

Dameon tossed the tablet to the side and stood on the sturdy island top. The others followed. Matthew's hand reached out for Emma to join, happily doing so.

Matthew played an imaginary guitar. The powerful sounds of the instrumental cover screamed. The four wildly jumped and moved to the new jam pulsing through their bodies. Elijah danced like the crowned prince of the art. Slightly off pitch but, eagerly encouraged, Emma belted the missing words from the track.

Dameon reached out, and snatched Emma, pulling her close. With euphoric energy, he sang with her in an improvised duet. A spin and tight hold around her waist, directed her to Elijah, who continued the vocals in Dameon's place. Dameon playfully danced against her. Emma pressed back into his body while Elijah continued to serenade. The quartet danced their hearts out. They sang at the top of their lungs to rock, country, and pop, and every other genre that dared to exist.

Dameon introduced lightly-poured margaritas to the party. He winked at Emma, who caught him make a separate, completely non-alcoholic drink for himself. Elijah whipped up colorful Mediterranean wraps, never giving his swinging hips a moment to rest. The festivities continued well into the night, only barely breaking for each to catch their breath, eat, and drink. The temperature of the room heightened. The planes sparkled in the night sky. Casinos dazzled through the windows with their neon glows.

Eventually, the party animals sprawled out on the round sofas. Smiling and breathing abnormally after the considerable cardio, Emma curled up under Matthew's arm. The music shifted into a quieter, slower, ambiance. Elijah snuggled against Dameon with a lazy grip.

As the moment wound down, her mind began to wander. The dance party was wonderful, fun, and beautifully innocent. But the thought crossed her mind, that it never would have happened if she followed through with her escape. Where would she be now if she had? In a police station? Finding a way to get back at Grant? Still running? No secrets.

"I... um..." she said uneasily. "I think I need to come clean about something."

Elijah's relaxed demeanor left his body. Matthew didn't cease holding her, but she could feel a muscle in his arm twitch, while maintaining his gentle hold.

Dameon grinned. It occurred to Emma that he was waiting for this. He was hoping she would out herself. He wanted to see if she would admit, to Matthew and Elijah, what she already admitted to him in the shower.

"I thought about running away today. I almost did."

"When," Matthew asked.

"When I went to the bathroom," Emma said. "It had a window. I was halfway out before I decided to come back."

An uncomfortable lack of words lingered, as low music continued to play. Emma's bicep unintentionally tensed, as Matthew's resting arm held tighter. She looked up to see him staring at Dameon. Elijah's eyes darted from Matthew to the man holding him. The two gained a nervousness, as they waited to see what their leader's reaction might be. Dameon adjusted into a further relaxing position, pulling Elijah closer as he did.

"Twenty-four hours," Dameon said. "That's what I was willing to give you, before I would say something, myself. I have to admit, I wasn't sure you'd tell them."

"You knew," Matthew asked, a hint of offense in his voice.

"Yes. I was entirely committed to telling you, but I wanted to give Emma a fair chance to do it first."

"Why," Elijah asked. "Were you afraid we'd catch you? I mean, we probably would have. But, what stopped you from trying?"

"No, or at least not completely. It wasn't just the fear of being caught I think... I think something in me actually wanted to stay."

Elijah's face showed a mix of pity and profound grateful feelings. His fears that revolved around allowing Emma out into the world weren't unfounded. But when offered the chance, she didn't take it. She chose them. Maybe it wasn't entirely with the most positive emotions on her part, but she did. If that wasn't the ultimate display of being trustworthy, she didn't know what else could be.

Elijah smiled through a stifled yawn, when Dameon tapped him on the leg with a playful slap.

"Well," Dameon said, "Thank you for this wonderful evening. It's been too long since we've danced like that. However, I'm afraid Elijah and I have some business to take care of, before he gets too tired to be any fun. And unlike you, he doesn't have a window to escape from, so—"

"Really," Elijah asked, with a groan and eye roll. "I don't suppose you would consider letting this one go?"

Dameon roughly kissed his cheek.

"Not a chance, Angel. Go to my room, I'll be there in a second."

Elijah got up lazily and started towards the stairs. Dameon wickedly grinned.

"And don't even think about falling asleep. I have plans for you."

Elijah let out another groan, waved, and blew a kiss good-night to Matthew and Emma, before disappearing to the second floor. Dameon stood next and stretched his back, his arms extending above his head. His defined abs showed off in a way that Emma guessed was entirely on purpose. Before leaving, his lips pressed to Matthew's.

"Good night lovers. And Emma," he said, grabbing her chin and giving her a far lighter kiss, "I'm proud of you. You really are a beautiful addition to our family."

Half way to the stairs, Dameon turned back, addressing Emma as he continued backwards with beckoning arms.

"You're welcome to watch again if you want. I can't promise it'll be pretty, but the offer is open. All you have to do is knock."

Once Dameon was out of sight. Emma tossed around the idea of watching what was in store for Elijah. Did she want to see? She wasn't sure if she felt any comfort in seeing Matthew's treatment be imparted on Elijah. An inkling of worry for him tugged at her heart. But maybe with her greater insight to Dameon, this time it would be different?

A tap on Emma's leg, signaled that Matthew was about to leave too. Emma's heart sank. She didn't want the day to end, and she wasn't entirely sure that he wasn't upset with her over the Huevos incident.

"I'll be in my room tonight," Matthew said, casually. "Try not to forget that this place is as much yours as it is ours. You can sleep in your room, wherever you want. Dameon and Elijah will definitely end up in his room for the night, so our shared room will be empty too."

"Wait. You aren't mad at me for trying to leave?"

He kissed her forehead, and smiled sweetly.

"How could I be angry that you chose us," he said. "Sleep well, princess."

Emma took a speedy shower, to rinse herself of the sweat that salted her skin from the dance. She dried, and laid naked in her white sheets. She looked around the room with new eyes, imagining the potential. Could she really make this room as hers, as Matthew and Elijah did for theirs? She tossed and turned, thinking about what her private sanctuary might look like. She couldn't make it more than an hour, before getting to her feet and leaving her room.

The penthouse was dark, apart from the ever present moon beams. Walking up the stairs without light brought back memories of the first night she snuck from her room. Seeing Elijah, Matthew, and Dameon naked, intruding on Dameon's private punishing session with Matthew, so much had changed since then. It wasn't really that long ago, yet so much had changed.

Emma thought of how much she may have already missed of Dameon and Elijah's activities. What exactly did the dom have in mind for his angel? He mentioned "sucking" during their game-time teasing, but how "punishing" could receiving a blow job from Dameon actually be? She imagined Dameon, his mouth taking in Elijah. Elijah, his beautiful golden curls, head back, his lustful groans, and being consumed with pleasure.

Emma knocked on the door. She wasn't sure what she would say. An awkwardness hit her stomach when it opened. A terrible feeling came over her, that she was intruding. Even after everything, she felt nervous at the idea of potentially being rejected when the door opened.

"I was," Emma said, shyly, "lonely." She cringed at her own words. "I was wondering if it would be alright if I–"

Matthew looked down lovingly at the green-eyed woman and gestured for her to come in.

Matthew closed the door behind Emma. His room was naturally darker than hers. The view of the strip added a permanent glow to her room. His desert view offered little light, blanketing the room in total darkness. At least, it would have been completely dark, if not for a significantly sized, highly detailed, moon-shaped, lamp next to his bed. Its deep yellow color bathed Emma's bare body in warm light.

"Dameon said you use your rooms when you need time to yourself. If you would rather be alone, I don't want to intrude."

Matthew brought Emma into a squeezing hug. His naked body smelled like sandalwood and a hint of coconut.

"We do, but that's not the only reason. Sometimes our rooms can let us have one on one time if we want. On nights like tonight, Dameon usually enjoys using his own room."

Emma relaxed under Matthew's warmth.

"I'm glad you're here," he said. "I don't really like to sleep alone either, and that big bed is a little much for one person, even me."

A loud swear from Elijah pierced the barriers the walls were meant to provide. Emma tensed. Elijah sounded strained, almost painfully so. What if Dameon was overdoing it? Emma recalled the memory of Matthew, barely able to breathe under Dameon's tight ropes. Matthew rubbed a large hand up and down Emma's back.

"He's fine," he said, with a breathy laugh. "I'd only be worried if Elijah said the safeword more than once. If he does, I'll check on them. But if he doesn't we can both assume that, despite the sounds, Elijah is fine."

Matthew turned to the California-king sized bed. He cozily invaded the space between the sheets and the comforter, then patted the mattress for Emma to join him.

Emma fit her lower body into his. Matthew snuggled her closer, molding her into his space. Emma reached for the moon-light on the bedside table, but Matthew snatched her hand. He wasn't gentle. His grip was too firm. He realized his mistake quickly, and released Emma's hand. With a hold that was still a little too tight, he held her shoulder instead.

"I'm sorry," he said. "I–"

Emma waited patiently for Matthew to find the right words. When he spoke, he sounded vulnerable and embarrassed.

"I don't like the dark."

Emma silently recalled the dim lights Dameon left on, during the night of their slumber party. She thought back to the day of the robbery, and what she read in Matthew's diary. "Is it because of when you lived in tunnels?"

The air in the room chilled.

"You left your door open, when you were out for the heist. I read some of the first journal. I feel pretty bad about it now. It was a pretty big invasion of privacy."

Emma stared at the closed door to the room. She felt Matthew take in a deep breath.

His hand slid away from her shoulder, to her neck, and a little too roughly played with her blonde hair. Matthew shook slightly. Being unable to see his face, she wasn't sure if he was shaking out of anger, nervousness, or embarrassment. He rolled her over to face him and continued to tangle her hair.

"How much did you read?"

Emma's stomach tied in knots, worse than the mess Matthew's restricting hand was making in her hair.

"Just the start. I saw what you did to your father, that you were homeless, and that you don't like the dark. That's as far as I got."

Matthew pressed his lips to Emma's forehead, then lightly brushed his nose against hers.

"It's not a secret, what I am, and what I can do. But if I'd rather not talk about it in detail, not yet, if that's acceptable to you. But please," he said, without really asking, "don't ever read another page."

Emma's heart pounded.

"I won't."

Matthew's grip tightened. A sharp breath sounded from Emma. Her fingers slid between his arm hair and his skin. Gliding ever so gently, she reached up to his hand and pressed him even closer to her head. His tense fingers relaxed with her touch. With the limited movement she was given, her face tilted to kiss the inner wrist of his arm.

"I won't do it again," she said. "I can understand not wanting to talk about it, but I do know what it's like to have a shitty father. I may not have killed mine, but... but I did burn his house down. I destroyed everything, and I wished that he burned with it. I've never told anyone that before, but it feels fair that I tell you mine, after reading yours."

Emma's hair was released. Matthew searched her face, trying to find words of his own. He moved in closer, resting his forehead to hers.

"Consider us even, Emma. I'm sorry, but there are terrible things in those journals. More than personal revenge is written in those pages. The people I've hurt, killed, and I... I don't want you to see what I wrote about them, or the things I wrote about you."

How could she not ask? You can't drop a couple of lines like that and expect nothing in return. Matthew saw Emma's struggle, and braced for the expected questions. She was following their honesty rule better than any of them could have expected. He knew he would be compelled to answer if she asked, and could see that she couldn't help herself.

"What kind of things? Not every detail, but I am curious, about what you wrote about me."

Matthew shut his eyes and made little creases in his face.

"It isn't good."

He looked into her forest-green eyes, curiosity begging for elaboration and created a few inches of space between them.

"I wrote about being pissed that Dameon wouldn't let me kill you."

She already knew about his early solution to get rid of her, but the words still managed to hurt and stir up traces of uneasiness.

"Then, after a bit, I started dreaming about you. I wrote down those dreams. They were violent and... I dreamed it, I wrote it, but I swear, I would never—"

Though Matthew's hand was no longer holding her back, her hair remained twisted around his fingers. Emma pushed through the pain of his presence in her hair, and reached to kiss his lips. Matthew let go of the strands only to press her body closer to his.

Emma ran her fingers through his chest hair and up to his neck. Her tongue found his. She bit his bottom lip, then looked into Matthew's eyes.

"Don't apologize for the things you want."

Strong hands pulled and rotated Emma to her back. Matthew hovered over her, hard and intimidating. He took in the curves of her body in the glowing yellow light. Butterflies filled her stomach. Her core clenched. She shivered between the arms of her captor, a murderer, the subject of so many of her nightmares, and fantasies. Emma's voice shook more than she wanted it to.

"Show me, Matthew, the things you want."

"Why? What would make you ask for something like that?"

Emma took a moment to think about it. Why would she ask something like that? Good question. She wasn't entirely sure. She only knew she wanted him, and always let her curiosity get the better of her. Maybe she just wanted to prove to him that she could trust him enough to ask? He was the one that set the precedent in the first place.

"You make me feel safe. Don't ask me why, I don't fully understand it either. You can be really scary when you want to be, and yet—"

Elijah cursed, loudly, desperately, again. The sound took Emma's attention. She looked in the direction of the shout, as if she could see through the headboard if she willed it hard enough.

Matthew grabbed an object from inside the drawer of the bedside table. Her reflexes responded with natural panic, when she heard the click of a switchblade open. Instinctively, Emma reached for the blade. Matthew caught her hands and pinned them above her head. Her breathing quickened. Her heart pounded.

"Do you still want to know what I've thought of doing with you? I'll understand if it's too much, given your history here. But if you really want to know–"

Emma could hear the sincerity in his voice. He wasn't challenging, or teasing, like she imagined Dameon would have been. He was gently, and sweetly, giving her a chance to stop it all before it began. Emma relaxed her arms best she could, but wasn't very successful.

"Yes. I do. I want to know."

Matthew closed his amber eyes. When he opened them, a previously restrained part of him was given permission to come out. Emma could see the little change, as he expertly twirled and snapped the weapon around his fingers.

"Are you scared," he asked, with a little more darkness in his throat.

"Yes," Emma breathed.

Matthew rested the cold of the knife against the tip of her left breast, hardening her nipple beneath it. Her sharp breaths sounded audibly. Her sex buzzed, and quickly became wet. She liked it. Why did she like it? Matthew teased her other side next, circling around the delicate area with the sharp tip of the blade.

"And," he said, in a dangerous voice, "do you trust me?"

Emma lost her ability to speak. She tried, but only trembling breaths could be produced as the blade skated side to side, moving a little lower with each pass.

Matthew was careful to never break her skin, but pressed just enough to leave the faintest pink trail. Matthew bared his teeth, looking like a predator ready to strike its prey. Emma's heart skipped a beat when he harshly devoured her mouth with his. His long hair isolated her face from the world.

Panting from both parties followed the hard kiss. A gasp escaped from Emma when Matthew stabbed the switchblade into the mattress. It was close enough to her side that she could feel its handle with every breath she took. His hands detained her hips as he pushed open her previously closed legs with his own. He readied himself near her opening.

"I asked, do you trust me?"

She did. She knew he could hurt her. He could break her. He could cut her to pieces, and yet she did trust him. So she answered with honesty.

"Yes."

Resolve graced Matthew's face.

"Do you want me," he asked.

"Yes. I trust you not to give me any more than my body can take. And yes, Matthew, I want you."

Matthew parted her with himself. Emma whimpered and tugged on the sheets below her as she felt Matthew push slowly in.

He was harder to take without lube, even wet as she was. He was almost too much. Matthew took it slow and gave her time to be ready for more. He filled her so tremendously. Despite being nowhere near her lungs, his hardness took her breath from her, making her gasp as he entered more and more. Strained, faint, cries left her lips. He let her hips move him in and out, getting used to what he could offer.

She tensed around his hardness and whimpered, as he pulled her hips to him, and pushed as far as her body would allow.

He pushed, pulled, and pushed, until her legs began to quiver and she let out tiny shouts of approval. Matthew picked Emma up, and wrapped her legs around his sides. He sat upright, his hard cock inside of her. Small sounds escaped her, as they shifted, trying desperately to take all of him. His full beard scratched at her, as his mouth played around her neck. She rocked her hips, driving him in and out in heavy breaths.

Matthew retrieved the switchblade. He held it, and traced the curve of her spine from her ass to her neck with the cold blade. Her skin reacted with the tiniest of bumps. Emma arched away from the blade on instinct. As she did, her breasts were shown off in a dramatic display.

Begging moans came from Emma, as Matthew took a breast in his mouth, knife still at her back. She felt its threatening sides press between her shoulders. Her moans turned to rhythmic cries, as she rode Matthew with increased vigor. He pressed Emma down to the bed. With one hand he rubbed his thumb against her clitoris, but with the other, he positioned the knife above her navel.

Just below her bellybutton he pressed the tip of the blade. Nervous hums pleaded in Emma's throat. Her skin started to strain against the steel. Her trembling fingers moved up her sides, and lightly touched the shimmering weapon.

The little circles of his thumb forced pleasure filled moans from her lips. Nervousness and the uncontrollable closeness of an orgasm mingled. He hadn't cut her, yet, but a sharp pain was beginning to take hold as he pushed the knife ever closer. A small whine escaped her lips as her legs tensed and her fingers inched up to the hand that threatened.

Matthew slammed the blade on the near table. Not a single drop of blood was taken as he did. Matthew wrapped his fingers around her neck. She pushed him into her, harder, nearly cumming. Matthew tightened his grip, expertly restricting her air and blood flow.

Roughly, mercilessly, he drove into her, again, and again. She choked on the breath she couldn't find. Her eyes watered, a few stray tears dampening her hair. Her legs begged to run but only slid against the bedding. Her sex greedily accepted Matthew's penetration. Her heart pounded hard with the rough treatment.

The yellow moon began to turn gray. Matthew spilled himself into Emma, and as he did, his squeezing hand released. Air rushed into her lungs. Endorphins flooded her brain. An orgasm more powerful than she had ever experienced before, forced a high scream. She pushed as hard as she could against Matthew, pulsing around him. Her legs pressed against him, as she continued to take every bit of him that he could give.

Matthew pressed his lips hard against her neck, then to her ear, where his words came out in a low rumble.

"I love the way you cum on me, little prisoner."

Emma swore. Every bit of her trembled bordering convolutions.

Slowly, messily, Matthew pulled himself out, and reached for the knife once more. Her chest rose and fell heavily, as he carefully placed the blade at her opening. Emma's bliss began to slip to fear.

"Don't move," he instructed.

Emma stilled best she could, but couldn't keep her body from shaking. She felt the tip of the metal against the lowermost point of her sex. She trusted him. She repeated it in her mind. She trusted him. He wouldn't. He wouldn't hurt her. She trusted him. When the pressure of the blade increased, her mantra wavered. Her voice cracked, and was raspy as she spoke.

"M... Matthew."

The mountain of a man hushed her sweetly, as he dragged the blade up, wetting it with their combined mess. His steady hand remained careful never to let it cut, or enter, her. Matthew lifted the glimmering switchblade and examined it, biting his lower lip briefly. He brought the blade up, and held it to her mouth.

"I want to see you taste us," he said.

Where the blade remained untouched by their climax, Emma's breath fogged its mirror finish. Her lower lip trembled slightly as she stuck out her tongue and licked the blunt side of the blade.

She swallowed their sticky conclusion, feeling his gaze as she did. Matthew threw the blade to the floor and kissed her feverishly, wrapping her tightly in his arms. When he attempted to release her, Emma desperately clung to him. Matthew kissed her cheek, and gently ran his fingers through her hair until her racing heart, and heavy breathing, eventually started to calm.

"Thank you, little prisoner. Thank you, for trusting me."

13 | Play Games Win Prizes

Dameon descended the stairs to find Emma and Matthew cuddled close on one of the curved sofas, with closed eyes. A plate of half eaten pancakes sat on the round table. He caught a peak across the penthouse at the kitchen counter. A discarded bowl that once contained batter, and a stack of enough fluffy breakfast to feed an army, was left out for anyone to grab.

Dameon ran a hand through Matthew's hair. The large man looked up and kissed the side of Dameon's palm, careful not to wake up Emma. It was useless. She picked her head up and smiled sleepily at the intruder.

"Good morning," she said, with a stretch of her shoulder.

Interest and curiosity gleamed in Dameon's eyes. He tilted Emma chin up to see new light bruising around her neck. It was incredibly faint, but just present enough for him to take notice. Dameon raised an eyebrow, and looked provokingly at Matthew. Emma reclaimed herself and snuggled harder into Matthew's warm chest.

"Don't worry," she said, closing her eyes again. "Everything is good."

Dameon chuckled and kissed the top of her head. When Elijah came down, he instantly noticed the smell of pancakes. He sighed with a prolonged, "Yesssss," and grabbed a plate.

"Wait," Elijah said, taking a seat on the sofa across from Matthew and Emma. "Who made these?"

"Emma," Matthew laughed. "Don't worry, I didn't touch them."

"You know cooking is a basic life skill," Dameon smiled.

"Microwaves and cereal exist for a reason," Matthew said.

"I assure you," said Elijah, with a mouth full, "those options are vastly overrated."

Elijah snuck an apologetic look towards Emma, on behalf of the awful cook in the family. Emma smiled back and snuggled deeper into Matthew. Dameon joined in the cozy breakfast together.

Emma's eyes popped open, remembering that Elijah may not have partaken in a night as enjoyable as her own. He looked fine, normal. Elijah caught her stare and puckered his lips. He read her mind with lightning quick analysis.

"Sorry if I distressed you last night. Actually, no. I'm not really. But an apology seemed fitting. It was this guy's fault anyway."

Emma observed the man, as Elijah mimicked her position and placed Dameon's arm around him to cuddle. Emma wondered if Dameon wasn't really as scary as he made himself out to be. Maybe Matthew really did enjoy himself during Dameon's so-called punishment. It certainly looked as if Elijah didn't have signs of any major damage or trauma. He looked just as loving and adoring as ever.

Matthew rubbed Emma's shoulder and repositioned himself to get off the couch. Emma nonverbally complained with a groan.

"Sorry princess," he said, sweetly. "I'd love to stay and lay with you all day, but I have been neglecting the gym for a little too long. If I don't get up and do it now, I'll probably end up staying here forever."

Emma pouted in jest.

"Aw," said Elijah, in that teasing way he was a little too good at. "What a mean man. Leaving this poor girl all by herself!"

Matthew rolled his eyes and headed upstairs to the mirror lined room. Elijah slithered out from under Dameon's arm. He crawled over the table, and onto the other sofa to hover over Emma.

"Careful," he said, mischievously. "If you keep looking at him like that, we are liable to get jealous. We might start to think that you like him more than you like us."

Emma's eyes darted to Dameon who watched the two like an entertaining show.

Emma looked back at Elijah, nervously, and shimmied back into the cushions for an inch of more space.

"You do, don't you? I have to say, I thought it would be me. I stitched you up, cared for you, protected you from your favorite while he was feeling murderous. I gave you a person you didn't have to worry about trying to sleep with you. And you favor him," Elijah asked, with a feral smile.

"Elijah," Dameon warned.

Elijah turned his head to Dameon, in minor annoyance. Dameon tapped his fingers against the armrest of the sofa. Amusement overlapped his cautious tone.

"You aren't being very fair, Angel."

Elijah snapped back to stare down at Emma. His shoulders relaxed. His face changed to something a little more sweet, but there was something disingenuous about his demeanor.

"It's okay honey," he said, with a quick kiss. "I don't blame you. He is impressive. He just has that special... Well, he is quite a bit bigger than us isn't he?"

Dameon laughed loudly at the progression.

"No!" Emma started. "I mean, yes he is, but no that's not why I–"

"I knew it! You do like him more. So tell me, is that why you decided to pay him a visit last night instead of us? I wasn't the only one making a bit of noise last night."

Elijah grinned sneakily. Emma blushed.

He won again. This game had Emma's head spinning. She had never been in a relationship with more than one person. What if she was breaking some kind of unspoken rule about not favoring one over another? Not that she did, did she? No, she liked each of them, just in different ways. It was too early to try thinking about this potentially complicated dilemma.

"Okay, okay," Dameon interrupted. "That's enough," he said casually. "Quit trying to pick on her over the dynamics of this relationship. It's cute how eager you are to dominate though. It's a new look for you. I like it."

Elijah took an imaginary hit to the chest.

"Cute?"

Dameon grinned in a way that reminded both who the most intimidating person would always be. Elijah held an expression that mixed irritation and the desire to antagonize the man.

"Between us, Emma," Dameon continued, "I don't think you have to be too concerned. His bark is worse than his bite."

Dameon stood from the couch. He reached to the ceiling and stretched his arms.

"My bite on the other hand—"

Dameon slid a hand over Elijah's shirt.

Elijah tensed at his touch. Emma could feel his nerves pass from his body to hers. Dameon traced his fingers up Elijah's spine, and rested an open palm on his shoulder, causing him to wince and hiss in pain. Emma's heart broke at the sound.

Dameon motioned for Emma to follow him into the study. Elijah moved, permitting her to leave the sofa. He followed the two, tilted his head and furrowed his brows. He watched as Dameon took a seat at the chessboard again behind the black pieces.

"Oh," he said, with a bucket full of sass. "So I can't risk scaring her with my games, but you can play yours?"

Dameon smiled, devilishly.

Emma took the chair behind the white pieces.

Elijah selected a blank canvas, and began dispensing a sunset pallet of colors. Emma pushed a pawn to begin the game. Dameon followed. Moments of silence passed with only the sounds of clicking pieces, Elijah's brush swiping across the blank space, and the occasional tapping of his water glass to clean the paint.

Elijah looked cautiously at the game.

"But really," he said, "You're so concerned with traumatizing the princess, but you want to play her?"

Dameon grinned and said nothing. Black's bishop took white's knight. White's rook took black's bishop.

"And it looks like she's playing to win," Elijah said, as he blended his orange into his yellow sky.

"What's so bad about winning every once in a while," Emma asked, coyly.

Elijah stopped and examined Emma for a moment. The game was moving quickly. Pieces were taken. Progressions were made. Dameon grew serious, realizing that she may have been an even greater opponent than he originally gave her credit for. Elijah broke the silence again.

"Why don't we use the term penis as much as we use, say, cock or dick?"

Dameon and Emma unsuccessfully tried to suppress their laughs. Neither wanted to be immature teenagers, but they couldn't help themselves. Dameon, never taking his eyes off the board, responded with attempted seriousness.

"There is nothing sexy about the word penis."

Elijah abandoned his unfinished work, and stood behind Dameon.

"Sure there is. It's just the anatomically correct name."

Dameon let out a breath of amusement and slight irritation.

"Would you prefer if I sucked your penis, or sucked your dick," Dameon asked, simply.

White progressed. Elijah gave a wink for only Emma to see, letting her in on yet another game he was playing. It was constant with him. Did he never tire of it?

"So you're telling me," he said, as he slid a hand over, then under Dameon's shirt, "that there is nothing sexy about this?"

He ran his hand slowly down Dameon's well defined front.

"You don't like when I touch the smooth skin over your tight abdominal muscles?" Dameon moved and lost his queen. Elijah went lower, reaching into Dameon's pants.

"When I massage your sensitive testicles, making your penis grow in my fucking hand? The feeling of me teasing the tip of your penis with my thumb?"

Dameon inhaled deeply, letting his head fall back into the crook of Elijah's neck. Elijah deviously nibbled at Dameon's ear and whispered.

"Penissss."

Both Emma and Dameon laughed. Elijah cut off the amused sounds by grabbing Dameon harder. Dameon groaned. He snapped his hand up to pull a fistful of Elijah's blond curly hair, and lowered his angel so that he could growl into Elijah's ear.

"You're cheating, Elijah," he said through gritted teeth. "There's nothing fucking sexy about anything you just said. You're just playing dirty."

Elijah wickedly smiled, looking at the board.

"You caught me, but I'm not the only one here willing to take advantage of you. I may not be a great chess player, but it looks to me like our Emma is willing to play dirty too," he said, slyly.

Elijah released Dameon. The overly competitive man looked back at his game, then at Emma. A white queen stood defiantly before a black king and two rooks. Dameon looked genuinely shocked to have been bested at his favorite game.

"And look at that," Elijah said, jokingly. "This one is you," he said, pointing out the helpless king, "And these two rooks are us. Look at how the sweet princess turned into a queen and dominated us all. But hey, at least... I'm... cute."

Emma wasn't appreciative of Elijah's commentary. But he was right, Emma had won. The flames behind Dameon's eyes returned. Emma began to regret her ambition.

"Dameon," Elijah said, with a sudden change of tone. "I was just playing. It's just chess. You said it yourself, we probably shouldn't–"

Dameon rose quickly from his chair, scraping it loudly against the floor as he did.

"Upstairs," he demanded. "Now."

Emma didn't move.

"Dameon," Elijah tried again.

Dameon didn't give Elijah any mind. He swept Emma up in his arms, and proceeded to carry her out of the study.

"Wait, wait! Hang on a minute," Elijah said, following close behind. "I get it. I got a little manipulative and played dirty. This is your game. I get it. But she's not like us. You can't–"

With a scan of his eye, Dameon opened the door to a room she hadn't seen before. He deposited Emma into the room, and blocked Elijah from entering with one hand on the door. Elijah's expression was serious in a way that scared Emma.

"I know it's not fair. We've been playing around a lot with her. I've been playing. But you can't do this. You can't play your games with her, Dameon. She's already here against her will. It's not the same as playing with us."

With his free hand, Dameon grabbed Elijah's face and roughly kissed him.

"Don't worry, Angel, I won't get too carried away. I'll just give her a taste of what I give you and Matthew. Besides, the lady won, she deserves to be rewarded. Wouldn't you agree?"

Elijah swore as Dameon pushed Elijah away and locked the sturdy door. A frustrated kick hit the door with a thud. Elijah's' muffled voice informed Dameon that he didn't like what was happening, and that he would be getting Matthew. Dameon only laughed and encouraged him to do whatever he needed to feel better.

The room resembled the study more than it did any of the fellow bedrooms. Deep browns and maroon colors covered the orderly space. Bookcases lined the walls, packed to the brim with fiction and non-fiction hardcovers. A dark bed proudly displayed iron bars for the base and headboard of the frame. Pillows and blankets of deep reds, purples, and black neatly rested atop the large mattress.

Dameon's face kept an analytical expression, as he turned to Emma.

"Are you upset with me? I mean, did I break the rule by using your distraction to my advantage?"

Dameon shook his head.

"Not in the least. You played well. You didn't break any rule by knowing how to win. However," he said, taking a step towards her, "I feel inclined to congratulate you for a job so well done. But, I also have the greatest desire to punish you because, as my partners love to point out, I am a sore loser."

Emma's blood chilled.

"Take off your clothes," he demanded, as he removed his own.

"And if I don't?"

Dameon grinned.

"I could take them off for you if you'd like."

Curiosity is a remarkable thing. Emma was horribly, painfully, terrified, but a part of her wanted to see what he would do next. What made the other men so nervous, yet still defend him? They both agreed he could get carried away. Would he get carried away with her? What did he do that worried them enough to try to protect her, while leaving them coming back for more?

Emma pulled her top over her head and stepped out of her underwear. Dameon moved past her, making her flinch as he did. He opened the drawer of a cabinet that matched the surrounding decor. Dameon rummaged through it for only a few seconds before pulling two ropes from the dark, wooden, furniture.

Emma panicked and tripped over her own feet, falling back and to the floor. Dameon descended on her as she crawled backwards. She trapped herself when she ran out of room, her back pressed against the wall.

"Wait! Wait!"

Dameon swung one of the smooth ropes behind her neck and shimmied it down to her waist, grabbing her hands as he moved.

"Please," she shook out. "Dameon, I'm… I'm scared."

The dark-haired man looked hungrily at her. He inhaled deeply and rolled his shoulders back.

"What are the safewords?"

Emma trembled in his hands.

"Dameon, when I watched you use the ropes on Matthew–"

He kissed the top of her head lightly.

"The safewords, say them."

"Yellow and red," she whispered.

"Good girl," he smiled.

"Please," Dameon said, smoothly, "Dameon stop, I can't take anymore, it hurts. These words will not help you. Do you understand?"

Emma nodded her head, feeling the words, yellow and red, on the tip of her tongue.

"You know the routine, little prisoner. I need to hear you say it. Do you understand?"

Emma's green eyes locked on to the deep-blue pair staring back, waiting for her to give her consent.

"Yes," she said.

Dameon waited a moment before speaking again.

"If you are too afraid, if this is too much, tell me now. Say red. Say it to me, and I will let you go right now. I'll back off. Is that what you want?"

"You promise it won't hurt," she asked, softly.

Dameon smiled with pity in his face.

"No. In fact, I'd be more inclined to promise you just the opposite. I can see you holding the final safeword in your mouth. You're thinking it. I won't stop you. I won't be upset. Just say it."

Emma swallowed hard and spoke softly.

"I don't want to say it, yet."

Dameon lifted Emma from the floor and led her to the bed, using the rope around her waist as a lead. He placed her near the edge and leaned her back. He pushed her further up the mattress, keeping her legs bent, feet flat on the soft blanket.

He pulled the line out from under her. With incredible speed, he wrapped the rope around her knee. He worked the cord between her thigh and lower leg, tightening the hold and pinching the circular bind in its middle. He formed a pattern that resembled a butterfly, as he repeated the knots lower and lower until her ankle nearly touched her butt.

The physical sensation of the rope wasn't painful, but the emotional feelings were explosive. He quickly and masterfully tied her other leg. She couldn't run or fight if she wanted to. Did she want to? Dameon was in complete control. Emma was at his mercy, and his alone.

"It is my intent to give you more pleasure than you think you can handle. But such a thing does not come without a little pain. I cannot guarantee that anything will stop on yellow. But if you can manage to say red, your wishes will be acknowledged."

Emma attempted to push herself up on her hands, about to debate over the use of the word, "acknowledged."

Dameon snatched her hands. Her back slammed back down to the fluffy bed. He brought her wrists towards him. With the remaining ends of the ropes around her ankles, he bound her wrists with very little slack. Emma felt completely exposed. Her restraints kept her legs bent, and hands near her feet.

She wasn't sure exactly how she felt, but she was undeniably wet. A flinch pulled at her shoulder, when Dameon leaned over her to meet her lips with a soft kiss.

"I'll show you what happens to my sweet partners when they win. You'll be rewarded princess. But my god, little prisoner, am I going to punish you. I'm going to make you beg me to take your prize away, and I'm going to love every bit of it."

Dameon knelt on the ground and pulled Emma close.

She felt so fucking vulnerable, and yet, a little eager. She pulled the ropes taut when Dameon's tongue touched her intimate center. Her legs tensed. He moved between her folds and pushed his tongue into her, fucking her in shallow, wet, movements.

Her sex warmed and ached against his mouth. Emma moaned, and a muscle in her leg twitched as he gave her a consuming lick. Her hips rose, as she tried desperately to grind into him, to part her legs further. His avoidance of her clit was madness, and she wanted his tongue to sooth the need. He paused, and blew softly at her wetness, sending chills up her spine and through her arms.

"Enjoying your reward are we," he taunted, kissing her innermost thigh.

.

Emma hummed with little "mmm" sounds of confirmation.

Dameon returned to her center, and trailed the short distance up, until he finally came to the most sensitive point of her body. He rounded it, maliciously teasing. Emma whimpered pleading sounds.

Pitying her lovely misery, he sucked against the little space, and flicked his tongue over the bundle of nerves. Emma clenched hard, and moaned beneath him. He licked the length of her again, and continued to worship her clit, sending intense pulses of desire through her existence.

Short cries of gratitude escaped her lips. The ropes strained against Emma's increasing enjoyment. Dameon took his time. He paused occasionally, teasing her with a random lack of attention more than once, prolonging her reward in the most terrible, wonderful, way. Emma pulled at the bindings on her wrists as her body burned with pleasure. Her arousal heightened as her tightened pussy threatened to orgasm.

"Dameon," she whimpered. "You're gonna make me cum! Dameon, I…I-"

Bliss flooded her body. Her hips lifted as far as they were able. She wanted to be filled. She ached for Dameon to give her his perfect, ready, cock and tend to her inner need. She breathed heavily, letting the orgasm roll from her head to her toes.

Dameon kissed her inner thigh again. As he did, she felt him smile against her smooth skin. Dameon pulled her aggressively closer and began ravaging her cunt. Emma screamed. Her overly sensitive clit sent terrible signals of pleasure and intense pain to her nervous system. She screamed out loud at the overindulgence.

"Fuck! Stop! Dameon! St… I can't!"

Dameon disregarded her begging and continued to devour her.

"Please!" she belted, at the top of her lungs.

Men slammed against the locked door, yelling.

"Dameon!" Elijah shouted. "Dameon stop! Let us in!"

Emma screamed wordlessly. Tears streamed down her face. She wriggled and tried to get away, but the rope was unyielding.

"Please, I can't… yellow, yellow, y-" she choked out.

Dameon ceased, only to swiftly slam his cock deep into her cunt. Emma cried out in pain, and wonderful relief. She pulled against the bondage. Her wrists burned in her struggle against the ropes. Her sex clenched. Dameon fucked roughly at the increased tightness, pulling at the cords for even more leverage.

"Please," Emma panted. "Harder. Yes. Harder, please!"

Dameon let out a rough groan.

"Oh, my greedy little prisoner."

Dameon gave her all she asked for. He pushed into her faster, harder, the sounds of their meeting bodies sending rhythms into the air. Dameon let out a guttural cry of his own. Through his cum, he kept pushing messily, until a high scream and considerable amount of wet left Emma in a small stream. She soaked the edge of the bed, the floor, and Dameon.

Matthew was first to barge into the room, Elijah on his heels. Matthew forced Dameon back onto him, restraining the spent man. Dameon caught his breath and smiled in satisfaction.

Elijah ignored the mess he stepped in, and looked helplessly at the knots. He accepted defeat before even attempting to untie the ropes, and gathered Emma up into a cradling hold. She shook uncontrollably and moaned in the aftershocks of cumming and squirting.

Dameon laughed softly, in near hysterics. To the surprise of the intruders, so did Emma. Elijah visually examined the messy, tied, woman. Matthew cautiously let go of Dameon, eyeing them both speculatively.

"It's fine Elijah," said Emma, trying to regain normalcy. "Matthew, It's… It's okay, I'm fine."

In a gentle movement, Elijah rested Emma's head into the mattress and stretched just beyond the two of them to reach for a pillow. Matthew glanced back at Dameon's door.

Dameon took full advantage of the moment of distraction.

"If that's the case—"

He moved in quickly. Dameon pressed his palm against her extremely overstimulated clit. Her nerves sent a shock that surged through her entire body.

"Red!" Emma screamed.

Dameon released her instantly, and raised his hands to the air. Matthew locked him back into his arms again. Elijah quickly gathered Emma once more, readying himself to fend off Dameon on her behalf. Emma rested her head in Elijah's arms and laughed with total exhaustion.

"Red," she said, softly and horsley. "Fucking red, Dameon."

Dameon reached for Emma's trembling knee, from beneath Matthew's hold. Emma mumbled a word close to, "wait," and flinched on instinct.

Matthew dug a hand around Dameon's shoulder. Elijah pulled Emma closer to his chest. Dameon raised his hands to the best of his ability, yet again, and spoke with sincerity.

"You have my word, the game is over."

Elijah gently laid Emma down, and slid away to the side. Matthew released, but monitored, the man as Dameon slowly stepped forward and sat on the bed next to Emma. Without struggle, he rapidly untied the knots and tossed the cords aside.

Emma rubbed her right wrist, noticing a series of darkening lines along her legs as she settled into a more relaxing position. Her limbs greatly appreciated the ability to straighten and bend at will.

Dameon shifted away to give her space, but was stopped when Emma reached out to take his arm.

"Wait," she said, her voice not yet smooth.

Dameon did as requested and sat back onto the bed.

"Dameon," she said, with a hint of insecurity. "I thought you said the game was over? Is this still part of the punishment?"

A puzzled expression furrowed his brow. Dameon tilted his head. He looked to his men for a clue as to what he may have missed. They looked as unsure as he was. Dameon moved a little closer, taking care not to touch her without her direct permission.

"The punishments and rewards are" he said, softly, pausing to survey the messy room, "concluded. What makes you feel you are still being punished?"

"Don't leave. Please," she asked.

Dameon's face reflected both pity and adoration.

"Oh Emma," he said, engulfing her in a warm hold.

He kissed her face twice and brushed away a few strands of her sweaty hair from her face.

"I personally don't believe I got too carried away this time, but I have to ask, did I push too far?"

Emma pondered the question before answering.

"Yes, and no. It was... a lot."

263

Dameon kissed her again.

"I know it was. If you don't want to be touched by me for a while, I'll understand."

"No!" Emma protested quickly.

He laughed in that breathy way he did, when he found her answers amusing.

"My intent may have been to offer a delicious dose of pain to your body, but not to your heart. If you want me to stay, to hold you, I will."

Emma reached for Dameon's hand, and held it close to her chest. Her pulse was only beginning to calm. Matthew gestured to Elijah to leave the room and allow the two to have a moment. Elijah hesitantly agreed, and quietly attempted to shut the door behind Matthew.

It was only then that Emma realized the door was ruined. Matthew had literally ripped it from its frame. Bits of wood littered the floor at the doors opening, the lock still in its activated position. Dameon chuckled when he noticed the same.

Dameon adjusted the two of them and laid down at her side.

"Emma," he said, pushing the comforter out from under them, then pulling it over to cocoon the two together.

"I care very much for you. I like the way you challenge me. I like the power you have over me. I like seeing what you do to the men I love. You've brought out sides of Matthew and Elijah that even I haven't seen before. And..."

For a moment, Dameon closed his eyes and sighed.

"And, I feel the compulsion to apologize to you, Emma. When I do fall, it's hard and fast. I'm afraid I can't help it. I love you, Emma. I wont ask you to lie to me, to say it back. I just need you to know it. You didn't choose to be here. You didn't choose me. I am a selfish man for wanting and enjoying so much of you."

Emma placed a soft hand on the stubble of his face. He pressed his cheek into it.

"You're right," she said. "I didn't ask for this. I definitely didn't ask to be locked away. The first time I saw you, I had never been more afraid in my life."

Pain formed creases above Dameon's eyes.

"But now," she continued, "I feel ashamed by it but, this is the only place I want to be. I'd be lying if I said I didn't want the ability to open every lock in this place. But if you gave me every key to the front door, right at this moment, I would beg you to let me come back, to stay after a walk to the park. You make me nervous, Dameon, you all do in your own ways. But I think I might also be falling for each of you too. I don't want this to end. The cruelest thing you could ever do to me, would be to leave me or force me to go."

Dameon quietly laughed to himself.

"Every key to the front door, huh? Are you suggesting that you would like one of my eyes to keep in your pocket? Sounds painful, even for me."

Dameon looked down at Emma with his dark, ocean-blue eyes. She smiled back at him.

"No," she said. "I think I prefer both eyes where they are, for now."

After a lovely moment of snuggling close, a protesting groan from Emma followed a playful nudge for her to get up from the bed. Dameon insisted that the two shower, but Emma was reluctant to end their cuddling.

"Princess," he whispered, "I can't abide by your willingness to risk getting sick, all because you wanted to be cozy over getting cleaned up."

Emma wrapped herself tighter under the velvety blanket.

"Who said anything about being sick," she complained.

Dameon stripped the comforter away, leaving her naked body suddenly cold.

"Ms. Biology did, that's who. Come on little prisoner, unless you'd rather be out of commission, while you deal with a UTI. Just imagine how left out you'll feel seeing us have all the fun without your participation. Who knows what rewards and punishments you could miss out on? The sooner you get washed off, the sooner we can get to the surprise we have planned for you today."

Emma's head popped up.

"We," she asked Dameon, with more exasperation than she intended.

Dameon's dangerous smile returned. He crawled over Emma, and placed his thumb on her lower lip. She opened her mouth slightly, letting him guide her. Her heart started pounding again. Emma turned her eyes downward with a face nearing shame. She wasn't sure she was physically capable of keeping up with their libidos.

"I don't think I have it in me, to go again so soon."

Dameon laughed wholeheartedly, picked up the woman, and carried her to his private shower that matched the dark decor of his room. He set her on a black, marble stone, bench and deposited rosemary smells into his hands. He guided her yet again into a relaxing meditative state. She breathed in the earthy smells as he lovingly cared for her body after inflicting such torment. His touch was gentle, his pace slow and healing. All the while, Dameon's words sounded in Emma's mind. He loved her.

14 | One Big Happy Family

Dameon led Emma to Elijah's bright room and knocked politely on the closed door. Dameon's hand rubbed Emma's arm through a silky robe in a tight hug at her side. Elijah opened the door expectantly. The concern he carried earlier, hadn't fully dissipated yet. He shot Dameon a disapproving glance as he took Emma's hand in his own. Before letting her go, Dameon kissed the side of her head and smiled with a wink.

"Ready to find Amy again," he asked, sweetly.

Emma looked up at Dameon with excitement. He nodded and left his princess in the highly capable hands of the transformative artist.

Elijah got straight to work. The talented man gently asked Emma to remove her robe, then sprayed her entire body this time. Getting the full body treatment felt a little like overkill, when before he only covered her top half. Although the coverage was greater, Elijah only sprayed enough to mildly tan her, rather than going for the full near-orange look.

Elijah reclothed Emma in the silk robe and sat her on the pink stool again, to begin her face makeup. He paused for a few seconds. A gentle hand ran up the length of her arm. He got on his knees, and knelt in front of her.

"Emma, are you really okay?"

She was caught off guard. Words spun in her mind before being able to speak. Elijah's face was filled with concern and question.

"Dameon's… kink, it's not for everyone," he said. "He can push too far, use his position of power to make you feel you have little choice. I didn't handle it as well as you seem to be, the first time he played his game with me. Ignoring a request to stop, only ending with a single word that can feel elusive in the moment, I just need to know if you are alright."

A twinge of pain found a place in Emma's chest for Elijah.

"Are you saying he hurt you," she asked.

A frown twitched at the corner of Elijah's mouth.

"The first time, yeah. I wasn't as prepared as I thought I would be. Now it's a game. I know him well enough to give him my complete trust. I know that it's just his way of playing the dom, and that he doesn't have any desire to actually hurt me. But that first time? I had a little too much trauma that still needed to be unpacked."

Emma reached for his hand, and squeezed his fingers.

"There are times, like last night, when I practically beg him to play with me in the way that only he can. But I didn't come into this like you. He and Matthew made their intentions clear from the start. I always wanted... I had the sincere choice to stay. You on the other hand? What has been a game for us, hasn't always been a game for you. I arrived with guarantees, and a clear entitlement to my own body. When you got here, your life and consent wasn't so indisputable."

Emma leaned down, and kissed Elijah with her unpainted lips.

"He scared me," she confided. "But even when I was afraid, even when it hurt, I think I believed that if I called red, he would stop. When I watched what he did to Matthew, I didn't have that same kind of faith in him. I don't think I had it until today. But Elijah," she said sweetly, "I really am good. I even... liked it."

The blond let out a relieving breath and returned to a standing position. Emma gave Elijah's hand an additional moment of compression, and smiled.

"Thank you," she said.

He returned the expression of gratitude and shook what he could of his anxieties away.

"I am curious though," she said, as he resumed his work, "I get why you are so concerned about Dameon, but why not Matthew?"

Elijah's head tilted like a confused puppy.

"Matthew? Why would I? He's not the dom type in bed. Well, he can be a bit of a switch, but nothing close to Dameon."

"Don't get me wrong, Dameon is definitely a lot. But Matthew," she said, with last night's knife work playing in her mind. "He's also into some pretty scary, dark stuff. Again, all good. I liked it. But I'm a little surprised Dameon is the only one around here you seem really concerned over."

Elijah didn't say anything. He lingered on her words. A thought crossed Emma's mind that hadn't before. Maybe Elijah didn't know. Matthew may have shown a part of himself to her that he hadn't let Elijah see. She then wondered if Dameon didn't know either. Elijah dropped the conversation, and continued distorting Emma's face.

Amy descended the stairs with her distinctive, confident walk. Dameon looked at Amy with a pleased expression. Her tan was less prominent this time, but still considerably different from Emma's. Elijah mentioned that it was important for Emma's natural skin tone to be more present than last time, but didn't explain why. When she asked, he wouldn't budge with an answer.

Emma did notice an inquisitive stare that Elijah fixed on Matthew, who didn't seem to notice. Matthew was more focused on, and amused by, Amy's significantly larger chest again.

"So," Matthew said to the room, "Are we ready?"

The questions rattling in Elijah's mind were temporarily put to the side, as Dameon wrapped an arm around Amy and teased.

"Yes, if our little prisoner can walk, that is."

Amy rolled her eyes and hugged Dameon around his waist, as if he were a close friend rather than the man that, only moments ago, nearly fucked her into oblivion.

"I don't know who this "little prisoner" is, but I'm ready to go!"

"Very good," Dameon said. "Then let's get out of here. We have shopping to do."

The four walked into the parking garage and into a private, walled off space assigned to their penthouse.

Inside, a V8, Maserati Quattroporte Trofeo awaited. It really was an impressive looking car. The exterior was black, and waxed to a near mirror-like finish. Its red brake calipers peaked though, giving an additional sporty look. Though a coupe may be the more traditional aesthetic, the four doors made perfect sense, if it was ever used as a getaway car for its thieving owners.

"No valet," Amy asked, saucily.

Matthew quietly explained that the secluded parking spot, and the expectation for them to retrieve their own car, were perks to owning the penthouse. It benefited them nicely, as they often needed to come and go and without the worry of watchful eyes. The privacy provided an untouchable feel, and it helped out when taking on more covert errands.

Amy smacked her gum.

"Oh yeah," she said, "Because this is so inconspicuous."

She slid into the seat behind Matthew, Elijah taking the other side in the back. Dameon took the front passenger seat. She initially considered asking why Dameon didn't drive. She knew that Matthew was their getaway driver. Were they about to steal something? Is that what they meant by going shopping?

Then she remembered Dameon's past. She wondered if he was still too traumatized to drive. She probably would be too, if her loved one died horrifically in a car accident. Though, it wasn't exactly an accident. Emma, instead, asked the other question that nibbled in her brain.

"How did you get the car so clean after I got blood everywhere?"

"Sebastian," Dameon said, simply.

Along the way, Emma got to learn a little more about Sebastian Fonsesca. He was a man of many talents. He sold much of their stolen loot. He ensured their car was detailed and fixed up. They trusted him with every secret they shared among themselves.

In the past, Sebastian set up meetings with other criminals. He passed along information to "his boys" if it could ever give them an upper hand. And for many years, Sebastian was more than just a useful criminal with a reputation. He was a part of their hodgepodge family. They talked about him with the sentimental respect owed to a beloved parental figure.

"All that and the man still runs a restaurant with the best steak in town," said Matthew.

Emma looked round at the spotless interior. He did a fantastic job. There wasn't the slightest hint that anything odd had transpired in the car. It occurred to her how strange it was to be willingly riding in this vehicle, with these men. Last time, she was sure they were about to murder her.

They drove through the bustling Vegas city streets. Men with stripper trading cards slapped the small laminated papers against their hands, peddling to tourists who tried to ignore them. Lights strobed and flashed despite the high sun.

People of all shapes and sizes sported three-foot margarita containers, and drunkenly stumbled around the sidewalks. Parents with children shuffled through the crowds, shielding their kids from obscenities as they made their way to the more family friendly establishments. Traffic inched them along until they turned into another concrete garage.

After a short trip to an elevator, Emma entered one of the largest malls she had ever stepped foot in. A confusing maze of escalators led up and down at least three levels, maybe four. White walls were plastered in advertisements, and the echoing sounds of shoppers filled Emma with excitement. She had forgotten for a moment about Amy, and quickly regained the false entitlement that she belonged in this place.

Elijah was obviously the most excited of the men to be there. He beamed at Amy, who matched his energy. He grabbed her hand, as if he were a kid in an amusement park, and whisked her away to the first shop.

Expensive clothes, that Emma would have been afraid to so much as touch, displayed themselves on tall modelesque mannequins. A sales associate politely asked if any assistance might be needed. Elijah never met her face with a, "Nope," and began snatching hangers from metal rods. He paused and looked back at Amy.

"It just occurred to me, I have no idea what you used to wear. Don't get me wrong, you are absolutely wearing at least some of what I pick, but what did you used to wear before Matthew snatched you up?"

Amy crossed her arms.

"You sure you can afford me?"

All three suppressed laughs, but couldn't fight their smiles. Dameon leaned in and whispered in her ear.

"Good girl."

Emma hid the warmth his words imposed.

"Well, before I knew I was gonna be, like, famous someday, and in my days when I didn't have money, I was a jeans and t-shirt kinda girl. Keeping it simple you know? Like, I didn't need brands to look cute. I know, right? Like, totally hard to picture."

Elijah spread his arms wide and presented the store's inventory.

"Well, money is no object today. What catches your eye."

Amy pointed at a summer dress with yellow and red flowers. Dameon retrieved the garment, and beckoned her to continue on. Elijah pulled clothes left and right, and handed her a heaping bundle to try on in the dressing room.

Matthew and Dameon took a seat, while Elijah followed her in, despite the protests of the poor associate. Once in the larger of the dressing rooms, Elijah helped Emma remove the deceiving bra.

"See why I laid off on the tan a bit? I want a better idea of how these will look on someone that isn't exactly Amy."

Emma nodded and happily jumped into everything Elijah threw her way. She tried on clothes for Emma in secret, happily getting Elijah's constant approval. Amy modeled extravagant outfits for the men, with the return of her large bra.

Matthew whistled. Dameon clapped. Their enthusiasm never diminished, as they watched their woman and Elijah thoroughly enjoy themselves. Occasionally, one of the men would toss a pair of shoes over the door, to both Emma and Elijah's delight.

Most of the clothing was for Emma, but a few items were picked just for Amy. She came out of the dressing room in white heels, white high-waisted pants with a pink swirling pattern, and a solid pink crop top. They were all

Elijah's picks, and Amy loved it. Dameon and Matthew placed the heaping pile on the counter to be rung up. Elijah snapped the tags off her current outfit and slammed them near the pile.

"She's wearing these out," he said, pridefully.

Store after store, Elijah pulled Amy around and dressed her up like his own personal doll, while being sure Emma got the final say in her new wardrobe. She wanted to feel bad about all the money the men were spending on her. She never experienced being so spoiled in her life. Clothing, shoes, makeup; anything she so much as touched with curiosity, was rung up and placed into the ever compiling shopping bags.

Dameon's pleasant smile, along with Elijah's bursting enthusiasm, made any guilt dissolve, with the confirmation that the men were enjoying her shopping experience as much, maybe even more, than she did. Even Matthew looked like he was having a good time.

The next lucky establishment, after about four different shops, sold lingerie. Matthew looked mildly uncomfortable in the space. To his credit, perhaps he wouldn't have felt so awkward if fewer of the women hadn't stared so lustfully at him, as they picked their own sexy undergarments. Dameon and Elijah received glances as well, but Elijah didn't seem to notice and Dameon replied with a cruel disinterested response.

Dameon picked a red one-piece, that was more straps than concealing fabric. Emma let a sly smile slip, seeing some resemblance to his bondage kink. Amy picked another red piece. It was more of a dress than the others, but the lower half was almost completely see-through.

A man of average height, a slightly rounded gut, and a goatee, ran his fingers under the garment in Amy's hand. He was heavily balding, the only remains of his dark hair neatly gelled around his ears and the back of his head. Slightly tinted glasses concealed his eye color, and a gray suspended, white button up shirt, let his prominent chest hair show through the top.

"I prefer the women in my life to be dressed in black, but for you," he said, looking Amy up and down, "I like to imagine you covered in red."

The world faded away. People continued to shop, laugh, talk, but Emma couldn't hear them. Dameon's face made it clear who spoke to her. Time stood still, and the warm atmosphere turned to winter. Matthew pulled Emma, slowly, and made himself a barrier between her and the intruding man. Elijah took a place between her and the stranger as well, nearly blocking her from view. Dameon looked inhuman, a vision of disdain and hate.

"Now, now, now," the man said, with ease. "Cheer up Lazarus. We're all here to have a nice time. I just happened to see you from across the way, and wanted to say hello to my dear son-in-law."

Matthew was cold, and intentionally intimidating, when he addressed the man in a rumbling voice.

"Hello Tony. Thank you for your kind words, but we were about to leave," he said.

Tony didn't mask his disgust for Matthew.

"Yes," he said, as if he had just eaten something sour. "I was simply offering an opinion on the woman's clothing, is that a crime?"

"Since when do you form opinions about women" Dameon snarled. "Don't pretend to have cared about any human being, other than yourself of course."

Tony smiled, as if Dameon told a funny joke.

"The pot said to the kettle," he grinned. "Here I thought Mr. Bale and Mr. Holden had you plenty busy. This though," he said, eyeing Emma past Matthew and Elijah. "Certainly an unexpected addition, isn't she? I'm a little surprised that she's your type."

Dameon's knuckles were bone white, as he clenched his fists together.

"Don't," he warned, with words laced in fury. "Don't you fucking look at her."

Tony smiled, his face unfazed.

"It's a real shame. I was in the mood to spend some money today, but then I remembered that I should probably skip the luxuries for now. Sadly, I only picked up this," Tony said, lifting a small paper bag. "Did you hear? Yet another of my businesses was recently robbed. I'm beginning to take it personally."

Tony eyed Matthew and Elijah, curling his lip as if he smelled rotting meat.

"You've always enjoyed a certain type of company. Tell me, you haven't heard anything about the unfortunate rise in lowlife activity, have you? No, probably not. I'm sure you'd tell me. We're family after all."

"Because you've always had a soft spot for family. If you want to talk to someone about it, why don't you chat with your son…oh wait!"

"Yes. Tragic," Tony said, coldly unphased. "Anyway, I seem to have changed my mind. You would probably get better use out of this than I would."

Tony tossed the brown bag at Dameon's feet.

"Please, enjoy your day. It's a lovely day! I will look forward to catching up soon, son."

Dameon didn't take his eyes off Tony until the man left the store, and retreated down an escalator.

Matthew picked up the brown bag, only to have it snatched from his hands by Dameon. He opened the unexpected gift, violently ripping the sides as he did. Inside was a simple dog leash and folded note. He read the note to himself, face twisting with every word.

In a blind fury, Dameon smashed the bag shut and stormed out of the shop. Matthew, Elijah, and Emma quickly followed him out. Dameon stomped his way over to a nearby trashcan, and chucked the bag, and its contents, at the concrete bin. But he missed.

The leash, the bag, and the note fell to the floor. Dameon stared at the missed shot and didn't move. His every pore was seething with anger. Emma looked down at the short letter on the ground.

"Lazarus,

Because I care, please take this. It's short and you would be wise to use it on the new bitch you have acquired. I'd hate to see her end up like poor Penny. But don't worry, I have friends everywhere. You'll be the first to know if I find her without her owner.

Your dearest father-in-law,

Tony"

Matthew whispered in Elijah's ear. The angelic man nodded. He wrapped an arm around Emma's waist and hugged her to him.

"Come on honey. We need chocolate, and I know just the place."

Elijah practically pulled Emma away from Dameon. She didn't want to leave his side, but Elijah reassured her that Matthew would take care of it.

Amy was taken to a decadent chocolate shop. The air was rich with fruity, sugary smells. The shop walls kept the dessert theme, with fudge-brown colors and deep red accents. To her surprise, chocolates weren't the only things the place sold. Behind the display counter of various treats, was a bar. Elijah led Amy to a stool and ordered on her behalf, one of everything and a glass of red wine.

"Elijah," Emma said, timidly. "Did you see what the note said?"

Elijah squeezed her hand under the bar, lovingly. He whispered in her ear.

"This is probably the most difficult lesson to learn, but also the most important. You're shook and feel seen. You got a small taste of that before, with El Tiburón. But even now, especially now, you can't lose Amy."

Amy snatched her hand from Elijah and waved her finger in his face.

"Listen honey, you can't grab my hand like that, and junk. Matthew takes good care of me and I'm not about to have him thinking I'm unfaithful."

Emma's pain lingered behind Amy's brown eyes. Elijah subtly nodded in approval.

"Calm your tits," he said. "You're not my type. But I did love shopping with you today."

Amy took a heavy drink from her wine glass.

"Totally! You didn't let me down. You're just the shopping buddy I needed in my life."

Emma needed the alcoholic drink. It loosened the stress in her shoulders, and inspired some of the confidence that Amy always presented to the world. The pair practiced creating and keeping conversations going with Amy. She did well enough, but her mind kept drifting elsewhere.

"Dameon seemed pretty upset."

Elijah gave her a quick warning glance.

"Yeah, he hates his uncle, or father-in-law, or whoever he is. He always gets uppity around the guy. It's probably nothing big, Dameon is such a diva. Not that I blame him, that guy always came off as a bit of a prick."

Amy placed another chocolate in her mouth, and washed it down with an additional sip of wine.

"Mr. Bale and Holden," she asked, in a hushed voice.

Elijah crushed a piece of chocolate between his fingers, and let the sticky, creamy, insides run over his thumb. He found Emma's eyes behind Amy's, and licked the filling before it ran too far.

"Yes, Amy. Matthew Bale, as you obviously know, seeing as how you two are dating. But yeah, Elijah Holden."

"Well, duh," Amy said. "Of course I know Matthew's name. I just never heard yours. You never brought it up."

It was a strange feeling that came with the new information. It never occurred to her that she never knew their last names. She had sex, crazy sex, with three men and never thought to ask. It's not like she couldn't understand why it was never brought up. She wasn't fond of hers either. It somehow felt too close to her roots, too close to her father.

Elijah tapped her subtly on the leg.

"You're doing better than most," he said, softly. 'But you're distracted. It's alright, but we should move before too much of Emma comes out."

Emma nodded.

As Amy and Elijah walked through the busy crowds, a hand slid around her waist. She jumped at the feeling, and gripped Elijah's arm. It was just Matthew. Dameon was at his side and looking moderately better.

"What's the matter babe," Matthew said, in an accusatory tone. "If you weren't doing something wrong, why would you be nervous?"

He pried Elijah away, and inserted himself in Amy's arms. The large man shot Elijah a distrusting look.

"Thanks," Matthew said, coldly, "but I'm pretty sure she looks better around my arm."

Elijah sidestepped away, placing Dameon between him and the giant. Elijah looked nervous.

"Calm down," Dameon said. "No one is trying to steal your girl. Besides, what would Elijah want with a woman anyway?"

"She didn't mind when I helped her out of her clothes in the dressing room," Elijah said, with an antagonistic tone.

Matthew took on a threatening stance, and reached for Elijah. Dameon held him back with one strong, extended arm.

"Don't," Dameon warned.

Matthew pointed angrily at Elijah over Dameon's shoulder.

"I saw you flirting at the bar. If you start getting too touchy-feely, I'll break every one of your tiny fingers," Matthew said.

"Baby," Amy butted in, trying to calm the increasingly scary man. "You know I only have eyes for you."

Matthew looked down at Amy, with a face similar to the one he gave Emma when they first met. He pulled off intimidating very well, a little too well.

"I hope so," he said. "Just don't forget your place. You're mine, and I don't like sharing."

Dameon pushed the large man back, and rolled his eyes.

"You're too territorial. Now come on, we have one more place to go."

The next shop was filled with high-end furniture. It was overwhelmingly packed with inventory, and Emma was afraid to touch anything.

Dameon managed to break Amy away from Matthew, and hid in a secluded corner of clutter. He dropped his false persona for the outside world, and held her close.

"I'm sorry for storming off," he whispered. "And I hope the show Matthew put on wasn't too much. We could tell you were shaken, so we gave Amy something to be shaken about. Matthew is good at being an asshole when he needs to be."

Emma held Dameon tight.

"It's fine," she said, quietly. "It was a good idea, I wasn't staying in character as well as I should have.

Dameon kissed the palm of her hand.

"You are very talented, Emma. You played the part beautifully, I was the one that lost it."

He leaned in for a kiss, but Emma backed away before he could do any harm to her makeup.

"I'm so proud of you, princess."

If Emma could blush past the heavy lines of her contour, she would have.

"We'll talk more when we're back home. But for now, we're here for your room. Anything you see, anything you want, it's yours. Try to have a little fun. Tony is gone, and we won't let you out of our sight. You're safe, and this time is yours."

Amy left their hiding place first. Dameon wandered nonchalantly to a different section of the store, randomly looking at the tag attached to an inaccurately designed globe.

Matthew found Amy, and pulled her by the waist with too much force. Elijah eyed the couple. Matthew growled quietly in his chest. He looked down at Amy with grumpy distrust.

This Matthew was clearly angry at her for being too close to Elijah, so Amy did the only thing she could think to do, to calm her controlling, jealous, boyfriend.

"Baby," Amy said, "don't be so mad. What would I want with Elijah anyway? You're my big, strong man. Besides, I haven't, like, seen it or anything, but I can't imagine he's half the man you are."

Amy's eyes drifted to Matthew's lower half then back up.

"Like, literally," she said. "A guy that short? It's gotta be proportional right? No thanks."

Elijah's jaw dropped at the offensive rapid fire.

Dameon also heard, and immediately pursed his lips. He grabbed the nearest item and read its description to keep from losing his composure.

To Emma's relief, Matthew took the bait. He puffed up his chest, his masculine ego thoroughly stroked. He eased up on Elijah's presence and kept a far more relaxed attitude for the remainder of their shopping trip.

If Emma could have named the theme of her selections, it would probably be titled, "colorfully chaotic." The bedframe was asymmetrical in every way. A standing lamp added to the collection was neon green. The bedside table was a dark purple. Everything chosen was a fantastic overcorrection for the bland room.

Against the wall of the store, were paints with flamboyant names attached. She chose a large can of witchy-cat black, and tiny containers of bright colors. Kissable-pink, it's-a-boy-blue, orange-you-glad, green-with-envy, and sunshine-yellow, made their way into Emma's final picks. She had a plan, and the men watched her shop unquestioningly, but curiously.

She admitted to herself that her choices rivaled that of a teen girl with a stolen credit card, but she would be damned if there was a speck of white or boredom to that room. The furniture was scheduled to be delivered later, but the paint was wonderfully available immediately. Emma relished the feeling of control over the place that was once used to confine her.

The group spoke very little on the way back to the car, their arms ridiculously full of bags. When the last door shut, the vehicle erupted in conversation. Matthew apologized profusely for his terrible behavior. Elijah poked at Emma in both offense and pride over her quick thinking.

"Half the man? Oh? Short so he's probably...You went straight for a dick-size jab? Okay, yeah. That's fine."

He crossed his arms, and faked a pout.

"I had to say something!" Emma defended. "If Matthew was playing an insecure man with macho energy, what would be a better way to validate him? It felt like a logical move."

Dameon laughed.

"You did the right thing," he said. "It was the perfect move. I just don't think any of us expected it."

Elijah rolled his eyes.

"Yes, yes, yes. It was the right thing to say. But you didn't have to be hurtful about it."

As traffic slowed to a series of sporadic stops, a quiet snuck into the car.

Elijah clicked the latch of his seatbelt, and slid to the middle seat. He wrapped a comforting arm around Emma and held her tight.

Dameon looked back and lost every bit of composure. He gripped Elijah's shirt with white knuckles and an anxious hold. One solid pull placed Elijah back towards his original seat.

"Dammit, Elijah! Seatbelt." he shouted!

Elijah leaned forward and kissed Dameon lightly on the cheek, before clicking his seatbelt back in place.

Emma observed the scene with peaked interest. He was genuinely afraid. It was an unusual state to see Dameon in. Angry, lustful, remorseful? Sure. His raw panic, however, was a new one. A trace of pity tugged at her heart, as she watched the nervous man.

Matthew reached out and intertwined his fingers with Dameon's.

15 | Pretty Water

Even with the door wide open, paint fumes filled the room. The wet walls shimmered with drying droplets of black. Dameon, Matthew, and Elijah opted to give Emma a bit of space, while she aggressively conquered her prison cell. With every black streak, she felt empowered, in control. Only the crown molding, baseboards, and ceiling remained of the old room.

The dark base color dried quickly. Emma opened the first of the small, colorful, containers, sunshine-yellow. She looked from it, to the black canvas, and threw it against the wall. It splattered messily, randomly, perfectly.

Emma felt a high from the chaotic technique, or maybe it was the chemicals. Regardless, the activity was not only fun, but intensely therapeutic. She continued opening and throwing colorful paints at the wall, until she noticed the audience of curious onlookers she had gained. All three peaked in from the doorway, grinning ear to ear. She paused, paint dripping down her arm.

"Too much?"

"Not a bit," said Matthew.

"It's just," Dameon said, "It feels like we are seeing so much of you. Not the prisoner, not the princess, just Emma. It's kind of cool to watch."

Emma chucked the last of the "kissable-pink," and watched the running paint with satisfaction. Once every color found its home on the walls, she went upstairs to rid herself of the paint that covered her arms and legs.

The distance from the fumes was very much needed. She took a quick shower, and changed into the first outfit she truly picked for herself since leaving Alabama. The top she chose was lightly colored, a mix of pastel pink, blue, and yellow. Its sheer material allowed her lacy, white, bralette to show though. Of all the expensive pieces of clothing bought at the mall, her well-fitting jeans felt the most luxurious. It was as if they were made for Emma's body.

A woman she didn't fully recognize stood in the bathroom mirror. Minimal make up highlighted her natural born features. It wasn't Amy looking back at her, it was simply her. It was her green eyes, her blonde hair, her pale skin. The woman moved when she moved, blinked when she blinked. The contentment, security, and happiness she saw, gave her the feeling that she was looking at a stranger.

She smiled at herself, and proceeded to find the people that brought this wonderful newness out of her. Emma paused at the railing, and rested her arms against the iron to watch the men below. Elijah and Dameon were bickering. Matthew was laughing at the two, as they pushed each other's buttons.

She didn't feel very much like a captive woman in that moment. She wanted to stay, to be with them. Matthew caught sight of Emma, and smiled with a funny look of awe. Elijah and Dameon realized their personal peanut gallery was distracted, and quickly found what Matthew was staring at. Dameon received her the second her feet hit the main floor.

"So this is Emma? It's nice to finally meet you."

She beamed and wrapped her arms around him. Comfort, warmth, and ease flooded her system. Dark-blue eyes reached deep into the soul of the woman that was finding a permanent place in their home and hearts. She could see the growing roots of Dameon's trust in his gaze, and felt her own twist and strangle what remained of her guarded pessimism.

Emma reached for a kiss, but before her lips could meet Dameon's, she was pulled away with enough force to knock some of the wind out of her. Elijah's arms lifted her from the ground, and spun her around. Emma laughed as the world blurred.

He faced her, and when her focus came back she saw the trickster intent behind his smile. Something unspoken was on his mind, but whatever it was, she could feel the beginnings of another challenging game coming on.

Matthew interrupted Elijah's stare, with an audible rumble from his stomach and exclamation of hunger. The party moved to the fresh air of the terrace. Dameon and Elijah grilled up a variety of colorful vegetables and kababbed steaks.

Hot food in hand, the four sat around the cozy firepit and watched the sun set over the dark mountains. The air chilled, but Emma evaded the drop in temperature with Matthew as her personal heater. She leaned into the crook of his arm, and trailed her fingers over his muscular forearm.

"When is your next heist," Emma asked, casually.

Dameon chuckled. He laid himself over the stone bench, legs bent, and head in Elijah's lap. Elijah moved his fingertips through the depths of Dameon's hair, massaging his head in a relaxing motion.

"Work, work, work, with you. Isn't it," he said.

Emma shrugged.

"You can't take away my favorite pastime now. I guess, I just wanted to know what was next."

Dameon took a deep breath. He closed his eyes to gain further immersion into Elijah's touch.

"I think it's best if we lay low for a little while. Tony is clearly on edge. He's likely expanding his security, and reach, as we speak. We'll need to see what he's planning, before our next push."

"Sounds to me like Emma is ready for bigger fish," Matthew said. "Thinking about hitting up a casino, sweetheart?"

"You can do that?"

The three men laughed.

"No," Dameon answered. "Despite what you've seen in movies, it's pretty much impossible, especially for people like us. We're already on Tony's radar, and we don't have the manpower for anything like that."

"Oh," Emma said, sounding more disappointed than she meant to.

Dameon laughed again.

"Not enough excitement at home for you? Getting bored already?"

"Maybe," Emma said, with a grin. "The sex may be great, but you guys can't possibly be occupied by video games and chess everyday. What else do you do for entertainment?"

Elijah ceased his pampering movements. The wheels in his head were turning. Dameon felt the shift, and held, yet another, telepathic conversation with Elijah. The dark-haired man bit his lip, raised his brows at the man, and nodded in approval.

Dameon got up with a low groan, and left the terrace to retrieve the music provoking tablet. Matthew could see what was being planned long before Emma, and rubbed her shoulder in anticipation.

"If it's entertainment you want," Dameon said, returning to the concrete bench, "Elijah can be quite the showman."

Provocative music played through hidden speakers around the firepit. Elijah rose with mock modesty, to whistles and claps provided by Matthew and Dameon.

Elijah moved with fabulous seduction before the three. Emma grinned as Elijah's fingers inched under his shirt, and pulled at the fabric. His well defined torso flexed, and teased, as the firelight danced with him. He rolled his hips, pulled at the waist of his pants, and expertly gave just enough to drive the need for more. He was, indeed, very good. The music pounded. Elijah lifted his shirt over his head and snapped it like a whip. Matthew bit his lip at the sound. Dameon grinned at his confident angel.

In time with the beat, he sauntered over to Emma, and placed a leg up on the hard seat. Emma's cheeks flushed and skin tingled, as the smooth-moving man grinded into the space above her. Damn. There wasn't a doubt in her mind that Elijah danced professionally before Dameon and Matthew. The man swayed with devastating perfection.

The grace of Elijah's body rivaled that of a Juilliard ballet master, or the most expert of strippers. His eyes burrowed into Emma's, as he slid his hands over his beautiful torso. He flexed and moved in front of her, compelling Emma to want nothing more than to run her tongue over his body.

A turn to the side placed him around Matthew, lightly pushing his knees apart. A roll of his shoulders and head, urged Matthew to reach out, but every move kept Elijah just out of reach. Caramel eyes focused on the nymph, requiring every ounce of will power from the big man to not claim Elijah for himself. Elijah winked, as he licked his lips and cruelly left Matthew, turning his attention to Dameon next.

"This show was meant for Emma, Angel."

Elijah placed a finger to Dameon's lips to hush him softly.

"What makes you think it's not?"

His bare back, now facing Emma, revealed three distinct bite marks. The most prominent of the bites, printed near Elijah's shoulder. Her stomach did a somersault, seeing the results of Dameon's inflicted punishments from last night.

Elijah gripped the shirt in his fist and swung it around Dameon's neck. He caught the other end and rotated to face Emma, the piece of clothing forming a loose noose around Dameon. He pulled the ends carefully, and grinded into Dameon's lap.

Elijah knew exactly what he was doing, and Emma was absolutely turned on. An image of sex and fantasy in reality, his hips over Dameon sent hard pumps to Emma's chest. With the release of one end of the shirt, he snapped the fabric again into the air. His attention fully on Emma once more.

Elijah wrapped the white shirt around his knuckles and pulled it tight. He straddled Emma, and wrapped the shirt behind her neck this time, pulling her ever so slightly forward. She followed as he commanded.

He rubbed the crotch of his pants over her jeans, and teased the space between his lips and hers. Emma reached for a kiss, but Elijah backed away playfully. She smiled and warmed at his erotic performance. He let go of the shirt with one hand and let the soft fabric caress her neck, sliding around with teasing passes. He flicked the garment away to the ground.

Elijah's fingers circled around the button of his jeans. With a thrust of his hips and snap of his fingers, he popped it open and slowly unzipped, while never missing a beat to the sexy music. Elijah pushed his jeans an inch down, then pulled back up.

Emma's underwear became increasingly saturated with her desire, at every reminder of the masculinity he possessed. He leaned forward, arms at either side of the desperate woman, and whispered in her ear.

"Meet me in my room in five minutes. Close the door behind you."

Emma nodded. She'd agree to anything Elijah asked in that moment.

He slid away, and with another roll of his hips, he pushed the jeans down. He shimmied out of the pants with grace and invitation. With the blow of a kiss in her direction, he turned and prepared to leave the firepit.

Dameon bolted to his feet and snatched his hand, not permitting his angel to go. He pulled Elijah back, and forced the dancer into his lap.

"Where do you think you're going?"

Elijah placed a pecking kiss on the interrupting man's cheek.

"I think I'd like to take a nice, relaxing, bath."

Dameon's face snapped to Emma, then back down to Elijah.

"With her?"

Elijah smirked at Dameon's tone of jealousy and surprise. Matthew mirrored the same look of astonishment. They stared at Elijah, who apparently suggested something completely unfair. It was as if he invited Emma to a once-in-a-lifetime party, and was rubbing the lack of invitation in Dameon and Matthew's faces.

Elijah stood with a cheeky shimmy. He threw a wicked grin Emma's way, and danced his off through the glass doors of the penthouse. Matthew and Dameon shot Emma envious glares.

"What," she laughed.

"He doesn't let us join his bath rituals," Matthew pouted.

"He doesn't?"

"No," Dameon said, with crossed arms. "He seems to think we'd ruin the experience, or whatever that means. But it's fine, have your no-boys-allowed night. Matthew and I will have a manly evening, with cigars, and poker, and balloons."

Dameon crossed his arms, stuck out his tongue, and blew a quick raspberry in the air.

Emma and Matthew's full laughs filled the balcony.

"Balloons," Emma asked, with a giggle.

"And we don't smoke," Matthew said, matching Emma's laughter.

"I don't know! I just said the first thing that popped in my head."

"Ha," Emma chuckled. "Popped."

Once at the top of the stone staircase, Matthew kissed Emma sweetly on the lips, and disappeared into the dungeon for the evening. Dameon pressed his lips to her forehead next.

"I don't know what Elijah's plans are, but I want to remind you that you have options, when it comes to where you sleep. I had hoped that after making the downstairs room yours, though it isn't quite done yet, you might feel more at home. I just want you to know, our room belongs to you as much as us."

"Thank you," Emma said, with a smile that brought one to Dameon's face as well.

He wrapped Emma in a tight hug that warmed her body and heart. Ending on that sweet note, he reunited with Matthew in their shared room; Dameon's, Matthew's, Elijah's, and hers. Their room.

Emma clung to Dameon's words and let them sit for a minute in her mind. For the first time in her life, she felt a foreign sense of security. She was home, wanted, and increasingly trusted by these people in her life. She took a deep breath, and held a feeling of comfort in knowing that her prison was being erased with every passing second in multicolored, drying, paints.

The door to Elijah's room was left ajar for her. She loved his room. If not for her overindulgence in her desire to overcorrect the prison, she imagined her space could have been similar to his. She understood it on a deeper level, the security, and freedom, to have a space that was all one's own. It really was a sweet idea.

The bathroom door, to the side of Elijah's bed, was wide open. When she stepped through, her jaw dropped. A round window separated two mirrors above modern rectangular sinks. Brushed silver, boldly, stood out against the white marble floor and bright, clean, walls.

At the center of the room, a huge round tub was the main focal point. The bottom quarter of the tub was silver, but the rest was perfectly transparent. The thick glass showed off a heavy swirl of pink water, with numerous metallic lines dancing aimlessly around. A fantastic layer of bubbles peaked and valleyed at the top. The air smelled strongly of roses, and a hint of vanilla.

Elijah rested his head on the edge, an image of total relaxation. He waved for her to join him, without opening his eyes. Emma shimmied out of her jeans and underwear. She unbuttoned her sheer collared shirt, and discarded the pretty bra. She stepped into the hot water slowly, allowing her body to acclimate to the change in temperature.

She took the opposite side to Elijah, eyeing him through the bubbly surface. The liquid felt like a bath of silk. The smooth viscosity caressed every crevice of her body. When she lifted her arm, sparkles clung to her skin.

"Tell me this isn't perfection."

"I think it's the most luxurious bath I've had in my life," she said, in absolute comfort.

Emma followed suit and closed her eyes, relaxing into the bone-warming surroundings. The water sloshed as Elijah moved over her. She opened her eyes. A pink hue, and glitter, imprinted on Elijah's skin.

He knelt with her between his knees. Behind her, he placed one hand on the edge of the tub. His free hand ran fingers through her blonde hair. Thoughts could be seen swirling behind his bright blue eyes, mimicking that of the metallic water.

Emma wanted to hear every thought, she wanted to ask a number of the onslaught of questions that flooded her brain.

"Just a minute, before you start up," he said, half smiling at the curiosity he could see bubbling in her. "No, I don't let Dameon or Matthew intrude when I'm having my me-time. This is where I come to relax, to think clearly, to decompress. Every time they've been allowed in, none of those things happen."

Elijah bent to take Emma's mouth with his. She hummed with the satisfying taste of him. His tongue played with hers until she was out of breath. He only released her to kiss her neck, her collarbone, her chest.

She didn't want him to regret his decision to let her be a part of his special time, but her body ached for him. Between the kiss, and the erotic dance performed by the fire, it was hard not to be turned on.

"So you're fine inviting me, because you think I'll be better behaved?"

"No," he answered, with a chuckle. "But I think I can make an exception this time."

Emma found Elijah's mouth again. Her tongue played feverishly with his. His words sent relief and excitement through her. Seeing the way he flexed and showed off, the way he teased? She didn't want to relax. She wanted to taste him, touch him, feel him everywhere. Elijah ended the kiss and held her in a serious gaze.

"I don't know if you've noticed, but I can get petty sometimes. Inviting you to what Dameon and Matthew can't have, part of it was payback. But all cards on the table..."

Elijah tilted his head slightly.

"My jealousy isn't just tied to them anymore. I feel a little left out. You've given yourself to both of them privately. I get it, they are big, strong, and bossy in all the right ways. But, I'm not the masculine man they are. I guess... I want to know if..."

Elijah paused for a moment, trying to find the right words.

"Do you want me, like you want them? Look, I know what I am. If I'm too feminine for your taste, not as... I'd understand, I would, I just–"

Emma splashed drops of the shiny water out of the tub, as she wrapped her arms around Elijah's neck, and shut the man up with a kiss. Bubbles lined her arms and dripped down Elijah's, sparkly, toned back and bitemarks. When Emma's lips retreated, she squished her cheek against his neck.

"Is this because of what I said in the furniture shop," Emma asked, with yet another kiss to his shoulder. "Because I didn't mean any of it, I swear. That wasn't me. It was all Amy. I never meant to actually be mean."

A silky hand slid down Emma's spine. Elijah's touch made her shiver, despite the heat of the water. His other hand tilted Emma's chin up to look at him. His beautiful face was stern as he studied hers with an air of challenge.

"Next lesson. We've all said and done things that we didn't mean, while committing to a role. You used the truth to create a believable lie, and by doing so you created an insecurity that would last beyond the fake persona. It's a good thing. It means you did well, and you, princess, did very well."

The complement stung. She didn't mean to hurt his feelings, though she clearly had.

"Now," Elijah said, "you have amends to make. How do you think you can do that?"

Emma's green eyes glowed with desire. A sensual hand of hers slid down Elijah's chest, past his sinful abs, down to his dick. She wrapped her fingers around him to make up for his wounded pride.

Though hard as a rock, Elijah let out a little laugh, and seized her hand. With an unexpected dominance in his eyes, he removed her apologetic gesture. He floated like a carnivorous predator above her.

"I'm going to need more than that, honey. Tell me why you want me."

"That's easy. You're hot as hell, and I really like you."

Elijah grinned and blew a clump of floating bubbles in her face. Emma shook them away.

"Boring," Elijah teased.

"Fine. Yes, I am attracted to you, but my favorite part of you is the way you feel like a friend."

Elijah raised a brow.

"Hear me out. I've only had one person I could call a friend before. Even then, it wasn't even close to the feelings I get around you. I want to tell you every one of my secrets. I love the way we play dress-up. I've never had so much fun shopping before. I like the way you keep me on my toes, and give me butterflies, when your eyes tell me that you've found an opening to play another game. I think you might actually be my best friend, pathetic as that sounds."

Elijah grinned. His eyes revealed his desire to take her then and there, but the game was still on. She knew it, and he could see she was more than willing to play.

"You only want me as a friend?"

"No," Emma said, saucily. "I said I like you as I do a friend, not that I don't also think of you as more. You really should listen better."

Elijah grinned at his own words and game being used against him.

"You're also the only person I've ever let touch my ass, so that's something."

Elijah speedily placed himself between her legs. He lifted Emma's hips from the bottom of the tub, and held her steadily with a single hand.

The muscles in her arms tensed, as she gripped the glass sides to keep from going under. She lifted her chin to prevent the water from covering her lips. Her feet slid against the slippery surface, useless and keeping her at his mercy. Elijah's fingers inched around her back side.

"Still? You mean to tell me that neither tried taking your pretty ass?"

Emma tried to shake her head, but couldn't without being submerged.

"No," she struggled out.

A shock filled her as Elijah inserted a finger into her. Her empty pussy tightened. Emma gasped, and instinctively struggled. Her position above the water was at risk, Elijah's hand keeping her in his control.

"I've been the queen of this home for many years. I've loved my men for a long time. We've shared everything, every secret, every plan, every kink. Until you came into our lives, that is. You, apparently, have seen sides of them, even I haven't known. So tell me your secrets, friend. What kind of dark kink did Matthew show you?"

Emma's stomach dropped. Her fingers were slipping.

Elijah ran a hand up her torso to rest over her chest. Her heart beat hard, as he threatened to push her under. The pressure on her chest intensified. Her upper body lowered. She arched her neck to keep her lungs filling.

"You– Are you upset with me?"

"No, silly" Elijah grinned. "I'm just being cute. Now tell me, what did that big, strong, usually submissive lug do that was so scary?"

"He used a knife. He didn't hurt me. He just… tested my trust."

Elijah pushed deeper into Emma's ass. Tiny moans escaped, as Emma accepted the longest of Elijah's fingers. He moved it with circular motions inside of her. She groaned at his lustful hand.

"And you liked it?"

"Yes," Emma nodded.

"And you liked it when Dameon played his punishing game?"

"Yes."

Elijah glared dangerously at Emma.

"I'd like to try something, little prisoner, do a little exploring of my own. Now, hold your breath."

She didn't. Instead of following the gorgeous man's direction, she breathed fast and nervously, above the floral water. She gripped the sides with every bit of her strength. As much as she wanted Elijah, he had a way of feeling like a loose canon. Dameon and Matthew had their ways of intimidating her, but Elijah played differently. There was an instability to him, she wasn't sure of.

Elijah moved the hand that pressed against Emma's chest, and rested it on her face. He covered her mouth in preparation. His eyes were feral, and a little terrifying.

"Come on, honey. You can't possibly be scared of little me, not when I'm half the man Matthew is."

After a few more nervous inhales, she took a steady deep breath.

Elijah pinched her nose and plunged her into the smooth water. The world muffled in sound. Her eyes shut out the stinging, soapy water. A second finger entered her ass. Her voice tried to sound but couldn't escape. She arched and struggled against the warm walls.

Elijah was medically proficient. Would he hold her under until she passed out? What if he drowned her, with the intention of bringing her back to do it again? The air in her chest beat against the confines of her body to get out. She choked at the lack of life-giving elements she needed. Her heart was bursting. Her ass tensed immensely around his fingers.

The world spun around her. Disorientation clung to Emma, as Elijah tore her from the pink water and bubbles. She gasped with a terrific inhale of air. She grabbed the dry sides once more, but her hands were slippery.

Elijah wore an expression of intense focus. He retrieved his fingers and supported her back, keeping her in his control. He pinched her nose again. She felt her warm quick breaths hit his palm.

"You really do have a funny way of inviting intrusive thoughts into reality. I'm starting to get the appeal. Get ready princess, we're going again."

Emma took a greater breath than the first time, and shut her eyes tight.

He drove her deeper, pressing her to the lowest depths of the tub. Her body didn't waste time to object. Her heart pounded. Her chest heaved fruitlessly. In a quick motion, Elijah's hard self entered her cunt. She sounded an unreleased moan in her mouth at his placement.

The hollow sounds of small moving waves rushed around her submerged flailing body. He'd never been there before. She wasn't even sure if he would want her in that way. But there he was, in one full and all consuming push. Distracted as she was, her legs squeezed around Elijah, giving him as much as she possibly could.

With a dramatic jerk, Elijah pulled Emma up. He released her face, to hold the back of her neck. Emma drew in a harsh breath that burned with the notes of vanilla. She reached out to wrap her arms above his shoulders.

Through every choke of air, she tensed around Elijah, her chest inflating to maximum capacity. She gripped his hair in her hands. His head tilted back with her clinging desperation. Emma rode Elijah like her life depended on it. Maybe it did, maybe it didn't. Either way, she couldn't deny her feelings. She wanted him like this. The feel of his cock inside of her, the heat of the water, the cold of the air; it was intoxicating. Elijah groaned at her grinding.

"Emma," he whispered. "Emma, please. Look at me."

Her hips slowed. Her breath was uneven. Elijah leaned back and relaxed into the water, staring up at the shimmering pink woman.

"You're fun, and don't get me wrong, I liked that a little more than I thought I would. But–"

Oh my god. This wasn't about him wondering if she wasn't interested. This was about him trying to be something for her. Fears of rejection started flooding her mind.

"Oh no! No, honey. It's not that," Elijah laughed. He kissed her quickly and feverishly. "Sorry, I should have chosen my words more carefully. You're perfect. I just don't know if I can be the dark, dominant, type for you. I want you, I do. I'm just no Matthew, and I'm definitely no Dameon."

Emma let out a breath of relief, and rested against Elijah's chest. His hardness was still inside of her, but she didn't move.

"I don't need you to be," she said, finally. "Elijah, I just want you."

Elijah's hands grabbed her butt and lifted, as both she and he rose out of the water. He carried her to his bed, albeit, with less effortless strength than the others could. He laid her on the covers, soaking them. He exited, pushed her up, and crawled over her.

"I'm afraid I'm not a natural dom. You think you can want that? Do you still want me, knowing the true sub that I am?"

"Yes! If it's all the same to you, I think the others have that covered." Emma laughed lightly. "Despite my history here, I don't need fear for my life to get my rocks off."

Emma and Elijah exchanged giggles.

"But," she said, "I don't know much about being a Matthew or Dameon in bed. Is that what you'd want from me?"

Elijah roughly pulled Emma on top of him. She straddled him, watching his playful mood spring to life.

"I am perfectly content in letting you play with me however you want. But... If you want to give it a try–? I don't mind playing a coach. It'll be fun to see what you can do."

"Put me in coach," Emma said, with a clap of her hands.

Elijah lit up. He nearly hurled her off, and rolled to the side of his bed. Emma lovingly laughed at Elijah's enthusiasm.

In a bedside table, with three drawers, Elijah kept a number of obscene items. He pulled open each, displaying his collection with showy hands. Emma's eyes widened, as she tried to suppress another giggle.

A rainbow of dildos, vibrators, clamps, rings, and beads cluttered the hidden storage spaces. In the bottom-most section, a leather strap-on harness was shoved into a corner. Emma pressed her stomach into the sheets, reached over, and dangled the harness with a single finger.

Elijah laughed so hard his body shook.

"Matthew and I may have a few things in common. We both love good dick, and we have a hard time throwing things away. Don't ask why I kept it, I really don't know. It's not like I've had a use for it in years, but if you're interested?"

Emma sat on her knees, eyeing the numerous black lines and silver buckles. She couldn't determine what was for the legs, and what was for the waist. She scrunched her face and smiled, as she turned the contraption over in her hands.

Elijah snatched the harness, and fastened her in. Emma kept her hands clear of his speedy work, as he bound the leather around her ass and waist. The key element was missing, but it didn't take Elijah long to find a moderately sized, bright purple dick. He put it in place, and examined Emma, making a square outline with his fingers to imitate the outline of a picture.

Emma laughed in near hysterics.

"I feel completely ridiculous. How can you take this seriously? I look hilarious!"

"Shut up. You look hot as hell! But If you ask nicely, I can show you just how well I can take it."

Elijah grabbed Emma's hand, and led her off the bed. He got on his knees. He intertwined his hands behind his back, and smiled at her. Emma stood over him, not really sure what to do.

"This is the part where you boss me around. Do your worst, honey."

"Um... okay, okay. How about, you want this dick? You, um, sexy slut, you?"

Emma snorted out a laugh. Elijah pursed his lips together in a comical frown, trying so hard to keep from cracking up with her.

Emma's laughter subsided, when Elijah caressed her calf and pressed his lips to the edge of her scar. He looked up at her with his big blue eyes, and licked his way up to her thigh. He pressed his lips up, and up, until he was at her hip. His fingers inched to her center, and tucked them under the tight straps.

Silly as she felt, his hands felt better. He followed the line of her ass to her middle. His thumbs massaged her open and shut, around the leather. He licked at her edges and placed a hand over the dick. He gripped it so tight, she almost became jealous of the thing.

He stroked the extension, and with his other hand, inserted two fingers into her. Emma felt an instability in her legs, as he moved in and out of her, matching the rhythm of his other hand. She groaned with the addition of a third finger, feeling her knees begin to come together. As he stroked, she could swear, she could almost feel his touch through the dildo.

Elijah irritatingly retrieved his hand. Her thirst for him grew, as she watched him suck her taste from his fingers. His doe eyes begged for her demands, as he went back to his original position with his hands behind his back.

"Well, princess? Would you like to show me what it's like to be your little prisoner?"

The feelings that passed through Emma, were very much to her surprise. Yes, she did.

"On the bed, Elijah."

Lust gleamed in his eyes. He bit his lip excitedly, and sat on the edge of the bed.

Emma placed a hand on his chest, kissed his lips, then shoved him back. She grabbed his, very real, cock in her hands and stroked. When he attempted to get up on his elbows to watch, she pushed his back to the mattress once more. Elijah's ass tensed, and hips moved to the movements of her hand.

She cupped his balls in her hand, and gave them a delicate squeeze. Elijah moaned loudly, when Emma suddenly took him in her mouth and sucked at his tip. She massaged his warm, sensitive areas, while taking him down her throat. She pushed through her gag reflex, hungrily devouring him. Seeing his pleasure made her so wet, and she wanted more.

Emma sucked hard on Elijah's cock, before releasing him. Elijah groaned from the depths of his chest. Emma watched him look down to her, as she moved her way up to his lips. Her tongue played with his, until she had kissed the breath from him.

"Want to be my good boy?"

Elijah nodded with affirming hums.

Emma guided Elijah face down, ass up. She felt the false cock in her hand, and with it, a lovely sense of control. As she readied behind him, Elijah grabbed for her and dropped to the bed.

"Wait! Wait," he giggled. "I love a rough time, but there," Elijah said, pointing to a bottle of lube in the top drawer. "If you don't mind? Please?"

Emma smiled. She reached back, snagged the container, and slicked the dick with a generous amount of the liquid. Elijah let out a breath of relief, as his face rested back to the mattress.

She readied again, apprehension beginning to get the better of her. She placed the tip against him. A shiver ran through Elijah's body, leading Emma to press her lips together and scrunch her brows. She took more delight in his eagerness than she initially guessed.

Slowly, she moved her hips, and pushed inside of him. Elijah's moans were so hot. She loved what she was doing to him. With a hand on either side of him, she pulled him to her, filling him with the purple toy. Open mouthed groans accompanied her newly found rhythm.

With every noise he made, Emma's intensity grew. Her speed increased, her own breathing audibly sounded. She was taking so much pleasure in the pleasure he was receiving from her. She wanted more of it, more of his panting, more of his little wines. The ache between her legs was becoming unbearable, but she didn't want to stop.

Elijah reached above his head to snatch a pillow. He pulled it close, and hugged it fiercely. He whined sharply, and pinched his eyes shut. Emma paused her rapidly roughening movements. She didn't want to actually hurt him, and she wasn't sure if he was enjoying it anymore, or in pain.

"No! Please! Please, don't stop. I'm begging, please. Don't stop."

The fire was instantly relit. She wouldn't stop, but she wasn't going to go easy on him either. She slid a hand up his spine and back down. With a smack to his ass, that stung her hand, she pushed ever so slowly in. He cried out at the contact, and pushed back to her crotch.

Elijah agonized at her pace. She kept the deliberate, unhurried rhythm. Drawn out moans made their way from Elijah, as she mercilessly stayed, terribly, gentle.

"Fuuck," Elijah breathily chuckled. "Fuck you. You're so mean."

"Aw, poor sweetie. You don't think I'm being nice? Show me how you like it. I'll give you what you need."

Elijah bared his teeth. He tossed the pillow to the ground, and pulled away. Swiftly, his arm grabbed her, and swung her beneath his body. He held her face and kissed her mouth. Before she realized what his other sneaky hand was up to, he ripped the unbuckled strap-on from her.

Emma screamed as he shoved himself in her pussy. He railed her, hard, jolting her body and consuming her at his will. A soft, "yes," escaped her lips with every thrust. His desperate chase drove her to absolute ecstasy.

"Cum, Elijah. Be a– fuck– be a good boy, and cum for me."

"Thank you," Elijah gasped. "Thank you. Fuck! Thank you, princess!"

The two orgasmed in sync, cum filling her cunt, and a wave us pulsing muscles contracting around him. Elijah buried his face in her wet hair. Sweat and perfume filled the air around the tapped partners.

Elijah pressed his lips to Emma's, sweetly, and smiled.

"Damn. It might be the orgasm talking, but Emma, I think I love you."

Emma directed Elijah off her, rolled over, and squeezed him in front of her. He backed up, pressing his back to her chest, and snuggled into her. Emma held him tight, and kissed the back of his neck.

"Yeah, probably. Because, I was starting to think the same thing."

16 | Desperate Times

Tiny leaves and spiraling vines made whimsical shadows in the morning light. Emma watched the hanging plants sway, as the air conditioner kicked on. Elijah ran his hand up and around Emma's shoulder. He pressed against her collarbone, pulling her back to his torso. Emma sighed as he nuzzled his nose around her neck and hair.

"Have I ever told you," he purred, "that you are an ugly sleeper."

A laugh burst forward, starting from Emma's nose.

"Good morning to you too."

"It's a cute kind of ugly. You sleep with your mouth open. It's adorable."

Elijah rolled his entire body over Emma, sprawling on top of her. He squished her into the mattress, as she wiggled to unsuccessfully get out from under him.

"Get off," she said, with a struggled laugh.

"My bed, my rules."

"That's not –oof– what you said last night."

Elijah made a show of rolling away and off the bed. Emma gasped for air over-dramatically, pretending to have been nearly crushed to death.

"Just wait 'til Matthew does that in his sleep. First time he got me, I thought I'd die. Speaking of which, you'll want a sports bra today. Matthew has plans for you."

"No," Emma said, frightfully. "Nooo."

"Yep. Get ready baby," he said, smacking her bare ass. "He's planning on making you sweat!"

Emma pulled the blankets over her head in protest.

"You can't make me. I'm pretty sure you three give me more than enough cardio."

Elijah reached beneath the comforter. He gripped her ankles and pulled. Emma laughed and shouted, grabbing the sheets. The corners snapped away from the mattress, and sent Emma flying to the ground over Elijah. He confined her playfully flailing arms, and wrapped her in a cute hold, kissing her cheek.

Downstairs, Dameon was sitting in a stool at the kitchen island. Emma gave him a little wave of her fingers, but he looked caught off guard. In his hands was an envelope. His eyes were lost in thought and hair was a mess. Maybe it was because he had just woken up too? Emma shrugged it off, and changed in her newly painted room.

When she returned, she was in a neon green bra, loose sleeveless top, and leggings. Dameon's fingers lifted the corner of a letter, preventing Emma from seeing the contents. As Elijah entered the kitchen, Dameon speedily folded the note and shoved it into his jean pocket. So much for no more secrets.

"Guess you don't want to share with the class," Emma asked.

Elijah dropped a frying pan on the stove, a little louder than necessary. His face remained casual, but a tension formed in his shoulders. Emma looked back to Dameon with increased curiosity. He looked guilty? Why? Before she could get the question-express to leave the station, Matthew could be heard coming down the stairs. Dameon gave a false half smile.

"Not exactly," he said. "We'll talk about it later."

"It's junk," Elijah said, with bite in his words. "It'll go out with the rest of the trash."

Matthew read the room and suddenly looked like he was contemplating going back upstairs. He didn't heed his instincts, and sat next to Emma instead.

"Fun night," he asked.

"Very," Emma said. "But you could have given me a heads up. I didn't expect Elijah to be the most dominating, ruthless, man in the penthouse.

301

He made Dameon look like a tame rabbit."

Matthew stared between Elijah and Emma in disbelief. Elijah's mood lightened and attempted to keep a calm composure. It didn't last long. He snorted a laugh that revealed her sarcastic fib. Dameon too, smiled at the absurd notion and let a little laugh out.

After a relatively light breakfast of eggs and sausage, Matthew tapped Emma on the shoulder and beckoned for her to follow him upstairs. Emma let out an exasperated sound and dramatically collapsed over the counter. Matthew laughed hard at Emma, pulling at her arm to get her moving. Elijah laughed as well, bending over the counter top to kiss her head. Dameon remained a little too distracted.

Once up the round stairs, Matthew opened the door to the gym with a gentlemanly bow. It was too early for a workout, but internally she was a little excited. He led her to a bench and removed several pounds from the bar above. Emma positioned herself with the leather seat between her legs. In the mirror, she watched Matthew place the round pieces of metal in their dedicated places.

He lifted the weights with incredible ease, as if they were made of feathers and not items that Emma would struggle to hold on to, even on an individual basis.

"Dameon has been working on plans to keep your mental health in a more positive place, going out, changing the room. Elijah has been teaching you how to pretend and cloak your identity. I want you to be able to fight if you need to. But before we do that, I need to know where to start. First, we're going to work on strength."

The bar above Emma looked silly. What once held well over three hundred pounds, was now fitted with a mere ten pounds on each side. Matthew instructed her to lean back and try to lift the bar from its place.

He stood at her head, a hand on either side of hers in case she needed the assistance. Annoyance that he thought she would need help for so little, sparked her determination. She gripped the bar, pushed, and embarrassingly, barely moved the weights. She shook and her arms strained as she lifted only once, holding her breath as she did.

Damaged pride reddened her cheeks. She was ready to hear Matthew laugh at her pathetic attempt, but instead of making fun of her, he assisted her in returning the bar to its place. He removed the remaining plates, leaving a naked bar above her and encouraged her to try again.

"This is kind of humiliating. Can we start with something else?"

"Nope, but don't feel bad. The bar alone weighs forty-five pounds. You haven't had the opportunity to train, so don't beat yourself up. That's why we are starting now. Try again. There's no shame in starting small. And don't hold your breath."

The empty bar was much more manageable without additional weights. Matthew counted out reps as she pushed the sparse equipment up and down, until her muscles burned. While she did, Matthew stood, palms up, ever ready to catch anything if she needed.

Her eyes drifted from the simple bar, to the space between the legs of his loose shorts. She cursed at herself for her dirty mind. She wanted, needed, a break from the seemingly constant sex, but here she was hoping for a peak up his pants. He noticed and poked a light-hearted jab at her, when her distracted mind caused the bar to unevenly tip to the side.

Instructing Emma not to leave the bench, and after a few kind affirmations, Matthew retrieved a small handheld weight. He straddled the bench just below the place that Emma's legs spread, and with a sweet hold, he pulled Emma into a sitting position. Chest to chest, Matthew lifted her arms up, wrapped her hands around the neoprene coated metal, and guided her hands back, behind her head.

"You know," he said. "We can still keep it interesting."

Emma pulled the weight up, then back down, feeling her arms object to the activity. She hadn't realized how out of shape she was until being here. Matthew's hands caressed her upper arms, keeping her form as it should be.

He slid his hands over her arms, lower, until his hands wrapped around her ribs. His thumbs stroked beneath her breasts. It felt nice, sweet, until it didn't. Matthew's thumbs touched a place in her ribs that almost made her drop the weight. Her stomach tightened, her lips pursed tight.

"Stop! Please, please, please! Stop touching me."

Matthew raised his hands, concern drenching his face. Emma swiftly brought the dumbbell forward and rested it in her lap. Breathy giggles sounded before she regained her composure. Matthew's face lit up, smile huge, and eyes provoking.

"Emma, are you ticklish?"

"Don't do it," she warned.

A lightning-fast hand touched the sensitive place at her ribs. Emma screamed a laugh, knees came up, and pushed against his attack.

"Okay, okay. I'll yield. Now, turn around. We're going to spend a little time in doggie-style."

Matthew led one of her legs on the floor, her other knee stayed on the bench. He placed the dumbbell back in her hand, and guided her through the motions of lifting it up and down.

The moment she had the hang of it, a large hand moved up her spine, sending goosebumps over her skin. Her sex tensed, feeling his hardness press close to her ass. What was wrong with her? A break! She needed a break. But the thought of his huge dick filling her up, feeling his– Emma swore with a breathy laugh.

Matthew laughed, teasingly, as he guided her through different ways to lift from her seductive position on the leather seat. She followed his instruction, and when her arms were too tired to take much more, lunges and squats followed.

Sweat damped her sports bra. Her body was numbing while adrenaline started pumping. Matthew took her hands in his at the catch of her second wind. They were ready to move on to the real lesson. Matthew stood behind her and slowly demonstrated the proper way to punch, moving her arms with his.

"Don't tuck your thumbs in, unless you want to hurt yourself. Doing that is a sure way to break a bone, and it's real hard to keep hitting when your hand is already done for."

The two of them faced the mirrored wall and practiced over and over. Emma's confidence was growing, feeling like a bit of a bad ass as she learned more about defense and offense than she ever had in her life.

"Alright Emma, hit me."

Emma's fists unclenched, and fell to her sides.

"I can't do that!"

Matthew laughed and casually beckoned her with four fingers.

"You won't hurt me. Trust me."

Well, she didn't want to hit him, but his sureness that, even if she did, she wouldn't have what it takes to do any damage? It irked her and created a competitive itch.

She threw a jab, holding back a smidge, but he dodged easily. She threw another, then another, missing every time. Each swing grew faster, more real, until one landed square in his hard abs. She withdrew her stinging hand, and shook it out.

As she examined her pink knuckles, Matthew tackled her to the padded floor. Emma fell with a grunt, as he pinned her down. She looked up at his excited face. He was playing, which relieved her. At least she didn't seem to have actually hurt him.

"Come on," he growled. "Get away."

Emma grabbed his wrist that pressed her shoulders to the floor. She wiggled, struggled, but he didn't move.

"You're not going anywhere like that, little prisoner."

She paused her fight. She stared into his wild eyes, breathing hard, feeling small.

"Another fantasy of yours," she asked, relaxing her hands on him.

Matthew's eyes trailed along her top half. His body weight shifted, adding more weight, depressing the mat below.

"Hands together."

Emma linked her fingers below Matthew's arms. A rough adjustment tore her hands apart, correcting her to replace her hands above his hold. He went back to pinning her down, when he instructed her to push down, hard, with everything she had.

When she did, her back moved up, his hands fell down to the floor. Her legs scrambled to scoot her body upwards. Matthew grabbed the back of her neck, pulled her face to his, and took her mouth with his. When he pulled back, he pressed her forehead to his.

"A headbutt will hurt you, but it's usually shocking enough to give an advantage. And never, ever..."

Matthew's hand squeezed her thigh, and brought her knee up.

"Never think you're above a kick to the groin."

"Still part of your fantasy," Emma teased.

"Absolutely not," he laughed.

A lent hand helped Emma onto her feet, as Matthew turned to the treadmills.

Emma's nervousness over looking foolish faded. She had to admit, she found more enjoyment in the training than she originally imagined. But when it came to running, it was her time to shine. Even on a machine leading nowhere, she felt a sense of calm in her fast pace. Matthew took his place on a second treadmill and kept up with her, glancing over at the electronic numbers on her screen with an impressed expression. Faster she pushed, and with the increased speed, she felt familiarity and security.

"Damn," Matthew said, between breaths. "What are you running from?"

Emma smiled, heart pounding, and feet swiftly tapping against the belt.

"Wouldn't you like to know," she teased.

Dameon knocked against the open doorframe, Elijah at his side. Matthew eased off the pace for a cooldown lap while Emma continued to sprint. Dameon raised a brow at her speed.

"We're lucky you didn't decide to make a break for it at Huevos," he said, with a smile. "I didn't realize you would have given us such a run for our money."

Emma beamed, and adjusted the settings on her own machine to a walking speed. Her heart pounded in her ears. Sweat spots clung to her shirt and pants. The chilly air of the gym pained her lungs. It felt terrible and wonderful all at once.

"When you're ready, we have something to show you," Dameon said.

Downstairs, smelly from the workout, Matthew and Emma met up with Elijah and Dameon. Elijah motioned for her to follow them to her room, where to her surprise, was a partially furnished space.

While she and Matthew were working out, Dameon and Elijah were busy putting together her new bed, a lovely dresser, a standing lamp, a large mirror, and a bedside table. The room that was once uncomfortably plain, now took on a shockingly put together vibe of dark and vibrant colors. It was perfect.

Emma's chest swelled with emotion as she stepped into the space that she envisioned. On the bed were a number of pieces she had picked out but were left unplaced in the room.

"We didn't want to do everything, but at least wanted to get the big stuff set up. We figured, you'd want to make most of the decorating decisions for yourself," Elijah said.

Emma spun around and pounced on Dameon and Elijah, wrapping them the tightest of hugs. Her eyes watered. This was hers. She wasn't sure if it could happen, but the room that once held such great fears and anxieties, the place of profound loneliness and pain, was now her personal room of safety and comfort.

"Thank you," she said, welling with emotion.

Elijah was the first to wriggle out of her hug.

"You can thank us after you've showered," he said, playfully.

Dameon rolled his eyes.

"Don't thank us Emma. It was the very least we could do, after the trauma we've put you through with this room."

With bubbling excitement, Emma entered the space. Nothing was hung on the walls yet, with the exception of one piece of artwork. She laughed as she took it in.

"What?" Dameon said, with a smile. "Did you think we wouldn't notice?"

Emma shook her head at the painting, her painting. It was the same one she attempted while waiting for the results of the jewelry store robbery.

"You're hilarious. But it's awful, and it's coming down."

"Aw, no," Elijah protested. "It's adorable!"

Emma allowed the wonky picture to remain, and began to go to work. She took a hammer and nail from a pile sitting on the bedside table.

Emma climbed atop the dresser for a better reach, and beat the nail into the wall. Thankfully, she hit a stud on her first try. She hopped down, retrieved a massive item from the bed, and hung it happily in its rightful place. The large clock silently ticked, as Emma continued finding a home for each of her lovely decorations.

Emma spent much of the day filling her room with the spoils of her shopping spree, only pausing for a quick shower, and speedy lunch break. By the time Elijah's chicken tacos came around for dinner, the delicious meal didn't stand a chance.

Elijah, as usual, had outdone himself. The bites were spicy. The corn, onions, lettuce, were crunchy in the best of ways. The various sauces were utter perfection. With a chef like him in the house, Emma found herself to be very grateful for the gym in the home. Sure, the training was great, but she'd probably have to make a habit of visiting the room just to keep fitting in her new clothes.

Dameon picked at his plate. Emma wondered if it was the run-in with Tony that was still weighing on his mind, or if his distraction was due to the mystery letter. She had never seen him do anything other than scarf down Elijah's works of art. Matthew and Elijah finished their meals fairly quickly, allowing Elijah to wiggle his way under Matthew's arm. Emma sat cross-legged on one of the green chairs and eyed Dameon with increased concern.

Dameon set his, finally, empty plate on the floor beside his green chair and looked grim.

"Sebastian got a hold of me today. Riel is dead."

Emma's full stomach churned. The others exchanged looks of shock, disappointment, and grief.

"I... I'm so sorry. My plan, I didn't want anyone to get hurt. I didn't–"

Dameon shot his head up to look at Emma.

"Don't," Matthew said. "It's not your fault."

"But it was my plan," Emma said, feeling tears begin to force their way out.

Dameon got to his knees, held Emma's upper legs together with sweet pressure. He waited for her attention before speaking.

"We would have prepared you better for this. It's always a possibility. Matthew wasn't just trying to make you feel better. It's not your fault, it's mine. I chose to target him, not you. Hell, if you want to hate someone for this, hate Tony. He wanted to send a message. He's the one that chose to kill him, not you."

It was nice that they wanted her to feel better, but it didn't curb the guilt. Sure, Tony killed him and Dameon picked the shop to hit, but it was still her plan. She was part of it. She was, at least in some major way, responsible for a decent person's death. It was overwhelming, horrible.

"Was that what was in the letter you got this morning?"

Dameon's reassuring hands froze. He went from comforting, to apprehensive. Sebastian didn't send the note. But if that's not what he was hiding, what was it? He was the one that was the biggest stickler over not keeping secrets. What had him so on edge, that he was so reluctant to share?

His hands left Emma. He returned to his green chair, folded his hands, and stared down at his thumbs. He wasn't the only one with a changed persona. Elijah's face grew irritated, while Matthew held him tighter.

"Carter sent us a party invitation," Dameon said.

Matthew's hand over Elijah's arm held the man even tighter. All attention to Dameon. Matthew's face was nearly unreadable to Emma, but Elijah's was not. He was furious at the mention of the sender's name.

"I think we should go," said Dameon.

"And why exactly do we need to do that," Elijah asked, viciously.

"Because," Dameon said, "I've ignored the last ten or so, and I was thinking–"

"No." Elijah said, with finality.

Emma felt a tingle of shock at Elijah's answer. It wasn't unusual for the man to be snippy, but this was different. Elijah held a power over this conversation that was potentially greater than Dameon's. He wasn't interested in entertaining the idea of accepting the invitation, and looked angry that Dameon would so much as ask for permission. Dameon's words may have taken their typical unquestionable structure, but nevertheless, he was asking for Elijah and Matthew's blessing.

"Elijah, I know you don't like it. But Tony is escalating. He knows about Emma, at least in some capacity. I don't know if I have what it takes to keep everyone safe. I... I want to go. Carter has a lot of power. If I ask for protection, I think there's a chance we can get it."

Dameon paused to watch Elijah's unyielding gaze. When Elijah didn't let up, Dameon continued.

"And to formally introduce the newest member of our family," he said.

"You really think that's a good idea," Matthew asked. "Meeting with that crew barely sounds like a lesser evil."

"I know it's not great, but–"

"No," Elijah said, again.

"Look," said Dameon. "I'm sorry. I really am. You know I am. But Carter is still an ally, of sorts. If we go and say we need some help, I'm pretty confident I can convince–"

"The answer is no, Dameon!" Elijah said sternly.

Elijah removed himself from his former place of comfort. He sat on the edge of his seat. His eyes burned into Dameon, with a hint of disgust. Whoever Carter was, Elijah wholly hated the person. Matthew's concerned expression and Dameon's desperation made Emma move uneasily in her chair.

"We've come a long way since then," Matthew said, trying to calm Elijah.

Elijah turned his fiery glare to Matthew in Dameon's place. He shoved Matthew's arm to the side and sat on the other side of the couch.

"I'm not saying I agree with Dameon," Matthew said, gently. "But you trust him, don't you? You know that Dameon would never ask this of us if he didn't think it was completely necessary."

Dameon's head sank. He stared at the floor. His movements made Emma nervous, but not in any of the usual ways. He looked ashamed. The last time she saw a look like that, Dameon had just realized how wrong he was to attack her. It was time to do what she did best.

"Who's Carter?"

Matthew's eyes lingered on Dameon for a moment, then rested on Elijah. Elijah heard Emma's question, but never looked her way. His attention was on Dameon, who continued to stare at the floor. Elijah cleared his throat, beckoning Dameon to meet his eyes. Elijah raised a brow, challenging him to tell Emma who this mystery person was.

Dameon took a deep breath and proceeded to tell Emma a story.

Carter was a major player in illegal activity in the city. In their early years, when Dameon, Matthew, and Elijah first started making moves to take Tony down, Sebastian played a significant role in shaping them into competent criminals. Sebastian encouraged a more vigilante-esque approach. However, when he discovered their methods of gaining information, he was disappointed at their recklessness.

Sebastian reluctantly introduced them to a valuable but very dangerous resource. Carter was, and is, a merciless, bloodthirsty, powerful, human being with a vast network of people to command. Upon being introduced, Dameon quickly became a person of great interest to the major criminal.

They both wanted Tony to suffer, to be out of their way forever. Dameon's thirst for vengeance proved to be a desirable quality to the organization. Carter was interested in building an empire with Dameon, and he found the partnership compelling, for a while.

Elijah was heavily unsatisfied with the direction Dameon's recollection was taking.

"Don't act like it was all business. Carter was a homewrecker." Elijah said, bitterly.

"Maybe, but—"

"Carter tried to take you from us!"

Dameon stood. Frustration returned, and with it a good amount of his authority.

"Not Matthew, Carter tried to take me from you. I was flown out to Paris because I owed a favor. I wouldn't have gone for any other reason."

Elijah rose to his feet as well. Emma didn't like this conversation. By the looks of it, neither did Matthew. He and Emma followed the other two with their eyes, like a riveting tennis match.

"You were flown out for a cute getaway and for a good fuck! And you did."

"We were sleeping with lots of people back then. How many people did you sleep with so we could get what we needed?"

"Not… like… that!" Elijah shouted. "Carter wanted to kill me! They tried to! Or do you not remember that part, because I sure do."

"Stop!" Matthew boomed.

Emma pulled her knees close, and held them to her chest. She balled herself up in the corner of her chair, while Matthew joined the other two on his feet. The room was terrible. Elijah was hurt and angry. Dameon was agitated. Matthew put an arm around each of the men and held them close.

"It was a long time ago," Matthew said, trying to regain some civility. "We all put a stop to the sex-for-information phase. Elijah, Dameon chose you. He chose you over Carter, over the easiest path to getting revenge. Carter could have given him the whole damn city, but he chose you. Dameon, you know it's not fair to ask Elijah to go along with this plan. Plus, it's way too risky. Carter has never played fair. We can't expect different now."

Elijah shoved Matthew's arm off his shoulder. Matthew willingly let both have a little space but his presence was reminiscent of that of a referee.

Dameon grabbed Elijah by the shirt and forced him close. Elijah tried to pull away, but with little luck. Emma's eyes widened when Elijah swung to slap Dameon across the face. The angry act was stopped short, when Dameon caught his wrist. He leaned to the blond and kissed him hard. Elijah wiggled under the advance. Dameon's other hand pulled Elijah's waist and held the struggling man in place.

A series of rapid "no's," left Elijah's mouth when Dameon allowed his lips the freedom. Emma's stomach felt sick.

"Matthew was gaining a reputation as a stone-cold killer. He was a prized collectible. He would have been their personal toy soldier, and he would have been used to death. Carter didn't have a need for a gifted grifter at the time. You were considered dead weight, and expendable to the organization. But do you know why the hit on you was really called out?"

Tears started to roll down the sides of Elijah's face.

"Let go," Elijah said, wriggling his wrist under Dameon's hold. "You're hurting me."

Matthew gripped the shoulder of Dameon's shirt, ready to yank him away. Dameon tried to roll Matthew's hand away unsuccessfully.

"Killing you," Dameon said, regardless of Matthew's presence, "would have fucking broke me. That's what Carter wanted. With you out of the way, maybe I'd be more willing to partner up. They all know better now. I made it clear, where my loyalties will always lie. Those people are too smart to think about getting rid of you this time, not now that they know that I'll kill every last one of them if they lay a hand on you."

Dameon dropped to his knees and looked up at his trembling, pissed off lover. Matthew's grip never faltered, still holding the shoulder of Dameon's shirt.

"I love you, Elijah! I regret ever letting Carter touch me, for letting it get that far. I know this is hard for you, but dammit, I need you with me. I swear to you, my only intentions are to ask for support, to protect our family. I understand what I am asking, but I don't know how long I can keep Emma safe. I know you care for her as much as I do. I'm not asking you to like it, but consider it, for her."

"Red," Emma said, calmly.

The occupants of the room turned side-tracked faces toward the woman in the green chair. It was as if they all had forgotten she was right there, and only her singular word reminded them of her presence. Dameon looked like someone had hit him over the head with a frying pan. Matthew glanced at Emma, but went back to monitoring the two men.

Emma stood to her feet.

"Red," Dameon asked, confused.

"Red," she repeated. "Full stop. I don't consent to this. If I'm really the root cause of this fight, then I'm telling you, no. Don't meet with this, Carter. You'll find another way."

Emma walked slowly to the men. She placed her hand over Dameon's that was still squeezing at Elijah's wrist. Dameon looked back and forth between Emma and Elijah. He unclenched his grip, and let Emma guide his hand down to his side.

"Is this really about protecting me," she asked.

"Of course."

"Then stop. Nothing any of you have done to me has hurt nearly as bad as watching you fight each other like this. Please, stop."

Emma's words cut deep. Pain erupted on each of the men's faces. Elijah's eyes bounced from Dameon to Emma. He scrunched his eyebrows together and ripped away from Dameon. He turned to Emma and grabbed her.

Elijah held the side of her head, and pressed his cheek against hers. His hand moved along her back and pushed her body into his as if he was trying to make them a single person. Elijah kissed the corner of Emma's eye.

"Do you really care for me," Emma whispered, past Elijah and to Dameon.

"You know I do." said Dameon.

"Then you'll find another way."

Emma looked between all three men.

"You're clever. You'll think of something. But please, don't do this. I can't stand it."

Dameon held Elijah and Emma in a gentle embrace. Elijah allowed it. Emma reached for Matthew, silently asking him to join. He did.

Dameon kissed Elijah's forehead, then Emma's. Emma tilted her chin and reached to plant her lips on Dameon's. Dameon slowly pushed Elijah and Emma backwards to the sofa, and sat them on the cushions. Over and over, he kissed their faces, their necks, their hands.

"I'm sorry," he said. "Please forgive me."

Elijah placed himself between Emma and Dameon, straddling her and facing the woman. He pulled Dameon's arms from behind him to wrap around his waist.

He held the back of Emma's neck and stroked the edge of her jaw with his thumb. He reached for Matthew's hand and wordlessly requested to be held. Matthew obliged and rested his forehead on Elijah's, with a large hand around the back of Elijah's neck. His other hand started at Emma's shoulder then ran down to intertwine her fingers in his own. This wasn't quite the conclusion Emma intended, but she didn't object. Seeing them use their loving touches was far more preferable.

Dameon's hands drifted down. He drifted beneath Elijah's waist band and found the man. Elijah's breath shook, and he reached to take Matthew's tongue. Another of Dameon's hands slid under Emma's shirt and sweetly held her side. Matthew let go of Emma's hand and placed his on top of Dameon's.

Matthew guided Dameon's hand up, until they felt Emma's breast together, pushing Elijah all the closer to her. Emma hummed as Dameon guided his and Matthew's fingers to roll over a nipple beneath her shirt. Elijah trailed Emma's jawline and inserted a thumb between her lips. Emma let him open her mouth. She arched under their hold and massaged the growth under Matthew's pants.

Elijah eyed the subtle striped bruises around her legs.

"Wait," he said.

Dameon and Matthew both paused their actions, with some apprehension.

"I don't want us to over-do it," Elijah said, softly. "Your body's been put through a lot over the last few days. You know you don't have to, right?"

Emma moved to press her lips to Elijah's neck, forcing out a sigh.

"I'll tell you when I've had enough."

Dameon passed a look to Matthew, who helped Emma up, and off, the sofa. Hand in hand, he led her up the curved staircase. On their way, Emma watched Elijah and Dameon linger behind on the couch. Dameon placed Elijah above him, and whispered something in his ear. Elijah attacked Dameon's mouth with his own, and grinded on top of him. Emma glanced up to Matthew, who was smiling sweetly and gratefully back at her.

"That's one way to diffuse a bomb," he said.

"It's not exactly what I planned, but I'm glad it worked."

Matthew led Emma onto the large, shared bed and crawled over her.

"You sure you're up for this?"

"I said, I'll tell you when I've had enough."

Matthew's tongue played in her mouth until Dameon and Elijah made it to the room. They were already naked. Dameon was fully erect and glistening, with the evidence of Elijah's foreplay. Elijah licked the taste of Dameon's skin from his lips, and descended on Emma and Matthew. While Elijah assisted Emma in the removal of her clothing, Matthew undressed himself quickly.

Dameon placed Elijah between Emma's legs, and himself behind Elijah. His hands rubbed against Elijah's smooth torso. Matthew bent to pay attention to Emma's chest with his mouth and hands. Emma moaned beneath them.

A hand of Dameon's, ran down to stroke Elijah. As he did, Elijah's dick teased Emma's sex. Emma let out wanting pleas at the touch. Elijah gave Emma precisely what she was asking for. She let out a gasp with his entrance. Their concern wasn't misplaced. She was becoming increasingly sore from the constant sex, and much of it rough.

He moved in her, smoothly and carefully, until Dameon bent him forward. Some level of alarm filled Elijah's face. He looked back at the man that readied himself from behind.

"I won't be able to last long if you do that," he warned.

"That's the plan. We'll make this one quicker," Dameon said, as he kissed along Elijah's spine. "I'm sure she'll understand."

Dameon passed a wink to Emma, who smiled gratefully in return.

Elijah wined out a moan. The sound made Emma hot. She watched, and felt as Dameon pushed Elijah deeper into her with Dameon's own thrusts. Elijah's arms trembled around her. He nearly collapsed on top of her, letting Dameon take his ass while Elijah took her. Emma ran her fingers through Elijah's soft blond waves.

Matthew positioned near Elijah's mouth. Elijah made a soft sound when Emma gripped his hair in her hands. She turned his head, placed a finger between his lips, and offered his open mouth up to Matthew. Elijah whined appreciatively at her control. Dameon groaned with incredible lust. Matthew bit his lower lip. Emma was prematurely spent, but seeing the way Elijah was being consumed, healing, made her want more.

"Fuck, Emma," Dameon swore.

Elijah choked greedily around Matthew's cock. Matthew overlapped Emma's hand at the back of Elijah's head, and gave a considerable amount of himself. Elijah accepted the gag that contracted around Matthew. Emma raised and lowered her hips, with a delicious lack of synchronization with Dameon. Elijah breathed hard through his nose and let himself be overwhelmed with the pleasure bestowed upon him.

Emma drank in the sounds he made, and increased the pace of her lower half. She clenched hard around Elijah. Dameon followed her lead, and grinned maliciously when he engaged Matthew in a silent conversation. Matthew left Elijah's mouth and continued the telepathic conversation with the blond man. Elijah nodded.

Dameon retrieved Elijah's wrists and pulled them behind his back. He let out soft, high, breathy, cries as Dameon thrusted hard behind him. Elijah made a guttural sound as the harsh man finished inside of his ass. Swearing snuck past Elijah's lips as his cum spilled into Emma.

Matthew slid an arm under Emma's neck, as Elijah quickly repositioned himself to lay behind her. He placed the back of her head against his stomach, and her body between his legs. Elijah snatched her hands, and held her to squeeze and pinch her own breasts at his direction.

Matthew took over Elijah's precious position between her, and shoved his massive cock into her. Emma shouted in equal measures of pain and desire. She breathed sharply while taking in his overwhelming offering. Dameon leaned close, to whisper in her ear.

"I want to taste you again."

Elijah stroked Emma's blond hair.

"Only if you want. I will understand if you're not ready." Dameon said.

Matthew forced a moan from Emma, with a deep thrust. Even so, she never took her eyes off Dameon. Her old nerves came back. She wasn't prepared to have a repeat experience of yesterday morning, not yet anyway.

"Will you..." she quivered, "again? You won't–"

Dameon kissed the tip of her nose in affection.

"No little prisoner. Not like that."

Emma nodded her head, though she knew by now what he needed to hear.

"Yes," she confirmed, aloud.

Dameon grabbed a pillow from the bed and slid it under Emma's ass.

Matthew and Dameon angled her so that as one filled her, the other was given just enough room. Dameon lowered himself above Emma and proceeded to lick at her clit. Emma shouted. Elijah's grip pinched her nipples tighter between their fingers.

Her feet pressed down into the mattress. She cried out as Matthew went faster, Dameon more wild. Emma felt the rush of stimulation and all-consuming pleasure as the second man filled her with yet more cum. She pulsed tremendously around Matthew as her orgasm flooded her body.

Matthew pulled out. Elijah let one hand free, and pressed his against her forehead. He forced her to look at him, while Dameon took Matthew's place between her legs. Before she knew what he was planning, Dameon sucked the cum from her cunt.

Emma screamed at the feeling of being drained of them. Her legs shook and body arched. Matthew came up to her side and placed his hand on her jaw. He opened her mouth, just as she had Elijah's. Dameon joined the others to kiss her open mouth. Only, it wasn't just a kiss.

He brought the warm cum of Elijah and Matthew to her, and spit it between her lips. Dameon placed a strong hand over her mouth, preventing her from spitting. She whimpered with her mouth full of their climax. She breathed hard and fast through her nose. He watched her with a trace of madness in his eyes, they all did.

She swallowed audibly, and brought devious grins to all of the faces. Matthew released her first, then Elijah, then finally Dameon.

"That's my good girl," Dameon praised.

Dameon fell to the bed, and pulled Elijah and Emma close. Elijah played with Emma's hair, while Matthew pulled in Elijah and Emma from the other side.

"We're going to Carter's stupid party," Elijah said. "But if anyone tries to murder me, I'm coming back to haunt the shit out of you, Dameon."

"Ghost sex," Dameon chuckled. "Sounds fun."

After a rather speedy shower to clean up, each of the four snuggled into the bed.

There was too much on Emma's mind, to allow her to sleep quickly. They were apparently going to a party, hosted by a person that obviously still had a massive negative impact on her lovers. She was rather proud of her ability to deescalate the argument, but Elijah's acceptance to go, somehow felt like a loss. That, and the thoughts of Riel, weighed on her enough to prolong her consciousness long after her partners were asleep.

A panicked swear jolted Emma from her dreamless sleep. Dameon hurled out of bed, tossing the covers indiscriminately, to flip on a light. Elijah jumped to his feet, frantically looking around the room for the threat.

Matthew stayed in bed, his back pressed to the headboard, his skin more pale than Emma thought might be possible. He shook his head, and uttered a series of panicked exclamations over his discovery.

"You said you were fine!" Matthew said, desperately. "You said you'd tell us if you needed a break!"

Emma stared, confusedly at Matthew, as if he was speaking in another language. His eyes were wide, and horrified, and swept over Emma's legs without wanting to touch her. Elijah mirrored Matthew's concern, and stared miserably at Emma. He seemed to be falling into Matthew's panic, while Dameon held an entirely different composure.

When Dameon saw the damage all the fuss was about, he tilted his head and laughed.

"What the fuck, Dameon!" Matthew said. "It's not funny. We hurt her!"

Dameon laughed louder.

Emma was literally bleeding on the bed, but only figuratively dying.

"I don't know how to fix this but... I'll be back. I'm sure we have something–" Elijah said, as he rushed to the door.

"Stop," Dameon laughed. "You ridiculous, ridiculous men. She doesn't need medical attention. She needs chocolate. And maybe some ibuprofen."

Elijah's bewildered expression faded into complete embarrassment at his remarkable misdiagnosis. He blinked hard, looked at the blood stained sheets and slapped a hand to his head.

"Oh my god," he said finally.

"What," Matthew asked, a little late to the party.

"Please," Dameon smiled, taking Emma's hand and giving it a kiss. "Forgive them. Matthew hasn't lived with a woman, pretty much ever, and Elijah was clearly caught up in the moment."

Emma pressed her hands to her forehead, and shielded her eyes. She was never one to be ashamed of something as simple as her period, but Matthew and Elijah's reaction was hilariously embarrassing.

Dameon scooped Emma up, and carried her back to the shower.

"Elijah," Dameon called back, with another laugh. "Maybe you can give Matthew a little refresher on the birds and the bees."

Dameon and Emma met the other two in the kitchen. The smell of fudgy brownies filled the air. Emma greeted Matthew and Elijah with an awkward smile. Dameon quietly laughed to himself again at the sight of Elijah, who was paying an unnatural amount of attention to cleaning a pan. Matthew watched his fingers tap incrementally on the counter.

"I can't exactly blame you, Matthew. But Elijah," Dameon said, with amusement. "You're the medic around here, and arguably, the more experienced when it comes to the female anatomy than either of us."

"I forgot!" Elijah said, defensively. "This might come as a shock, but I haven't exactly had to think about periods on a regular basis. As a man, living with a bunch of men, it hasn't been on my mind for the past however-many years."

Both Dameon and Emma caught each other's rolling eyes.

The brownies were just what the doctor ordered. While Elijah shed most of his embarrassment, poor Matthew was still struggling.

He wouldn't look at her. Emma was beginning to feel offended by the treatment. It wasn't her fault her body decided to obey mother nature. Maybe he thought it was gross, but he didn't have to sit there making her feel like an alien for it. It was a natural part of life, and she wasn't going to feel bad about it.

"Okay, Matthew," Emma said, with a mouthful of brownie. "What's the big deal? Maybe you haven't been around this much, but if you're going to have me here, you're going to have to get used to it a little. I can't exactly turn it off."

Matthew didn't meet her gaze.

"I really thought we... I... hurt you."

Emma put a pause to her delicious prescription. She rounded the counter to hug Matthew but he made the first move, lifting her from the ground and holding her close like a doll. Her toes grazed the floor and when the heels of her feet returned, she kissed him while her fingers touched through his beard and to his jaw. She tried to offer some comfort by reassuring him that she really was fine, but all he gave back was a harder embrace.

"It does bring up a question though," Elijah said. "You've been here for nearly two months. Were you... late?"

Dameon raised a brow. He clearly hadn't done the math. Maybe he forgot just how long she had been with them? Worry showed in the little creases of his face.

"When you held Matthew in that first time," he said, "You seemed so sure. I assumed you were protected, had an arm implant or something. We've been so reckless. Are... Have we been risking getting you pregnant this whole time?"

Emma shook her head but her mind lingered on thoughts far from pregnancies and periods.

Two months? Had it really been that long? That short? Her time in the penthouse felt like years. All that time in isolation, everything that happened, it was all contained in the span of a couple of months. Her feelings for these men had grown into something so strong, but in only months? Maybe she really had lost her mind through the trauma and sudden affection, after a lifetime of feeling so alone.

"Look," Dameon said, softly. "I promise I won't be upset because we gave you every reason not to trust us. I swear, I won't be mad. I just need to know if we need to get you something and–"

He took a mindful breath, attempting to choose his words carefully.

"I want to know, were you strategically trying to get one of us to knock you up?"

"No!" Emma said, a little too defensively.

Dameon raised a questioning brow.

"No! I haven't had a period in over a month, but that's not unusual. I'm still on the birth control shot. I have only a month left, apparently, but until then I'm good. It does that to me, makes me pretty irregular. Do you really just think that I would try to save myself by getting pregnant?"

Dameon shrugged.

Irritation came back to Emma in full swing.

"Maybe," Matthew said. "It would be a hell of a card to play."

"Well I'm not playing cards, and I'm not playing you. But I am going to need something fairly soon, if I want to keep pregnancy out of the equation. It's not like I planned on being here for two months."

"Sebastian can help with that," Elijah said. "He's how I get most of the drugs we keep on hand. He can get a hold of anything, we can get you covered."

Emma's eyes darted down to her hand, as she felt Matthew take hers in his. He was gentle and searching for the right words for what was on his mind.

"I didn't think about asking. Do you want kids? I mean, in the future?"

There was sadness in his voice. None of them had talked about this yet. It was a rational question. If they wanted to keep her on a long-term basis, maybe even forever, it was a reasonable thing to ask.

"Do you," she asked, curiously.

"No." said Matthew and Elijah in unison.

An uncomfortable silence fell in the room. Elijah suddenly looked sorry over his quick answer. It made sense to her. Given their criminal activities, having a kid would be a pretty big issue. Not to mention, the fact that none of these men imagined having a woman as a partner in their future. Having kids wasn't a risk to them before she was brought into their family.

"But do you," Dameon asked. "Please. Try not to let us dictate your answer. We never talked about this before, but what you want in life matters to me. I want to know."

"I really don't," she said. "I never have. It never felt like something I wanted before."

"And now?"

Dameon looked at her with his deep-blue eyes. Elijah and Matthew exchanged glances. It almost sounded like Dameon was considering the possibility.

"I… Do you want kids, Dameon?"

All eyes were on him. He looked thoughtful and a little disappointed. Emma wasn't sure if he was saddened by Emma's lack of desire to have children, or something else. But it made her almost feel guilty for her answer.

"No," he said, finally. "But I feel like I'm taking something away from you."

Emma laughed.

"I do not want a baby," she said. "I don't ever want to be a mother. Probably for some of the same reasons you guys don't want to be fathers. I'm not particularly interested in continuing my family line. Also, I'm not some baby making machine. Just because I'm a woman, doesn't mean I automatically want a child."

Dameon stretched his arms over the counter, and let out a sigh.

"We've got to get a hold of Sebastian," he said, with a relieved smile.

17 | How To Make Friends

Clothes littered the floor of Emma's new, beautiful room. She and Elijah had been looking for a specific dress for what seemed like hours. It didn't take long for her natural messiness to make its mark on her private space.

They chose to divide and conquer. Elijah searched upstairs, in a closet of their shared room. Emma checked her own closet for the third time, it had to be there somewhere. It wouldn't have been such an issue, if purchases from their excessive shopping spree didn't take up more space than her personal closet could afford. Elijah reassured her that she wasn't alone in her dilemma. He too had more clothes than he could fit into his room.

Elijah joined Emma to search through her closet once more when, Dameon knocked against the doorframe to Emma's room. He held the garment with a single finger, dangling the dress. Elijah rushed over and instantly snatched it from his hand.

"Yes!" Elijah exclaimed. "That's the one."

The dress was a dark gray, almost black. It hugged her every curve. Its outermost sheer layer was covered in a sparkly, glitter-looking material. The outfit was on the shorter side, but the high sleeveless turtleneck cut made it a little more modest.

Elijah moved the hidden zipper up, along her spine and ending just below her hairline. He looked her over in studious observation. It fit Emma like a glove. He stood behind her in a long glowing mirror that touched the floor.

Emma couldn't shake the feeling of exposure. It wasn't the dress' fault, but rather the lack of Amy looking back at her. Her skin tone was natural, and freely revealed the light bruising around her legs. Her green eyes were hers. Her makeup was elegant, but only complemented her born features, rather than trying to hide them. She certainly looked gorgeous, but too much like Emma to go outside.

Elijah smiled, but she could see the same fear in his own bright blue eyes. From his pocket, his hand retrieved a silver locket. He opened it in front of her. A tiny picture of Dameon, Matthew, and Elijah, smiled back at her.

"I know," he said. "It's kind of cheesy."

Emma closed the piece of jewelry and rubbed it between her thumb and finger.

"I love it," she said. "It's really sweet."

Elijah clasped the necklace around her, and handed Emma a pretty, light-blue wig, cut in the shape of a short bob. The wig hung limply in her hands while Elijah hid, and adjusted her natural hair.

"Sweet? Or a gentle reminder of how much you love us, when you meet Carter?"

His tone was joking, but there was a seriousness hidden behind the words. She couldn't be hurt by the wary sound in his voice. If he almost lost Dameon to Carter, she could understand why he might be worried about Emma. She didn't have near the accumulation of trust Dameon had, but nonetheless, they were going.

Even with the false hair, she still felt that she resembled herself entirely too much. Elijah explained that the hair was less about concealing her identity, and more about doing the opposite. She needed to be noticeable for the night. She needed to be perfectly recognizable after being introduced. This version of Emma was who they would ask protection for. When Carter's people were introduced to this easily distinguishable look, they would know that she is who they need to look out for.

"You know we don't have to go, right," Emma said. "We can still call it off."

"No," Elijah said, solemnly. "Dameon is right. We slipped up, and underestimated him. We won't do it again. Besides, we couldn't keep you a secret forever. If Tony knows, Carter is sure to find out, maybe already knows. It's better to confront it on our terms."

Vegas, like any other city, was one of numerous atmospheres. There were homes, schools, grocery stores. There was the new-downtown full of modern buildings, bright lights, and the most sought after casinos. But further on, was the old-downtown. Entertaining lights still played, but there was a seedier feel to the area.

But they weren't going to the older tourist attraction. Beyond the gleaming lights and crowds there was a darker place, where street names turned to letters, and homes lacked the typical track-housing feel. Matthew drove to a location where any hope of security vanished. Dark alleys, the wandering lost, drug dealers, and predatory stares, seemed banished to this place.

The car parked a considerable distance from Carter's venue, though Matthew made a verbal note that it might not be there when they returned. Emma made a mental note to thank Elijah and Matthew for her lesson in high heels. If they hadn't entertainingly shown her how to stride in the shoes, the walk would have been nearly impossible.

The streets seemed to absorb light like multiple black holes. On foot, they passed garages and abandoned looking buildings. Each pounded with the music of different parties. Emma's nerves could be felt in her throat when the occasional passerby eyed her uncomfortably.

Heavy bass beats sent vibrations through the pavement, as the four well dressed people approached a shady looking stucco building. Two bouncers guarded a graffiti-covered door. They were large, but Matthew was bigger. Before noticing the newest guests, the paid muscle was busy intimidating a group of troublesome teens begging to get in. When Dameon, Matthew, Elijah, and Emma came into view, the guards straightened.

One of the bouncers reached for a radio to inform others of their attendance. Emma knew her partners had made a name for themselves, but seeing the reactions of the two guards gave real weight, and a deeper understanding, to their reputations.

Matthew pulled one of the teens by the shirt. A laughably fake ID fell to the ground.

"Trust me kid, unless you have a death wish, you'll run home."

Matthew pulled back his dark blazer, to reveal a gun strapped to his side. The child and his friends stumbled over each other, as they rushed out of the neon painted alley. Dameon visibly approved. One of the bouncers asked for the weapon before entering. Matthew obliged, and shoved the handgun against the man's chest.

"I expect to get this back when we leave," Matthew demanded, with an aggressive push.

The man nodded profusely. The other men opened the door for the four, and they stepped into Carter's domain.

Sex, music, and precariousness swam in the atmosphere. Lights cast a green glow over the dancing people on the floor, on poles, and sitting at private tables. A hall to the side held room after room, had guests pulling each other through doors, wanting a more private experience.

Dameon led the way to a lonely table in a corner, and placed himself between Elijah and Emma. Matthew sat at Emma's other side, keeping her secure between him and Dameon. Emma wanted to feel as untouchable as her three men, but couldn't find the courage in her chest.

They leaned back and surveyed the room with menacing personas. She was bringing the credibility of their group down. She could feel it. She was in over her head here. Why was Amy so easy to channel, but here, Emma felt like a sitting duck?

She recalled the advice her men peppered her with before coming. Try to refrain from speaking. Don't ask questions, they wouldn't likely be able to answer with honesty. Trust no one. Anticipate violence. No public displays of affection. Don't question any demands they made, and believe that everything they might do, was to keep her safe.

A familiar face neared the table. A wide smile accompanied the man, along with two young, barely dressed, women. Both hung around him, under each arm. His silver hair and intense eyes were instantly recognizable.

327

Sebastian was dressed just as well as his boys, with the exception of an abandoned jacket. The top couple of buttons to his white dress shirt were undone, though it remained tucked neatly into his dark gray pants. A smile flickered across Dameon's face, but disappeared quickly.

"Please excuse me ladies," Sebastian said, dismissively, "I have a little business to take care of."

One of the women, heavily busty with dark hair and deeply tanned skin, pouted. A warning look of impatience stifled her sultry attitude. She reached for her friend's hand, and nervously backed away into the crowd.

Sebastian leaned over the table, palms flat. He met the eyes of each of the men, then rested on Emma. She could understand why the two women were so quick to run. An air of authority and danger surrounded El Tiburón. His hard stare led Emma to reach for Dameon's hand beneath the table.

Dameon held her reassuringly, with strength in his grip, before leaving her to cross his arms in front of his chest. A new song played over the loud speakers, as El Tiburón's expression turned to a mix of seriousness, and challenge.

"I have a reputation to maintain," he said. "El Tiburón has never let the prettiest lady in the room go without a dance."

Emma's discomfort was completely visible, as he waited for her to entertain his request. "Come, you have my word that I'll be a complete gentleman."

Emma turned to Dameon, still unable to hide the panic in her face. She needed him to say no, to keep her with them. Of all of the people in this place, El Tiburón was the last person she was willing to be alone with, close though he might have been to them. Dameon didn't look at her when he nodded approval to the man.

Emma was screaming on the inside, and sure her concern leaked through to her outward appearance. Matthew got up from his seat, without needing to be told. El Tiburón practically dragged Emma out of the booth. She caught Elijah's eye, who broke character just long enough to send her a quick wink.

El Tiburón led Emma from her protective men, and onto the dance floor. As he did, men held their women closer, while a number of feminine eyes stole a look at the handsome man. He spun her in an elegant twirl, and faced her with a piercing stare.

Around them, the room grinded, and looked to be engaged in sex more than dance. Sebastian took Emma in a way that reminded her very much of Dameon, Elijah, and Matthew, when they taught her how to ballroom dance. He led her back and forth, far slower than the Cha Cha, but with greater expectation for her hips to roll with every step.

Emma caught on fast and found El Tiburón's rhythm, that somehow aligned perfectly with the erotic and ominous sounds that filled the room. He pulled her close, his lips nearing her ear, but never touching more of her body than the hands he was guiding.

"Tell me Emma, what do you have planned for my boys?"

Her heart caught in her throat.

"You know my name?"

"Mija, my boys tell me everything."

"Everything?"

El Tiburón smiled, devilishly. His leading hand turned her around, and faced her away. He directed her to look towards the table across the room, seating her watching partners. His arm came down before her, holding in a way that was reminiscent of Matthew's hold, when the men were trying to decide whether or not to accept Grant's arrangement. Despite the familiarity of the hold, Sebastian kept a respectful and gentle touch. He didn't grind against her, like the others in the crowd. He didn't press her body to his like the song encouraged. He danced, but with the restraint of an instructor paired with his student.

"They said enough," El Tiburón said, continuing to move his feet in suave motions. "They like you, want to keep you. And my Dameon seems to think he's fallen for his cute... what did he say? Prisoner? Or do you prefer princess now?"

Emma shivered in El Tiburón's arms, as he swayed side to side with her. His hold gained pressure that may have felt like a hug in another moment, but here, it felt very much like a reminder of his influence. Her feet continued to move at his command. From across the room, she made eye contact with Dameon. His face was hard, all of theirs were. He watched with no intention of stopping the smooth man behind her.

"You offered to sell me," Emma said, looking for an ounce of confidence. "Do you wish they had taken you up on the chance?"

"No," he said. "I will never want that for a girl. It's vile, and people that engage in that behavior are despicable to me. But I would have done it for them. Those boys are special to me. Dameon put them, and you, in a terrible position. I gave him a way out, but know that I would have been sure to make him regret it. Not only out of pity for you, but for him. He's better than that. They have been mine long before they were yours, and I will do just about anything to keep them from getting caught."

"Why?"

"They told me you like your questions," he chuckled. "They are my boys, the sons I never had. So I ask you again, what are your intentions with my children."

El Tiburón spun the woman to face her yet again. His face was grave, though his body continued to dance as if it was as natural as breathing. The music shifted songs with new heart thumping beats, but equally sexual lyrics. El Tiburón's movements slowed to a halt, but kept her hands in his.

He should have more lines in his face for his age. Yet in those he had around his eyes and that faintly rested along his forehead, stories could be told of a man that had been around the block. The things he must have seen, done, to survive in this world of crime and uncertainty were on display, and embedded in his light eyes. His white significant stubble, with hints of black, also could have aged him, yet somehow only made him all the more attractive. It's no wonder he had a reputation of dancing with any woman he wanted. Who would ever say no?

"I don't have any ill-meaning intentions. When I am with them, I feel at home, even happy. For what it's worth, I didn't want to come here. They said it was risky, but I said no. I don't want to see them get hurt."

"That would be a great answer for any other parent. But it is not

330

comforting to hear how willing you are to avoid self preservation. You should be begging for greater protection. I don't trust you, little girl, though my boys seem to. When something is too good to be true, I've learned that it usually is. Until you give me reason not to be kind, know that you are safe with me. But if you break my boys, I will break you in turn."

Nods of understanding moved Emma's head up and down. As far as meetings with the boyfriend's parents go, this was probably the worst in history. Well, it could have been worse, but it wasn't pleasant. El Tiburón was a fascinating combination of lovingly parental, and dangerously criminal. She had no doubts, he would hunt to the ends of the Earth if she were to break their hearts.

"Thank you," Emma said, sweetly. "Not just for the security, but for loving them the way you do. They deserve to have someone looking out for them."

Sebastian let a smirk creep up into the corner of his mouth. Emma couldn't be sure if he liked what he heard, or if he felt impressed by the deception he thought she was hiding. It was in that curl of his lip that she finally saw it. Dameon. He may not have been his biological father, but he was completely influential to the person Dameon was. His dominance, intimidation, the undeniable feeling that he could burn the city to the ground if pushed a little too far. But also, the undying loyalty he had to those he loved.

El Tiburón led Emma back to the table with her lovers waiting. Though in this place, they felt less like the men she cared for, and more like the criminals she encountered at their first meeting. They were on edge. Yet even so, they made up three of four of the most powerful looking people in the room, only rivaled by El Tiburón himself. Dameon didn't move a muscle as Matthew got up to place Emma back into her safe position between him and Dameon. She felt a comfort in being back with them, her protectors at either side.

"Satisfied," Dameon asked, without the slightest acknowledgment towards Emma.

"Not at all," El Tiburón said. "But the night is young, and there are many women that would love a piece of this."

"You old dog," Dameon said, cracking a smile.

"Watch your mouth boy," El Tiburón said, with a mischievous grin. "I didn't become The Shark to be called a dog by the likes of you."

The silver man tapped his knuckles twice on the table, before retreating back to the party. As he did, multiple women closed in on the prize of a man, and practically threw themselves at a chance to dance with and, Emma presumed, a shot at fulfilling his hopes of a more eventful evening.

Emma looked from one man to the other, but none gave her so much as a glance in her direction. They were too busy being on guard, and surveying the room for possible threats. It was good, she concluded, that they were being so careful, but she very much would have liked to get a shed of emotional comfort. She could understand why they wouldn't, but it still felt uncomfortably cold. There was no room for sweet hand holding or softness here. Her sense of relief was soon dashed, when Elijah swore under his breath.

A paid woman, wearing a metallic outfit, with about as much fabric as one of the swimsuits Emma was given, approached the table. She leaned over low and with seduction. She was sexy with long dark hair, and a body that looked built for her work.

She crawled on top of the table and began to dance on her knees to the rumbling tunes. Dameon nodded to Elijah. The blond stood and reached for the woman's chin. She did her best to continue, but trembled with his touch. It curdled Emma's stomach to see someone so deeply afraid of Elijah.

"Your services are not required here," he said, with venom.

"I'm supposed to," she secretly begged past her dancing. "Carter said I have to," she whispered. "Please!"

Elijah held a merciless stare. A stone dropped in Emma's stomach when she saw the enormous fear that gripped the woman. To the people in this place, they were dangerous, revenge hungry, murderers. And with that thought, Emma felt terrible for the woman before them. She jumped slightly, when Elijah snatched the woman's hair in his hand and brought her close. The poor woman looked on the verge of tears. She tried to plead to Dameon, though Elijah never gave her the ability to turn her head to face the leader properly.

"I'm sorry," she said. "I'm sorry. I have to. They said Carter could kill me if I don't."

"You know who we are," Matthew questioned, with a growl.

The tears began to flow as the dancer closed her eyes. She tried to nod, but Elijah didn't give her an inch to do so. Matthew stood to join Elijah, and came equally close to her personal space.

"Then you already know what I'll do to you if you don't leave. You can deal with Carter, or you can deal with me."

The woman sobbed at Matthew's presence. She was shaking. Dameon did nothing. He didn't move a single muscle in his face or otherwise. It was horrible to watch. Emma moved to comfort the woman, but Dameon snatched her shoulder, and led her back to her seat.

Another woman approached. She was stunning. Her skin was darker than the night, eyes so brown they seemed like all pupil, curly hair cut shorter than the men, and tall as the Stratosphere. Her salmon-colored dress showed off her elegant, perfect, curves.

Not another one. Emma's heart ached for these women being forced into this position. Dameon caved and reached for Emma's hand beneath the table and held tight.

"Elijah," the new arrival said, smooth as silk. "and Matthew. So violent. This is a party. You wouldn't want to offend your generous host by denying such a gift would you?"

Elijah let the woman go with so much force, she nearly fell off the table. Matthew returned to his place, and sat tall next to Emma.

Elijah glared at the new woman, right hand forming a white knuckled fist. The new woman's eyes hovered over Elijah and looked amused at the anger that radiated from the man. The lady dismissed the terrified stripper, who frantically ran to a small group of other women, who received her as if they never expected her to return. The remaining woman bit her lip as she drank Dameon in.

"Carter," Dameon addressed.

The woman grinned.

Emma's head spun. Carter was a woman? She wasn't sure why this surprised her so much. They all talked about sleeping with both men and women. She had only assumed.

An insecurity settled in Emma's chest. Carter was gorgeous. Worst of all, she was Emma's opposite in every way. She glowed with power and confidence. Emma couldn't hold a candle to her. Dameon's stare didn't ease her nerves. Though he held Emma's hand out of sight, his gaze betrayed a glimmer of desire. They all could see it. Carter could see it.

"Come with me, Lazie," Carter said.

The ghost of a snarl, barely hid in Elijah's face. If given permission, Emma was sure Elijah would rip Carter to sheds. His hate was overflowing for the woman. It's no wonder he hated Emma so much, when Dameon decided to keep her. He thought Dameon found another woman that could want to break up their happy family. Carter didn't attempt to conceal the fun she found in Elijah's discomfort. Her body language seemed to say, "I could take him from you if I wanted, and you know it."

Not tonight, no thank you, I'm good, or I'd rather not, would have all been acceptable responses Dameon could have given. But instead, he stayed silent, and released Emma's hand. Dameon didn't offer eyes of comfort. No promises to come back. He simply got up, rounded the table, and stood close, just as she demanded.

She offered her hand. He took it. He kissed the top like a prince acknowledging fellow royalty. Elijah burned. Emma could understand his jealousy. Matthew, however, seemed unphased.

Carter led Dameon to the dance floor. The people parted for her. Her guests seemed to feel an unspoken rule to keep their distance, as if touching the woman without her permission would end in death. Maybe it did.

Carter wrapped Dameon's arm around her and smoothly, slowly, swayed her hips. Dameon's body moved in a trance at her will. It was unbearable. When Sebastian danced with Emma, he at least kept his movements respectful. Carter allowed no such thing.

They looked complete, perfect. It killed her. It destroyed Elijah. Matthew only watched with a protective stare.

"Oh," was all Emma could say.

"Yeah," Elijah said.

"Quit pouting," Matthew said, sternly. "She's only temporary. If he doesn't make her happy, he doesn't have a chance at making any of this worth it."

Dameon pressed his hips behind Carter, as she ran a graceful hand up his arm to rest on the back of his neck. He pressed his cheek to the side of Carter's face and whispered secret things into her ear. She smiled. She pushed her ass against his crotch. Dameon visibly breathed in her seduction and tilted his chin, in that way men do when wanting to thrust into the person rubbing against their dick. His hands slid over Carter's body and dug his fingers around her hips, pulling her closer.

Emma stood. Matthew pulled her arm aggressively to sit her back down.

"What are you doing?"

"Not pouting."

Matthew moved faster than Emma could register. He dragged her to the side, and out of the booth by the wrist. He led her to a little secluded corner behind a velvety purple curtain, out of sight from the party-goers. He slammed her against the wall with too much force. His caramel eyes burned into her. His grip was starting to hurt.

"You're out of your depth here. We're outnumbered. Every person in this place, besides El Tiburón, is hers. This is not like home. You can't push buttons here."

"You can't expect me to sit and watch that."

"Yes I can, and you will. You think this is bad to watch? This is nothing! Carter is the type to make us "watch" while she bleeds you out for hours, only allowing the relief of death if we offer it to you. Don't make me see that. I don't know if I could do you the kindness of ending it for you."

His eyes were desperate. He was afraid more than he was angry. They may have acted big and tough, but this place scared the shit out of Matthew, just as much as it did her.

Nosey steps joined them behind the curtain. Matthew jumped at the unannounced guest and pulled out a hidden sidearm. He pointed it directly at the intruder's face, at Elijah's face. Elijah's expression dropped, and he hoped that Matthew had the sense not to be too trigger happy.

Matthew showed instant regret, and pulled Elijah in for a strong hug. He apologized. They talked. Emma wasn't listening. She found her opening. Her temper was lit and not even they could stop her.

She slid past Elijah and Matthew. She avoided their detection, until it was too late for them to react. Emma made her way through the crowd of people that were practically having an orgy on the dancefloor. She tapped Dameon's distracted shoulder.

"May I," she asked, sweetly.

Dameon shook his head subtly. His eyes were wide and horrified. He was begging her to go back to the table without his use of words. He was playing a game of chess in his mind, she could see that. But it was too late. Emma made her own move, and she couldn't back down now.

"Well," Carter grinned. "You are either very sweet and ignorant, or very stupid and reckless."

Dameon gently, slowly, pulled Emma behind him.

"Respectfully, I would appreciate you not speaking to my woman like that."

Multiple onlookers were forming but never allowed the dancing to truly dissipate. Emma was causing a massive disturbance, but what could she do? She had gone too far, to simply bow out and claim she didn't know better. A real target was placed on her by her own doing, and there was no reversing it now.

"Ha," Carter laughed. "Respectfully?"

"I'd like to think I'm more sweet and reckless," Emma said, interrupting Dameon's rescue.

Dameon held Emma defensively behind his back. His grip around her wrist made her hand go numb.

Carter backed up ,without conveying the feeling of truly backing down. "What kind of friend would I be, to rain on your parade? Enjoy yourselves. It's a party after all," Carter said, then proceeded to walk away.

"Wait," Emma said, with all the strength she possessed.

Carter turned and laughed at Emma's arrogance, curious to see what the audacious woman had to say.

"I think you misunderstood me, I wasn't requesting a dance with Dameon."

Carter's eyes lit up. She moved alarmingly close and looked down at the smaller woman with blue hair.

She stepped between Dameon and Emma. Carter waved Dameon dismissively away. Dameon, slowly, carefully let go of his princess, and took a step back. Carter took Emma's waist and pulled their bodies together. Dameon said nothing, and retreated to the side of the room.

Elijah and Matthew split, and circled to the other walls. The three watched as Carter took control of Emma. Sebastian took a position in a corner, shooing away his latest dance partner. Each of her trusted men watched her closer than the secret service.

Carter's hands moved up Emma's back, to her shoulders, then let one hand trail back down. She lowered, until the hand rested at the top of Emma's ass. Emma wanted to stay strong, but the alluring woman really was a lot to take in.

Carter danced, rotating her hips in the most fluid, and devastatingly perfect, way. She inched Emma around the room. The four men moved through the people, maintaining their best line of sight.

"Tell me, Emma," she said. "Have you ever been with a woman?"

Emma shook her head. She hadn't. The thought clouded her mind. She never objected to the idea, but never really had the opportunity to try either. Too late, Emma realized that they were in the hallway of rooms. Carter's strategically dancing people blocked Dameon, Matthew, Elijah, and Sebastian's vision.

Men and women near Emma grinded on each other, forced tongues in mouths, and gave in to their most basic needs. Carter opened a door and led Emma in. She felt scared, isolated. They couldn't see her, protect her. Her men had no way of knowing, or hearing, what was about to happen.

She really bit off more than she could chew this time. She was on her own.

The room was small with a glow that shifted from red, to blue, to pink. The walls visibly vibrated with the rhythmic sounds. Papers with numbers, love notes, and disturbing photos littered the walls and door. On a small corner shelf, markers and pens waited for more poorly made decisions.

A single chair was present, that Carter placed herself in like the royalty she was. Emma stood awkwardly before her. Her heart was in her throat, and threatened to make her sick. Carter reached between her legs, and retrieved a long barreled handgun from under her seat. She sat tall, and held it in a relaxed grip while she studied Emma.

Emma couldn't take the anticipation anymore. She opened her mouth to speak but was cut off by the queen in the chair.

"Take the wig off."

Emma hesitated, but did as requested. Her blond hair messily fell to her shoulders. Carter stood and placed the cold barrel under Emma's chin.

"So," she said, face too close to Emma's, "Ignorant or stupid?"

Emma's legs felt weak. They shook violently beneath her. She tried to back up but Carter matched her steps, until she was backed against a wall. A warm tear fell from Emma's eyes.

"Stupid," Emma answered.

"You follow Dameon's honesty rules?" Surprise coated Carter's voice.

Emma tried to nod but was blocked by the forceful gun.

"Yes."

"In that case, what makes you think you're better than me? Why should Dameon Lazarus, my Lazie, choose you over everything I can give him?"

"I–" Emma shook. "I'm not. I'm not better than you. And... I don't know. I think... I think Dameon thinks he can save me. He seems to like that. Maybe that's why he can't choose you. You don't need saving."

Carter removed the gun, and replaced it with a hard hold that dug into Emma's cheeks and wrapped around her chin. Carter kissed Emma. It wasn't kind or even desiring. It was purely a show of power.

"I always take what I want," she said. "Do you know what I want?"

Emma shook her head to the best of her ability.

"The fucking world," Carter said, in Emma's ear. "I want everything."

Carter licked the round end of the gun from its base to the tip.

The gun moved down, along Emma's dress. The tiny front sight of the gun lifted the hem of Emma's short dress. Carter jerked it upward, ripping, and forming a long slit up to her hip. Emma gasped at the harsh sound. Back down the gun went. She felt the warming weapon slide up her leg and push up against her underwear.

Emma would have dropped to the floor, but Carter held her up by the grip on her face and the barrel that threatened to find its way inside of her. If it did that to her dress, what would it do to her body, even if Carter didn't shoot? She was wearing a tampon. Would it make it hurt worse? Did it matter? Emma pulled at the woman's grip but Carter didn't budge.

"What is it you want," Carter asked.

Emma cried. Tears flowed freely and ran streaks of mascara and eyeliner down her face. She couldn't speak.

Carter forced the loaded weapon higher, until Emma's underwear strained against her hips, and she could feel it beginning to enter.

"Them," she cried. "I want Dameon, Elijah, Matthew. I... I love them. Fuck you! They are the only thing I want any more. I love them!"

Carter removed the weapon, and let the scared woman fall.

She placed the gun on the seat of the chair, never turning her back to Emma. When she approached, Emma pulled her knees together and interlaced her fingers around her legs to hold herself shut. Carter tilted Emma's head up, and reached for the locket. She opened it and examined the contents. Carter ripped the necklace from Emma's neck. She looked around the room, ripped one of the love notes from the door and wrote on the corner. She tore the corner and folded it as small as possible to fit it in the locket. Carter returned to Emma.

"Get up."

Emma obeyed.

Carter shoved the necklace to Emma's chest.

"My Lazie says you've caught Tony's interest, which means you have my interest. You are only alive because you entertain me. Few people have walked away after showing the nerve you have tonight. Fewer have tried. You aren't a weak woman if you can tame those three, especially the beast, Matthew. I like your grit, but don't push your luck."

Emma clung to the locket, as if her life depended on it.

"I was going to tell Dameon no. I was considering getting rid of you before you ever left this building. Dameon, however, might still prove useful to me, but I can't use him if I take one of his lovers. Even I had to learn that lesson. And you… I like you. I don't know what your plan is, but I want to see how it plays out. You can tell Dameon he has a deal."

Carter retrieved the blue wig, and tossed it to Emma. The music stopped. Both of the women looked around the small room with alarm. Carter burst out of the door, with Emma on her heels.

A deafening bang exploded in the air. Emma watched as Matthew pulled the trigger on an unknown man. Blood splattered on the surrounding people. Armed men and women pointed their guns at him, Elijah, Dameon, and El Tiburón. Blood pooled beneath the dead man.

There was no panic to be found among the people, prepared to execute the four men at the center of the room. Only Dameon's furious booming voice made noise in the room.

"I said, where is she?"

Elijah and Sebastian held their own guns, and scanned the crowd. Dameon appeared to be the only person in the building not holding some type of weapon. Carter looked back at Emma and smiled. The terrifying woman snatched the ash-blue hair piece from Emma's hands. Carter strode to the men on display, with grace, and a total lack of fear. Her hand instructed Emma to follow. She did as she was told.

Emma wasn't nearly as comfortable in the center of the ready weapons as the others seemed to be. Even Elijah had a hard resolve in his stance, gun ready to be shot. Dameon's eyes widened when he saw Emma. A tiny hint of horror flickered in his eyes. Carter stepped through the puddle of blood, and stopped at the dead man on the floor.

"Aw," Carter said, with false sorrow. "I liked Ronald," she said, as she turned the corpse's face with her high heeled shoe.

"Carter," Dameon started.

"Listen up!" Carter commanded the room, ignoring Dameon's plea.

Carter roughly pulled Emma in front of her, and shoved the blue wig over Emma's blond hair. It was ill placed, and her natural hair showed through the bottom of the short false hair.

"This is Emma Kincaide," she shouted. "If you see her, be ready to start shooting. Anyone perceived as a threat to her, is to die immediately. You will protect her, retrieve her, and bring her to me at my command. Is that understood?"

The room erupted, "Yes, boss," in a unison that mimicked a military response.

Carter shoved Emma to Matthew, who held her arm with a strength that would surely result in bruising the next day. Carter sauntered over to Dameon and placed a hand on his face.

"Get the fuck out, Lazie darling."

They didn't need to be told twice.

18 | Old Promises

Matthew remained silent for the walk back to the car, which thankfully was tag free and still there. Once in the car, his communication didn't improve for the duration of the drive. Dameon, on the other hand, spoke scolding words over Emma's disregard for her own life and rash actions. He spoke loudly, she didn't hear. Emma only stared out the window and watched the lights of the city pass by.

Eventually, Dameon paused his reprimanding attitude until they made it to the safety of their home. Emma walked in first, avoiding the attention Dameon continuously pushed for. Matthew immediately shed his blood-stained clothes in a trail, as he went up the stairs to shower. Elijah followed Dameon's lead, arms crossed, and equally displeased.

Emma continued to ignore them, and walked in the direction of her room. She opened the door, but Dameon snatched the handle and slammed it shut. He smashed his fist against the door.

"Have you been fucking listening? Every rule we gave. Every single one! You couldn't sit quiet for just one night? One night," he shouted, too loudly.

Emma looked at the floor.

"No," she said, solemnly.

Emma reached to open the door again, but Dameon refused to move. Elijah looked exasperated, clenching his jaw with a grind of his teeth.

"Just let me go!" she screeched. "Let me have some fucking control over my own damned body, and take a fucking shower! You said this room was for privacy? Well, I need that! Let me be fucking private!"

Elijah lost every drop of anger. Finally, he saw through his frustration and noticed Emma's torn dress. His eyes filled with regret. He shook his head, trying not to believe all of the scenarios racing through his mind. His disappointed crossed arms shifted to a stance that looked more like he was attempting to hold himself together. He put a hand on Dameon's shoulder, and inched him back.

"Don't," Dameon said. "She could have died, she could have–"

It took too long, but the realization eventually hit him. He snapped his attention back to Emma, a barrage of questions wanting to escape. He didn't fight it, when Emma pushed his hand away, scanned her eye, and slammed the door behind her.

Emma tried walking to the bathroom, but her feet decided to run. She braced herself on the edge of the countertop, and looked at the woman in the mirror. Emma threw the messy wig to the ground and stared. Her reflection was beaten, bruises started forming where Matthew grabbed her. Running makeup, puffy eyes, and smudged lipstick told the story of an abused girl.

She rid herself of the ruined dress, and steamed the bathroom with burning water. She sat in the tub, where the shower drenched her curled up body. Emma cried. She cried with sound, with snot leaving her nose, with jolts beating the feelings from her insides out. Pain, violation, and the remnants of immobilizing fear, kept her in the water until her skin was pink and pruned.

Emma unfolded her new dark blanket, and wrapped herself between the sheets. She wanted to be alone. She wanted the feeling of her, and only her in this space. She soaked her pillow with her overwhelming thoughts.

She hated herself for her stupid temper. She hated Dameon and Elijah for bringing her to the party. She hated Matthew for exposing her to the horror of seeing a person murdered before her eyes. She hated Grant for his part in it all. She hated everything. She didn't want to go to Carter's. She tried to tell them, no. Emma wished she could disappear into the blankets and just feel nothing.

Emma's tears reached the extent of their capacity. Her eyes closed. She surrounded herself in pillows, and laid there for an eternity in a night.

When she opened her eyes, Carter appeared in her bedroom. Dameon must have let her in, but how? Only Emma had the ability to open her door now, with the addition of the scanner. When she saw the image of terror, in her tight pinkish dress, she screamed. Carter rushed Emma, putting a knee to her chest, and gripping in a way that prevented Emma from breathing.

Dameon entered the room. He leaned against one of her white walls. Emma tried to call for him, but when he came closer, it was only to fondle Carter's breasts and kiss her neck. He placed his hand over Carter's, and pressed harder over Emma's mouth and nose. Her chest heaved, and body struggled, under their weight. Her white walls closed in. They were hurting her. They were killing her.

Emma jolted upright in her bed. Wet spots on her pillow displayed evidence that she had been crying in her sleep.

It was still night. The walls were colorfully painted, not white at all. Dameon was nowhere to be seen, nor was Carter. The moon lit her room, as did the shining lights of the city. Emma read the large metal clock on the wall. She wasn't asleep for longer than a few hours. It was a dream, a nightmare. She grabbed a robe from her bathroom, deciding she had more than enough time alone with her thoughts.

She reached for the door and thought about the way she left Dameon and Elijah. Poor Elijah. He had been so sensitive to the idea of her being taken advantage of. When she locked them out, it was without a real explanation. What did she leave them thinking had happened? She never hated them, she was just hurt and angry.

Guilt crept into her gut, when she wondered what Dameon and Elijah must have been thinking. Emma opened her door, silently as possible. Against the opposite wall in the hall, were Dameon and Elijah. A single blanket covered them as the sleeping men slumped over each other in a seated position.

Elijah opened his eyes first. He tapped Dameon's arm frantically. Dameon looked at his partner, dazed. When he fully woke, it was with a dramatic start. He attempted to jump to his feet, to reach out and hold Emma, but Elijah held his arm. His expression reminding Dameon to wait for Emma's permission, keeping him on the floor.

Dameon stared back at Emma with desperation, then to his sleepy partner for guidance. Elijah only shook his head. He knew. He knew she might not be ready. Elijah always seemed to know. Emma clenched the edge of her fuzzy robe. She got on her knees, meeting them at their seated level.

"I'm sorry," she said. "She... I'm not as hurt as I probably led you to believe. I–"

Dameon reached for her hand, but Elijah snatched it back yet again. Dameon's hair was frazzled. Shadows darkened under his eyes. He looked terrible. Emma crawled closer, and rested her hand on their shared blanket.

"Can we go to bed? Please," she asked.

Elijah nodded.

Matthew wasn't in their room. A significant part of Emma wanted to go to his room, to check on him. But the more she thought on it, the more she convinced herself that he might need space too. They were all patient enough to give her the privacy she needed after the debacle, the least Emma could do would be to let Matthew have the same.

Emma was first to crawl into bed. Dameon and Elijah stood at the side. Neither could be sure of what she wanted or needed, and both didn't want to be intrusive after everything. Emma smiled weakly at them. She held Elijah, and guided him behind her to hold her tight. He did exactly as instructed. He squeezed her beneath the blanket, with the strength of someone trying to press the pain away. Dameon laid in front of her, and lightly touched his fingers to her cheek.

"Please tell me what happened. Elijah doesn't want me to ask, and I know it's not fair to so soon. But it's killing me, wondering, imagining."

Elijah somehow managed to hold harder. He was loving, careful, and well versed in the needs of someone that was hurt in a way he was personally familiar with.

"She pulled a gun on me. She threatened to use the barrel to– She didn't.

345

She just held it against my–" Emma choked. "It tore my dress. She– She was going to put it– Dameon, I don't want to think about it right now."

His hand shook in a way she instantly recognized. His eyes held a hate, she had only seen reserved for Tony. He was bloodthirsty and pissed beyond measure. Emma's self pity dropped, to make room for apprehension over Dameon's anger.

"I'll kill her," he said, through gritted teeth.

Emma's eyes pleaded. Dameon didn't seem to notice.

"I'm going to rip Carter's dead heart from her chest for the way she touched you, deals be damned."

"No!" Emma whispered. "Please, don't let it be for nothing. Don't ask Matthew to kill anymore people because of me."

"Not Matthew," he said. "Not this time. I brought you there. I personally will make her beg for your forgiveness. I will break her bones, one by one, for every tear she caused you to shed. I will make her suffer, until she admits her mistake."

Elijah kissed the back of Emma's head.

"We all will," Elijah said. "Dameon wants revenge, but the truth is, so do I. Carter is going to pay for hurting you."

"Please," Emma begged. "Don't. I don't want it."

Emma started to cry again.

"Is it too much to ask that you just let it be, and stay here with me?

"Yes," Dameon said.

"No," Elijah contradicted. "You have us. We will love you until the end. Dameon is angry, we both are. When she came after me, it was part of a bigger plan. I can see that now. But she hurt you just to stroke her ego. That said, Carter's fate is up to you. If you want us to stand down, we will do as you wish. How we proceed is your decision."

Dameon hated Elijah's compassionate words.

"But," Elijah said. "if Carter tries to touch you ever again, we will not ask for your blessing. We will kill her."

"Carter crossed a line," Dameon said. "If you ever reconsider, know that we will be ready. I should never have taken you with us."

Dameon grabbed Elijah's waist and pulled him, and therefore Emma, close. He kissed Emma's forehead and surrounded her with oceans of support, love, and regret for his decisions. This is what she needed. She needed them. She needed love, not more violence. Emma sobbed quietly until she fell asleep in their arms.

Dameon was awake. Elijah was awake. When Emma opened her eyes, their desire to stay by her side warmed her heart. They snuggled together until Emma's stomach rumbled in hunger. In the kitchen Matthew was sitting at the island.

He hunched over a bowl of sugary cereal, crunching quietly. Dameon grabbed three more bowls. Elijah went for the milk. Emma sat gingerly next to the big man. He turned slowly to face her. She smiled with an apology filling her face.

"Don't," Matthew said.

Emma stared down at the speckles on the countertop. Matthew placed a large hand on hers. She slid hers away. Her feelings of guilt bubbled in her chest. He never would have murdered that man if she didn't overstep. He'd still be alive if she didn't lose her temper, and try to be bigger than she was. Because of her, another man died. She pained at the body count she was beginning to rack up, even if it wasn't directly by her hand.

"Please," Matthew said, painfully. "Please, don't be afraid of me."

Emma's head popped up. Dameon and Elijah attempted to watch Matthew discreetly. They were failing. Matthew wasn't looking at her, only at the hand he assumed that she rejected for all the wrong reasons. Emma pounced on Matthew with open arms. He flinched under her sudden embrace. A slow hand met Emma's over his shoulder, and pressed into her with a hold that was pleasantly too tight.

"Matthew, I'm not scared of you. But I am sorry. You killed a person because of me. Please, forgive me. You were right. I was reckless, and I'm so sorry."

Matthew's heart pounded. He pulled her closer onto his lap, and buried his face in her hair.

"You aren't at fault for my trigger finger. I shouldn't have gotten distracted. I let you fall into her trap, then I abandoned you last night before even seeing if you were alright. I'm sorry for letting you see the murderer I am, and for being worthless afterwards. I wasn't exactly great company."

Emma smiled.

"It's okay. Me too. I can't say I understand, but I get the desire to be alone. I needed some time too. But Matthew, I'm not afraid of you. I just—"

Emma recalled last night, the words that Carter pulled from her desperate lips. The honesty rule had really sunk its teeth into her. She spoke the only thing that could come to her tongue while Carter interrogated her.

She cared greatly for the three men, before Carter forced the words, but she wouldn't let herself admit the whole truth until the truth was pressured out of her mouth.

"I love you," said Emma. "And I'm not afraid. I love all of you, so much."

She looked around the room. Each of the men stared at her.

Great depths of emotion surged through the three with her words. Matthew looked as if her declaration pierced his heart. That elusive mix of gratefulness, joy, and the pain of feeling undeserving of those simple words, surged through his being. When she looked at Dameon and Elijah, they too looked like they had been physically shot by a bullet of emotion.

Three days had come and gone since the rotten evening. Nightmares seemed to take a routine place in Emma's nights, but her understanding lovers were always there to bring her back to reality. She was safe with them. The world was right with them, in their home.

Less time passed than Emma expected, before comfort regained its rightful place in the home. Their leisurely days of baking with Elijah, working out with Matthew, and even playing innocent games of chess with Dameon without repercussion, facilitated a place of healing. Emma's discomfort over Carter may never completely disappear, but she felt good here. There was only one thing missing she decidedly wanted back.

The noises of engines roaring played through the surround sound of the house. Matthew leaned on the armrest of the couch. Elijah and Emma took a more competitive position in their chairs, as brightly colored cars raced around an animated track. Dameon groaned next to Matthew with his losses, as expected, but Emma was getting much better this game. As a result, she began to enjoy it just as much as Matthew and Elijah.

"Alright, I'll say it first," Matthew said as his car pulled behind Elijah's. "Is shark week about over?"

Elijah and Dameon both glared at Matthew.

"What," she laughed, eyes not leaving the screen.

"Well," Matthew said, "we've all been abstinent for a solid minute. Didn't seem fair for us to have fun when you can't. But... I'm just asking."

A distracting thought ran across Matthew's face. He let his car drift off to the side of the track while studying the woman committed to the race.

"Shit," he said. "I'm sorry. I'm an idiot. If it's 'cause you aren't ready after what happened at the party, I get it. Shit, I'm sorry. Please, pretend I didn't say that."

Emma looked around at the men and gawked. Her lack of focus dropped her placement to dead last, even more rapidly than Matthew's driving mistake and Dameon's typical performance.

It wasn't Matthew's realization, that they may not have been touching her because of Carter, that caught her off guard. That was fine, and honestly, didn't bother her. If anything, she found that idea sweet. The events of the party were rapidly becoming just another traumatic event of her past. She had plenty up to this point, and the lack of penetration was somehow making it a little easier to move on from.

It was the idea that they would be reluctant to have sex with her while menstruating, that floored her. Elijah paused the game.

"I thought you weren't having sex with me because of Carter."

"That's exactly why," Dameon said. "None of us wanted to push you. Your period just coincidentally lined up."

"I swear," Matthew said. "That really was the reason. I just... I forgot for a second. I don't know how I did. I'm sorry."

"It's fine," Emma said. "But you are not about to tell me that this is where you draw the line, are you," she asked them. "The Carter thing, I can understand, but were you really not going to have sex with me because I'm on my period?"

None answered.

"Oh my god! With all your guy's kinks? Are you really about to be prudish now?"

Matthew looked at Emma with confusion in his brow. It really never occurred to them before. They just assumed that she would be off limits a week every month. Knives, ropes, sure, but a little blood was too much? Seriously?

"I'm not asking you to eat me out, clearly you're too squeamish for that, but are you about to tell me that you've never had period sex? Not once?"

Dameon laughed. It felt good. They all needed to hear it. Elijah smiled and giggled in his chair. Was he blushing?

Matthew maintained a stare that showed that the proposal was beyond his imagination.

"No," Dameon said. "None of us have. I don't think any of us had really thought about it before. Is that something you want? It sounds messy, but if you are asking…"

Emma couldn't believe her ears. She narrowed her eyes.

"That's it," Emma said, challengingly. "My turn to play a game,"

Matthew and Elijah shifted uneasily. Dameon slid to the edge of his seat and raised a brow. He placed his elbows on his knees and waited with peaked interest.

"If I beat all of you, even Matthew and Elijah, you give me the reward I deserve for the win, today."

"You're sure you want to play these games so soon," Dameon said, seriously.

"But–," Matthew said.

"Absolutely," Emma cut off. "I've seen how much you hate to lose. How badly would it kill you to see that I not only beat you, but that I got the hang of this game better than you with less practice?"

Dameon's eyes moved up and down Emma. Her words irritated his competitive drive in the way she hoped it would. It did bother him that she was getting good, while he still struggled so terribly with the video game. She could see it with every loss, but he was loving this. Matthew and Elijah exchanged uncomfortable glances.

"Game on," Dameon grinned.

A bundle of nerves, Elijah pressed a series of buttons to start the race. Matthew and Elijah made their opinion on her provocation clear. They were playing to win. So was she. She wasn't starting out great, but there were multiple laps for her to catch up. Dameon, predictably, was dead last. He knew he would lose. This time, however, losing for him also meant winning.

Emma, Elijah, and Matthew led the way. She pulled in front of Matthew, his worries over playing her game were getting the better of him. Elijah was gaining distance. Emma glanced at the man. He was fully concentrated and unwilling to give her first place. She looked back to the screen. She'd never win at this rate. Elijah was too good.

"Shark week huh," She said, inquisitively. "Funny name for it. Are you implying that you'd be interested in sharing me with Sebastian one week a month? I hear sharks like blood."

Matthew audibly let out a noise of disgust, and fake gag, at the intrusive imagery Emma provoked. Dameon gave his complete attention. A fire lit behind his eyes. The joke drew out some of his possessive nature.

"He's old enough to be your father," Dameon said, flatly.

"I bet he likes to be called Papi," said Emma.

Dameon looked like he wanted to jump her bones right there, and make her regret her words. Matthew pulled a throw blanket from the side of the couch, and threw it in her direction. Multiple "ew's" sounded, as he dropped back significantly in the race.

Nice, but not the one she was trying to get to. Elijah managed to ignore her instigating. She kept her finger on the gas and got to her feet. Emma moved to the center of the room, and sat on her knees, legs spread. She rocked her hips. She breathed quick and loudly. Emma moaned at the screen. Elijah only became more serious. Emma swore and moaned a breathy sound as she held the controller near her crotch, over her jeans.

"Elijah," she whined. "You're so good. It's not fair. You just keep going!

And here I thought you didn't like to play rough with me."

Elijah's eyes were fixed on the television. He pretended to ignore the distractions but Emma could see her silly plan working.

"Mmm, Elijah," she groaned. "I see why you like to win. It vibrates so much harder when you're in the lead. It feels so good. Oh yes! Yes! Elijah!"

The blond's eyes looked over to Emma. He knew what she was doing. It wasn't true. Nothing about the mechanics of the game changed when your place in the race improved, but he couldn't help but look. He watched as she moved up and down on her knees, moaning and making sounds that demanded his attention. Dameon couldn't stop little laughs from escaping at Emma's erotic, and comedic, distraction.

"Look out!" Matthew shouted.

Elijah crashed into a side wall. He swore with a toss of his controller.

Emma jumped to her feet. She pulled ahead, and won in the last few milliseconds.

She grinned at the man. Elijah scowled back at her dirty trick.

Emma threw her hands in the air, and danced at her successful attempt to win at any cost. Dameon stood and tossed his own controller to the sofa. He offered his hand to Emma. She took it with a wicked grin of her own. Matthew dropped his controller and looked nervously at Elijah. Emma smiled at the tragic looking men in the room.

"Don't worry, Elijah," she said, teasingly. "I won't ask you to join. I get why you probably wouldn't want to."

Elijah slumped back into the green chair with relief.

"Much appreciated," he said, with a giggle.

Emma retrieved her hand from Dameon, and placed both of hers on Matthew's knees. He stared at her devious expression with specific nervousness that she had only seen reserved for Dameon. She could see why Dameon liked this. It was a delicious interaction. She leaned over him, playing with his reluctance.

"Afraid of a little blood," Emma asked, teasingly.

"Yes," Matthew said, with a hint of plea in his voice.

Emma met his lips and kissed him sweetly. Matthew was at war with himself. She could see he wanted her, but he wasn't comfortable with this new activity he never planned for. Was his nervousness based around the fact that he had simply never had period sex before, or was it because he was the only one of the men that had actually spilled the blood of others, many others? Emma liked this game, but she didn't want to actually hurt Matthew. She knew there was a chance that his aversion might be deeper than a little surface discomfort.

"Just Dameon," Emma said. "You have fun with Elijah."

Matthew pulled Emma in, and kissed her roughly, his beard scratching at her chin. When he released her, he took a calming breath and mouthed the words, "Thank you," as Emma stood upright.

"This is the last time I'll ask, little prisoner. Are you sure you're ready," Dameon asked.

Emma pulled Dameon to the stairs and bit her lip.

Elijah passed a concerned look to Emma, as he moved to the sofa to cuddle close to Matthew.

"Calm down boys," Emma said, with a grin. "This was my game. I survived the first of Dameon's punishments and rewards, I'll be fine this time too."

"They know I was holding back," Dameon growled.

It was, in fact, Emma's idea. It's what she wanted. But when Dameon closed the broken door to his room, butterflies filled Emma's stomach. She liked the nervousness he gave her. She trusted him, and loved the way he pushed her back against the damaged door, to receive his sweet hand in her hair. He kissed her gently at first, then wickedly. She took his tongue with passion of her own. His other hand squeezed at her breast.

"Anything I should know," he asked, inquisitively. "It seems you may be more experienced at this than I am."

"Some women say it's easier, some hate the experience." Emma said, breathlessly.

"I'm not interested in other women, princess," Dameon said, coldly.

"For me," she said, feeling his hand tighten in her blonde hair, "I'm more... sensitive. But I don't want you to hold back this time."

"Yes you do," he whispered.

Emma's skin froze.

"Let me clean up a little first," she said.

Dameon grinned.

"You have ten minutes, little prisoner," he said. "Every second after, is a second more you will owe me."

With a final kiss, Emma excused herself to the bathroom to prepare. She freshened up, while Dameon took her moments of a quick shower to prepare for whatever it was he had on his mind.

When she stepped into the room, multiple ropes rested on the bed. For a split second, her stomach turned slightly. Was she really ready for this so soon after her incident with Carter? Yes, she was. It was her body, and her choice to be here. She wanted Dameon and the games he offered.

"Four minutes and sixteen seconds," he said, as he laid her onto the bed. "That's what you owe me."

"Wait," Emma said, feeling cheated. "You're only giving me four minutes with you?"

Dameon laughed, dangerously.

"Oh no, my little prisoner," he purred. "That's what you'll give me. When you're taped. When you can't speak. When you can't take a moment more. You'll endure four minutes and sixteen seconds of overindulgence."

An intense mixture of anxiety and desire exploded in her. It may not have sounded like a large number, but those additional minutes of overwhelming overstimulation sounded like potential torture. Dameon's fingers, chillingly, ran down one of her legs, straightening her limb to its maximum length. He wrapped a smooth, dark, rope around her ankle. He tied it tight to her and pulled, to attach her to one of the bars at the foot of the bed. He repeated the process to her other leg, pausing on the way to kiss her scar. When his lips touched the white healed mark, a sensitive tingle shot through her nervous system.

A rush of anticipation pulsed through Emma, as her naked Dameon crawled onto the bed and lifted her arms above her head. There, he bound her wrists together in a tight knot that fastened her to the top bars of the bed. Dameon slid his fingers along the rope, and met her hands.

"You are mine," Dameon said, in a low voice. "But this," he said, placing the end of the binding material in her hand and closing it, "is yours. Pulling this will set you free, and is as good as red."

"I thought you said you wouldn't hold back," Emma instigated, with a shake in her voice.

"I have every intention of using you the way I want," Dameon said. "But the final choice will always be yours. Anyone that attempts otherwise, should suffer for giving you anything less. Now give me the safe words."

"Yellow and red," Emma said, softly. "But Dameon, I–"

Deep-blue eyes burned into her soul when Dameon placed his hand over her lips and shushed her. He stood at the side of the bed, crossed his arms, and watched. He didn't touch, he didn't move. He just stood, staring at her. Insecurities gnawed at the woman, as Dameon took in every bit of her helpless composure. He stepped slowly around the bed, studying her increasing breaths. From the other side of the bed, he retrieved something she couldn't quite see.

Dameon leaned over Emma. His impressive size was fully hard and ready to take. Dameon placed his lips on hers and delicately played with her tongue. Emma closed her eyes. She wanted to enjoy this part, the pleasure before the pain. He nipped at her bottom lip and, without warning, slid something small and cold into her.

In an instant, she felt the incense vibrations. She cried out and pulled on her restraints. Dameon's grin hovered an inch above her quivering lips. In his left hand, he waved a little remote.

"The little numbers go to ten. This," he said, pressing a button and making Emma clench around the toy, "is only three, my sensitive little prisoner."

Dameon pushed himself off the bed. He walked to the broken door, and hauled a large bookcase to slow any potential saviors. His muscles tensed as he did. Emma tried to move her knees together, but the ties refused her the comfort.

Dameon chuckled at her attempt and hit the button again. Emma whined with the buzzing feeling and panted. Dameon leaned against the wall and stroked himself to her writhing. Emma attempted to calm herself. She tried to breathe through the buzzing between her legs. Dameon joined her on the bed and held her head in his hand.

"Open up princess," he said.

She did with heavy breaths and a begging face. She couldn't take the discomfort of being watched anymore. She wanted his touch. She needed to feel more than his eyes on her. Dameon placed himself in her mouth. She felt him against her tongue, sliding over him, under, around. Emma shivered. When she did, he pressed the button twice.

Emma whimpered around his cock. She sucked him feverishly, as if doing so could relieve the intensity happening between her legs.

"That's my good girl," he growled.

The miserable, wonderful feelings surged through her. Emma's screams muffled in her full mouth. She begged fruitlessly until he gave so much of himself she could barely breathe. Her body tensed hard, and muscles protested, as she gagged and choked on him. Her body tried moving in every direction to no avail. It was madness.

He pulled away with ruthless speed, causing Emma to gasp out loudly, catching her breath. Dameon's unforgiving thumb pressed the torturous button two more times. A guttural scream sounded from Emma with the increase.

"Look at the lovely mess you're making."

She did. Between hard breaths, Emma looked down. Blood had made its way to the comforter.

"Dameon!" she cried, "It's... it's... too much!"

"No," he said with a chuckle, "not yet it's not."

Emma flinched dramatically with a final press of the remote. Her heart skipped a beat at the sudden silence that sent shivers through her body.

Dameon cut off the vibrations with the last press, and dove his fingers in to retrieve the little toy. Emma hummed at the intrusion and the unannounced lack of vibrations. Sweet relief flooded Emma's brain and body when Dameon plunged his dick deep into her. His red soaked fingers gripped her waist.

She moaned gratefully when Dameon gave her as much as her pussy could possibly take. His hard dick expanded her and rubbed against her walls in glorious pumps. His head tilted back, and he took her with merciless pushes to her core. He drove in and out, hard, satisfyingly, perfectly. Her muscles tightened and contracted. Emma felt her orgasm nearing. When the urge to chase it surfaced, a panic accompanied. She knew what would happen if she did, what Dameon would make her feel.

"Dameon," she begged looking down at his red lower self. "Dameon?"

A dark smile pulled at the corners of Dameon's mouth. He pulled away but not out, and wrapped his fingers around his large cock. With a deep thrust he examined his messy hand with immoral arousal.

"What's the matter, little prisoner," he asked. "Not afraid to cum, are you?"

Emma groaned at his unyielding movements that tugged at the edges of her orgasm.

"Yes," she admitted.

A clean hand swiftly gripped around her chin, his fingers digging into her cheek. His face was so close to hers, challenging her to prolong the inevitable conclusion her sex could no longer withhold. She couldn't stop. She was cumming around him, and he could feel it all.

He cursed at her panting, her subtle shake, her eye roll she tried so hard to conceal. She pulsed around him when she finally gave in and let the waves of pleasure win. Dameon groaned in her ear and placed the little messy toy on her clit.

"Four minutes and fifteen seconds," he growled.

"Wait!"

At full power, Dameon turned the toy on.

Emma let out a gut wrenching scream.

Ten seconds felt like thirty. A minute felt like an eternity.

She cursed in loud cries, as tears fell down the sides of her face, and into her hair. Emma felt herself cum a second time. Her heart was bursting, her head spinning, her cunt sending every signal biologically possible to make it end.

"R... R... Yellow," Emma whimpered.

Dameon chucked the toy across the room, slamming it into a nearby wall. The relief of feeling Dameon and only Dameon, sent ripples of pleasure down Emma. Her eyes rolled back again. She whimpered heavily nearing the border of crying. She pulled against her restraints, realizing a soreness in her ankles and wrists.

Emma's eyes widened, and her breathing quickened, once more when she felt the unbearable warnings of yet another orgasm being coaxed into existence.

"No," Emma whispered, with exasperation. "You... you can't. I can't!"

He could, and she did. With a final deep push, Dameon made her cum for a third time. With her, he followed in a warm finish.

Emma pulled her emergency line. The knots around her wrists fell limp. Dameon's head jerked up, as if the silent motion set off a deafening alarm. He untied her remaining limbs with quick fingers. Her legs instinctively came together and pressed tight, as Emma rolled onto her side to curl into a loose ball. Dameon cautiously climbed in bed beside her and pulled her back into a caring hold. A soft pillow was placed under her head making a red streak across its top.

"I'm a mess," Emma said, weakly. "Your pillow, it's–"

"The pillow," Dameon said, softly. "You, me, the blanket. Yes. But we've washed more blood away than this. And even if we can't, it's a small price to pay."

Dameon wrapped an arm around Emma's knees, and hugged them closer to her body.

"Do you feel safe?"

Emma turned to face her loving, punishing, painfully gorgeous man.

"Yes," she said, heart still racing. "I feel properly wrecked, and will probably need some time to recover after this one, but yes. I know I'm safe with you."

Dameon pressed his lips to Emma's forehead, extracting whatever strength that may have remained. She wanted to sleep, to fall into a world of calm and comfort, but Dameon's teasing hand tilted her chin in annoying authority. He shook his head with a funny smile.

In a smooth singular movement, he snuck an arm under Emma's knees and his other under her shoulders. He stood with the spent woman in his arms, and carried her to the darkly decorated shower.

Emma washed up with an all business attitude. Her shaky legs agreed with her speed. They called for a nap as much as the rest of her. She was rinsing the rosemary soap from her legs when she looked up at Dameon. He'd done very little to clean up just yet, and was staring at the shiny red, still clinging to his hand.

"Hey," she said, sweetly. "Are you okay?"

Dameon didn't answer, but his eyes snapped to the freshly scrubbed woman. Emma stood slowly and led him into the path of the running water. The blood vanished under the stream and down the drain.

"If you don't want to do it again, you know that's fine, right," Emma said. "It's just a week. And you don't have to stop with the others on my account. It doesn't have to be the end of the world."

Dameon shoved Emma against the cold shower wall. Her back arched in protest to the temperature, and her weak legs threatened to give out. He held her by the shoulders and kissed her violently. When he allowed her a breath, Dameon pressed his body against hers and bent to kiss against her ear.

"We made a deal," he said, harshly.

"I haven't forgotten."

"You can't tell me it isn't my fault that Carter attacked you."

A brand of fear that Emma hadn't felt in a while towards Dameon, reared its head. He was angry and beside himself. Though she did feel scared by his rising temper, it wasn't what he'd do to her that frightened her, it's what she was afraid he was about to ask of her.

"I hurt you, by putting you in her hands. I knew the risks, and put you in danger anyway. You promised me that you would never let me get away with harming you again."

"Stop it, Dameon. I'm not going to hurt you. I care too much for you to cash in our deal now. I won't do that, especially for something that you didn't even do!"

"Then let me kill her. How can you want her alive after assaulting you? Let me end her."

"No! My answer is no. Quit blaming yourself for my dumb choices, and stop asking for permission to take revenge on my behalf. Of course I want Carter to drop dead, but you saw her numbers. I can't risk you getting hurt going after her. I'm not willing to lose you over this, plus he'd never forgive me if you died now."

"He?"

Emma's eyes widened. Guilt sunk in her gut at her accidental word choice. She was talking more than she was thinking, and her feelings managed to escape before she had the chance to filter them.

"I–" she started, considering backtracking.

"Don't break our rule now, Emma. Tell me exactly what you meant. He?"

"I guess I did stick around long enough for raw honesty to become second nature," Emma admitted, in a small voice.

She didn't want to say what was on her mind, but felt knew he wouldn't accept anything less.

"I was thinking about Matthew. He's done so much to keep you from personally killing anyone. If you died trying to be a murderer, I don't know if he'd ever be able to face me again. Elijah might hate me too, but at the moment, he seems just as pissed as you. I think he'd put all the blame on Carter, but Matthew? I don't think he'd ever shake the blame for my part in your death. Everything he's done for you would be for nothing, if you ran off to fight Carter over my mistakes."

A gentle hand moved around Emma's waist and pulled her into the warmth of the shower. Emma's knees were visibly shaking before Dameon wrapped her in a strong embrace. His warm hand rubbed heat into her cold back.

"I can't lose you, Dameon. Not only would it destroy me if something happened to you, but I'm pretty sure I'd lose Matthew and Elijah too. Matthew needs you, and I can't give Elijah what he needs to keep him. We all need you. Don't ask me to risk everything over this. The answer is no. Just let it go and stay ours. That's all I want."

19 | Checkmate (Dameon)

Dameon leaned over the railing of the terrace. He looked down at the street, at the cars, at the people going about their lives. He felt the beginnings of a laugh linger in his throat. It was funny. How many times had he considered it? Just a little will power and he would be over. He'd be done with the pain of losing his other half, the better half.

It's true, what they say about twins. He felt it. His body ached and burned before he even got the call. Dameon leaned an inch farther. He could never do it to Matthew and Elijah. He knew his oldest friend, and first love would never survive. He saw the remnants of the scared kid he befriended behind Matthew's eyes on the day he offered Emma his life.

Elijah wouldn't fare much better. He'd probably find some way to blame himself, though it could never have been his fault. Now, he had Emma to worry about as well. Fuck. Would she really mourn him? He'd mourn her.

None of the hypotheticals mattered in the end. He'd never do it. He had people that loved him, and that he loved in return. He didn't even want to nowadays. Besides, he had too much work to do. He still had Tony to break. Sure, a few low level hits would be a small thorn in his side, and offing the ones responsible for Penny's death... Tony very likely didn't lose a minute of sleep over them. But in time, he would take down his entire empire.

Baby steps. But he wasn't taking baby steps anymore. In fact, he wasn't making any moves. There he was, looking over the balcony, and hiding in his ivory tower. He needed to do something about Tony, for Penny, for

Emma's safety.

A thought rattled in his brain for the past month that made him sick to his stomach. Maybe revenge wasn't all it was cracked up to be? Sure, he wanted to avenge Penny, but he also wanted to live. He wanted a life of peace and calm with Emma, Elijah, and Matthew. He'd fought for so long, it would be nice to move on. But just as the thought attempted to settle, he wondered if such a life was even possible.

Emma startled Dameon when she showed up by his side. She didn't seem to notice. She smiled thoughtfully, as she looked out to the cityscape. They really did a number on her. The woman that he fucking kidnapped, abused, and manipulated into loving him. Yes, he loved her too, but that wasn't the point. The point was that she had no business being next to him, smiling like she chose it all.

Her face turned. Shit. He was learning to agonize over that look. It was the same look she would make when full of uncomfortable questions or observations. Dameon braced himself for the inevitable.

"Dameon?"

He raised a brow and waited.

"I want to go to the convenience store. The one a couple buildings down. It's close, and I'm getting good at my Amy makeup, even without Elijah's help."

He noticed. The woman fell into Amy's character so well, she barely needed Elijah's coaching anymore. It had been months since Carter's party, and they still used Amy on the rare occasion to keep up appearances. If Tony, by some small chance, only knew of Amy, maybe seeing her with them would keep him off the real Emma's scent. It wasn't likely, but a man could hope.

Dameon was sure he knew what Emma was asking for, but played dumb anyway, hoping she would reconsider.

"I don't see why not. Any of us would be more than willing to take you."

Emma looked disappointed. Good. Don't ask.

"I want to go alone," she said.

Fuck. No. No, she couldn't go alone. Tony made his threat clear. It wasn't about keeping her from running, she had already proven that they'd broken her enough to make her willingly want to stay. No, Amy needed a shadow any time she left the house. Sure, anyone would hate the lack of basic freedom to go where they please without a bodyguard. But she wasn't just anyone.

"No."

She looked offended.

"Do you really not trust me? Haven't I proven myself to you?"

Dameon rubbed the headache, forming under his hair.

"Of course you have. But why do you want to go alone?"

Emma was clearly set. She wasn't about to let this go.

"I want to buy period supplies without you, Matthew, or Elijah," she said with some force.

"After everything, you don't want any of us to see you buy a few pads or tampons?" he said, with a grin.

He was getting to her. Her eyes betrayed flustered feelings and her grip on the railing tightened. Dameon was going to need to play dirty to win.

He spun the woman around and pressed her against the glass. Emma's breathing grew heavy. His dick hardened at the sight of her breasts rising and falling. He loved these games, even if he didn't always love the reason for playing. He teased her want for him, hovering his lips just out of reach. Dameon played with the straps of her shirt that barely contained her.

His ego throbbed with her wanting eyes. He wanted to squeeze her, to lick, suck, bite. But this wasn't about him.

"You have every bit of my trust princess. But the situation has changed," he said with a hint of desperation. "It's not the fear of you betraying us that keeps me from wanting you to go alone, it's the fear of losing you. You're aware that Tony knows Amy, and has eyes everywhere. Amy can't go anywhere alone."

"Then blue hair it is. Tony may have eyes, but so do Carter's people."

Dameon lifted Emma and sat her dangerously on top of the railing. He had her, he'd never let her fall. She knew this, but no amount of trust could make a person be at ease in such a risky position. She trembled under his

364

hold. She clearly wanted to hide her fear but her eyes betrayed her. Emma's painted nails, courtesy of Elijah, dug into his arms. Dameon hated himself for loving it as much as he did. He could practically taste her anxiety as she accepted the power he had over her.

"If you are looking for adrenaline," he said playfully, "I assure you, I can give you plenty here."

He slid a hand under the back of her shirt, touching her soft skin. He could feel it when she took a terrified and shaky breath. Play the game man, keep it in your pants. Have a little control. Emma tried to speak a few times but words didn't sound. He was winning. He could see it in her disappointed face.

"I don't want to be your little prisoner any more," she said, bravely, yet quietly.

The words felt like a punch to the gut.

The height of the building suddenly felt more tangible. He'd never let her fall. He'd never let her go. She knew this, didn't she? Was she finally through with them? With him? Dameon placed Emma gently on her feet and stepped back. He shouldn't have pushed so hard to intimidate her.

"If you hate the name, we can drop it."

He knew that wasn't what she meant. Emma closed the distance he created. Her face was saying goodbye. He could feel it.

"I want to put our deal behind us, Dameon. I want to end it. My room hasn't felt like a cell in a long time. You've made good on your promise to get me out of the house, and I trust you never to hurt me again. But I think you know, it will always hurt me, in some way, to stay this way without any real freedom, forever."

Dameon felt sick.

"So I want a new deal," Emma said. "You promise me my freedom, to let me come and go as a please, to not follow, to trust me with your secrets–"

Dameon closed his eyes, waiting for the incoming request to never come back. He knew the day would come. It had to. No one could ever be happy being a prisoner. No matter the love poured into her, no matter the gifts, or increasingly regular outings, she'd inevitably want what any human being needed. She needed her freedom.

"You give me that," she said, "and I'll promise you my life."

Emma's face was sweet, genuine. She meant every word. He wanted to save her, protect her, love her, the same he did for Matthew and Elijah. But Elijah was always quick to remind him, he could never save her like this, not when he made the call to hide her away. Nevertheless, a teasing brow raised on Dameon's face.

"Did you just propose to me," he asked, with a smile.

Emma laughed with a cute smirk. He liked seeing her happy, even more than he liked playing games.

"I suppose so," she said, sweetly, "but only if it would count for Matthew and Elijah too. I wouldn't want them to get jealous."

She was getting cocky. He wondered if Elijah was rubbing off on her, or if this is how she was before him. He couldn't know. There was still so much about her that he didn't know.

"I," Dameon said, reluctantly, "I don't want to lose you."

Emma wrapped her arms around his body, stood on her toes, and kissed him.

"You'll never have me, until you let me have myself again. You want to make things right? You want to fix it? This is the only way."

Dameon squeezed Emma too tight.

"Deal," he said.

She held him just as hard in return.

When Dameon informed Matthew of the decision, he was not impressed with the decision. It didn't matter. She was already gone.

Elijah was shockingly on board. Well, maybe not shockingly. He and Emma had a bond that was different from what Dameon and Matthew could have with her. He and Matthew could certainly understand what it was like to have a messed up childhood, but they at least always had each other. Elijah had no one. Emma had no one. He often knew what she needed better than Dameon or Matthew could. Elijah wanted her safe, but he also wanted her to thrive.

Matthew had every desire to see her happy, but more than that, he wanted her safe. He knew better than Elijah, about all Tony could be capable of. Elijah may have been quick to hop aboard the revenge train, but he didn't see Tony in his early years.

Elijah saw Tony, the untouchable millionaire, sitting on fat stacks, living easy. Matthew and Dameon saw the mobster version of Tony, the man that was quick to inflict pain and suffering when slightly inconvenienced. Maybe the man had grown soft, but Dameon would bet the tower in his name, that he hadn't.

"We couldn't keep her locked away forever," Elijah said, trying to comfort Matthew. "Plus, you know she would have eventually hated us, if we tried."

Matthew stood to his feet, rejecting Elijah's attempt at offering a calming hand. He was fuming.

"And you just gave her the keys, added her scan to the door, and gave her the best of luck?"

Oh yeah. He was pissed.

"And a phone," Dameon said, bluntly. "She's only going to the corner store and back. She needed this, Matthew. She needs to know she has our complete trust. She needs–"

Dameon took a deep breath.

"She needs to stop being treated like our prisoner, and start being treated like one of us. We all face risks going out there alone. We have to accept that she will too now, and we can't shelter her for the rest of her life."

Elijah smiled, clearly approving.

"Do you love her," Dameon asked.

Matthew paced.

"Of course I do!" he shouted. "But I'm fucking scared! What if Tony finds her? What if… what if she doesn't come back? What if she runs?"

Elijah spoke softly.

"Then she would be giving us exactly what we deserved in the first place."

Matthew halted his marching.

"We're all attached but–" Elijah said, sweetly, but was cut off before he could finish the loving sentiment.

Dameon's phone rang.

Dameon looked at the buzzing device. It was her. She was fine. She was probably taking advantage of every drop of her newfound freedom. She would be fine. The room read Dameon's face and mirrored his concern. He answered.

"Tisk, tisk, Lazarus. I did warn you, didn't I?"

Dameon put the call on speaker and placed the phone on the coffee table. He'd break the damn thing if he held it any longer. Not to mention, the others would need to hear. He knew he wouldn't want to relay whatever he had to say.

"Well," Tony asked, smugly.

"I hear you," Dameon said, through gritted teeth.

"Good. Here's the deal, you and your little club come down to my place. If you do, I won't touch the girl. If you don't... I'll take it as a sign that I misjudged your relationship with her, and write it all off as a messy loss. I want all three of you here. If it's just you, she dies. No guns. And tell your big friend to be on his best behavior. I don't want to have to eliminate him just because you can't control your muscle."

The room was quiet.

"I'll assume you're thinking it over. I'm giving you an hour. I'll look forward to seeing you soon."

Not a person moved. No one spoke. They just sat there.

Dameon knew it was his fault. If he didn't bring Emma home, if he didn't keep her, if he tried harder to keep them from forming an attachment to her this wouldn't even be a discussion.

He would have to let her die. Could he live with himself if he chose that? No, absolutely not. But he wasn't about to let his lovers pay for his mistake. He couldn't lose her. He couldn't lose them. What the hell was he going to do?

"So... we're going, right," Elijah asked, without really asking.

"No!" Dameon shouted.

Matthew and Elijah looked at him with pity. He hated it.

"Dameon," said Matthew, standing at his tallest, "we knew this was how it could end. Not just because of Emma, but the whole thing. We chose a life of violence and we knew it would probably end with violence."

Dameon upended a sofa. He kicked it over, and over again, until his foot ached.

"No! No! I can't! I won't let him do this! I won't!"

Matthew gripped Dameon's arm, and pulled him in. Matthew's temperature was hot. He was scared, Dameon knew it. Elijah was too. They all were. He couldn't let Tony win like this.

"He already beat us," Matthew said, with an unbearable calmness. "If he gets us, Emma might have a chance. We both know that he's sick enough to make her live, knowing we are gone."

Matthew grabbed Dameon's face. He hated it. He hated being handled like he wasn't their fearless leader. Still, at the moment, he knew he needed it. Matthew knew it, that's why he did it. He always knew how to reach him.

"If Emma survives, we can rest easy knowing that she'll make him pay. She'll fucking ruin him. Tell me I'm wrong."

Dameon knew he was right. She had a rage he'd only seen when looking in the mirror. When Matthew killed, he was uncannily calm. Elijah could get pissed, sure, but Emma had the desire to inflict pain if pushed far enough. He recognized her anger when she lunged for her ex. He witnessed it first hand when she threatened to cut his dick off, when he offered her the chance to get even with him. She may not have done it, thank god, but she considered it.

If she found out Tony was responsible for their deaths, she'd unleash hell.

"I can't ask you to do this," he choked.

Elijah wiggled his way under Matthew's arm, and held both of them.

"You don't have to," Elijah said.

Elijah tried to sound sure, but there was so much fear hidden under his voice. Matthew nodded in agreement. Dameon swore. He took Emma because he thought, in his moment of idiocy, that he could save her, keep her safe. Now, at least he had a chance to actually do it. He cursed under Matthew's strength and Elijah's bleeding heart. Dameon broke away from his men and spoke unquestionably.

"I'm driving."

Dameon raced through the city. Why worry about traffic tickets if you weren't around to pay them?

He drifted to a stop in front of a mansion. He didn't do it for flare, but rather to release a little anger. The three stepped out of the car and were instantly met with multiple guns pointed in their direction.

More than one kept their weapon on Matthew, and for good reason. How many of them were hired to replace the men he personally killed? Matthew was a damned boogeyman to these pricks. Tony walked out with an ugly, beaming, smile.

"With about half an hour to spare," Tony yelled, from behind his guards. Fucking coward.

"Come," the man said. "We have lots to talk about."

"Show us the woman and you have a deal," Dameon shouted back.

Tony removed his tinted glasses and cleaned them with his shirt.

"No. But you have my word that she currently remains unharmed. She'll stay that way as long as you do as you're told."

He gestured at the armed men.

"Not that you'll get far if you don't."

Dameon, Matthew, and Elijah glanced at each other. Brave faces, all around. Good. They would give Tony as little satisfaction as possible.

They walked together into the house. Past the huge front door, past a set of stairs, and down a hallway. They moved in silence. Elijah was losing it. He tried to keep a straight face, but Dameon could see the panic emanating from his being. It killed him to see it. Tony unlocked and opened a door in the quiet hall and gestured for the men to enter. Matthew was instructed to go in first, then Elijah.

The door was slammed shut, with Dameon remaining in the hallway.

"No! Wait! Matthew! Elijah!"

Another door was opened behind Dameon, while guards held the violently struggling man back. It took three of them, but they managed to push him into the room and cuff him to a metal chair.

"Tony," he begged. "Tony, you want me. You don't give a shit about them. Just–"

A fist met the side of Dameon's face. His ears rang. The room spun. For a quarter of a blissful second, he couldn't think.

"You think I'm going to let the monster and your pet go after the shit you pulled," Tony spat.

His breath was a mixture of salami and booze. Another hit to the face. Dameon wasn't sure if it hurt more or less than the first. The metallic taste of blood filled Dameon's mouth. He spat onto the floor. A single white molar clicked as it fell to the concrete floor. Yeah, the second hit hurt more.

"Wait," shouted a male voice. "Wait, wait, wait."

Dameon looked up from the growing red puddle on the floor. He must have been hit harder than he thought. His brain wasn't working. In front of him, was the ex. Emma's ex, standing in front of him, pushing Tony out of the way.

"You're going to ruin it," he complained.

"You're Gt–" shit what was it… "Grant! Grant," he said, confused.

It didn't make sense. The thin man with dark brown eyes looked at Dameon with absolute disgust.

"You really don't remember me, do you," he asked, rhetorically.

Sure he did. Emma's ex. Maybe he got the name wrong? He didn't know what the hell was going on. Why was he here?

"I guess I don't blame you. It's been a while."

Dameon's jaw was becoming increasingly more painful. The hole where his tooth had been, was suddenly a lot more noticeable.

"What are you talking about," he asked, though the blood in his mouth nearly got in the way of his words.

"I'm fucking Greg."

Nope, nothing made sense. Clearly the first punch knocked him out. This was all a dream, or hallucination. The dead don't talk, or walk, and they definitely don't demand the kidnapping of their dating partners.

"But–" Dameon asked, playing along with the shitty dream. "How? You're dead."

Greg smiled, but looked irritated.

"No, the girl, Penny, she died. I, on the other hand, managed to survive. I, understandably, felt like keeping a little distance would be my best move. You know, since dear dad here tried to kill me. So, I made a new me, and wouldn't you know it, ten years later I ended up back here anyway. Funny how the world turns. Guess family always comes back, well, maybe not yours."

How couldn't he have seen it? His brown eyes, hair color, height? Sure, ten years could do a lot to a person's looks, but how could he have missed it?

Tony faked a cough to shut his son up. One secured Dameon's head, another held his body. Dameon tried to struggle. He was confused, and when he saw the knife, panicked. The fear was overwhelming.

Before the end could be dealt, Tony grabbed Greg by the collar of his shirt.

"You will wait for my orders before proceeding. Are we clear?"

Greg nodded to his father, then to the henchmen.

The guard pointed the blade at the corner of Dameon's right eye.

It pushed. He screamed. He screamed from the depths of his soul. It was excruciating, all consuming. It dug. He tried to fight. It pried. He couldn't possibly scream and cry louder. Please pass out, Dameon begged his body. Please. Die or pass out, come on! Anything not to be here. End it! Make it stop! But he didn't.

Freezing air hit his empty eye socket. He was dying. Nothing else existed in that moment. He cried. He wondered how he was crying. Could half of him cry without an eye there? The pain! The pain was too much.

Dameon didn't fight when the guards uncuffed him. He fell limp, as they dragged him from the room. Why? He had legs. He could run. He couldn't see well, but he could run. A momentary burst of will was snuffed out by a hard punch to the gut when he began to struggle. Tony kicked his side, his arm, his stomach. For some reason, the blows to his body made his face hurt. Everything hurt. It was too damn much.

He didn't realize he was in the room with Matthew and Elijah until he heard the yelling. Elijah screamed through his cries. Matthew roared and pulled against chains. Dameon joined his loved ones, arms chained above their heads from the ceiling. Elijah could barely touch the ground. A duet of screaming and shouting his name bounced off the concrete walls.

Tony stood in front of the three, the door behind him, arms crossed and stone faced.

"You should have known better, Lazarus," he said. "You should have known I wouldn't wait around to take you out. I've killed better men for much less."

Dameon couldn't speak. He could barely think.

"Before you die," Tony said, coldly, "I want you to know, it was the girl. Emma, she did this to you. Know, this was all because you chose the wrong house, the wrong girl. It took a little longer than I would have preferred, for you to let her off the leash. But I'm glad you did Lazarus. She might just be my favorite asset. I'll let you marinate on those thoughts, before you're sent to meet your pathetic sister."

Tony produced three black canvas bags, and placed them over each of the men's heads, leaving Dameon for last.

"Get used to the dark. The next light you see, will be the fires of Hell. Enjoy."

Tony's footsteps distanced. A light switch clicked off. The door to the room closed. Uncontrollable sobs erupted from Elijah.

"Dameon," he whispered. "Matthew? I'm– I knew this was coming, but now that it's here? I'm really scared."

Dameon's heart crushed.

"D... Dameon," Matthew stuttered out. "It's so dark. Elijah? Dameon?"

Dameon broke. It was harder than he could have predicted. He wanted to pretend that they would face their deaths like the strong men they were. They would do the right thing. They would save the princess. But she wasn't their princess, she lied.

"She didn't really do this," Elijah cried, "right? She... she wouldn't."

"Why wouldn't she," Dameon said, defeated.

All was quiet, with the exception of Elijah's crying and Matthew's small panicked sounds as he breathed.

"But... I really thought," Elijah said.

"What? You thought she cared about us? We fucking kidnapped and tortured the woman. When given the chance, she played every one of our games. She gave us every little thing we ever asked of her. Even if she is, or isn't, working with Tony and Greg, she said exactly what she needed to in order to get us here."

"Greg," Matthew asked, after a long pause. "As in, Tony's son? But I thought–"

"Yeah, so did I," said Dameon. "But turns out, Grant is Greg. Fucker survived. Greg is who asked us to take Emma, if they were even dating at all. Maybe it was all a set up from the beginning. I don't know. I don't know what's real anymore. All I know is it hurts and I'm just ready for it to be over."

Elijah made an attempt at being comforting, but his tears got in the way. "I'm still real, Dameon," he said. "I'm... I'm here."

Dameon attempted to cry. He still wasn't sure how it worked.

"I know, Angel. I know. I'm sorry. I'm sorry for all of it. Matthew? My love, please. Please don't be scared. We're all here. We're here and... and–"

Dameon couldn't. He couldn't think of a single comforting thing to say.

"I love you," he told them.

They waited for the end.

The door opened. It felt like an eternity, and yet like they didn't have enough time. Dameon's body ached. He felt cold. He lost so much blood, he was surprised he held on this long. He was glad he did. He wanted to be with Elijah and Matthew when the time came. He didn't want to leave them.

The light never came on. Dameon's hood lifted.

Emma stared back at him. There it was, her bloodthirst. Her eyes were wild. Loathing gleamed in green, even despite the darkness of the room. He hated her. He missed her. He wanted to hurt her. He wanted to hold her. She looked at the empty hole, where his right eye used to be. Sorrow, regret, any hint of care, it couldn't be found on her face. The only emotion she exuded was pure hatred.

Dameon opened his mouth to speak her name, but was stopped when she put a finger to his lips. He didn't have the strength to fight, not even with words. She removed her finger and pressed it, coated in blood, to her own lips. A stamp of red printed on her mouth. She leaned close.

"Shhh," she whispered.

He recognized the movements. He felt the irony in his bones. It was she that had a dark bag over her head. It was he that pressed his finger to his lips to quiet the woman. He was getting the same treatment he had given her in the back of that moving truck. He was bleeding out then too, but not like this. He wasn't going to walk away from this.

She replaced the bag, leaving him in the dark. He couldn't hear her. Quick steps from the hall to the room sounded, followed by heavy masculine breathing. Tony? Greg? The man joined Emma, and the light flipped on. His hood was ripped away. A gun pointed at Dameon, square in the face.

A deafening shot was fired. Elijah and Matthew's anguish and pain, screamed from their bodies. They lost him. He was gone.

20 | Red

Golden keychain in Emma's hand, a phone in her pocket, and with a smile on her face, Emma walked into the elevator. She didn't really need period supplies. The guys actually did a fantastic job of keeping her stocked. Emma knew the excuse had a high probability of failing, but she had to try. She needed a decent reason to get out, and without the watchful eyes of Elijah, Matthew, or Dameon.

Using the affectionate pet name as leverage, was a last resort. The image of Dameon's pained face, printed itself in her memory. It devastated him to hear how serious she was about leaving. Their "little prisoner." She wasn't that anymore, though she would be lying to herself to say it didn't give her mixed emotions.

Emma studied her reflection. She was incredibly Emma, minus the blue hair and locket that was required for her exit. She was about to walk through the front door of the building. She was about to be a free woman for the first time in too long. Every step filled her with satisfaction.

A bell rang at her entrance to the shop. There weren't many people, but she couldn't shake the feeling that something was off. Her intuition was burning. Maybe she was simply being anxious over being so exposed for the first time in months. She was bound to feel that way for a while.

She took a mental inventory of her surroundings. One woman in sweats and an old t-shirt sitting at a slot machine, one man in a hoodie getting a drink in the refrigerated section, and the cashier. Emma grabbed a candy bar and soft drink.

Emma was nearly knocked off her feet by the man in a hood. She didn't catch his face before he sprinted out the door without paying. The cashier yelled in frustration but didn't pursue. He only swore and pounded a fist on the counter. It was enough. She didn't want to take chances now. She felt eyes on her, even then.

Emma reached into her pocket to retrieve the cellphone that was no longer there. In its place was a note simply saying, "It's about time. See you soon." Her chest pounded. She stepped up to the flustered cashier and paid for her items, before asking for the store phone to make an urgent call. The man unhappily obliged.

The call was unnerving. Gnawing feelings of indecisiveness settled in her gut. She could just go back. Maybe she didn't have to do this? Still, she gave the information she needed to, explained where she was, where the men were, and mentioned the note in her pocket.

Her conversation was met with sickening joy on the other end. After hanging up, she lingered in the store, unsure of what exactly to expect. Were Tony's men about to flood the streets? Would Carter's? It's not as if she had much of an opportunity to work out the details of her call. She had only just gained access to the outside world, and now the damn phone was stolen.

No one seemed to be around, but her stomach never let the feeling go, that everything was about to go sideways. There were too many players to worry about. She sipped her drink until it was finished, ate the chocolate, and tossed the rubbish into a nearby can. The bell rang again with her departure from the shop. Enough time had passed, she needed to get back.

A different man with reddish-brown hair eyed her from across the street. Emma pretended not to notice her stalker as she made her way casually back to the penthouse. He matched her steps from across the street, then into the grand building. He belonged to someone. Tony? Dameon? Carter? She couldn't be sure of much, besides the fact that this man was clearly on a mission that revolved around her.

She wished the note, and call could have been a little more clear. She called the elevator, scanned her card, pressed the button for the top floor, and watched the doors shut, almost. At the last moment, a hand stopped the large doors from closing. The goon got in next to her and stood uncomfortably close.

"Going up," Emma asked, politely.

He said nothing, only crossed his arms and waited.

The ride up took an eternity. They both knew a fight was coming but both also knew that there was nothing to do until the elevator permitted them to get to their end destination. They stood in silence, waiting.

When the pleasant dinging sound rang, it might as well have been the bell to begin a boxing match. The man lunged at her. Emma leaned against the handrails of the elevator's interior and kicked him in the gut. She was given enough of a headstart to undo the first of the locks. The man tore her away from the door and ripped the keys from her hand. She bit his hand on her arm and broke his nose with a solid punch, thanks Matthew.

She scanned her key. The man grabbed at her wig, which came off easier than he expected. She turned to hit again, but it was her turn to receive a fist to the face. Her vision blurred with dizziness and watered instantly. He dug his fingers into her arms and picked her up.

Emma headbutted the man, damaging herself, as much as him, in the process. She kicked again, this time, landing square in his crotch. He fell to his knees and curled up with loud swears. Emma scanned her eye. The door unlocked. She rushed in.

The man's hand attempted to catch the closing door, but was met with a series of very broken fingers, as she slammed over and over, hearing his bones crack. He retreated, leaving Emma hurting and out of breath on the other side. There was no getting in without her. If he didn't know that yet, he would realize it soon enough.

There were no words of worry. No commotion involving panicked men bombarding her with questions as to what had just happened. The penthouse was silent. She called for Dameon, Matthew, and Elijah in a desperate voice. Nothing. They were gone.

Emma replayed the conversation over the phone in her head, as she lifted a toppled sofa. Once returned to its rightful place, Emma did the only thing she could do. She made the call, not entirely sure if it was the right move. Now, all that was left was to wait.

Over half an hour passed. Emma rested on one of the rounded white couches with an ice pack to her face. In a startled jump, she turned to the direction of the front door, when she heard keys fiddling with the lock. A whirl of the scanner permitted the people on the other side to enter.

There were only three people out there that could do such a thing. Yet none of the men that stepped into the penthouse were those people. Grant led four threatening men into the empty home. He looked around, face full of disappointment and disgust.

Finally, he acknowledged Emma on the sofa. Her mind and heart raced.

"Grant!" she said, breathlessly.

Grant carelessly tossed a ball, wrapped in cloth, on the coffee table. Emma's curiosity never knew bounds before, this moment would be no different. She unfolded the cloth to reveal a deep ocean-blue eye. She darted her hand away from the detached body part. Her stomach threatened to expel vomit onto the floor.

Emma looked at the brown eyed man. He seemed to be waiting for her reaction. She stood with pain and longing in her eyes.

"Grant!" she cried, as she threw herself into his arms.

Emma gripped his shirt tight. She pushed her body to his, and held him as close as physically possible. Tears streamed down her cheeks. She reached up and pulled him close for a kiss. Her lips met his in obsession and desperation.

"Thank you! Oh my god, thank you!"

Grant's mouth twitched. Emotion surged through Emma's body.

"I take it, you got my note," he said.

"I did!" Emma said, through her tears. "You can't imagine the things they did to me, the things I had to let them think."

She sobbed in his arms.

"I hated having that fight before all of this," she said. "I'm so sorry."

Grant slowly twirled a strand of her blond hair around a finger.

"Are you saying that being with these pretty-boy assholes made you miss me?"

Emma sniffed and nodded.

Grant tilted her chin up.

"I seem to recall something about wanting to destroy me, after handing you over to them?"

Tears streamed down her face.

"You know I didn't mean it. I couldn't let them think I was completely weak, not that it mattered. They were so horrible!"

Emma tried to smile, but only broke back down to sobbing into Grant's chest.

"Please, don't let those people touch me ever again."

Something dark flashed in Grant's eyes that reminded Emma a little too much of Dameon. Grant kissed Emma's head, and wrapped an arm around her waist.

"We have to move," he said. "I have a lot to catch you up on."

One of the henchmen rewrapped the eye on the table, and placed it in his pocket. Grant led the way outside.

Grant opened the passenger door to his Corolla for Emma. She stepped inside and clung to her seatbelt. They weren't going home. Grant wasn't going in the right direction for that. Where was he taking her if not back home?

"So, you had the pleasure of meeting Tony, in person," he asked, bluntly.

Emma's nerves made her fingers tremble, as she closed her eyes and nodded.

"And what did your captors have to say about him?"

"Only the basics. Tony killed Dameon's sister. He also murdered his own son. Avenging her was the reason Dameon kept hitting Tony's businesses. Dameon nearly killed me over that bit of information. Oh Grant, I've never been so scared in all my life."

Grant eyed her a few times before returning his attention to the road.

"You can probably stop calling me Grant. I'm back to Greg now."

Emma stayed quiet. She looked down at her hands, trying to keep her composure, and listened, hard.

"Greg?"

"Yeah, but don't feel too bad about not knowing. Not even Tony knew I was alive, that he failed to kill me. I mean, he still got the Lazarus girl, and that was the real big fish anyway."

"Why... why didn't you tell me?"

"I've been in hiding, Emma. Of course I didn't let you in on that detail. I made a new life for myself. I didn't want to be a part of Tony's mafia dreams. But things change. Plus, can you imagine what they would have done to you, if they found out who I was? Who you were with?"

Emma nearly lost it, but didn't want to ruin anything. She couldn't believe the words that were hitting her ears. Her heart thumped in her chest.

"I wish you had told me," she said.

"Yeah, well, everything moved pretty fast after Lazarus robbed the pawn shop, didn't it?"

The Corolla paused at a guarded gate. Dameon, Matthew, and Elijah's empty car sat at the entrance with three of the doors left open. Emma's eyes lingered a little too long on it. Greg ignored the vehicle and parked on a semicircle in front of an expensive, large, home.

Greg shut off the engine, got out, and opened the door for Emma. She took his hand as he offered it.

"I look a hell of a lot different than I did the first time I met the Lazarus son," he said. "When he and his crew broke in, it didn't surprise me that he didn't recognize me. It had been ten years, after all. But I knew him. He always talked a big game, but could never go through with most of his threats. The big guy, maybe. But Lazarus wouldn't be happy about it."

Greg guided Emma into the home. The setting could have been used in the filming of a mafia movie. The dark, casino-style carpet, oil paintings, and gaudy white pillars gave the home an almost comically tacky feel. This was clearly Tony's home, and his Godfather influences were made abundantly clear.

Emma was led down a hall and into an office, Tony's office. It was dark with a large collection of dusty, untouched books. Greg offered her a seat near a large dark wooden desk. He sat in the partnering chair to Emma's. She wondered if Tony would be joining them soon in his empty chair.

Greg never ceased his studious gaze over her. From the moment he walked into the penthouse, he kept a cautious eye on her. She crossed her legs, and held her hands together. She looked shyly around the unfamiliar room.

"When he took you, I made sure Tony knew. He wanted Lazarus' kid more than anything, but the guy was always careful not to give him the opportunity. Thanks to your help, I gave him that. So we waited. Today was your first time out, unaccompanied, by one of Lazarus's henchmen. So our people made a move. Looks like my father and I both got what we wanted."

Emma focused on her fidgeting fingers. She tried to speak but nothing came out.

"Guess you're probably pretty angry with me," he said.

"Well, yeah. But at least you got me back. I was so scared."

Greg stood to retrieve a plastic bag that was sitting on Tony's desk chair. He pulled out a tie down made for securing furniture in the back of a pickup truck. Emma jumped to her feet.

"Grant–" she started to beg.

"Yeah, sorry." he said, without much apology. "Your appreciation for the rescue is adorable, but the men in the other room seem to think you are worth dying for. So just in case, I think we'll take a few precautions. Also, it's Greg."

Emma hugged one of Greg's arms.

"Please!" she begged, pathetically. "Grant, I mean Greg, please don't. Dameon, I mean Lazarus, he would tie me up. He made me– Greg, please! I don't ever want to be restrained like that again. I've given you everything, you can trust me! Please, don't do what he did. I don't think I can take it. I love you! If you love me too–"

Greg shoved Emma back into the chair and began fixing her to it. He knotted the ties around her wrists and ankles. Emma pulled lightly against the ties and breathed hard.

"You said they are here," she asked, in a shaking voice.

Greg gave her an interrogating look.

"You promise they can't get me?"

"Not likely," he said, simply. "Tony plans on letting them sit for a few days, or until he's done fucking up Lazarus' brain and body."

Greg rolled his eyes. He didn't seem to hold the same appreciation for prolonging their deaths as his father. He clearly wanted them out of the way quickly. Greg saw something flash in Emma's eyes. Finally, he smiled.

"They really trained you well, didn't they?"

Emma blinked.

"Let's see just how long you can keep it up for, shall we?"

Greg smacked Emma's inner thigh and squeezed. He leaned down, and invaded her mouth with an intrusive tongue. He unbuttoned her pants, and shoved his hand down. He pushed two fingers up. A numbness followed, until the need to throw up surfaced.

The door to the office opened, without a knocking warning. Tony was about to step in, when he saw his son in the midst of an assault. Greg removed his hand, painfully.

"I was just–"

"What makes you think I want to hear, or care about, what you were doing," Tony said, sounding inconvenienced. "While I'm sure it wouldn't take you longer than two minutes, I don't have time for this. Miss Kincaide will have to wait to be disappointed. Meet me in the other office, seeing as mine is apparently occupied."

"I'll be there in a minute."

"You'll be there now. We need to talk about your inappropriate use of my resources to retrieve the girl. You're a fucking idiot for bringing her here."

"She's harmless! I have her tied to a chair, what is she going to do?"

"No one is harmless, Greg. You're proof of that."

"I gave you Lazarus! You should be thanking me! I–"

"You are an insubordinate little prick, and the reason one of my men is without a god-dammed trigger finger. Now let's go, before I decide to finish what I started with you. I will burn you, you slippery shit. And this time, I'll watch to be sure you don't get to come crawling back."

Tony left, without closing the door behind him. Greg turned to Emma. He leaned over her, cutting off the circulation to her hands as he squeezed her wrists.

"I'll be back. When I am, we'll pick up where we left off."

In an instant, Emma's demeanor shifted. Her weak and pleading eyes turned sharp as daggers. Her trembling lip swapped for a dangerous snarl. Every muscle in her body was tense and ready for a fight.

"I will fucking end you," she growled.

Greg looked very satisfied with himself, turned away, and closed the door to the office.

The bondage was weak and amateurish. With only minor abrasions, Emma was able to get one hand free in less than a minute. In under five, she was completely untied. She scanned the room and quickly found a suitable weapon, for the time being.

The door handle rotated. Emma quickly and quietly moved her chair so that the man would need to step completely in the room to see her. If it was Tony, things would get complicated. If it was Greg... good.

An unknown guard entered the room. Emma kicked the door closed and stabbed the man in the neck with a letter opener. She ripped his vocal cords enough to render him unable to scream. He instinctively reached for his neck. A bad move, he should have reached for his gun.

She leapt on the man and stabbed over and over, until he no longer moved. It took longer than she imagined, but it was of little consequence. Emma grabbed his hand gun and a knife far better suited for her needs. She peaked out the door and calculated her next move. The hall was empty.

Silently, Emma made her way through the home. She opened every unlocked door she came across. One room had two men chatting about how stingy Tony was with their pay. The man didn't know how right he was. They weren't paid enough for what was coming. Emma burst through the door and closed it behind her.

"Help!" she whispered. "They're out there! They're coming to get me!"

She made her way quickly to the stunned men that didn't know whether to point their guns at her, or to go out and see who the "they" might be.

"Please!" she cried, tears streaming down her face. "Don't let them get me!"

With a speed the guards could never have anticipated, Emma sliced the throat of one, then stabbed the other in the gut.

She jumped on the back of one of the men, doubled over and holding his belly. She pulled at his hair, and cut well past the esophagus. They took so much longer to bleed out than in action movies, yet not quick enough for her liking.

Emma found this somewhat inconvenient, though they didn't pose a threat to her as they twitched and desperately tried to grab at their wounds. When they stopped their struggle, she retrieved their automatic rifles. She pulled their straps over her head, and collected them against her back.

Onward she pressed, finally running into a formidable room with a greater number of terrible people. No stealthy kills this time. Emma swung one of the automatic weapons around and sprayed the room. They didn't stand a chance, and neither did her shoulder.

She didn't anticipate the kick back and painfully learned her lesson. Stupidly, many men rushed into the room. She simply hid behind the open door once more, then mowed down the men that picked the wrong man to work for. Emma was too close to some, splattering pieces of them over her and sending destructive bits of bone flying and threatening to avenge their former owners.

Outside, chaos was ensuing. Shots were being fired, screaming and shouting over radio calls were filling the property. Good. Tony's operation would crumble before the sun would set. Emma's personal rampage continued, getting more reckless and taking more chances as she moved. Even as others shot at her from corners, rooms, and some running down the halls, she stood her ground. These assholes chose the wrong profession.

Two guards stood anxiously at one particular door. Emma caught a glimpse from around a corner. It must have been where her men were kept. What else could be so valuable? Unless it was Tony and Greg. Though they weren't her first priority, she wouldn't object to paying them a visit first.

Emma didn't give the guards a chance. She shot each of them before they had time to react to her presence. The door was fairly heavy. The walls to the room were thick. She wondered if the soundproofing was to keep noise from getting in or out. How much of the devastation outside could be heard from that room?

The light from the hall revealed three men, her men. Elijah was practically dangling by his wrists from the ceiling. Matthew was trembling and terrified. Dameon swung limply between the two. He looked broken, gone. Was she too late? She saw his eye on the coffee table.

She lifted the bag from the limp person before her. One eye looked up and met hers. He was alive. His eyelid was still attached, but a gaping hole was all that remained of his right eye. Blood smeared over his pale skin. Defeat weighed on his limp body. He was the image of a man that had already accepted his end.

Death would not snuff out the light in Dameon's eye. Today, Emma was death, and she had another claim to make. She was going to kill Grant... or Greg. She wanted to make him suffer for every drop of blood spilled, every ounce of pain he extracted from her lover. The guards were dead outside. So much noise was made. He could run, or he could investigate. Emma wasn't sure which he would choose.

Priorities changed when she saw her lover in his state. She wanted blood. Emma wanted to get the drop on Tony and Greg. She wanted to trap them, and take the revenge she was owed. Dameon wasn't the only one that could hold a grudge.

Dameon's jaw trembled as he tried to speak. She put a finger to his lips. Don't say a word, she thought. Don't let them know. She hoped with all of her soul that he would understand. She placed her finger against her own lips, and shushed the broken man. The pain behind his face broke her heart. Rage shoved her sadness to the side. She replaced the bag over his head, stood behind the door in the dark, and waited.

Footsteps ran towards the room. Emma hoped it wasn't another guard. It was not. Tony flipped on the light to the room. The man was out of breath from either running or panic. Emma hoped it was both. Tony snatched the bag from Dameon's head and threw the damp cloth to the ground with a slap. He pointed a handgun at what was left of Dameon's face.

The shot rang and bounced off the hard walls of the room. Elijah and Matthew screamed in a song of pain that was sure to haunt Emma for the rest of her life. They didn't know. But how could they? Emma rushed to Elijah, Dameon, then Matthew, and tossed their blindfolds to the floor. Shock, confusion, and terror absorbed their faces.

Tony fell to his knees at Dameon's feet before toppling over as he bled out in growing puddles. The pattern of the handgun's design stamped in Emma's tight grip as she glared at the dying man. It almost didn't feel fair. Tony wasn't only hers to take. Dameon and Matthew hated him for much longer than she did. Even Elijah could have some claim over the awful man.

With great effort, Tony rolled over to look at the woman that pulled the trigger. Struggling breaths wheezed in his chest. His eyes bolted to the doorway, where Greg took in the scene, jaw agape and shocked at the damage done.

Greg panicked but didn't look particularly remorseful over his father's slowly dying body. Greg spun around the room and found Emma. He looked like he was about to say something when Tony kicked his son's legs out from under him. The wounded man scrambled to his feet and ran for the door, a thick red trail marking his exit. The coward slammed the door behind him, taking full advantage of his headstart. Greg looked up at Emma, pleading from the floor, covered in his father's blood.

"Wait, wait," he begged. "I would never! He made me! I love you, Emma! You know that right?"

Emma cocked the gun and tilted her head. She looked like a deranged animal. She was covered in carnage from head to toe.

"I told you I would destroy you, Grant, or whatever the fuck your name is."

"You fucking bit-"

Emma dropped the handgun. She retrieved a tactical knife, and stabbed Greg through his right eye. The man let out a blood curdling scream. He was far from dead. Greg retreated backwards until he hit the wall.

Her rattling hand lifted, to touch the knife, to confirm what had happened. Greg sent echoing screams bouncing off the walls. Emma pointed the last of her loaded rifles at him. She pulled the trigger, feeling the pressure of the little piece of metal against her finger, and painted the room red.

Emma stood too long, looking at the mess she made. What was left of Greg was unrecognizable. A part of her forgot her mission. She was locked in place, motionless, unfeeling, and disbelieving of the events that lead her to that moment.

"Emma," Elijah asked, distantly.

She looked at the blond on his toes. It took a moment for reality to rush back. But when it did, it came back with a vengeance.

Life sprung back into Emma's eyes. She looked around the room. Keys hung on the wall behind them. She rushed to snatch them. The chains were held by large locks after being wrapped around permanent fixtures for this very purpose. She shoved the key in, turned, and the chain unwound around the metal bar.

Elijah hit the ground with a thud and groaned. Emma wanted to help but scrambled to Matthew. He didn't fall at all, but eyed Emma with caution. Neither had time to ask questions, as Emma was already unlocking Dameon's chain. Elijah and Matthew brought him gently to the floor. Each still had handcuffs around their wrists. Emma found the key and unbound them quickly.

Dameon was barely conscious.

"We need to get him home," Elijah said.

"What are you talking about," asked Emma. "He needs a hospital, a real hospital!"

"No," said Matthew, angrily. "Tony still has docs on his payroll. They won't know what happened yet. They'll be sure Dameon dies, before ever finding out that Tony might already be dead first."

"Even if his people aren't the ones to get Dameon," Elijah said, "a hospital will ask questions, and I think... I think I can save him."

Emma reached for the handgun she dropped earlier. She checked the cartridge and slammed it back into place with a loud click.

"Fine," she said, bluntly.

A thought crossed her mind, the keys. The security of the penthouse was severely compromised. It was only lockable with the retinal scanner without those keys. It would be better than nothing, but having the ability to fully lock the door would be a greater comfort. Emma looked at the bloody carcass on the floor.

Greg's pants were somewhat intact. She searched through the gore and into his pockets. They weren't there. Her heart sank. They'd have to figure that part out later.

"Let's go," she said.

Tony locked them in whilst making his cowardly retreat, but Matthew made quick work of breaking down the door. He picked Dameon up, and carried him, while Emma tossed an automatic rifle to Elijah. He took it in stride. Confusion hit Matthew and Elijah as they heard the warzone occurring outside the house. Emma led the way, unfazed by the shouting and shots.

Beyond the front door, chaos ensued. Men and women were using Tony's partially concrete exterior gate as a barricade, while two armies defended and attacked. One side clearly had the advantage, and it was not Tony's.

Carter and her soldiers were taking down Tony's men with lethal ease. The menacing woman stood, machine gun in hand, and clearly enjoying herself. Her people protected her like the queen-bee she was, out numbering Tony's at least three to one.

Carter led her swarm, screaming like a maniac and grinning as she sprayed. Her enjoyment amongst the destruction was put to a pause when she saw the near lifeless body in Matthew's arms.

"Lazie? Dameon? Dameon!"

Emma, Matthew, and Elijah ducked behind the concrete barrier. Carter joined them, attention on her past-paramore.

"He's not dead, is he," she shouted, over the sounds of gunfire.

"Not yet," said Elijah, shaking his head. "but we have to move now."

The stomachs of Emma, Matthew, and Elijah collectively dropped when Carter swung her weapon behind her back, reached out, and grabbed Elijah's face with both hands. She brought him to her, and pressed her forehead against his. She closed her eyes, looking angry, in pain, and desperate. It was strange seeing the human behind the entity of raw power.

Emma's finger readied over the trigger of her gun, waiting for Carter to give her an excuse.

"Save him," Carter said. "Or you'll have me to deal with."

"Save your breath," Elijah said through gritted teeth. "I don't need your threats to keep my Dameon alive, Carter."

A bullet grazed their protective barrier, sending bits of rock into the air just above Matthew's head. Each of the people instinctively ducked further, except for Carter. Howling a war cry from her chest, she sprayed bullets with little regard for even her own people.

Carter pointed a finger down to Emma, the thrill of the battle returned to her face.

"Thanks for the call," Carter shouted, with an angry smile. "Tony's empire falls today. You are looking at the biggest boss of Las Vegas, and I won't forget your part in this, friend."

Carter paused, just long enough to cup her hand around her mouth, and yelled through the chaos.

"El Tiburón! You can leave the fun to me now!"

Emma peaked from around the barrier to see the silver man shooting with expert precision. She gasped when an enemy force ran from behind him, screaming and ready to stab the ally in the back.

El Tiburón grabbed the arm of his assailant in the nick of time. He pulled hard towards him, throwing off the attacker's balance. El Tiburón twisted the arm with a snap, and used the assaulting blade to pierce its owner in the side twice, then forced the man to slice his own neck with vicious strength.

El Tiburón looked at Carter, and ran with a slide home in the dusty desert ground. When he saw Dameon, Sebastian crawled to Matthew's arms. He took his adopted son in his arms, and stroked his bloody hair back. His chest heaved as he held his mangled child. He held the boy's head, the greatest fear of a loving parent, flooding his eyes.

"The path to the penthouse is secure." Carter said. "Go!"

Matthew scrambled to his feet to retrieve the car. Emma followed close, providing cover for the large target. Matthew revved the engine and slammed on the gas, barely giving enough time for both of Emma's feet to find the floor of the passenger side.

Close, yet safe as possible, he slammed on the brake to allow his lovers and El Tiburón into the back seat. Sebastian gripped Dameon, as if holding the life into his son. With a grateful nod to Carter, Matthew peeled away, sending a cloud of dirt into the battlefield, and leaving the place to the new change of command.

21 | Actions and Consequences

The Maserati swerved like a bat out of hell. It was a wonder they didn't get pulled over. Emma twisted around the front passenger seat, to see Elijah and Sebastian attempting to clean Dameon. A concerning amount of blood drenched his clothes. Emma didn't have time for panic. Now was not the time.

She searched around her seat for the supplies she knew would be available for a time such as this. A dark bag rested at her feet. Emma unzipped it, and found what she hoped for. It was a self-made emergency kit, like the one Dameon used when the roles were reversed. Emma retrieved a clear baggy with clothes and tossed them back.

Elijah silently, and quickly, pulled off Dameon's clothes. He dressed him in the clean replacements over his nearly lifeless body. Emma kept searching and found a pair of sunglasses and duct tape. Matthew wordlessly glanced periodically over, as Emma recreated the blindfold they used to get her to the penthouse. This time, the goal wasn't to keep its wearer blind, but to conceal the damage beneath.

Matthew kept eyeing the bloody woman with apprehension, as she passed the glasses back to Sebastian. He took them, as he continued to clean the face that they were intended for. Emma ignored Matthew's looks. She didn't have time to answer or ask questions. She dug for more clothes and found them. They were men's, but they'd have to work. She stripped in the front seat, and used the inside of her soiled shirt to clean off as much blood from her as possible.

Emma opened up the mirror of the car's visor and saw an unspeakably gruesome mess. Matthew reached to the side and passed a water bottle to Emma. She drenched her hair and washed her face and hands the best she could. It wasn't great, but passable. She tightened the drawstring of the trunks that were entirely too big on her, and sunk into the seat.

They screeched into the private parking area and Elijah leapt into action. He tried to pull Dameon's body out of the car, until Matthew took over. With more strength than Elijah could manage, he wrapped a limp arm around his neck as Dameon attempted to stand at his side. Elijah placed the sunglasses over the swollen and damaged face. Sebastian took Dameon's other arm and made a poor attempt at a "Weekend at Bernie's."

Even dressed as he was, he didn't look fine. They'd have to be fast. Matthew and Sebastian practically dragged Dameon through the lobby, and into the elevator. The smallest amount of luck sided with them, when not a single drop of blood was left along the way. Once in the elevator, the large man picked up his lover's legs and cradled the man. When at the door, Emma scanned her eye to get them safely inside.

Elijah rushed to the emergency room, his entourage at his heels. Matthew laid Dameon onto the table with unbearable care. Elijah made a loud command for blood. Matthew rushed to a steel refrigerator and came back with a clear bag filled with blood that had Dameon's name scribbled on the outside with marker.

Of course they kept each other's blood on hand. The sight barely surprised Emma at this point. Elijah readied an IV and a stand for bags to hang on.

"Talk to him Emma," Elijah commanded.

Nothing. Not a single word came to her mind. Emma's shock seemed to finally be setting in.

It was gone. His eye was gone. The image of Greg's mangled body intruded in her mind. All the men she killed seemed to linger at the corner of her vision. Flashes of Dameon, Elijah, and Matthew chained to the ceiling distracted her, making her forget what was needed of her. The floodgates of panic finally cracked and broke.

393

Instead of providing comfort, Emma rushed to the trash can and proceeded to vomit the candy bar and soda from earlier. A terribly sweet hand rested on her shoulder. Sebastian looked gravely at the operating table while Emma puked, and Matthew took Dameon's hand.

"Hey," Matthew said, just above a whisper. "Hey Dameon. You're going to be fine. Elijah's got you. We're home. You're going to be okay."

Dameon groaned, and let out a lengthy sigh of relief.

"I just gave him some Morphine," Elijah said. "It'll probably make him pass out, but he'll feel a lot better."

With shaking legs and a foggy head, Emma returned to the side of the increasingly relaxed man. Dameon opened his remaining eye, horror flooded his blood-soaked face as he noticed her presence. He couldn't move, be it from exhaustion, his nearness to death, or bone chilling fear.

"You," Dameon said, deliriously, "you killed me!" He attempted to retreat into flight mode, but his pains didn't permit it. "I saw you! You shot me, but then– you killed Tony. I... I– You did it! You killed us! You did this!"

Sebastian pulled Emma back with a stern, yet calm, hand against her shoulder. Matthew placed a large and loving hand on Dameon's cheek. He stared at his lover. The regret and desperation racing through Matthew's mind couldn't be parted from his face.

"No one can hurt you here. You're safe."

Dameon looked as if he was about to fall asleep. His eye rolled back for a moment. He managed a long blink, then fell totally limp. Matthew snapped his attention to Elijah. Elijah checked a monitor he inserted over Dameon's finger and continued his work unfazed.

"He's just asleep," Sebastian said. "You should go, both of you. Elijah needs to concentrate, and work fast. You two will better serve him by not being here."

Matthew nodded. He looked at the bruised, broken, and bloody, body. If it wasn't for the occasional movement of his chest filling his air, Dameon would have looked dead already.

"I'll see you when you're all fixed up," Matthew whispered.

He gave Dameon a kiss on his forehead before leaving.

The door was shut. The hall was deafeningly quiet. Emma walked as if she were in a trance. For some reason, she ended up in the kitchen. Matthew followed at a distance. Emma felt it, the divide. She felt the anger he was directing towards her. He blamed her. She could understand why. It was her fault. If she hadn't left, hadn't pushed so hard to go out on her own...

She placed a hand on the fridge. Why? She couldn't eat if she wanted to. She looked back at Matthew. The large man held his stance of intimidation, the same he used when surrounded by enemies. She recognized it, but she couldn't be scared. She didn't have any room for more fear, only anguish.

"Tony said you set us up."

Emma didn't say anything.

"Tell me you weren't working with him. Tell me you didn't do this."

Emma blinked and let go of the fridge. She wasn't hungry. She wasn't anything. But in that same breath, she was feeling too much. A red handprint left a mark on the refrigerator's handle. She thought of Greg, the nothing she left of him. Her heart started to pound again. She kicked the door, denting it, and stormed out of the kitchen.

Emma headed for the stairs but Matthew's hand grabbed her wrist. She struggled hard, hurting her hand as she pulled. Emma yelled with feral overexertion at Matthew. He released her with a push away. Matthew called after her as she marched up the stairs, asking if it was guilt that brought her to their rescue, if she was really playing them all along. His anger grew with her ignoring response.

Emma burst through the door of their shared room. She threw open the bathroom door and slammed the water of their shower on. She pulled off her shirt, balled it up, and threw it to the floor. Matthew grabbed her arm and jerked her towards him. Emma tried to rip herself away but he didn't let her go this time.

"Answer me!"

"Don't you dare question me!" she roared.

Her legs shook and gave out. Matthew let her fall to the tile floor.

Red. There was red on the door handle, on the shower walls, on the floor where she collapsed. His face betrayed a look of conflict. She did feel guilt, but not for the reasons Matthew shouted about.

She was to blame. She insisted on putting everyone in danger so she could go out. She was pissed with herself for it, but what stoked her burning anger the most was the questioning of her loyalty. Did she not prove to what lengths she would go for them?

She thought back to what Greg said. He mentioned that Tony was playing mind games. Telling them that she betrayed them sounded like something Greg would do for the hell of it, or just to try to extract a little more pain. If his father was anything like him...

Emma untied the shorts. She crawled out of the large clothes and sat under the cool stream of water. Her side rested against the freezing wall. She didn't look at him.

"I never worked for Tony, but that doesn't mean it wasn't all my fault. I killed people, Matthew," she said, with a cry in her throat, chopping her words as they pushed past her lips. "I ended so many lives. I almost got you killed. I– Dameon might– It's my fault, but, I don't ever want to hear you question my fucking loyalty again."

Matthew approached slowly. Emma listened to his steps, the sounds of his shoes and socks had been abandoned. He walked into the shower with the remainder of his clothes still on. He stood just outside the cold stream. She felt him towering over her. She opened her eyes to watch red and a few chunks of human remains run down the drain.

He stood at the corner of her vision as she stared at the flowing water on the floor. The temperature around her body warmed. It was only with this change that she realized she had been shivering. The warmth was hardly enough to provide any real comfort.

A large shirt fell to the floor. Emma heard the distinct sound of a zipper, and snapped her eyes up. He pushed his underwear down with his pants, and stepped out of them. Fear and distrust gnawed at her gut. Matthew sat on the bench and watched the pale woman on the ground. They sat in silence for a while. Both tried to let the warmth wash away some of the day, but relief would elude both of the traumatized people.

"I'm sorry," he said, finally. "I let the bastard influence me. I was scared and angry. I was wrong to question you."

"Yes, you were," she said, softly. "But I forgive you."

A hand of Matthew's reached up and grabbed a bottle of shampoo. It was very much needed. They smelled of sweat, fear, and metal. Matthew silently offered some of the soap to Emma, and scrubbed his own hair. He stood to rinse it out then swiftly, silently, washed his body. Emma only sat with a small pool of untouched soap in her hand. She watched little shimmering swirls move around, as she manipulated the cleaning liquid in her palm.

Matthew gently pulled Emma to her feet. He took what he gave her, and proceeded to gently wash the gore from her hair.

"Try to close your eyes," he said, ready to rinse out the suds.

Emma shook her head, increasing the speed with every turn.

"I'm sorry, Emma," he said. "I'm sorry for yelling. Please, trust me, even if it's just for the next few seconds."

Emma kept shaking her head.

She knew he would take it personally. He probably hated that he was so quick to use his murderous, intimidating persona against her. But Emma couldn't do it. She couldn't shut her eyes. She didn't want to face what waited for her in the dark. Her victims lingered just out of sight with her eyes open. She was sure they would come for her if allowed access behind the darkness of her eyelids.

Matthew accepted her reluctance, and guided her head back. He shielded her eyes from any stinging soapy residue. Once clean, he moved a large hand slowly down her back. A different emotion took over Emma. Thoughts of Greg's intrusion soured Emma's feelings, and sickened her. She snatched Matthew's hand and shook as she gripped tight. Matthew eyed her hand with an interrogating stare.

"No," he said, pain lining his denial. "He didn't. Fuck, Emma. After everything, please. Don't tell me that on top of everything, Tony's people touched you."

Emma's hold tightened around his hand.

"Grant, or Greg," she said. "Whatever his name is…was. Just his hand, but yes. He would have done more, he wanted to. But then I… I killed him, so he didn't get the chance."

Matthew released Emma and backed away. Her body was bruised from the elevator fight. The side of her face, where she was punched, was gaining colors of purples and blues. She felt his stare and the inferences that accompanied it.

"He didn't do any of this," Emma said, waving over her battered places. "One of Tony's guys got in a few hits to get the keys. He apparently lost a few fingers, but I still lost the keys."

Matthew was furious. His anger wasn't directed at her anymore, but at the assholes that hurt her. Murder returned to his eyes. It didn't matter. There wasn't anyone left to kill. There was a good chance her attacker wouldn't have survived Carter if he went back to Tony's place. And as far as Greg went… she took care of him.

Anger bubbled in Emma's gut. She felt discomfort when Matthew touched her. She knew why. Greg left an unseen mark that Matthew picked up on. It wasn't fair. Why should the dead man's touch have a lasting influence over her love for Matthew, and her desire to be held by him? Rage boiled under her skin.

Emma hated Greg. She hated Tony and everything he did to Dameon, to her, to Matthew and Elijah. The fire roared in Emma's chest. She was broken, hurt, but more than that, she was pissed. Emma felt Greg's tongue being forced down her throat. She felt the intrusive push of his fingers into her. She thought of the torture he put Dameon through.

Emma looked at Matthew with fire in her eyes. He took a cautious, additional, step back. He looked almost afraid of her.

"Kiss me," she demanded.

Matthew shook his head.

"Get his taste out of me. Please, Matthew. Kiss me. Take me," she said, through gritted teeth.

"I don't think I physically can," he said, sadness coating his words. "You can't tell me what you're asking for won't be painful emotionally, maybe physically too. I get that you're angry, but I can't get it up, knowing what it could be doing to you. I don't want to hurt–"

"Fuck pain!" she yelled. "Get him off of me!"

Matthew took a few anxious steps to her. He pulled Emma's face to his, and kissed her. He pressed his lips to hers, and poured every bit of loving emotion he could find into her being. He held her in an embrace that fused the broken pieces of Emma together. He overwhelmed her with his warmth and gentle power.

She wanted to hold him back but couldn't. Her arms were pinned to her sides while he acted as her personal cocoon. He wrapped himself as completely as humanly possible around her. He squeezed out the fear, the guilt, the regrets. It's not what she was asking for, but it felt like what she needed.

The water shut off. Matthew dried Emma, then himself, with haste. He picked her up and carried her to bed, where he wrapped the two of them under multiple blankets. He didn't make moves to take her, only continued to hold her against him. Matthew kissed her while tears silently flowed from both partners.

Emma closed her eyes.

In the darkness, a sound took Emma's attention. A distressed golden dog, dug at the floor. She watched him look around, desperately for his owner. The dog cried and howled in grief over Riel, who would never come back. He didn't know why, only that he was gone, his walks were gone, his friend. Sloshing echoed, as blood dampened the floor, coating the pet's feet and nose.

People pulled themselves from the walls, and surrounded the edges of the bed. Gunshot wounds littered their bodies and their faces. Their blood flooded the floor. The levels rose higher, until the bed floated on the river she created. Her victims watched her powerless, immovable, body next to the mangled corpse of Greg. She could feel the wet, viscosity of blood that touched her skin as a bullet-shredded arm of Greg's ran up the side of her body.

Emma woke with gasping screams, and a jerking fight. Matthew bound her arms, and pulled her into him. He whispered words of comfort and calming sounds. He reminded her where she was. She was in their room. She was safe. The blankets were soft. His body was warm. His heart was beating with hers, and she could feel the truth in his words.

Once limited to light shaking, Matthew lifted Emma into a sitting position. He left for less than a minute to grab a glass of water from the bathroom. He verbally continued to guide her back. The water was cold, and real. She felt the process of liquid filling her mouth, running down her throat. Air entered through her nose and out her mouth. She was safe.

"Matthew," she asked, quietly. "How do you do it?"

The large man looked down with uncertainty at the naked woman.

"All of those people," she whispered. "There were so many. I can't stop seeing them. I can't stop feeling the throats I cut open. I can't stop feeling the gun fighting back, when I pulled the trigger. I can feel it like it's happening now. I can smell it. I can't stop seeing it!"

A strong arm pulled Emma onto Matthew's lap. He pressed her tight against his chest and stroked her hair. He breathed deeply until she followed his lead.

"Childhood fears," he said, softly, "aren't the only reasons I sleep with lights. You never forget them. You'll eventually calm down. But you'll never really forget what you've taken. Some nights are better than others. The haunting is strongest right after the kill, but I'm sorry. You just... keep going."

Emma flinched periodically in his arms at the memory of her own savage actions. She tried to rationalize that it was all to save her lovers. She told herself that her victims chose to work for Tony, a terrible human. Maybe that was enough to make them bad people?

She couldn't shake the feeling that some might have been perfectly fine human beings. People with families, people that just made a few bad choices. She made plenty of bad choices. Did the lives of three outweigh the many lives lost? She didn't stop to think about it then, but it was all she could think about now.

Elijah interrupted Emma's spiraling thoughts, when she saw him in the open doorway. He was exhausted. Blood stained his clothing. His body slumped against the frame, letting his head rest against the wood. His face was solemn and he looked moments from passing out. Emma and Matthew jumped out of bed to receive him. Elijah let out a long breath.

"He's alive," he said. "He'll... he'll survive. I want to keep him close to the med room for now."

"We could put him in my room," Emma offered.

Elijah nodded. Emma rushed to grab a robe. They would need her to open the door. She wrapped the tie around her waist quickly, and was about to run downstairs, when Elijah stopped her.

"Wait," he said. "Just the door. Don't go to him, please. He's not ready."

Emma paused. She wasn't ready to see him either, but that didn't dull the sting of being asked to stay away. She pushed the feeling deep down. She had a way to help, it was a small thing, but only she could do it. Emma nodded, and continued past Elijah to ready the room.

She turned to look back. He was watching her. Too many emotions flowed behind his gaze to decipher what he might be feeling. Matthew already had his moment of confrontation, but Elijah hadn't yet. How much of Tony's lying did he believe? Even if he didn't trust a word of Tony's, the man just spent hours trying to repair his loved one over the damage she caused. Would he be able to forgive her after that? Her questions would have to wait. Dameon needed her door open.

Emma hurried down the stairs. She placed her hand on the handle, and looked at the scanner. Her mind lingered on the front door. She stared at the high-tech lock. It felt wrong, needing to access her room this way. Instead of scanning her right eye, as she had previously always done, she tried her left. It didn't work. Tears formed.

Dameon's access would be denied if he tried to get into his own home. They would need to reprogram the lock. Emotions swelled in her chest again.

"I thought about it too," Elijah said, at the end of the hall, "the scan."

Emma turned to face him. How long had she been standing behind her?

Elijah shed his shirt at some point. His hands and face had been washed, but his pants, and parts of his arms, were still covered in terribleness. Emma's clean nakedness beneath the robe felt unfair. She turned back to the lock and opened her door. She propped it open with a heavy, metal statue of flowers for a doorstop.

Elijah entered the open room, and helped get the bed ready for its new occupant.

"Matthew assured me that Tony was lying," he said. "I believe him. I believe you. But Dameon– He isn't himself yet. Until he's better, I think you might– it might be better if you were to keep your distance. Just for a little while."

Emma nodded. Matthew's work at piecing her together was coming undone. Her heart was shattering. She fell to her knees, at the edge of her bed, and sobbed. Her tears rendered her blind. The thought made her cries only intensify. Dameon. What if his impairment would affect his painting, his chess playing? What if his other eye was damaged too, but she didn't notice in the chaos? What if he could never trust her again? She didn't notice that she had been repeating out loud, that it was her fault, until she felt Elijah's hand on her back.

"It's not," he said, smoothly. "We couldn't keep you here forever. You can't blame yourself for the actions of a villain."

"But," Emma choked out, "Greg used me to draw you out. If I... If–"

Another hand found Emma's shoulder. It was Sebastian. Emma looked up with blurry vision. The older man offered an open hand. Emma took it.

Sebastian led her from her room, up the stairs, and into the room of hers and her lovers. Matthew was gone, probably to help Elijah move Dameon. Sebastian gestured for her to sit on the edge of the bed. As he took a place next to her, she wrapped the robe tighter, holding the edges shut with white knuckles.

She hyperventilated, fighting another round of sobs. In a hold she couldn't recall experiencing before, Sebastian pulled her close, and wrapped an arm around her head to cradle her near.

"There is a time to be strong, and there is a time to feel the pain. Let it out mija."

She did. Emma broke fully, completely. Her body wrenched, as she wetted Sebastian's dirty shirt with her flowing tears. Every bit that had yet to come out, poured from her eyes and left through loud, unhindered cries.

"You called in the cavalry. You did the right thing. Tony was prepared to take everything from Dameon, more than just an eye. The boys downstairs are only alive because you got them out."

"But–"

"And even if Tony didn't have you, he would have found another way. We all know how this kind of life ends. You gave them the best chance they could ever ask for. You can choose to blame yourself, but I don't. Elijah and Matthew don't. Dameon will come around, he's just a little lost right now. I don't even think he understands that he's home. He'll get there."

Emma wrapped her arms around him, and continued to cry. He pulled her closer and rubbed his hands over her back. She held onto his bloody shirt, as if everything would disappear if she didn't. Sebastian held her head to him, kissed the top of her hair once, and rested his chin at the crown of her head.

"Thank you, Emma," he said. "You saved my boys. You saved them! Don't ever forget that."

When Elijah appeared in the room, Sebastian hugged Emma once more. He left to give the two privacy.

Emma joined Elijah for a second shower. She wasn't ready to be alone, and neither was he. Downstairs, Sebastian and Matthew tended to Dameon. Together, Emma and Elijah got into the big bed, and snuggled close, until Elijah fell asleep in her arms.

Emma did not sleep. She couldn't. She didn't want to see the faces again. More than the fear of seeing her dead victims, she discovered an anxiety of seeing Dameon in her dreams. Despite Sebastian's kind words, she wasn't able to entirely shake the guilt, even though his parental love comforted her in ways she would forever be grateful for.

It didn't matter that she didn't want to fall asleep. Life didn't allow for such a luxury as the days passed. Elijah and Matthew took shifts to be with Dameon and Emma. Since that day, neither man was comfortable letting either out of their sight for longer than a few minutes.

Sebastian came and went from the penthouse, dealing with the politics of Tony's end, and lending careful counsel to Carter. Elijah or Matthew, depending on the shift, tried to bring their princess back. They watched shows with Emma, read books, even played a few friendly video games.

Dameon never left Emma's room. He was sentenced to the same prison she was once given while he recovered. Emma fully adopted Matthew's habit of leaving lights on. For four nights, Emma slept, with either Elijah or Matthew, while the other accompanied Dameon. The separation and division of the household weighed heavily on each of them.

Emma watched Greg pry Dameon's eye out of his head. She heard his screams while Dameon screamed the question, why she would do this to him. He shouted that he trusted her, that she betrayed him. Her victims lined the bed night after night, and drowned Dameon in their river of their blood. She watched Dameon gurgle and choke on the results of her desperate actions.

Greg's shredded arms, torso, and face demanded her body, while she fought back in slow motion. Her arms weighed a ton each, and moved as if the air around her was unnaturally dense. The bed burst into flames as Greg shook Emma, violently, reminding her that everything was because of her. He would never let her sleep. She would never know peace.

Matthew's hands were on her shoulders. Emma was screaming. His movements were light but indeed shaking her awake. She gasped on the air in the room. Elijah sat in the bed, balled up with red, watery, eyes. He watched her sanity slipping, and it was killing him.

"Will it always be this bad," Elijah asked Matthew, in a whisper.

Matthew didn't answer. He motioned for the water near Elijah. The cup was passed, spilling little splashes on the bed. Matthew placed it in her hands, and grounded her again. The glass was smooth. The liquid was almost cold. When the edge touched her chattering teeth, it made the smallest clicking noise. The bed was warm. His hands were strong, and lovingly firm on her. Matthew glanced at Elijah.

"We need to let her see him," Matthew said. "He's ready enough, and she needs it."

Elijah nodded, in cautious agreement.

Emma anxiously followed the two men to her room. She stopped in her tracks before reaching the door. She thought of every terrible scenario. She tried to prepare herself for the hatred, or panic, her presence could bring out in him.

"We'll be right out here," Elijah said. "The door will be open. If you need us, we'll hear."

Emma took heavy steps around the doorway.

Dameon was laying in her bed. He looked relatively comfortable. He was reading a book. The sight brought her a mild comfort. A black band was wrapped diagonally over Dameon's head to cover his missing body part. When he heard footsteps, he turned.

His left eye darted from his partners in the doorway, and to Emma. His face illustrated his nervousness. Emma wanted to run. She wanted to hold him. She wanted to hide.

"It's okay," Elijah said. "We'll be close."

Matthew and Elijah backed away and sat against the hallway wall, to wait patiently for the results of the reunion of the two. Whether the meeting would go well or poorly, they would be ready.

Emma took uncertain steps towards Dameon. He tensed at the enclosing space. A hand snapped to the uneven headboard, and gripped nervously behind his head. Emma shook her head. She couldn't do this. He was terrified of her. Her eyes burned again. They seemed to do that all the time now. She looked towards the door and considered running.

"Don't," Dameon pleaded. "Please, Don't."

She was scaring him. She couldn't do this. Emma's feet sped towards the hall.

"Don't leave," he shouted. "Please?"

Emma stopped, just short of the doorway. She spun to face the man on the bed. He looked pained. His breathing was heavy. He shook his head in desperation.

"Please don't go," he begged.

Slowly, Emma approached the bed. She crawled up and neared herself to him. Dameon's tense muscles returned. He sat straighter. She got closer. With oceans of apprehension, her fingers pressed against his bare torso.

He was horribly bruised. His ribs were black and blue, his face was still swollen. She leaned closer, but he turned away. Dameon shut his eye and winced, not at her touch, but at her proximity. Emma fought through her trembling, to place her hand as lightly as she could against the least damaged portion of his face. He took in a sharp breath.

"I'm sorry," he said. "I'm sorry I couldn't protect you."

Emma's heart bled. He wasn't the one that needed to apologize. With every ounce of care and precaution she could manage, she gently sat herself on top of Dameon, placing him between her legs. A fluffy comforter separated them. Emma slid her hand over his on the headboard, and guided him to her waist. Once placed, she held his face delicately, and turned him to face her.

"I'm sorry I ever asked to leave," Emma said, through tears.

Dameon shook his head again.

"It's not your fault," he said.

Emma couldn't stand his forgiveness. She reached to kiss Dameon, but he turned again.

"Wait," he started. "You don't need to do that. I'm not as pretty as I used to be," he said, with a forced laugh.

Emma's hand softly moved up the side of Dameon's face. She started to lift the black band away, when Dameon snatched Emma's hand. His hand was shaking and his lips pursed.

"I don't want to scare you," he said. "It scares me when I look at it. You shouldn't have to see it."

Tears escaped from her eyes. It suddenly felt unfair, like bragging, being able to so easily cry.

"Do you still want me," she asked.

Dameon's visible brow furrowed.

"I don't remember what I said, Emma, but Elijah told me the jist of it. My mind wasn't right. I do. I want you. I love you. I always will. Nothing that has happened could change that."

"Then you'll have to let me see someday. For as long as you'll have me, I want to be with you. I don't ever want to leave your side again."

Dameon shakily ran his hand from hers, down her forearm, up to her shoulder, and down to her waist again. Emma slid her fingers under the band. Dameon shut his eye and waited, holding his breath. She removed it.

When he looked at her, his deep-blue eye stared back to observe her reaction to the empty hole revealed. Tingling filled her stomach and hands, as if she accidentally skipped a step on the stairs. She trembled over him. Tears flowed along the left side of his nose, but slowly pooled in his empty socket. He could cry, but without the roundness of his missing piece, there was nothing to direct the streams down, it only flowed back into the dark place.

Emma leaned close.

Dameon flinched back.

She stopped just short of his lips, waiting for him to come to her when ready. His fingers found her long hair. He ran them up, and caressed her, in the way he used to. He closed the distance and pressed his lips to hers. Warmth and explosive emotions consumed her. The guilt over the pain she caused, burned in her. Her desire to make amends, made the heart in her chest pound. She would spend the rest of her life making this up to him.

The tears that gathered in the empty space, spilled over, and onto Emma's face. Dameon felt it and jolted back, bumping his head against the headboard. Emma smiled with a light, breathy laugh. She rubbed the back of his head with one hand, and wiped the salty water from her face with the other.

"It's okay," she said, with a genuine smile, and a wipe against her arm.

"It's not," Dameon said. "It's disgusting."

Emma took the corner of the comforter, and dried beneath both sides of his face. Dameon pounced forward to wrap Emma in a strong hug. She winced when he unintentionally squeezed against her most sensitive injury. Immediately, he let go. He lifted her shirt, just enough to see the healing bruise around her side. After a check up from Elijah, he informed Emma that her attacker from the elevator seemed to have bruised a rib or two. It mirrored Dameon's own nearly broken ribs. Anger snuck into his demeanor.

"You're hurt."

"Just a little. You should see the guy that did it. He wasn't as lucky."

Dameon smiled proudly. It turned too quickly back to a frown. The guilt between the two proved too insidious to let them be just yet. Matthew knocked against the frame of the door. Elijah raised a witty brow, as they took in the scene of Emma on top of Dameon, with him pulling up her shirt.

"Looks like it's going better than expected," said Elijah.

"Already back to leaving us out," Matthew grinned.

Dameon replaced his black covering. He pulled Emma's waist into him in a small, single, jerking motion. He carefully moved his hand beneath her shirt, to her back, and rubbed gently. It felt good, healing to feel a part of his old demeanor returning.

"Don't be silly," he said, teasingly. "I'm just grateful she pities me enough to pretend I still do it for her."

"I don't know who you think is pretending," Emma said. "You look like a sexy pirate now, and we haven't had fun with role-playing yet. Sounds hot."

Dameon turned his head to her, with his raised brow. She smiled sweetly at him. A genuine, lovely, beautiful smile graced his face. The world wasn't fixed, but it was getting there. Her ghosts may have continued to linger, but for the first time, she felt distance from her haunting victims.

Emma cautiously closed her eyes, and let the darkness find her. They were there, but they couldn't touch her, not here. When she opened her eyes, Emma found Matthew's understanding gaze in the doorway. He smiled back at her, and wordlessly confirmed that it would get easier.

She had them, all of them. A wholeness that eluded her over the last few days found its way back into her soul. It was the greatest peace she felt, since before her departure on that awful day. She was home. As long as she was with these three, she had faith that the wounds seen and unseen might someday heal.

22 | Vows

With Dameon's return to the penthouse, so did a pleasant contentment. It was comforting having their family back together. Music played in the home again. Joking and wonderful bickering came back. A place of love and correctness found its rightful place in their home. Dameon still needed care and Emma continued to have the occasional night terror, but they learned to live again, with Matthew and Elijah's undying support.

Sebastian became an increasingly more constant addition as well. More than once, he brought his famous steaks over for dinner from Huevos. He helped in any way he could, to get Dameon and Emma back on their feet, and in a healthier headspace. Emma grew to deeply love the man. She missed him, when he needed to leave for days at a time. She understood exactly why Dameon, Matthew, and Elijah felt so close to him.

The man behind El Tiburón was their father. After Carter's siege on Tony's estate, Sebastian made it very clear that he regarded Emma in the same way he did his boys. As far as he was concerned, she was his child as much as the others. For the first time in her life, Emma had the family she never thought she'd have. With the exception of the occasional PTSD flair, she'd never been happier.

Dameon had taken to wearing his black band daily. Though better options existed, he didn't like the look of any of the traditional eyepatches. Elijah insisted that there were better options, but Dameon's vanity took priority. Emma didn't mind. She felt he looked like a dashing adventurer from a fairy tale.

One relaxing day, Dameon leaned his head over the back of his green chair. He stared at the ceiling, blatantly irritated. Matthew selected a new track to start another race. Elijah supplied the living room with sweet snacks.

"Shouldn't you be taking it easy on me," Dameon asked, pitifully. "Won't playing these games strain my vision or something? I lost my eye. Must I lose what's left of my dignity too?"

Elijah massaged the tops of Dameon's shoulders.

"Aw," Elijah said. "Poor baby. But you aren't fooling anyone. You're fine," he said, with a loving tap on Dameon's arm.

"It was worth a shot," Dameon chuckled. "But really, I think I might actually be getting worse. I hate this stupid game."

"Yeah," Matthew said. "Well, three of us love it, so suck it up. Game on."

He really was worse. Emma couldn't decide if his impairment had anything to do with this poor performance, or if he had finally stopped trying at the only activity he wasn't good at. She fell pretty far behind the two best players in the room as her mind wandered.

While she was grateful for much of the returned normalcy, there was one thing that was still missing. Though emotionally intimate, none of them attempted to initiate any physical acts. She knew why. Dameon and Emma weren't treated like fragile glassware anymore, except for in that regard. They didn't want to rush too much physical strain on the two, and three, definitely, didn't want to push Emma.

Matthew, Elijah, and Emma had also been giving Dameon time to come to terms with his newfound insecurity in his appearance. It occurred to Emma that the main culprit of their avoidance, might actually be little more than a lack of communication. Elijah won the round. Dameon groaned. Emma placed her controller on the armrest of the sofa.

"When will sex be back on the table," Emma asked, bluntly.

Matthew looked at her with a surprised smile on his face. Elijah also rose a brow in her direction. Dameon smiled, but the corners of his mouth were less enthusiastic than Emma had hoped.

"Hum, I don't recall us having sex with you on the table," Elijah said, playfully. His tone then took on a more serious delivery. "But really, we figured when you were ready, you'd tell us. We didn't want to be the first to ask."

"Well I'm ready. Let's go!"

Dameon laughed softly and leaned back in the chair.

"What exactly do you want," he asked. "You and I still have fucked up ribs. I watched you drop to the floor yesterday over a sneeze."

"Then we'll go easy," Emma said, sweetly. "I'm not asking to have my brains fucked out, though the idea of having less floating around in my head, does sound enjoyable. I just… I miss you. In the spirit of our special rule, I've gotta say, I'm starting to feel like none of you are interested in touching me anymore."

The men exchanged glances.

"It's not that," Matthew said. "It's just–"

"What," Emma asked. "This is me being as obnoxiously clear as I can be. I miss you! Thank you for caring enough to give me time, but I don't want anymore tiptoeing. I miss being with you, and I'm starting to worry that there's more to it than moving too fast."

"What do you mean," Dameon asked, seriously.

Emma took a deep breath.

"Are you afraid of me," she asked. "I mean, are you freaked out after I… well… murdered a ton of people, and lit the powder keg that led to a mob war?"

Dameon rose to his feet. His steps were deliberate, before he knelt before her. On his knees, he placed himself between her legs and pulled her to the edge of the sofa. His words rumbled in his chest.

"Yes. We are afraid. We all knew the rage you could harbor, but none of us realized the magnitude of what you were capable of. You aren't our captive. You don't need our protection. We've been waiting for the day that you are healed enough to see if–"

Dameon paused to look back at his partners. Matthew was stone faced, but Elijah nodded for him to continue.

"You don't have to stay," Dameon said. "Tony is gone, and we've put you through enough trauma. None of us would blame you if you decided– when you realize you don't need us anymore."

The words rattled in Emma's skull. When she looked around the room, she could see that Dameon's sentiment was felt in the others. They really thought that she would come to the conclusion that she didn't need them? They were expecting her to just leave? Despite the fact that she rampaged for them, this is what they thought would happen?

"We love you, Emma." Dameon said. "We obviously don't want you to go, but you can. You can leave and never look back at the pain we've caused. You can move on and never have to look at my face and the reminder it brings, that we were the ones that needed saving, not you."

How did the conversation turn to this? Dameon wasn't asking her to leave, but the understanding on Elijah and Matthew's faces agreed, she could. She was not under any obligation to stay. The thought filled her with joy at her absolute freedom, but also pain. She was not, nor ever would be their prisoner again. She was, in their eyes, their equal. More than that, they saw her as someone capable of even more than they were.

Emma lowered herself forward and pressed her lips to Dameon's. He held her, and savored every moment she gave to him. He was treating this moment as if it would be the last with her. He kissed her like it was goodbye.

"How many armies do I have to obliterate to show you that I care," she asked, with a smile. "There is no one I would rather spend the rest of my life with, than you three. I love you. I don't plan on going anywhere."

The cushion to the left of Emma sank, as Matthew took his place at her side. He pulled her waist to him in a squishing hold. Elijah joined to her right, knees pressing into the sofa, and arms wrapped around her top half and head. He kissed her playfully, sweetly, romantically, along her cheek and to her lips. She was surrounded in every way. This is how she wanted to stay for the rest of her life.

"I'm so glad you are a ridiculous human being," Elijah whispered.

"We belong to each other," Matthew said. "And we belong to you, for as long as you'll have us."

"Till death do us part," She asked, with a hint of request.

"For all of eternity, Emma," Dameon said.

The dungeon called. Dameon, Matthew, Elijah, and Emma answered.

Among the lovers, Dameon was clearly the most nervous. Matthew was first to hastily remove his clothing, then Dameon's shirt. Elijah kissed Emma, while pushing her pants to the floor, only releasing their kiss to get the pants totally off.

Emma led Dameon to the bed, and laid him down on his back. He lifted his hips as she pulled his underwear down and past his feet. She crawled over his body, recovering bruises fading, but ever present. She stripped herself of her shirt to reveal her own, that still showed in yellows and greens.

Gentle hands trailed up her legs, past her waist, and rested above the tender marks. Elijah finished undressing quickly, and kissed Dameon's hand over Emma's ribs. He continued to press his lips up Dameon's arm and to his shoulder. Matthew took Emma's mouth with his own before bending down to show her bare chest appreciation.

Emma moved her hips forward and reached behind her to stroke Dameon's hardness. He breathed deeply in satisfaction at her touch. Matthew reached down to ready Emma. His eyes requested her attention, as his fingers waited for confirmation before her entrance. She nodded. He accepted.

A single large finger slipped into her already wet self. She breathed in sharply and gripped Dameon tighter. Dameon's sounds followed Emma's. He found Elijah, and wrapped a hand around him, inviting a groan from the blond man.

Emma tried, but couldn't reach Matthew. The unfairness anguished her. She lifted away from Matthew's hand, and positioned Dameon to replace the former occupant. Slowly, she descended on him. He filled her terrifically, something she missed for far too long.

Emma's eyes asked for Matthew. He rose to kiss her again, while she turned her hand's attention to him. He moaned softly against her lips.

With a sweet pull upward she instructed Matthew to move higher. Emma bent to meet him halfway and took his ready self into her mouth. She moved her hand up and down his shaft, as she licked and sucked at his incredible size.

She rode Dameon with increased delight, while Elijah kissed Dameon passionately. Elijah moved to adore Emma's chest. The faster she moved, the more Dameon matched her pace beneath her.

Panic took hold when Dameon felt his eye covering shift. He reached for the fabric with both hands to hold it in place. His breath quickened with worry. His men stopped to give him time to find the comfort he searched for. Emma did not.

She leaned forward, chest on his chest, and placed her hands on either side of his face. Her fingers slid under his own protective grip on the black cover.

"No," he said, with fear in his voice. "Please."

Emma bit her lip, and smiled wickedly. She pressed her lips to the side of his face, feeling his rough stubble.

"Lover," she said. "No and please aren't the safewords."

Dameon swallowed a sound of nervous desire. His face betrayed anxiety, and absolute pride, in his princess. He swore under his breath, as the ghost of a smile attempted to push through.

"I don't want you to have to see it when we're like this" he said.

"I do. I want to see every bit of you. You are loved, and Dameon, you are very much wanted."

Emma disregarded his plea that touched the edges of yellow. She pushed part of the fabric away, leaving his insecurity still covered. Dameon nodded his consent.

"Look at you," she teased. "You should know better. I need to hear it. Do you want this?"

Dameon lightly laughed at the role reversal. He was scared, but his trembling hand was willed to cease its transparent worry.

"Yes, princess. If it is what you want, it's what I want."

Dameon allowed Emma to remove the entire piece of remaining clothing without interference. She ran a careful thumb over his cheek bone, and embraced the side of his face. She leaned closer and whispered into his right ear.

"You are so incredibly, perfectly, fucking, hot. You always will be."

Emma's forehead pressed into Dameon's neck, and she moaned loudly at a deep, and hard, thrust provided by Dameon's dick. Her hands buried themselves beneath Dameon's body and gripped the blanket beneath. He snatched the abandoned black band, and seized her wrists.

When she lifted her head, he wrapped her wrists together with the cloth, and tied a knot at incredible speed. He held her bound hands in his between his chest and hers. He motioned for Elijah to get behind her. Elijah obeyed after a heavy kiss to Dameon. Heat and an overwhelming sensation of love surged through Emma, as she watched Matthew take Elijah's place at Dameon's lips.

Dameon's demanding presence returned. He looked whole again. A sharp gasp uttered out, as a finger of Elijah's entered her ass. Her ribs warned of their displeasure with the sudden tensing of muscles, and quick respiratory actions. In a moment of distraction, she forgot her hands were bound, when she reached for the blanket beneath Dameon once more. She pulled against the restraint, enjoying the pressure on her wrists.

Elijah introduced another finger, readying her for him. Emma whimpered at the feeling, and tightened around Dameon. He groaned in Matthew's mouth at her clenching. Matthew devoured his lover in desperate want.

Slowly, gently, Elijah's lubed up self entered her. Emma cried out in little spurts, as he filled her inch by inch. Her fingers searched desperately for something to grab. Dameon took pity on her and offered his own hands in her palms. She squeezed his fingers. Dameon released Matthew, and looked down at Emma. The side of her torso pained but she chose to collect her pleasure regardless. She moved her hips into them and rocked with moans of threatening discomfort and intense desire for more.

"Emma," Dameon whispered. "My princess, my little protector."

Emma's eyes darted up to see a smiling Dameon and Matthew. She

416

paused. She looked back to Elijah. He slid a hand up and down her back and smiled too.

"Your... your what," she breathed.

"My lovely," he said, with thrusts, "strong, ruthless, little protector."

Her heart burst with happiness, excitement, and lust.

Emma's pace returned. She rode Dameon and Elijah with a fierce rhythm. She took them completely, and with power. Her heart raced. She begged for Matthew, who eagerly placed himself in her mouth, and a hand in her hair. She felt thrilled with the complete feeling. She loved this. She missed this. She could live in this moment of perfection forever, and be in bliss until the end of time.

Emma moved hard and fast over the two. She took greedily from Matthew. Elijah was close. She could feel it in his grip around her hips. With a few final, deep, pushes, he pulled out and finished on her ass.

Dameon grinned and gave wordless permission to Elijah. The beautiful blond man pulled Emma up, and away from Matthew. He pressed her back to his chest, and held tight with one arm across her collar. His other hand wrapped around her neck, and moved her face to the side. She looked up at him behind her. He may have finished, but he wasn't done.

"You're going to love this," he grinned.

Without warning, Matthew picked Emma up. The sudden emptiness sent tragic feelings through her body. Matthew faced her away from Dameon to face Elijah. Matthew placed her ruthlessly back on Dameon's cock. Emma shouted at the entrance. Dameon groaned deeply at the feel of her.

Elijah kept her gaze, as she writhed over the sensation of Dameon, now filling her ass. She breathed heavily through her gasps. Her ribs heavily protested, but the rest of her told her bruised bones to kindly shut up. It was too much, but she loved it all the same. Elijah placed a hand on her chest, and leaned her back against Dameon who wrapped his arms around her to massage her breasts. Emma whimpered through the intense amount she was receiving.

"Relax, honey," Elijah whispered. "I know it's a lot, but I dare you to tell me that it doesn't feel like bliss."

Elijah moved to her side, running light fingers over her trembling leg. He licked from her sternum to her navel. He stopped at her clit, and licked once with a sweet, mischievous, smile. Emma pulsed around Dameon, drawing a curse from his lips. She whined gratefully, and looked for Dameon's face. When she found his lustful stare, he pinched the sensitive tips of her breasts. Her hands snapped to hold his rough taking hands.

When Matthew took Dameon's previous place in her pussy, he expanded her to her absolute limit. A nearly screaming moan erupted from Emma.

"Don't worry, sweetheart," Matthew said. "I'll be gentle."

Emma looked down at the massive man, slowly entering and filling her. She watched as his cock disappeared into her desperate cunt, over and over. Elijah grinned at her show, and interrupted with a kiss that poured every bit of passion and love into her that his soul could offer. A large hand massaged Emma's hip as Matthew pushed in and out at a maddening, careful, perfect pace.

She was dizzy with the overwhelming amount. Emma wondered how she could possibly take so much, yet she did. She did, and it was ecstasy.

"My brave protector." Dameon whispered.

His words pushed her to the edge. Elijah's unrelenting tongue surged heat, and needy desire, through her. Dameon continued with Matthew. She couldn't take it anymore. She was consumed by their passionate touches, cumming around her gifted men. Elijah gave her just enough space, to whimper aching groans, at his satisfied smile.

Matthew thrusted through her waves of orgasmic pleasure, as he and Dameon spilled into her. She gasped as much as her lungs would allow, until they sweetly gave her rest. Dameon unbound her hands and assisted her back, to lay peacefully chest to chest. Matthew and Elijah rested at either side of Dameon.

"For better or worse," Matthew said.

"In sickness and in health," said Elijah.

"For the rest of time," Dameon smiled. "We promise. Do you?"

Emma looked up at the three faces.

"I promise," she smiled. "I do."

She wasn't sure how long they were asleep after their shower. The setting sun peeked through the opening of the ajar door.

Matthew excused himself from the beautiful moment. After an exchange of kisses, he got dressed. Apparently, he planned on picking up groceries earlier that day, but a pleasant distraction changed his plans. While he certainly didn't mind the change of plans, they were getting very low on food, and he'd never hear the end of it if Elijah wasn't given his preferred supplies for cooking. With some reluctance on Emma's part, he left the penthouse.

Elijah abandoned the bed with Matthew. Despite the shower, he had his heart set on one of his bath rituals. It didn't take Emma long to realize that they were giving Dameon time to have a private conversation with Emma. A hint of nervousness hit her. It must have been big to leave such a lovely moment.

"Matthew, Elijah, and I have been talking. We think it might be time to leave."

"Leave?"

"The penthouse. We've drawn a lot of attention to ourselves this year. We've accomplished what we set out to do, and more. Tony's empire has been destroyed thanks to you. There's not much here for us anymore."

"But," Emma said, saddened by the words. "This is home."

Dameon brushed a stray hair from Emma's face and kissed her.

"As long as we are together, we are home."

Confliction and questions danced in Emma's mind. She didn't want to leave the penthouse. She enjoyed the room she made. The thought of leaving their personal rooms to some random buyer, the memories made in the dungeon, she didn't want to leave it.

"Where would we go?"

"We aren't sure yet. Elijah obviously wants Cuba, Matthew and I are fairly indifferent. But the final decision is yours, as much as it is ours."

More questions were interrupted by a jarring BANG.

Dameon and Emma jumped at the sound. Both scrambled out of the cozy bed. They snatched robes on the way out of the room, and scanned the open second story. Elijah's door was open. Something small was on the floor just outside the door.

Dameon's color drained from his body when they approached the item and saw what it was. His eye. His eye was used to attempt to unlock the room. When it didn't work, it was abandoned, and the door had been blasted open. Emma rushed in behind Dameon.

Tony stood in the luxurious bathroom, gun pointed at the angel in the pink tub.

The man was ragged, in the same clothes he wore when he fled Emma. Old blood stained his shirt and pants. His tinted glasses were broken and askew. He looked deranged and hellbent on getting his revenge. They took his son. More importantly, they took his position of power, and handed it to Carter.

Elijah gripped the edges of the bath. Terror lined every inch of his face. Tony's finger took only a moment, and yet an eternity, to pull the trigger. A deafening noise rang out.

"No!" Dameon roared.

Wordless screams from Emma, echoed against the walls.

Dameon charged at Tony. Emma ran to Elijah. The pretty water grew red. With every passing moment. The once beautiful swirls were quickly polluted with horror. With every ounce of Emma's strength, she pulled Elijah from the tub. She pressed with all of her weight on the gushing wound that resided on his red and pink chest.

She didn't know what to do. Elijah couldn't tell her what to do. All she knew is that the blood needed to stay in. He needed it. She had to keep it in. It needed to stay in. Just stay in! Please! Please just stay in. Her hands were shiny and red.

Dameon struggled with Tony. Another ear-ringing shot sounded. The glass portion of the tub shattered. Blood and water flooded the floor. Dameon fell to the floor, as did Tony. The gun slipped from Tony's fingers, and slid near Emma. Just a moment. She would be back in just a moment.

Emma left Elijah to grab the weapon. Tony lunged for her. His leg prevented him from reaching the gun first. Dameon was holding him back by the ankle. Tony kicked Dameon's face, in the perfect place to cause the maximum amount of pain. For good measure, he kicked once more at Dameon's bruised ribs. Dameon curled in agonizing pain, while trying to catch his breath.

The gun was slippery in Emma's hands. She was covered in Elijah's blood, and the nature of the life-preserving liquid did no favors for her grip. Tony pinned Emma to the ground. He took her hand with the gun in his, and smashed it into the hard tile on the floor. Pain consumed her hand but she didn't give up.

She knew she couldn't win and clicked a mechanism on the gun. Tony slammed her fingers into the marble again and again until a bone snapped. Excruciating pain crawled up her hand and through her arm. She screamed in rage and sorrow, when he pointed the gun at Dameon and pressed against the trigger.

Dameon didn't hesitate. He kicked Tony with his remaining strength, and retrieved the gun for himself.

"The safety!" Emma screamed. "It's on!"

Dameon flipped the tiny switch and fired. He fired again, and again, until the magazine was empty. Tony was gone, this time for good. The villain of a man died too quickly in a pool of his and Elijah's blood.

Elijah! Dameon and Emma rushed to his side. He wasn't moving, he wasn't anything. He couldn't!

"Don't leave me! Ange... Ang-"

Tears choked Dameon's helpless, desperate, cries. Every muscle in Dameon's face, in his body, was etched in excruciating pain, as he lifted his lifeless lover, and squeezed him to his chest. He ran Elijah's golden hair through his fingers. His head fell limply back.

"No. No, Ang- Elijah? Elijah! Don't you fucking leave me! Don't go! Please, please come back!"

Emma sobbed hysterically with her entire body. She held his hand, but he didn't hold hers back. Matthew's presence joined the room. Emma could barely see him fall to his knees through her tears. He crawled through the water, through the tainted sweet smells. Matthew gripped a cold hand and broke.

"Bring him back," Dameon begged. "Please! Bring him back!"

23 | Life After Death

L as Vegas had one last surprise for Emma. The sun didn't shine. Like a true outsider to the city, she was under the impression that the desert offered year-round warmth. It did not. A breeze forced a shiver from her bare legs.

Her short black dress wasn't appropriate. If Elijah picked out her outfit, she would have been better dressed. Dameon removed his dark suit jacket, and placed it lovingly over Emma's shoulders. He wrapped an arm around her waist from her right, while Matthew held Emma's shoulders from the left.

She soaked in the warmth of Matthew and Dameon squishing her together. She needed it. The bitter air insidiously seeped into her bones. Sebastian stood close, staring at dark granite with simple engravings. Emma's eyes roamed around the graveyard. So few would ever know what rested below their feet, or the emptiness that accompanied them. Sebastian falsely coughed to smother the sound of a sniff.

"Don't start that," Matthew lightly laughed.

"Start what," Sebastian defended, while puffing out his chest.

Dameon smiled sweetly at the fatherly figure. He wrapped a caring arm around Sebastian's shoulders, and pulled the tall silver man near.

"Most never get out of this life," Sebastian said. "I'm glad I could help one more time. It's just hard to say goodbye."

"Then don't," Dameon said. "Come with us."

"I've been doing this longer than you've been alive, boy," Sebastian said.

"I don't know if I have retirement in me."

"All the more reason for you to join us," Emma said. "You could use a break."

Sebastian smirked at his most recently acquired child. His eyes spoke the words his mouth refused to sound. He wanted to leave, to run off with his kids and enjoy however many years he may have left. A thousand beautiful outcomes tempted his soul. But he wasn't ready, not yet. Maybe he never would be.

There's a saying about old dogs and new tricks, but with Sebastian, Emma could see the conflict brewing in the man. Could he leave after rising so close to the top? He spent a lifetime playing the political game in the criminal world, and now he was reaping the rewards with Carter. Yet even with his current success, something in Emma's gut told her that their farewell was not permanent. He'd be back in their lives someday, and they would welcome him with open arms.

The grass shuffled from behind the group of people, all clothed in black.

"You wouldn't be attempting to take El Tiburón from me, would you?" a sultry voice chimed in.

Emma spun around first. Carter walked with unnatural grace over the grass plots in vibrant red heels. The small party gave their full attention to the lady in dark, fashionable pants and rose-red top.

A defiant and tense stance took over Dameon's posture. Matthew switched from grieving mourner, to grumpy bodyguard in an instant. He snatched Emma and placed himself between the criminal empress and his little protector.

Carter strode with indisputable power towards Dameon, initially ignoring all others. She extended a hand, accented with meticulously manicured, rather short, gold nails. Dameon took it, cautiously. Though a tree's worth of olive branches had been exchanged between them, the unexpected visit put each of the men and Emma on edge.

"I was out for a drive today," Carter said, casually. "Before I knew it, I found myself considering renegotiating our arrangement. I was really looking forward to adding you to my arsenal, Dameon," she said, with a mocking pouting lip.

"Carter," Dameon warned.

"Calm down, lover," she said, with a satisfied sigh. "You offered your services for Emma's when you came to my party. I'm no longer in need of that, and frankly neither is she."

Carter's eyes trailed up and down Emma.

"Emma here," she said, "clearly doesn't need anyone's protection. But that is neither here nor there. I've accepted that her part in giving me the city, and your pretty view, makes us even. Not to mention, El Tiburón would never approve of me using you for anything fun."

A soft touch from Emma's hand made contact with Matthew's side, instructing him to let her step in front of her giant human shield. He didn't like it. She could feel it in the way his body moved with rigidity, and stayed ready to make a move if needed.

It wouldn't have made much of a difference. Carter's crew stood at a thoughtful distance, enough to give her the privacy to talk, while still maintaining the ability to gun down anyone at her will in a matter of seconds. Emma stood between her men and Carter, her voice unwavering and strong.

"Then why did you come here Carter?"

"Despite what you may think of me, it does bother me, what happened in the penthouse."

Carter paused. Something resembling a genuine tone, and dangerously close to an apologetic note, touched her words.

"I didn't think Tony survived. I was sure we'd find his body in a gutter somewhere, eventually. Failing to intercept him was a poor way to repay you. I never apologized for it."

"Well, he's definitely dead now," Emma said, with bite to her words. "And saying you never apologized isn't exactly an apology."

Dameon shot a warning look at Emma. She was irritated that Carter would show up and insert herself into their private moment.

"You're right, and I won't. It worked out pretty well for me! That said," Carter said to Emma, with challenge in her tone, "I could always use a fighter like you. If you are ever in the mood for a little more action, I would love to see... more of you. I can't help but feel like you only just got started. You could be fun to keep."

"I think you know who I've chosen to keep me. And, I've had enough action for one lifetime, thanks," Emma said, as she took a step forward.

Emma's face was hardened, her own intimidating aura, undeniable.

The men could be felt swapping anxiety and excitement back and forth behind her. Their little protector, the fierce adopted daughter of El Tiburón, stood toe to toe with Carter and didn't show the slightest trace of fear.

Carter flashed a brilliant white smile. Her eyes lit with predatory glee. Emma's defiance was feeding adrenaline into Carter's insatiable nature, but neither was willing to back down.

A trace of blame still festered in Emma's chest over Elijah. She should have killed Tony when given the first chance. Carter had a whole army patrolling the streets, yet the snake still managed to slip past every one of them. Emma's blame shifted.

If her people had caught him, if they could have simply finished him off... Emma wondered, more than once, if Carter intentionally let Tony go, knowing that he'd come for them. It would be a risky move, but perhaps an easy way to get rid of her last potential bit of competition. Maybe it was paranoia, but at the end of the day, it didn't matter. She hated Carter before, and she would continue to hate Carter into the future.

Carter broke the staredown to glance past them all, to where Elijah remained. A sheltering and angry streak reignited in Emma, something that happened increasingly often when it came to her men. To her surprise, Carter's smile wavered, and diminished, into a subtle expression of regret.

"He made the right choice," said Carter, in an almost kind voice. "Enjoy the peace, Elijah."

Carter looked back to Emma, offering only a half-smile.

"We know," Emma said, with gritted teeth. "We all made the right choice."

The tall woman took a number of steps backwards, taking in her last sight of the little family she wanted so desperately to control. She never stopped wanting Dameon. She would always be on the hunt for muscle like Matthew. She'd forever be jealous of Elijah's place in Dameon's heart. She even wished to keep Emma close, if for nothing more than to see if her murderous rampage was a one-time fluke, or the awakening of a monster that even Matthew couldn't compare to.

Carter's eyes rested on Sebastian.

"El Tiburón, you know your girl is right. Now's your chance to have what anyone else in our line of work doesn't get. You can make a difference around here if you stay, but for a limited time, I won't hold it against you if you leave."

"Would you? If given the opportunity," Sebastian asked, grumpily.

"Not a chance," Carter laughed. "I intend to die on a pile of money, old and out of touch, at the hands of the next rival. I have no desire to give this up."

Carter met Dameon's eyes one last time. She grinned and turned, to walk back to her waiting car. Multiple guardians awaited her return with crossed arms and a professionalism that could rival the secret service. Carter didn't look back, as the largest of the guards, a man with two missing fingers, opened the passenger door for his boss.

She stepped into the black vehicle. The engine started, and the tires rolled at a respectful speed at the resting place for the dead. Carter continued to face the road, but Emma could swear that, through the tinted window, she could see a hint of remorse, as Carter disappeared from Dameon's life for good.

Emma looked back to the stones that peppered the green turf. As she surveyed the quiet graves under the gray sky, she saw Elijah.

His golden waves were bright, in spite of the dull atmosphere. They blew lazily with the breeze that chilled Emma's skin. His eyes held every bit of blue the sky was missing. His smile was teasing, beckoning Emma to join him.

Emma walked past Matthew and Dameon to one of the stones protruding from the ground. She ran her hand over its rough surface. It all felt surreal. Less than a year ago, she never could have guessed that her life would end up here.

Elijah's hand touched her shoulder. Maybe the floral sweetness she smelled came from the offerings that topped the remains of loved ones lost, but she was sure at least some of the scent was him. Emma looked up at his happy eyes.

Elijah grinned at her with mischief in his soul. He bumped his hip against hers, and instantly regretted it. His hand shot up to his chest with a groan. Emma giggled. Dameon wrapped sweet arms around his angel and kissed his head.

"Ready for Cuba," Dameon asked, smiling.

Elijah beamed.

"You're a lucky kid," Sebastian said, with watery eyes.

"Of course I am," Elijah said, pulling Emma and Matthew closer. "I'm going to Cuba!"

"Please, Sebastian," Dameon asked, once more. "Come with us. It is your homeland! If not for yourself, do it for us. We could use a citizen that could help keep us under the radar."

Dameon embraced Sebastian. The older man hugged his son with ferocity and care. He patted the dark-haired man on the back, and wiped the beginnings of a tear with his shoulder.

"Get out of here," Sebastian said, lovingly.

Emma looked at the stones again. She read the names. Dameon Lazarus, Matthew Bale, Elijah Holden, and Emma Kincaide. Here, they were laid to rest. As far as Las Vegas was concerned, they were gone. They were free to live out the rest of their days in a cozy home in Cuba with each other.

Even if there was anyone left that might hate them enough to want to harm them, they'd have a hard time finding them now. Sebastian saw to that, with a perfect forgery of their deaths and new identities. Though their first names remained the same, they each shared a single last name, a final gift from Sebastian.

The name Fonsesca was given to each of his sons and his daughter, on their new documentation. In this way, they would always be his, and belong to each other. Emma cried tears of happiness when the announcement

428

was made, and would be lying if she said that her partners didn't do the same.

One by one, the family entered the Maserati. Before Dameon could shut his passenger side door, Sebastian placed his hand on its corner. He held it open, resting his temple on his knuckles as he peered into the vehicle. He smiled in a bitter sweet way that only a parent can, when the kids leave the nest. His children didn't rush, letting the moment between them burrow into their hearts.

"I'll see you again soon," Sebastian said.

"Don't take too long, dad," said Dameon.

Sebastian's lip trembled slightly.

"I'm proud of you," he said. "All of you."

A final sniff and hard tap to the edge of the door sent off their departure. The door shut with a muffled clap. Emma and Elijah waved from the back, as Matthew sent a grinning two-fingered salute to their father. The sports car gently rolled out of the graveyard, and onto a mostly empty side street.

The drive through Las Vegas felt like moving through a dream. It's a funny thing, the feelings a person can have for a simple structure of concrete, wood, drywall, and glass. Emma looked out into the distance at a dim tower touching the cloudy sky.

The top floor of that building was her prison, then her home, and now only a piece of her past. She had grown to love, and find comfort, in its walls and its stone floors. It was a place she came to associate with safety and security. But after Tony, and his vengeful mob-boss intrusion, it turned into another place of discomfort. Too much blood had been spilled over the home.

Even after Sebastian, the man they would forever hold in their hearts as their adoptive father, and his trusted hand-picked team of cleaners, were finished making it look perfect again, Emma couldn't scrub the images from her mind.

Only a few months ago, her heart pained when Dameon suggested leaving their home. Emma didn't initially feel ready to leave the penthouse forever. Despite everything they had been through, everything she had done, she hated the idea of painting every room in a neutral eggshell-white. It felt wrong, the thought of strangers moving in, having never known of all the love and pain that existed in those spaces. But when Tony's final blow hit her family, the home had lost its luster.

When the terrible memories tipped the scales from home, to place of misery, Emma suddenly desired to never set foot in the place again. Dameon, Matthew, and Emma were reminded of Elijah's brush with death, every time he flinched after being hugged just a little too hard. Even now, he was still recovering from the gunshot wound. They agreed in unison that they were ready to leave, to move on with a life far from the devastation they accumulated in the town and the penthouse.

It took longer than they had hoped to sell the building. The economy was in shambles, but there were always rich investors itching to get their hands on the jewel of a tower. Dameon, being the sole owner, met up with a few interested buyers yet none felt like the right person.

In the end, and with a heated discussion amongst their family, it was decided that Carter would be the most fitting new owner of the building. If she hadn't brought the cavalry when they needed it most, the family of four may not have ever made it out of Tony's compound.

While they didn't trust, nor like, Carter by any means, it was a decent parting gift for the newest crime boss of Vegas. When Carter's offer was accepted, the four not only received enough money to live in retirement for the rest of their lives, but also the kept the knowledge that they would hopefully, forever, be in her favor.

Emma placed the city in Carter's hands, and Dameon gave her a new base of operations befitting the empress she became. Elijah wasn't thrilled, but came around when Matthew revealed to his lover that they were leaving Vegas to live out their retirement in Elijah's dream location, Cuba. By the end, when the home was packed, the furniture sold, and the money filled their bank accounts, they were each at peace with the idea.

When Emma, Dameon, Matthew, and Elijah arrived at the busy airport, the tower was just out of sight. Emma stood on the tips of her toes to get a final glance at the place when she felt a hand on her shoulder.

Dameon caught her green eyes, understanding reflected in his remaining dark-blue eye. The elastic string of his black eyepatch bent a few of his dark hairs out of place. She ran a gentle finger under the strap and fixed his hair to its rightful perfection. Dameon's thumb brushed against Emma's pink, chilly cheek. He closed the distance between them and bent for a kiss.

Centimeters before his lips could meet hers, Emma jumped at the sound of plastic wheels hitting the pavement with a crack. Both turned their attention to a bickering Matthew and Elijah. Emma giggled at Matthew's exasperation over Elijah's remarkable ability to overpack.

"Four bags? You really needed four? And why are they so heavy?"

"So sorry," Elijah said, rolling his eyes. "Not all of us are as happy as you are to wear the same clothes over and over again, like a cartoon character."

"I don't– it's a standard outfit. Shirt, pants, underwear, socks and shoes," Matthew said, counting off his basic necessities off on the tips of his fingers. "You don't need much more."

"Maybe you don't need more. I, however, am not willing to be caught underdressed and unprepared for any situation."

Dameon turned to Emma with a devilish grin. He spun the blonde woman, and wrapped his arms around her in a binding hold. His warmth transferred to her cold body, thunder rumbling overhead. Emma shimmied her back closer to Dameon's chest.

"You're sure you want to live the rest of your life with those two," he said, jokingly in her ear.

A wholehearted laugh found Emma that shook from her body to his. A low chuckle rumbled in him that warmed her even more than his embrace.

"I wouldn't have it any other way," she said.

A loud whistle echoed in the crowded lot. Matthew and Elijah snapped their attention to Dameon in an instant. He waved his hand over, instructing them to wrap up their banter and get moving. Elijah popped the metal and plastic handle from two of his bright blue suitcases and walked with sass radiating from every step.

Matthew puckered his lips and narrowed his eyes at the pretty blond man.

The giant heaved Elijah's duffle over his own bag, and onto his shoulder. He wheeled Elijah's fourth piece of luggage behind him. Upon rejoining the group, he unsuccessfully blew at a few stray, long, brown hairs in his face, that tangled in his beard.

Dameon ran his fingers through the long waves out of pity, then gripped the large man's chin.

"You're cute when you play the strong man," Dameon said, biting his lower lip.

Matthew's eyes lit up, a breath puffing up his chest.

Elijah's gaze darted between the two, then landed on Emma. A mischievous grin and quick raise of his brows graced his angelic face. He leaned close to Emma, to whisper a hopeful note that the four would find a way to join the mile-high club once the plane was in the air.

"Adorable," Dameon said. "You think I'm going to wait for the plane to take off?"

The leader, the giant, the angel, and their little protector, made their way to the automatic doors of the airport. They walked away from their city, a different kind of adventure waiting. A new life was ahead of them, a life of peace, minimal crime, and far from the old one so full of grudges and revenge.